The Lost Lovelies Foundation

BETH WILSON

First published in 2020
by Laneway Press
Abbotsford Convent
St Heliers Street
Abbotsford VIC 3067
www.lanewaypress.com.au
info@lanewaypress.com.au

Set in Garamond 11pt.
Layout by Red Bilby Media
www.redbilby.com.au

Proudly printed in Australia
by McPherson's Printing

Cataloguing-in-Publication details are available from the National Library of Australia
www.trove.nla.gov.au

ISBN: 978-0-9923433-7-8 (print)
ISBN: 978-0-9923433-9-2 (epub)

Dedicated to
Isa May Wilson
1920 – 2016
who believed in her children
as only a mother can.

1

Martha

In twenty years of practice as a midwife, I had never lost a mother or baby.

It had been a source of pride. Nursing was my life, caring for others my passion. I consider myself to be a professional and caring midwife. I especially love working maternity. There's something special about ushering new life into this world, and I love being the one women turn to in their hour of need. Whether it is standing up to gynaecologists on their behalf or just holding their hand as they push through the pain, I want to be there, right beside them.

Anita was one of those women who glow in pregnancy. She was beautiful, in love, and that baby was so wanted. Michael, her husband, came to all the pre-natal appointments and was a happy, involved father-to-be. His love for Anita was like a badge pinned on his chest.

They chose the new Melbourne Birthing Centre for the delivery rather than the main hospital next door because they were a couple who didn't believe pregnancy and birth should be overly medicalised. That arrangement suited me too. The centre was classified as part of the hospital, which meant I was protected by the hospital's insurers.

Anita and Michael presented two days before her predicted due date, but I wasn't worried. Some women deliver early, others late; that's the nature of childbirth.

Later, I wondered if it was fate that made the baby come early.

Oh god! Would anything be different?

If the baby had arrived on time, that girl wouldn't have been there.

Heath would have been okay.

Anita and Michael would have had the chance to be fabulous parents.

I wouldn't have had my name dragged through the mud.

I know there's not much use going over what might have been, but I can't help it. I do it every time I remember that day and I remember that day, every day. Sometimes I feel guilty, other times I just feel so very sad. Traumatic memories sneak up on me when I least expect them. The only thing that helps to diffuse the pain is doing my best for others; to stand beside them when they need me the most.

It was a good birth.

Anita was healthy and, of course, the obstetrician arrived just before Heath popped out. Typical man. He turned up after all the hard work had been done and elbowed me out of the way to do what I craved the most. I wanted to be the first person to hold the new, healthy baby in my arms.

When Dr Stevens placed the little baby boy in her arms, Anita shone like a star … a different kind of star to the one she eventually became. Her face was bright with love and wonder, as if the birth had infused her with joy. I had seen this transformation from woman to mother many times. It was always wonderful and with Anita it was incandescent.

Michael had been beaming and crying from the moment he heard Heath's first wails. He looked so proud as he held his newborn son in his arms.

Later, when Anita was sleeping peacefully, Michael nodded his head towards the camera on the bedside table. 'Martha, will you take a photo of me and Heath?'

I was happy to oblige. I took the photo and then Michael went to get a coffee while I placed Heath back in his crib.

I saw him settled and left to check the woman in the adjoining room. We're not supposed to leave our patients, but what can you do when there are so few rostered nurses on duty and someone else needs your care? I was only away from Anita for five minutes, but when I got back the crib was empty.

There was no baby.

It had been a long shift, so I rubbed my eyes in disbelief.

That didn't help. I looked over at Anita, who was still asleep.

No baby in sight.

At first, I thought Michael must have come back and was holding the baby. But no, he strolled in alone with his coffee. He went straight to Anita and sat watching her as she slept, a happy expression on his face.

I was totally bamboozled.

Where the hell was the baby?

Had another nurse picked him up? I looked around the room and then checked the corridor.

A cold sense of dread was creeping through me as I rang for backup.

Leanne, the only other nurse on duty—and a friend since our student nursing days—came in smiling. I hustled her aside.

'Where's the baby?' I whispered, trying to keep my voice down. I didn't want to alarm Michael or wake Anita, but I was starting to feel desperately afraid. My voice quavered and my stomach clenched into a knot as I tried to control my emerging panic.

'What?' she asked, looking completely blank.

'Where the hell is the baby, Leanne? What have you done with him?'

'Me?' She cried out as if I'd hit her. 'Me? He wasn't in my care, he was in yours!'

Michael looked over at us, oblivious of our panic, and his gaze came to rest on the crib. 'Where's Heath?' he asked with a smile.

I didn't know what to say. Doubt creased his brow and he rose. I began to sweat as panic gripped me.

I shifted towards the door. 'I'm going to report this. Leanne, you stay here.'

'No, you don't,' Leanne said, ducking past me. 'I'll do that. You stay here.'

She left me with Michael, who was beginning to look frightened. I tried to conceal my feelings, but he could tell something was wrong. He became increasingly agitated. He darted over to the empty cradle and looked up at me with a dazed expression, and I could sense his confusion. His gaze roamed desperately around the room, as if looking about would somehow make his son materialise.

'Where's Heath?' he demanded. 'Where's our son?'

'We have to wait,' I said, trying to sound calm.

'No! You can answer me right now. Where is our son?'

I choked on a sob. 'I don't know.'

2

Martha

The foundation has been taken over.

I'm free.

My reputation is intact. I am now a woman of considerable means and have my independence. My new husband and I are the proud owners of a stunning house high up on a heath-covered cliff at Hideaway Bay, with astonishing views of the headlands and the Great Southern Ocean.

We stroll along the beach picking up little shells, marvelling at the waves, the sky and the cape. The tide is out, allowing us to observe the teeming life along the margin of intertidal rocks. Gerard is enthralled. 'It's incredible how these creatures have adapted to being covered by the ocean part of the time, and at others exposed to the hot sun or the drenching rain as the tides ebb and recede.'

I agree with him as I gaze at the grasping tentacles of sea anemones and shining green and silver periwinkles in a shimmering rock pool. These amazing plants and animals put up with many challenges yet they thrive despite the pounding surf.

Gerard momentarily leaves my side to throw a stick for the dogs and a sudden blast of icy cold air hits my face. I suddenly feel isolated, alone and on trial, almost like I had all those years ago. It was like hundreds of eyes were on me back then, all the time. I don't know why I feel so panicked—Gerard is nearby, so are the dogs. I look around the beach, searching for watchful eyes, but I see no-one.

As if demonstrating its own enduring power, the ocean sends a freak wave rushing towards us. Gerard races back to my side, the dogs running beside him, and as we dash across the wet rocks to the dunes Gerard slips and twists his ankle. He gives a yell of pain, wincing as I help him to safety and sit him on a rock.

'Go easy, love,' he groans, as I examine his ankle.

'I don't think you'll be doing much walking for a while,' I tell him. 'The kiosk isn't far. I'll see if Bobby can drive us back home.'

Bobby is glad to oblige and bundles us into the car. As we weave down the snake-like road through heath-covered dunes, I mention the creepy feeling I'd experienced on the beach.

'You're not the first ones to get freaked out there. It's the site where settlers massacred dozens of local Aboriginal people last century,' says Bobby.

I shiver as I think about how some crimes never really get erased. The worse they are, the longer they're remembered. Gerard and I exchange a glance and I smile reassuringly at him, trying to put my spooked feelings behind us.

When we get back to the house, Bobby helps Gerard inside and I make him comfortable with paracetamol and pillows. I invite Bobby to stay for a beer, but he refuses. 'Thanks, but it's getting dark and I've gotta lock up the kiosk.'

Before leaving, he stands at the windows, gazing out at the sea where the sinking sun is lighting up the flanks of Cape Hideaway. 'Geez, what a great view you guys have got. I've lived here all my life and I've never seen the bay from this perspective before.'

I wonder about his words and how our jobs, our beliefs, and even our houses, limit the perspective we have on the world. I see Bobby out, thanking him profusely, and hurry to tend to my injured husband.

***

Gerard and I sleep late. There's no need to rush, not anymore. It's pleasant to lie in bed listening to the seabirds crying and the little heath twitterers and warblers singing. I try to guess what song comes from which bird.

I arise at my leisure and check on Gerard's swollen ankle. 'Hmm, breakfast in bed for you today.'

Gerard indicates he'd rather sit by the windows than stay in bed, so I help him to the living area and sit him at the table overlooking the sea. I set him up with a coffee pot, toast, and a book on Joseph Stalin before calling the dogs for our morning walk.

I want to go down to the sea using the shady green path carved through the heath. The dogs, however, have their own plan. They're keen to go inland to hunt for rabbits. I turn my back on the sea and wander down the dusty back lane after the eager dogs. Fat sheep in paddocks pause, grass dangling from their mouths, to gaze at us as we pass. The dogs ignore them—it's underground mutton they're after. We pass a few lonely looking farmhouses built in hollows to protect them from the wind, but it is the ancient cypress trees lining the lane which harbor the rabbit burrows that interest the dogs.

While I wait for them to scout for prey, I take in the rolling green hills, the azure blue sky dotted with white puffs of cloud, a gentle sea breeze and the shimmering horizon. I feel liberated. I am intoxicated by the immense space and the smell of the countryside—a heady mix of salty air, eucalyptus and wild garlic.

I take another deep breath and feel years of stress just melt away.

It's been a long time since I've been in a space with no other people in sight or sound, just the songs of birds, whirring of crickets, and the odd baa from fat sheep. It gives me the same feeling of freedom and happy immediacy that I'd known as a child.

This was my grandmother's birthplace and I plan to be buried here, eventually. Strange, how things come full circle. My mother left Hideaway Bay when she was twenty years old with Dad, who took her away to Mariner's Point, a six-hour drive away, never to return. She never forgot this place and it's only now I can understand why. She fed the imaginations of her six children with stories about Hideaway Bay's secret places and the adventures she had with her brothers. She always promised she would bring us here one day to visit Gran and Poppa, but that wasn't to be. Breast cancer took that dream away.

The dogs have finished hunting for rabbits, at least for the moment, so I decide to take them to one of Gran's secret places. There's a freshwater lake nearby, filled from underground springs that never dry out, even in the drought years. Apparently, there's also a limestone cave system that stands above the lake. I'm eager to finally see them.

It's a hot walk, so as soon as the dogs see the water, they bolt in, happily swimming and doing laps. I stand at the edge, watching in delight as Lost and Found play. They bring me such joy with their unquestioning loyalty and their appreciation of the natural world. I haven't had any dogs in years and am constantly surprised at how happy they make me. They are exactly the elixir I need, bless them.

They swim back to me, shake their fur, and stretch out full length to dry off, their tummies on the cool, wet basalt. They look so refreshed that I chuck off my shoes and jeans and wade into the dark lake myself. The water makes my skin tingle and I float on my back with my eyes closed, letting the water soothe me, listening to the breeze and the magpies.

This is freedom. No rushing about, no-one else's demands to meet, no cause to be betrayed.

Feeling restored, I take myself out of the water and lay on the warm rocks to dry my skin under the sun. Pulling my clothes back on, I call Lost and Found. We climb up to the caves above the lake. The impressive outcrop of limestone stands like an abandoned temple in the most unlikeliest of places—a cow paddock. The caves are above ground and I call out 'helloooo' to test for echoes. This startles the dogs into barking and their barks echo back to us causing more barks until I quell the pandemonium with calming pats.

Gran called these the Ghostie Caves. Easy to see why. There is a limestone column in the largest cave where petrified tree roots thrust upward from the rocky floor. It's a quiet, cool place overlooking the lakes and the foaming ocean beyond the dunes. I feel privileged to be standing on this ground. It feels sacred.

The strong aroma of cow manure makes it hard to dream, so we wander back down the dusty track towards the old township. Grasshoppers click across our pathway, announcing our trespass.

Small things become beautiful out here.

I pause to admire how abandoned rusty chicken wire and tangled barbed wire in the top corner of a paddock looks like it's been wind-sculpted and glazed by the salty air. We come across a swampy natural spring that serves as a dam for the cattle. Its grasses hide birds so small they can dance on the leaves of floating water plants.

Among the gossiping reeds are seven gliding black swans. They watch as the dogs scramble happily into the water to say hello. Disturbed, the biggest bird turns its lovely head and sounds the alarm, a high-pitched call to flee. The other swans respond by lifting their white-tipped wings and stretching their impossibly long necks as they rise from the water. I find their awkward beauty to be deeply moving, their ascension to the sky a privilege to watch.

The dogs are eager to continue exploring so we ramble on to the abandoned settlement. There's not much left of the old township of Hideaway. It's all ghosts now. A solid stone church still stands, built, according to The National Trust sign, in 1884. I peer in through the narrow, pointed windows and expect to see a holy place. Instead, I see it's been renovated at some point and turned into a holiday house. It doesn't look like it's been inhabited for ages.

I am surprised how territorial I've already become. I don't want tourists coming here and asking questions. I don't want to share anything about this place at all.

A bossy fantail seems not to approve of my sticky-beaking and tries to drive us away by spreading its white-edged tail wide and swooping at my head.

'Okay, little bird, I'm not going near your nest,' I tell it.

The dogs look startled, wondering who I'm talking to. They're so funny.

On the hill above the township is the cemetery. I open the squeaky wood and wire gate that could do with oiling and surprise some grazing rabbits. They bolt, with Lost and Found hot on the trail.

Wandering through the quiet graveyard, I relish the shade afforded by huge old pines, radiata and cypress on one side, and the remnant eucalyptus forest on the other. Belladonna lilies bloom around the dead. I wonder why these flowers always seem to thrive in country graveyards. This is a fair dinkum Australian bone orchard where I am afforded glimpses of the births, deaths and soul of the old township.

I find the Protestant section and the graves of my great-grandparents, Henry Robert and Ada May, side by side, buried three years apart. Gran and Poppa are buried beside them. Mum is buried in Marine Point, which seems sad to me now, as it's so far away from where she grew up. There are other Mayne graves here, including that of Uncle Charlie.

I remember Uncle Charlie from when he came to Marine Point when I was five years old. He stayed for about a week and I don't think I'd ever seen Mum so happy. We kids were happy too. Uncle Charlie told great stories and played the mouth organ. We sat around the open fire in the good room at night while Mum and Uncle Charlie drank tea, and he would play while we sang *You are my Sunshine, Hang Down Your Head, Tom Dooley*, and *Irene Goodnight*. I seem to recall lots of train songs because Uncle Charlie could make great train sounds on the mouth organ.

And then he was gone. We stood out the front and waved. A cloud of dust rose around us as his car pulled away and the light in Mum's eyes went out. We talked about him for days—no, years. We were so sad when he left. That night, Mum, washing dishes in the kitchen, softly sang *Andy's Gone a Drovin'*.

Standing in front of his grave today, I'm surprised at how sad I feel knowing how much Mum missed her brothers.

Memories—they are the reflections of our lives. The echoes that we create by our deeds.

I plan to come back and tidy up the graves, but for now, my husband needs me. I quickly stoop to pick some pink heath. It'll look nice in a vase.

'Come on, dogs, we've got better things do with our lives than hanging around talking to the dead.'

Wandering back to the house, I think about the foundation and Anita and everything that happened at the end. Things started with such purpose and hope but spiralled out of control.

After all the media fuss, the ombudsman processes—it's just so good to be free of that now. I have Lost and Found for company, and Gerard. The ocean, the birdsong, the hidden lakes and caves from Gran's stories—I'm unwinding.

At last, I'm coming down from all the bullshit.

3

Martha

Just before Anita stood up to go to the lectern, she squeezed my hand and whispered, 'Wish me luck!'

I laughed. 'You're so good at this you don't need luck.'

Her eyes sparkled in anticipation. 'Right on, Martha. I'm gonna blow the roof off this joint.'

I watched as she stepped up to the microphone, accompanied by the sound of rapturous applause. I was sitting next to Gerard and caught his eye. We grinned at each other, knowing that with Anita's innate charm she would win over the entire room in moments.

I felt the energy of expectation filling the room, as my friend smiled broadly at her guests. Anita was a brilliant speaker. She'd always pause for a moment or two to let the tension build to the right level. Anita held the pause, slowly scanning the room, gracing individual tables with a smile, nodding to some of the celebrities and acknowledging individual supporters before beginning to speak. Her voice, warm and seductive, carried beautifully throughout the room.

'My dear friends, thank you. Thank you all for joining us on this special day. I can feel the love in this room. I know how many of you have suffered at the hands of criminals. I too have suffered so much, but I have endured. And now, we finally have a way to end our suffering and prevent others from suffering as we have. Together, we will triumph over evil. Goodness and justice will prevail.' Anita paused for a moment to allow the audience time to applaud energetically.

It was the tenth anniversary of the founding of The Lost Lovelies Foundation. Our annual fundraising luncheon—our biggest event of the year—had turned into a full extravaganza to commemorate the occasion. There were 500 attendees, including our volunteers, who were enjoying a full luncheon service at the Grande Hotel, attended to by the hotel's premier

10

waiters, the best corporate musicians money could buy, and of course, the star of the show, Anita Hammond-Jones—media darling, socialite, and founder and CEO of The Lost Lovelies Foundation.

Anita flicked a strand of golden hair behind her ear and resumed her speech.

'Ten years ago, my baby was stolen by a desperately unhappy girl who was unable to care for herself, let alone my son. When the police finally tracked her down, my beautiful newborn baby was dead.' Anita lowered her head and stopped, her voice choked with emotion. Her eyes glistened with tears but she raised her head and resumed. 'I only held and fed him once. I never got to take him home. Instead, while my breasts ached to feed him, she let him starve.' She gave the audience a sad smile. 'Heath would have been ten this year.'

The room was silent, and I tried to balance feelings of pride and admiration for everything that Anita had accomplished over the last ten years with my own remorse. I knew it wasn't my fault—the Coroner had cleared me—but guilt and self-doubt were never far from the surface. I tried to push my feelings away, just as I did every time Anita told her story. I reminded myself that her compassion towards me mitigated these feelings.

Anita held her head high. 'I know this girl was desperate and mentally unhinged and served her jail time. She's now in a psychiatric institution, and that is the best place for her. She's safe there. She must never, never be allowed to kill someone else's child. I don't waste precious time hating her, although I do abhor what she did,' Anita said.

Anita never said her name, she only ever called her 'the girl'.

Anita spoke with renewed vigour. 'In the early days I almost forgot how to live. I went to one psychiatrist who wanted to drug me up. Another one told me I was suffering from post-traumatic stress disorder. He told me there were some things you just don't get over, that I just needed to go through the stages of grieving.' Anita's gaze swept the room. She was disdainful. 'I was in disbelief. "Stages?" I asked the man. He answered me smugly that it was okay for me to just "survive".' Anita gave a sniff of disbelief. 'How can any person survive such grief?'

Anita shook her head. 'He told me it was okay to be a survivor. He said I didn't have to be a superhero, I could just live. It was a proclamation that was amazing to me. I asked him how he knew such things and he told me he was an expert. "In what?" I asked and he replied, "Grieving and human suffering."' Anita shook her head again. 'I asked him if he'd ever lost a child. Needless to say, his response was completely unsatisfactory. He said, "You don't have to personally experience trauma to understand how clients suffer and survive. My training allows me to do that."'

Anita made a disdainful face. 'When I left his clinic, I knew I had turned a corner. His words fired me up and I decided I wasn't going to be someone talked down to by those who didn't truly understand my grief. I wasn't going to stay at home and be useless. I wasn't just going to survive, I was going to thrive. I was going to be a leader and help parents just like me.'

I shared a smile with Gerard as Anita upped her pitch and pressed forward confidently. 'As all of you wonderful people know, I started The Lost Lovelies Foundation not long after Heath's death. He died on either the first or second of September; a day that should have been full of hope.' Anita slapped the lectern. 'At first, I could do nothing, not a single thing! I was crippled with grief. I couldn't go out or talk to anyone, other than the police and a few journalists who have become friends, and who dealt with my loss so sensitively.' She looked over at the media contingent on the far side of the hall and gave them a gracious nod of her head. 'Speaking of which, I want to acknowledge those of you from the media who are here to support us today. Without your help this foundation could not have achieved so many good things for families who have lost a child.'

Applause filled the room. The official photographer lined Anita up in his lens and his camera flashed and clicked.

Anita quietened the cheering. I knew this portion of her speech well; this is where she went from victim to advocate.

'My loss helped me see there is a distinct lack of protection for victims in our laws. As a society, we are vulnerable to violent criminals who have no regard for the law. I made it my mission to support other families who have lost children to crime. The Lost Lovelies Foundation will continue to support parents whose children have been the victims of criminals.' She slapped the lectern again. 'Our quest is for justice! We strive to have the voices of pain heard and heeded. We have lobbied our political leaders for sensible laws to prevent offences against children taking place. Our achievements to date have been sensational, but our biggest battle is to have the Victims' Voices Bill passed. This initiative will ensure anyone who has harmed a child will not be allowed out of prison or custody without the express consent of the parents or carers of the lost baby or child. I urge you to support this Bill in whatever capacity you can.'

The applause was prolonged and intense. I added my own applause to the cacophony.

The Victims' Voices Bill had been Anita's idea. As her profile and her contacts had grown over the years, backing for the Bill gained more support. I wasn't a huge fan of the idea at first, but I'd watched as ridiculously short sentences were handed down to perpetrators and was appalled when the villains were released, only to reoffend. Time and time again, families had come to the foundation for support and I saw firsthand the suffering that came from inadequate sentencing and a lack of properly supervised parole.

Anita had grown more fervent in her championing of the Victims' Voices Bill as the end date of Jennifer Harris's sentence loomed. She was successful in lobbying government to make sure Jennifer was not released at that time but detained in an institution, and she wanted to make sure it stayed that way. Anita had ramped up the publicity and got me to seek out as many lobbying opportunities as possible for the Bill. I started adding articles on the progress of the Bill to our newsletter and this led to additional support from those who believed in the Bill almost as passionately as Anita.

Anita's voice drew me out of my reverie. 'I want to especially thank our magnificent volunteers. Please stand up if you are a Lost Lovelies volunteer.'

About twenty people rose and they stood shyly while applause enveloped the hall. I joined in enthusiastically, feeling so proud of them. They were a dedicated bunch who freely gave their time and energy to the foundation and were responsible for many of our fantastic fundraising efforts. Several were trained counsellors who assisted our beloved, overworked Leanne, who ran the Lost Lovelies Listen Line. Leanne had been on duty with me on the day Heath was taken, and, despite everything, remained my dear friend.

Anita signalled to the volunteers to be seated. 'Our volunteers are unique. They understand the people who come to us for help. They offer peer support, which is a proven model of care. Their important contributions have gone towards making the first ten years of The Lost Lovelies Foundation so amazingly successful. We love you all.'

Anita began to speak a bit faster now; she was drawing to a close. 'And now, dear friends, enjoy this celebratory luncheon and each other's company. Once again, I thank you all, and I'll try to speak with each of you personally during the next couple of hours. Please don't forget to purchase a red gerbera and wear it proudly as a symbol of our love for the Lost Lovelies. Also, there are raffle tickets and envelopes on your tables. The prizes are gorgeous and are all donations from our generous sponsors, Beauty Is Skin Deep, Pharma One, and Live Before You Die. Let's give them a round of applause.'

Anita quickly shushed the audience by waving her outstretched hands. 'Also, take the time to check out the fantastic items in our silent auction and place your bids before dessert is served. Thank you, I love you all very much.'

After the applause died down Anita worked the room, making sure she stopped to talk to guests at every table. I shadowed her, taking notes and contact details as she networked. There were members of the police force, all in their dress uniform, including Deputy Commissioner Lalor. I was intrigued to see his uniform was a much brighter blue than those of the other officers and I wondered if the Chief Commissioner's would be even bluer. He kissed Anita and asked her if she'd consider giving a short address at the annual police ball. She agreed and I added it to my notes.

The media table was towards the back of the room and included television reporters, gossip-hunters from the social pages, and news reporters. Jamie O'Dhea from *The Watcher* was there, looking handsome in a casual sort of way, wearing an open-necked white shirt and dark jeans. He and Anita embraced and I smiled, knowing they had been sharing more than just interviews.

There were also representatives from the research sector, which was great. Anita was introduced to Professor Louisa Moore's latest student, Elissa Mustaffa. I watched the young woman with interest. Our annual grant allocations were looming and Professor Moore had nominated several of her students in previous years for a piece of the funding pie. Anita had some misgivings about Louisa Moore, who was fiercely independent, but her students' work had the potential to bring academic respectability to our cause. I thought Elissa looked like a good candidate. She was young, seemed bright, and a bit starstruck by Anita, as so many people were. Anita moved on, but I noted Elissa's details—under the watchful eye of her professor—and advised her where the grant application forms could be found on our website.

By 4.00 pm the luncheon was over. Anita had kissed and farewelled the last of her guests and the volunteers were doing a clean-up of the hall under the supervision of Leanne.

My feet were killing me and I just wanted to kick off my shoes. Anita and I retreated to a private suite where Jamie O'Dhea was waiting.

Anita kissed his cheek and turned to me with a satisfied smile. 'Martha, darling, there is a nice cold Bollinger in the fridge. Can you open that for us? I have earned a drink and so have you. Five hundred guests at $500 each—that's wonderful for our work.'

'Of course, Anita.' I poured three flutes of champagne and Jamie handed one to Anita. She sipped daintily at her glass at first, then she smiled and drank the rest down in one swallow.

'Gosh, that didn't even touch the sides. Top me up, dear Martha.'

I refilled Anita's glass, something I'd done many times before.

'Ohhh, I have sooo earned this champagne.' She kicked off her Italian shoes and clinked glasses with Jamie. 'What a wonderful audience today,' she said, followed by a happy sigh.

Jamie put his arm around her shoulders. 'They loved you.'

Anita laughed. 'I loved them. Did I tell you I'm thinking about changing the name of the foundation to The Empty Arms Foundation? What do you think?'

Jamie looked thoughtful. 'I like it, but the current name has so much goodwill.'

I agreed. 'It's a great name, but The Lost Lovelies Foundation is so well known. If you changed the name you'd have to start over with new publicity and promotions, and even stationery.'

Anita considered this for a moment and nodded. 'Jamie, as usual, Martha is right. The name stays. Here's to The Lost Lovelies Foundation, you and I, and to our loyal Martha.'

I raised my glass, but the two of them were now looking rather hungrily at each other, so I smiled and put down my glass. 'I'll leave you to it. I need to make sure the donations are securely stored and get everything back to the office. You have a late start tomorrow, so I'll call you at about ten to go over your schedule.'

I don't think she even heard me.

I wandered back out through the hall to check on the clean-up progress when I noticed Gerard leaning against a wall, looking like he was waiting for someone. He smiled at me. 'I thought you might like a lift home.'

I was pleasantly surprised. 'That would be nice, but I have to go back to the office. Still a few things to get sorted before I call it a day.'

'No worries,' said Gerard. 'I'll drive you. Save you having to hang around waiting for a taxi.'

I was pleased because I really was tired, and I liked Gerard. He had a calm way about him and despite what he'd been through in his own life he never expressed any anger. He wasn't bad looking either, not that I was interested in anything more than a reliable professional relationship. The cause was all that really mattered.

'How very kind of you, Gerard,' I said. 'I'm just about pooped, so I'd love a lift.'

He helped me carry out our banners and other gear the volunteers and Leanne had tidied up for me, ushered me to his car and opened the door. 'Your chariot awaits, madam.'

When I was settled, he closed it gently. I felt rather spoiled to be chauffeured about, especially given how much running around I did for Anita. It was nice to have someone looking out for me for a change.

On the drive to Yarra River Hospital, the home of the Lost Lovelies, Gerard congratulated me on the event. I quickly corrected him. 'Anita's the star attraction. Our success is down to the work she does.'

Gerard agreed, but he said, 'I don't think you give yourself enough credit, Martha. Your organisational skills are fantastic. The guests at the lunch know they had a great time, but it wouldn't even occur to most of them that putting a big event together requires an enormous amount of work.'

I had to agree with that.

Gerard was a courteous driver who slowed to allow a jaywalking duck and her babies to cross the road. 'The effort you put into looking after everyone was impressive. I wonder if Anita appreciates that?'

'Of course, she does,' I replied. 'She's always grateful and quite lavish with her praise.'

'I'm sure she's generous in her praise for the things she notices, but you're so efficient that a lot of things get done without her noticing.'

Well, that pleased me no end. And suddenly, I began to notice Gerard.

4

Jamie

I walked from the street into the darkness of The Journo's Club. A bit knackered from last night's romp with Anita, I hoped a hair of the dog might help. Anita took what she wanted in all ways. It was as if she was so badly done by she was entitled to have whatever she fancied, including me. That suited me just fine.

Adjusting to the gloom, I noticed Jack Ruler's trench coat on the rack. I gazed about and spotted my old mentor sitting alone at a table near the bar.

'G'day, mind if I join you?'

'Pull up a pew,' growled Jack.

'Beer?' I asked.

'Why thank you, mate. Don't mind if I do.'

I waved to Aunty Thelma who brought two beers, full strength for Jack and a light for me. I felt a stab of concern for Jack as he gulped down the brew. I predicted another attempt at rehab for him before too long. For the moment though, I put my pessimistic thoughts on the backburner. Getting his hot takes was always a joy, so I asked, 'What do you think about the next election?'

Jack rolled his eyes. 'The boss has made it clear we are to support the government and belt the hell out of the opposition.'

'We go through this bullshit every four years,' I grumbled. 'I'd like a chance to write the truth for once.'

'Whatever that is!' Jack snorted, winding up for a rant. 'What other choice is there in this fuckin' one news empire country? Journalists are supposed to go against the flow. You know you're a journalist when there's a disaster and everyone else except you is running away. But in Australia you do what the old boss man says because he's filthy rich and he's been running this country for years.' Jack coughed and hacked for a moment. He stopped to draw breath and took a big swig of beer, which seemed temporarily to heal him. He wiped his mouth with the back of his hand. 'How's Daisy and the kids?'

'Yeah, they're good. Daisy's gone back to teaching. She's got a job working with special needs kids and she loves it.'

Jack watched me out of the corner of his eye. 'Are you still rooting that foundation woman?'

I was taken aback. How did Jack know? I decided the safest way to prevent the wily old fox from getting a rise out of me was to remain silent.

Jack took another long swig of beer. 'The old man uses journalists in the same way sharks hunt. He sends the young bucks like you in to get the stories, to persuade the targets to trust a journalist. In return, you build up their reputation and turn them into a name. You write some nice stuff and they get more famous. They think they've got the media on their side, but when they begin to fall that's when the sharks start circling. The more you promote them the higher they go, and the higher they go the further they fall. People, especially women, like to share their innermost thoughts with journalists and that's why we sleep with them.'

Jack's critique was interrupted by a violent fit of coughing. I averted my eyes until he'd got rid of whatever crap was obstructing his breathing apparatus. I felt my old mentor's hand clap my shoulder.

'Still alive, Jamie!'

'Jesus, Jack,' I complained, juggling my beer, 'you nearly knocked the glass out of my hand!'

Jack released my shoulder and went for his own glass.

'What have you been working on?'

'The Victims' Voices Bill. What do you reckon about it?'

Jack immediately snapped about. 'That's her agenda, Jamie, lad. Have you forgotten everything I taught you? There might be a story there, but you've always got to be an outsider, a stranger, because if you're not a stranger, you're an insider, one of them. You should be after what she wants hidden and if you don't do that, you're nothing more than a publicist. You might as well get a job being a spin doctor for some bent politician.'

I was surprised at how indignant that made me feel. His words reduced Anita to an amusing little yarn, but she was much more than that. How many people would be able to drag themselves up by their bootstraps after having their baby snatched? Anita had courage; she was determined to fight for what she believed in. She stood up for traumatised parents and she didn't let the knockers faze her. I respected her energy and her commitment.

Yes, a journalist is always after stories, but Anita was different. We'd been on and off over the years, more on than off of late. She was great in bed, but afterwards she'd turn away from me and curl herself up in a little ball. I wanted to understand her better, to get a handle on her contradictions.

I couldn't wait to be with her again. Not that I'd ever tell Jack.

Instead, I asked Jack if he wanted another beer.

'Well, I'm not exactly dying of thirst.'

I ordered two more beers from Aunty Thelma. His beer had been on the table for less than a minute before it was gone. Jack wiped his mouth and continued with his cynical but insightful ramblings as though he'd never stopped. 'It can take a long time to get to the real story. Sometimes it hasn't happened when you get on the scene and so you hang around until it does. There's no law against enjoying yourself while you're waiting. Just don't ever become an insider. Stay with her until she becomes a loser, that's where the real story is.' Jack looked down, surprised to see his glass was empty.

I shifted in my seat, staring at my own untouched beer. My editor wanted the puff human interest pieces. Who would ever suggest that parents who'd lost a child because of a crime wasn't a good story? Anita's work was worth supporting.

Jack suddenly stood up, somewhat unsteadily. 'I'll get us another beer.'

I smiled and shook my head. 'No, mate. I'm taking you home.'

Jack gave me an appealing look. 'Just one more, mate?'

'Nah, it's home time. I've learned a lot from you, mate, and I need you stay alive long enough to teach me even more.'

Jack moaned. 'I need a slash.'

I sighed. 'Alright, go do what you've got to do. I'll get your coat.'

I collected Jack's trench coat from the rack, said goodbye to Aunty Thelma, and waited outside the men's toilet for my old mentor to come out, just as I'd been doing ever since I was a cadet.

My mind drifted, but one thing was clear. I was hooked on Anita, had been for years. I knew it was a rookie mistake and I should know better, but somehow my feelings about her got in the way of my better judgment.

I'd first seen Anita with Michael at the interview they gave after Heath disappeared. Michael was supposed to do all the talking, but the scrum wanted to get to her. Anita surprised everyone, and possibly herself, by rallying and stepping up to the mark. She answered every question thrown at her clearly and calmly. Sure, her voice quavered when they mentioned Heath by name and that only made them happier—'grieving mother shows pain in public' is pure gold—but it was a good story and Anita was brilliant.

I watched as she struggled to make them see her perspective and I admired her fortitude and patience with some of the total drongos from the gutter press. I decided to wait until they'd all left to try to talk to her.

When the room was almost empty and Michael was busy talking to two police officers, I approached Anita, introduced myself and smiled sympathetically. 'That must have been so tough on you.'

Anita looked me right in the eye. 'They didn't scare me. I've got more important things to worry about. My baby has been taken. There's nothing worse than that.'

I was impressed by her strength. I offered her a quiet, off the record chat. Her gaze never left mine as she took my business card.

It wasn't until months later that an opportunity arose for us to be on our own together. There'd been another child murder and Anita, in supporting the bereaved parents, granted me an interview. Even better, she persuaded the parents to give me an exclusive. It was a page one story picked up by the radio jocks all day and it got a mention in the public broadcaster's main evening televised news. I asked her if she'd accept my dinner invitation as a thank you. She agreed and I took her to a charming little French place by the river. Anita opened up to me that evening, and one thing led to another …

I sighed. I wasn't ready to let Anita Hammond-Jones go just yet.

Jack came staggering out of the men's toilets and I helped him with his coat. 'When are you gonna get rid of this coat, Jack?' I ribbed him. 'It makes you look like a flasher.'

He grinned. 'I like it.'

As we walked to the cab rank, Jack took me by the arm. 'Jamie, I meant what I said. You're a good journalist, but you'll lose your credibility if you let yourself be seduced by your subject and get caught up with her and her causes. You've got to be the observer, not a player.'

After I'd poured Jack into a taxi, I tried to call Anita but only got her voice message.

'It's Jamie, call me back when you can.'

I was hoping she would.

5

Louisa

I love the Bluestone University at this time of year. The old magnolias in full bloom are just gorgeous with their honey-scent sweetening the air. They bring an exotic touch to the native shrubs and flowering gums that attract and shelter the blue wrens and finches.

On this fine day, I was escorting Judge Clifford Jamieson back to his car after his delivery of a guest lecture to my criminology students. It was something of a coup to get a sitting judge to give a lecture and the theatre had been packed with my students from all years, undergraduate and graduate.

I'd known Cliff for many years. We did our articles year together at the Government Solicitors Office. That was a busy and exciting time. Cliff and I spent long nights researching and preparing briefs for court. Our days were devoted to running from our office to the courts to barristers' chambers and back to the office and back to court. Being a litigation lawyer was a bit like being a cerebral athlete.

After completing articles, Cliff became a judge's associate and after that a prosecutor. For the next fifteen years, I worked as a criminal law barrister. This meant we were on different sides, but when our paths did cross outside court we greeted each other as old friends. Cliff ended up married with two children and would proudly show me photographs of his wife and kids over the years. Cliff was later appointed to the bench of the Supreme Court. I'd survived a failed, child-free marriage, and work at the Bar was drying up, so I decided to pursue my real passion—academe. I loved research and teaching and tried to give my students as much of a taste of the real world as possible. That's why I asked Cliff, soon after his ascension to the Bench, to give a guest lecture.

It had been a lively session. My students were in a unit of study that focussed on the human rights of perpetrators, and as an offshoot of that, victims' rights. It seemed timely, with the very public and somewhat aggressive campaign by victims' groups to get the Victims' Voices Bill passed. I was keen to hear from Cliff what his views about this Bill were, especially as sentencing seemed to be one of the major issues of contention.

'Do you have time for a drink?' I asked.

He thanked me with a smile but shook his head. 'I'd like to, Lou, but I'm driving.'

I grinned. 'Does that mean I can't give you the nice bottle of red in my bag to thank you for coming out today?'

Cliff shrugged his shoulders and, ever the gentleman, guided me around a muddy puddle. 'Well, that's not such a hardship. I can always have a drink when I get home!'

I laughed and handed the gift bag to him. 'It's been good to see you again after so long. You know, I've always wanted to know something. You were such a fiery and formidable prosecutor, but you never really told me if it was hard to make the transition to unbiased judge.'

We dodged a gaggle of students near the library and crossed a courtyard that led towards the car park. He searched his pocket for his car keys.

'Well, these days I have to view cases through a wider lens. So, yes it was a big change for me, making unbiased decisions based on all the evidence. It's easier now.'

I'd always assumed it hadn't been easy, but it was interesting to hear him say so. He'd certainly copped some flak. 'You've had some tough media commentary lately,' I noted. I apprehensively recalled my own article that was generally critical of the judiciary.

Cliff shrugged. 'It comes with the job. Every judge, especially those who were once prosecutors, have been accused of being a turncoat. I don't take much notice of it.' Cliff suddenly stopped and turned to face me. 'It was great being a prosecutor. I could thump on the table and bang on about things like retribution. I didn't have to worry about the motivations or vulnerabilities of the accused, that was the job of the defence—people like you, Lou. Do you miss the Bar?'

I had no hesitation in my reply. 'Not a bit! I loved the work, but it was hard yakker. I'm content with university life, as is my cardiologist.'

Cliff snorted and opened his car door. 'Well, my dear, thank you for inviting me out to visit the next generation of lawyers. I've had a busy week, so I'm looking forward to a quiet night reading the full text of the Victims' Voices Bill. Have you read it yet? I'd be interested in your opinion.'

The Bill. It was all my students were talking of at the moment. As a criminologist, I was well aware of the war of words and the tensions between those who wanted to provide more inclusion and support in legal processes for victims of crime and those who were concerned about the human rights of accused persons. Of course, there were also a host of views in-between.

I sighed. 'I have indeed read it, and I've read the media reports on the Bill and they worry me. Papers like *The Watcher* are baying for blood without weighing up any of the consequences for the administration of justice. I mean, for a start, where are we supposed to put all these people who could be held indefinitely? I went out to the Billabong Centre last week to have lunch with Helene Morton. Her facility is chockas. The staff are run off their feet and there's precious little time for any therapy, it is just containment. We're creating colonies of outcasts.'

Cliff looked deeply concerned. 'What worries me is this proposed law can exclude the discretion of judges in sentencing. As it is, I'm having to apply the minimum sentence laws that oblige me to impose punishments that I know are disproportionate to the offences committed.' He gave me a little smile. 'I've also just read your research article, Lou, the one in *The Journal of Judicial Affairs* on the changing role of judges in sentencing and the impact of their sentencing remarks.'

I made a face at him. 'Oh, you mean the one that contained some criticisms of the judiciary? What did you think of the findings?'

'I agree with your conclusions that judges have an important role to play in educating the public about what kind of considerations we take into account when determining sentence lengths, and in advising the public why certain behaviours are classed as criminal. We judges complain that the public don't understand what we do, but we don't do enough to explain our work to them.'

I nodded. 'I agree. Your remarks in R v Warburton are a good example.

You said to a man who had murdered his teenage daughter, "You behaved as if she was your property that you could do what you liked with, and, when she told you she was leaving home, you viciously stabbed her in the kitchen in front of your other children. This kind of behaviour deserves the harshest condemnation and punishment." Your words condemned the individual offender, but also sent a message to society at large that domestic violence will not be tolerated.'

Cliff seemed happy with that, but he pressed me with a dark look. 'But you are also critical of us?'

I nodded again, with a cheeky smile this time. 'Well, Cliff, you know we academics have to include some criticism otherwise we wouldn't be seen to be doing our job.'

He laughed. 'I can't speak to that, yet your research indicates there is significant discrepancy between individual judges in sentencing practices?'

I nodded, my smile fading. 'Yes, I did find that. My major concern is that while the sentencing remarks send a message of denunciation, they seem ineffective to the public when a short sentence is given. Warburton got eight years and a non-parole period of five. Most members of the public would think that was inadequate, especially when the remarks were "this kind of behaviour deserves the harshest condemnation and punishment". The public and advocacy groups, such as The Lost Lovelies Foundation, latch on to such discrepancies and use them to stir the pot.'

'There was expert evidence to show he had fully cooperated with a men's anger management program and was utterly contrite,' said Cliff. He gave a little shrug. 'Well, I guess judges are only human. We are fiercely independent and sometimes that means it's difficult to ensure consistency of decision making.'

I laughed. 'The court administrators don't describe managing judges as "herding cats" without good reason.'

Cliff put my gift on the back seat with his briefcase. He got into his car and put down his window.

I leaned down to look at him through the window. 'I have nothing but the highest respect for judges, Cliff. The ability to exercise discretion in deciding individual sentencing is important. One size doesn't fit all.'

He revved the engine of his BMW and smiled. 'I'm glad you see it that way. I'll be interested to talk to you again, Lou, after I've read the Victims' Voices Bill.'

'Take care, my friend.'

I watched him go and returned to my office in the law building. My last duty of the day was a 5:00 pm appointment with my new Masters student, Elissa Mustaffa, who wanted some guidance on her thesis topic.

Elissa turned up right on time. She was a bright looking young woman, dressed simply in a cream-coloured blouse and black slacks with lace up shoes. She'd been in Australia since her high school days, and she had high expectations of herself. She was eager to get her education and then head home to Malaysia. She missed her family.

I invited her to sit with me at the table and poured a cup of herbal tea for each of us. 'So, Elissa, what did you think of Judge Jamieson's lecture?'

She picked up her tea and blew on it to cool it down. 'I found it interesting. He was good at getting the students to explore sentencing principles. But then again, in contrast, when we were at The Lost Lovelies Foundation function the other day, I could see Anita's point of view and that of her guests. So many people have suffered in losing a child through crime.'

I nodded.

Elissa's brow furrowed. 'Anita Hammond-Jones is charismatic, no?'

'She certainly knows how to woo an audience,' I agreed. 'Tell me, have you thought much about your thesis topic?'

She gave me a wry smile. 'I think about little else, Professor Moore.'

I nodded. Choosing a thesis was never easy. 'What are the most important things you would like to understand about offending and our criminal justice system?'

She looked thoughtful. 'What I want to understand is why people can be so cruel to each other.'

That surprised me. 'You could have explored that question by doing psychiatry,' I pointed out.

Elissa confessed she had considered that but thought the course was too long. 'You have to complete a medical degree before you can even begin psychiatry. Perhaps if I wasn't so lonely for my family, I would have reconsidered, but I am happy I have done criminology because it helps me understand society as well as people, and anyway, criminology borrows a lot from psychology and psychiatry.'

I was impressed. Most students just accept what you teach them, but Elissa obviously thought deeply about her studies and the place of criminology in the overall context of the law.

'Well, now that you've seen the families at the Lost Lovelies luncheon and heard Judge Jamieson speak, has that influenced your choice of topic?' I asked.

Elissa nodded. 'I see there are contradictions that need to be researched. There is a clash between the quest for justice, that can include revenge and the place of rehabilitation and even forgiveness. I would like to explore some of the issues raised by Judge Jamieson by interviewing more judges to understand their reasoning better.' Elissa stopped abruptly, and said, 'I hope this doesn't sound too pretentious, but in trying to understand cruelty, I begin to think the most dangerous people are those who think they are right.'

I considered this for a while. 'Do you mean people who think they're right or people who know they're right?'

Elissa looked pensive. 'That's what I want to find out. I have read as much as I can about the Heath Hammond-Jones case. I wonder about this so much. First, the parents and the baby are victims. The midwife is implicated. Should she have left the baby and mother unsupervised? The offender, Jennifer Harris, has she received an appropriate sentence? Shouldn't she be free by now?'

I nodded. 'She's still detained, even though she's served her time. They kept her in using the Mental Health Act.'

Elissa frowned. 'That seems most unfair.'

'It's a legal anomaly that's been justified by the government on benevolent grounds.'

'How can continued detention be justified on benevolent grounds?' she asked incredulously.

'She is being held under the Mental Health Act so they can claim she is receiving treatment and that it is of benefit to her.'

'That's supposed to be benevolence?' Elissa looked troubled.

I imparted my years of experience on the matter. 'Beware the therapeutic state, Elissa.'

'Meaning?'

'Meaning, when the State purports to be helping someone, their human rights can go out the window. If the Victims' Voices Bill is passed, there's a chance Jennifer Harris will never be released, even if she has no mental illness.'

Elissa was looking confused and I wasn't surprised. I was having trouble comprehending this proposed scheme too. It went against all the principles of criminal justice that I'd ever believed in.

'What would be the grounds for holding Jennifer?' Elissa asked.

'It would be justified on the grounds that her victim, Anita Hammond-Jones, believes her to be a continuing threat to public safety.'

Elissa frowned. 'That would mean Jennifer could be incarcerated forever. How to reconcile these things? I believe this requires research.'

I liked this rather intense young woman and we talked about how she might begin to test her ideas. 'We have to refine this so you have a workable hypothesis. First, we need to think about the available data. Crime statistics, as I'm sure you know, are notoriously problematic.'

Elissa agreed. 'Yes, I have learned they never tell you how much crime there is, just who got caught and convicted.' She paused with a frown. 'Do you think people affected by child murders would be a suitable cohort?'

I had a feeling she was going to tackle this sensitive subject. 'Yes, they would be a suitable cohort. But as you saw at the Lost Lovelies function it could be harrowing. Are you sure you want to expose yourself to that?'

Elissa nodded. 'I can think of nothing more cruel to do to a person than kill their child, so, yes. I know it will be difficult emotionally as well as intellectually, but I think I have sufficient maturity to deal with that. I would like to understand the reasons why lobbyists like The Lost Lovelies Foundation think it is necessary to have a Victims' Voices Act and why they don't trust the judges.'

Well, that got me fired up too. This topic would be sure to attract a grant from The Lost Lovelies Foundation, but only if the application was carefully phrased so Anita, or more likely that sharp-eyed assistant of hers, wouldn't toss it out. I printed out a Lost Lovelies grant application form and gave it to Elissa. 'I think it's a great topic, but it needs further refinement to ensure it's doable. I'd like you take this form home and think about how to apply for a grant without alarming the funders. There is a possibility that the end results won't flatter their organisation. Perhaps you can word it to focus on the judges, as opposed to the intentions of lobbyists.'

Elissa took the form and scanned it briefly. She folded it up and put it into her bag and stood up to leave.

'Professor Moore?'

I looked up. Elissa stood in the doorway, a frown spread across her face.

'Do you think they'll pass the Bill, even with its flaws?'

I shrugged. 'Just look at what they passed during the pandemic.' I tried to give her a reassuring smile. 'It's currently with the government's legal people, so hopefully they'll pick up the most obvious flaws. Parliamentary scrutiny follows that. With any luck, the problems will become more apparent to its supporters by then.'

We arranged to meet again in a week's time.

6

Martha

I called Anita to go over her schedule for the day.

Yawning and complaining, Anita grumbled, 'I'm not really with it yet. A bit of breakfast by the riverside might help. Why don't you meet me at Rivers and we can talk while we eat?'

I'd be waiting forever if I agreed to that. 'Counter-offer, how about I drop by and pick you up?'

'Martha, darling, that would be fabulous,' she mumbled.

So, I drove to her house just south of the Yarra River, the same house she'd shared with Michael. She wasn't ready when I got there so I waited in the kitchen. The place was a mess. There were dirty dishes and glasses in the sink and several empty champagne bottles on the table.

While Anita showered, I washed the dishes and put the rubbish out. I decided to give the floor a quick wash, but I couldn't find the mop, so I went in search of it. As I passed what should have been Heath's nursery, I took a quick peek inside. It was, as always, impeccable. The blue bassinet remained unused and the bluebird mobile I'd bought for them still hung sadly over the empty cradle. The little teddy bear sat on the chair, just as it had ten years ago. I quietly closed the door and returned to my chores. When Anita was finally ready, she didn't even notice I'd cleaned the place up.

At the café, Anita ordered pomegranate juice, eggs Florentine and the newspapers. I had a hot chocolate and poached eggs on toast. Walter brought us a complimentary sparkling mineral water, not a rare occurrence when Anita flashed her beautiful smile. To her delight, the gossip column in the paper featured a photograph of her with the governor's husband, Edwin Singh. The caption read, 'Anita Hammond-Jones radiant in Roland Crawfish.'

Anita clapped her hands in delight. 'Yes! Radiant, I love that! That's how the media usually describes English princesses. This kind of publicity is gold for the foundation.'

I took a sip of my hot chocolate. 'Don't forget, at noon you go to the gym for an hour. Your personal trainer can't make it today but has sent his friend who, he assures me, is well-trained and talented.'

'Is he a hunk?'

'Naughty girl!' I grinned at her and then looked at my planner. 'At 1.15 pm you shower, get dressed and we'll get a taxi to Channel 3 where the hairdresser and make-up artists will look after you. We need to be there by 2.15 pm to pre-record for *Today, Tonight and Tomorrow*, which goes to air tonight at 6.00 pm. The topic is the Bill.'

Anita was pleased. She loved talking about the Bill. Getting it on the parliamentary legislative calendar was a major effort, so to have a national program willing to talk about it could only boost her push for it to succeed. Her eyes shone. 'We've worked so hard for this! I think we're nearly there, Martha. I've got a really good feeling it's finally going to be passed.'

I returned her smile. 'Me too.'

Anita took my hand. 'No bereaved parent will ever have to be insulted by their child's perpetrator being free to re-offend.'

'That's all down to you, Anita. You've worked hard, much harder than any other victims' rights groups.'

'Because of us, Martha,' Anita corrected me. 'You've been there every step of the way.'

I felt so proud of us, as Anita smiled at me. We had worked hard and sacrificed much, especially lately. It had been at least a week since I'd been out with my walking group, and I'd had to reject several shifts from the nursing agency. Still, the cause was worth it.

I put aside the schedule. 'With an election due before Christmas, the Bill must get through by then.'

'I'm confident,' said Anita with resolute firmness, 'and I'll take my confidence into the recording studio.'

'After recording, it would be good if you could come back to the office. There's a few things that need attending to,' I said.

'Okay. Will you stay and watch the show?'

I nodded and tucked into my eggs. 'I can stay until seven tonight, but then I've got a shift. I picked up three nights at St Stephens.'

That made her smile. 'Oh, that's great. We can watch my interview together before you head off to save lives. I'm thinking of wearing something pink, you know, nice and soft.'

Anita had an extensive wardrobe for Lost Lovelies publicity. When we got to work, she mused over a dozen outfits before ultimately deciding on a Sally Slate pink and pale gold suit with fringed hems, a pink satin blouse and white boots of Spanish leather. I laid the clothes out for her (all gifts from our generous donors) while she was at the gym.

Later, we took a taxi to the studio. Anita talked a lot about Marcel, the guy who took over from her personal trainer.

'Oh, Martha, I was looking around for him when he scared me by coming from behind. I turned and found myself looking into the face of one of the most gorgeous looking men I have ever seen. I thought, whooey, he is so sexy! I even asked him if he was a gypsy.'

'Anita!' I was shocked. 'You didn't ask that, did you?'

She smiled. 'He didn't mind. He just said "oui" in a really sexy way. He's got this dark, curly hair and these amazing, flashing dark eyes, and long-lashes and a lovely smile. And after our session, when I was puffing and covered in sweat, I was towelling my face and hair and Marcel asked me out for coffee, calling me "mademoiselle" and everything. Naturally, it was a no-go, but Marcel promised to watch the show and said he'd see me on Tuesday at nine for our next workout. Guess what he did next, Martha?'

I raised my eyebrows. 'I've no idea.'

Anita's eyes shone with excitement. 'He put my hand to his lips, ever so gently, and brushed my fingers with the most seductive little kiss.'

I just managed to avoid snorting, as I thought, uh-oh, here we go again. Instead, I asked, 'Is he really French?'

Anita laughed. 'Oh, he's just so French.'

'Hmm,' I grumbled. 'He sounds a bit too French to me.'

We eventually made our way to the studio, and the driver turned to Anita with a curious look on his face. 'Are you famous or normal?'

Anita flashed a smile. 'Famous.'

I paid the driver with a foundation credit card, and he grinned as he jumped out of the car to assist Anita with her door. I noticed he didn't come anywhere near mine. Oh well, I was used to playing second fiddle to Anita.

'When can I see you on the television, madam?'

Anita slid her legs out the door. 'Tonight, Channel 3 at 6.00 pm.'

'Okay, okay.' He grinned at her. 'I will definitely watch.'

After walking down corridors lined with glossy photographs of television stars, past and present, we were guided into the studio by a handsome young man who introduced himself as Jason. He had plugs in his ears, receiving instructions from someone, somewhere, invisible to us. Anita was swept into make-up, while I sat on a comfortable couch in the waiting area doing everything in my power to resist the large bowl of lollies that sat on a coffee table beside the magazines.

Anita soon returned, all made up and glowing. 'What do you think, Martha dear?' she asked, pouting, and poking out her bum with her hands on her knees. I laughed and wolf whistled, and she was quickly whisked away into the studio by Jason.

I watched the filming from the monitor in the waiting area. The set looked like a lounge room with pot plants and pale green furniture. It was the perfect backdrop for her pink and gold suit.

It didn't take them long to get started. Anita was sitting alone in an armchair facing her three inquisitors who were on the settee. They were Souzi Court, Zaria Singh, and Jonny Willow, a current affairs veteran who'd been gracing our screens for decades.

After the introductions, Jonny handed over to Souzi. 'How are you able to be so brave after losing a baby in such awful circumstances?'

Anita gave her a beautifully practised sad smile. 'I do it for other parents who have lost a child to criminals.'

Souzi quickly turned to the topic of the Bill. 'Anita, you seem confident that your perspective on victims' rights is the correct one. We know, however, this is a controversial issue and there are opposing views. How can you be sure you have the right answers?'

This was tricky phrasing from Souzi, but I was unnecessarily nervous because Anita, as usual, was fabulous. Her reply was simple. 'I was a mother. My baby was stolen and left to starve. When you've been through what I have, you know what's right.'

Souzi pressed harder. 'Anita, the Victims' Voices Bill, if passed, would take away significant and long-accepted human rights of offenders who have served their time and are eligible for release. Those people could have done all the right things, such as completed behaviour modification programs and engaged in good behaviour. Aren't they entitled to be released?'

This made me uneasy, but Anita smiled her Mona Lisa smile and in a gentle voice said, 'Souzi, the cold hard facts are these: a baby was taken, my baby, he was starved, and he died. It is not an isolated case. Only last year another child killer was released on parole. He was well-behaved in prison, completing anger management training and other rehabilitation programs. He knew he only had to behave himself for five years and then he'd be free. He didn't change. In fact, he reoffended within weeks of release. He just pretended to rehabilitate and now we have another traumatised, grieving family and further public mistrust of our criminal justice system. It's always the innocent who suffer.'

As the interview went on, I was more and more proud of Anita. Souzi had thrown difficult questions at her and she just took it all in her stride, amazing woman that she was. I was relieved and pleased when the interview ended. At times, I was cringing at the audacity of some of the questions, and although Anita didn't show it, I knew her well enough to realise she'd be fuming.

When it was finally over, Jason brought Anita back to the area where I was waiting and handed her over to me. She grabbed a handful of lollies and he showed us out, reminding us the show would be going to air that evening at six. He thanked Anita and asked if he could call her sometime.

Anita flashed her beautiful smile. 'Yes, any time at all. Just call and Martha will arrange everything.'

7

Martha

I sorted through the mail. There were donations of money and services, letters of support, accounts, and a small letter with a handwritten address. I picked up the silver letter opener, the one with the ruby and little pearls, and slit it open.

The letter was from Dr Helene Morton, Jennifer Harris's psychiatrist, and someone I'd known from my nursing days. I frowned.

Dear Ms Hammond-Jones,

May I begin by congratulating you on the success of The Lost Lovelies Foundation and the wonderful work you do for people who have suffered such terrible losses. I am a forensic psychiatrist and in my work I see some tragic cases.

It is one such case that I am writing to you about. I am the treating psychiatrist for Jennifer Harris, whose story you are sadly all too familiar with. Jennifer was only eighteen when she committed the horrible offence of taking your baby after losing her own to a stillbirth. She served prison time and is now a patient at the Billabong Forensic Centre.

Following prolonged therapy, Jennifer has made significant progress and is currently free of any symptoms of mental illness.

As her treating doctor, I am convinced Jennifer is no longer a danger to anyone and she would greatly benefit from being allowed back into the community. As you know, the Tribunal charged with deciding these matters is the Mental Offenders Review Tribunal. The MORT will be meeting in three months' time to review Jennifer's case.

The MORT is required to take into account the views of families of victims. If the Victims' Voices Bill is passed, it will be compulsory for the Tribunal to detain an offender if a person 'significantly affected by a crime against themselves or a close family member, opposes the release of the offender'.

I was wondering if you could give me some time to talk to you about Jennifer and explain her progress. Not a day goes by that she doesn't express her deep remorse at what happened …

I couldn't finish reading the letter. How insensitive of Helene Morton to expect Anita to have sympathy for her child's murderer! What planet was she coming from?

'Martha? How did we do with donations today?'

I hastily stuffed the letter back into the envelope, gathered up the mail and took it into her, the letter hidden in the mix. Anita could get righteously fired up and it was always interesting to watch her explode.

'We've done well. There was a cheque for $45,000 from the Racing Authority and another for $10,000 from a secondary college where the kids went out collecting for us.'

Anita laughed. 'Oh, the sweet darlings. What fabulous teachers they must have. What's this?'

I went to hang up some of the new dresses Anita had received gratis from designers hoping she would wear it at a big event. I was neatly stacking some shoeboxes when I heard a gasp. Anita's face was burning brightly.

'Anita, are you okay?'

She thrust the letter at me, an expression of pure fury on her face. 'Put this shit in the shredder,' she hissed, jumping to her feet. 'I need to get away from here. I'm going to the parlour to have a nice facial peel.'

I was hesitant to stop her because she was always calmer after a treatment. 'Is that a good idea given you've got a photo shoot tomorrow? You don't want to look too peeled.'

Anita went pale and she sat back down. 'Heath's ten year memorial, of course.'

My heart went out to her. 'How about I book the facial for Friday? Your skin can settle before facing the cameras again.'

'Oh yes,' she replied weakly, staring blankly at her desk. 'Martha, can you please pour me a gin and tonic?'

I slipped the letter into my pocket and brought her the drink. 'Let's go through the rest of the mail.'

***

At 6.00 pm I poured a flute of champagne for Anita and a glass of sparkling mineral water for me. I served some of Anita's favourite truffle and turmeric crackers and switched on the television.

Anita, her pain boxed away once more, gave a shriek of excitement. 'Oh great, they've made me lead interview and I've got the promo spot too!'

The two female interview panelists looked leggy and gorgeous in contrast to the craggy-faced veteran, Jonny Willows. As I had anticipated, the lounge set with pale green furnishings complemented Anita's suit really well.

She was pleased. 'It's always interesting and a bit unnerving to see the final interview after they've edited it. You can never be sure what they'll cut.'

I quietly agreed.

Jonny opened the segment. 'The government has prepared a new law that is expected to go before parliament soon. No one has worked harder than our next guest, Anita Hammond-Jones, in lobbying for this reform. If the Bill gets passed it will allow victims of crimes against children to have the final say about whether the offender who harmed their child is released or remains in detention.' He turned towards Anita. 'Anita, you are the founder and CEO of The Lost Lovelies Foundation. Please tell us what prompted you to establish the foundation.'

The angle of the camera gave the impression that Anita was looking straight into Jonny's eyes. 'I was a happily married suburban housewife. My husband, Michael, was a professor at the Bluestone University.'

I relaxed and took a sip of water. So far so good.

'We lived in a lovely house in South Riverside. It wasn't long before I became pregnant. We were happy, my parents were thrilled and—'

'Tell us a little about your parents?' Jonny interrupted.

'They're country people, orchardists, living near Ballarat. I was their only child, so they were over the moon about a grandchild. I dreamed of my baby visiting his grandparents in the country.'

'You were expecting a little boy?'

'Yes, Michael and I decided we'd learn the baby's gender early so we could plan the nursery. We worked on it together and it was, and still is, beautiful, with blue—'

'The nursery is still there?'

'Yes, I couldn't bear to change it.'

'Was it a straightforward birth?'

'Yes, the birth was remarkably quick and without complications. I held Heath in my arms, and I have never before or since experienced such a feeling of overwhelming joy, completeness and sheer unadulterated happiness.'

She was so good at this. I'd never have been able to appear so calm in the face of such questioning. In fact, I hadn't. I hated being questioned when I had my 15 minutes of notoriety.

'What happened next?' Jonny asked.

'I slept for some time after the birth,' Anita said, her face etched with grief. 'When I woke up, I could feel something wasn't right. Michael was there, as were Mum and Dad. It was Mum who told me the dreadful news.'

Jonny's brow creased in sympathy. 'Take your time, Anita. How did you feel at that moment?'

'I asked what was going on, if Heath was sick, but my mum said it was worse. "Heath has been taken," she said. Well, I couldn't believe it, Jonny. I asked her what she meant by "taken" and she told me that my baby had been stolen.' Anita paused, her eyes looking watery. 'I think I started screaming because the doctor and a nurse came in and injected me with something and I don't remember anything until the next morning when I woke up.'

'What happened when you woke up?'

'They told me a teenager had given birth to a stillborn child. She took my sweet little Heath. They found him days later starved and frozen at a construction site.'

'And the teen?'

'Oh, she was there too, in a stupor,' Anita replied. 'The police charged her with kidnapping and murder. She was deemed fit to plead. A jury found her guilty and she was sentenced to just eight years. She'd already been in custody for two by the time of sentencing, and after three years, she was shifted out of the prison system to a psychiatric institution.'

'Let's move ahead to the work you do now,' said Jonny.

Anita nodded. 'I came to realise the only way I could survive was by doing something to help other people who had suffered like me. I started The Lost Lovelies Foundation in memory of Heath and others who had lost a child through criminal actions. The foundation turned ten this year.'

'Anita, you have been a strong advocate for the rights of victims to have a say in the sentencing of offenders,' Jonny interrupted.

'That's right, interrupt the grieving mother,' muttered Anita.

'Yes,' said Anita. 'I was approached by a group representing victims of crime. They wanted me to support them in making sure governments and courts included victims' views in sentencing. The courts had been far too lenient and there were several disasters when the parole board released offenders and failed to supervise them.'

'What disasters?' asked Jonny.

'In one case a pedophile who had abducted and raped a five-year-old girl was jailed for five years. He was released at the end of his sentence and six months later he did the same thing to another little girl. In another case, a child killer was released on parole and also re-offended. The system has failed those kids and their parents.'

Jonny raised an eyebrow. 'Do you oppose parole?'

Anita sighed. 'The parole board people keep saying, oh well, they have to be released some time, it's better to have them on parole so they can be supervised. But they weren't supervised, and I asked myself, well, why do they have to be released at all? If they are a danger to kids, they should never be released. Some people say, "what about their human rights?" and I say what about the human rights of me and my child and all the other Lost Lovelies? What about them?'

It was at this point in the interview that Souzi Court took over the questioning. Anita burned as she watched. 'Fucking bitch,' she muttered.

I refilled Anita's glass.

Souzi gave Anita a patronising smile. 'Anita, do you think people who have been convicted of offences against children should be locked up forever?'

'That depends on the circumstances of each offence,' replied Anita.

Souzi looked bemused. 'Don't judges take that into account when they sentence offenders?'

Jonny spoke before Anita could respond. 'Anita, we've run out of time, but I thank you for sharing your story with us. You are a courageous woman.'

'Thank you, Jonny.'

'Thank you, Anita.'

'You were fantastic,' I told her.

Anita smiled. 'It's about helping others, Martha dear.'

'Well, you know I think you're marvellous, but I didn't like that Souzi Court woman at all.'

'Fucking bitch. When she smiled it was like being questioned by a well-groomed racehorse.' Anita glared at the television, now on mute. 'Did you notice how much they cut? Zaria Singh asked some really good questions about supporting victims of crime.'

I drained my glass. 'Yes. It looked like she just sat there doing nothing.'

Anita scowled. 'They edited out all the positive things I said about the foundation and how much we've achieved.'

They did leave the last part of the interview just hanging there, but I decided not to say so. Instead, I tried to be positive. 'You handled it all beautifully.' I put down my glass and stood up. 'I've got to run, I've got a shift at St Stephens. We've an early morning with the memorial shoot, so I'll call you at five and I'll pick you up at six. And don't forget we've got the board meeting on Friday and there are a lot of papers to prepare.'

Anita poured herself another drink and waved me off.

As I drove to work, I realised I still had the letter from Helene Morton in my pocket.

8

Helene

I sighed as I got out of the car and looked at my workplace. The mental health facilities in our state were well-designed for their time, but now they're run down and dismal. If it weren't for the clients, I'd have hated going in there every day. But the Billabong Centre was my baby, and I was its director. It was located way out the back of the old Jamieson Centre, the high security asylum for offenders who were found unfit to plead, and who languished behind its bluestone walls and barbed wire.

Conrad was waiting for me on the walkway with an eager smile on his face. Because staff numbers were so low, I always agreed to requests to accept work experience or placement students. Conrad, a trainee psychiatrist who was in his first year of postgraduate studies, was shadowing me for a few weeks. Conrad wasn't sure which branch of psychiatry he wanted to specialise in and was keen to familiarise himself with forensic psychiatry.

'Good morning, Conrad.'

'Good morning, Dr Helene. I saw you pull up, I hope you don't mind that I waited.'

I gave him a warm smile. 'Not at all.'

We walked companionably along the path together. There were a few tough succulents and geraniums that survived the lack of care in what was left of the gardens. Photographs of the place taken about fifty years ago show the gardens looking well cared for and lush. In those days, the patients were allowed to work around the facility, keeping it clean and freshly painted. This was said to be really good for clients with depression. But the trade unions protested saying the work should only be done by their members. The government of the day agreed, but they didn't provide any extra funding to pay for the work. So, the patients lost their activities and the facility deteriorated.

I sighed inwardly, trying not to let my mood infect Conrad.

I'd seen yet another article in *The Watcher* extolling the virtues of Anita

Hammond-Jones, and it was playing on my mind. I'd tried to contact the woman multiple times in recent months, but to no avail. Had she no idea what that terrible Bill would do to the clients here? We hadn't had a suicide in the five years I'd worked at Billabong, though there had been some attempts. I put them down to a loss of hope. Boredom at Billabong was a perennial problem and we were always looking for ways to tackle this challenge.

With the festive season approaching, I decided to call a meeting of the clients and nurses to discuss what we might do to cheer things up a bit.

I sent Conrad to round up everyone and readied myself for the day. I dropped into my desk chair and switched on my computer. I stared at my planner, the date of Jennifer's MORT hearing circled. I only hoped the letter I posted to Anita would get through where emails and calls failed.

Jennifer Harris had come to us at the end of her sentence. She should have been released into the community long before now, but strenuous lobbying by Anita led to a nervous government certifying Jennifer under the security provisions of the mental health legislation. This was a rare move and caused a lot of controversy at the time. Some people saw it as draconian, vindictive and possibly unconstitutional on human rights grounds; others argued the crime Jennifer had been convicted of was so dreadful it warranted special measures. Anyway, Anita won, Jennifer came here, and the public soon forgot about her.

I put my both hands on my desk and took a few deep, calming breaths. If that Bill passed, Jennifer would never be free.

Jennifer was as much a victim as a perpetrator. Her history was complex and not one I'd ever wish on anyone. Some of the circumstances leading up to her offending were unclear, as Jennifer had remained mum on the particulars.

What troubled me most about the whole situation was the way the psychiatric services were being used as a dumping ground for people considered to be blockages. Jennifer was just one of many. Psychiatric services ought to be dedicated to assisting people with mental illness by providing shelter and therapy—that's what they were designed to do—but the self-interested politicians were always keen to harvest the law for votes and we copped the fallout. Jennifer, in my opinion, was not mentally ill.

Unsurprisingly, Jennifer was often surly. She was even more so now that she had cottoned on to Anita's latest ambitions. She was a smart girl and had been studying remotely. Her legal studies made her well aware of what would happen to her if the Victims' Voices Bill was passed. Yet through all this, Jennifer was respected by the other clients. She tried not to let her confinement get her too down, despite her odd surly moments. The Bill hadn't passed yet. There was still hope.

I made my way to the main room. I looked around and was disappointed to see that Conrad had managed to round up just five clients for our first meeting. I could only suppose they were there because they were bored. However, Jennifer was there, along with Yvette, Tonya, Maddie and Jason, and that was something.

I mentioned the boredom issue and was unsurprised to see rolled eyes and hear snorts of derision.

Jennifer spoke first. 'You wonder why we're bored? Have a look at the activities list!'

I frowned. 'I didn't know we had one.'

'Exactly,' said Jennifer. She looked away in disgust.

'There might as well be none,' said Yvette. 'Do you know what's on it?'

'No,' I confessed. 'Juan, could you go and get it for us?'

Juan, one of our wonderful nurses, fetched the fly-spotted whiteboard that had 'Activities' scribbled at the top. Under Monday was written 'Bus Outing'.

'How long is it since any of us went out in a bus?' Jennifer demanded.

'We used to have bus trips,' I said. I was going to say more, but then I remembered when a reporter from *The Watcher* spotted us on an outing and ran the headline, 'Baby Killer's Picnic'. Of course, there was a comment from Anita who was typically vitriolic and kicked up so much fuss that the bus outings were stopped.

Under Tuesday, the activity listed was 'Yoga and Mindfulness'. Another disaster.

'Sorry, the funding ran out for yoga.' I was aware of the glares sent my way. 'Point taken. Okay, let's start again. Jennifer can you be our scribe? We can include whatever you want.'

I gave Jennifer the marker. 'Who has a suggestion for Sunday?'

'Prayers,' said Maddie sarcastically.

We all laughed as Jennifer wrote it down.

'Monday?' I prompted.

'Hip-hop,' said Yvette, beginning to look interested.

'Wednesday?' I could see the energy and interest start to appear in their eyes.

'Choir practice,' said Maddie. The mood in the room subtly changed. Everyone seemed to be considering the possibilities. Conrad looked over at me and smiled.

As the meeting neared its end, Jennifer reluctantly suggested, some of her surliness lingering, 'Why don't we write our own Christmas musical?'

Maddie looked doubtful. 'Where'd we get our audience? The Jamieson Centre?'

'Well, we could invite them if the Royal Family are too busy to come,' said Jennifer dryly.

Jason snorted. 'Yeah, Christmas could be busy, like, for them, but it could be pretty fun to ask the Jamieson people and all the inmates and staff of Billabong.'

'Clients, not inmates,' I reminded him.

He shrugged. 'We're not clients. Clients get to decide if they want something. Being here feels like being an inmate, so why pretend we're here with rights? Call it like it is, I say.'

This wasn't a new conversation for us at Billabong. The staff and I tried to use language that promoted a positive culture, but the clients saw things differently.

Conrad sensed the conversation veering away and guided the subject back to the musical. 'How about we incorporate everyone's experiences into the performance?'

Jennifer nodded. 'That's a great idea. I'd like to start work on a song called something like *Christmas Without Hope*.'

That sounded grim, but we agreed to write and stage a performance together. I decided I'd get Conrad to write a grant application for funding from a not-for-profit organisation. We wouldn't need much.

The meeting ended on a positive note. Maddie and Jason, and even Jennifer, promised to get a few more of the clients involved by the time of the next meeting.

I went back to the office and made some observations in client files, noting in particular that Jennifer continued to engage with other clients despite her keen awareness of the impending Victims' Voices Bill reading. I sat back, staring at my computer screen. By the end of the year, that horrible Bill might be an Act.

Indeed, it might be a Christmas without hope.

9

Gerard

I was at the Lost Lovelies office to do my usual audit of the books. Martha looked particularly lovely, and as there's no fool like an old fool, I suggested it would do her good to have a break and invited her over to the pub. She readily agreed. I had another reason to speak to her, and I didn't want to do it in the office.

We chose a table in the beer garden by the native mint trees. Martha said she liked the little bees that buzzed in among the mauve flowers. When we were settled with our drinks, she opened the conversation in a direct fashion. 'You know, it's been years since we first met, but you've never really told me why you joined the foundation.'

I felt my usual surge of panic rearing its ugly head whenever I was asked questions that opened old wounds and Martha, bless her, picked that up straight away. An apologetic expression crossed her face.

'Sorry, Gerard, I didn't mean to pry.'

I pushed away my fear. I didn't mind sharing my story, not with her. She knew most of it already.

'Well, you know I got a call from Anita about twelve months after the crash that killed my family.'

Martha nodded.

'She told me about the foundation and asked if we could meet. I didn't have much else to do at that time and my sister told me it wouldn't do me any harm to get out.'

'That was really courageous to meet with someone while you were grieving. A lot of people isolate themselves,' said Martha.

I felt a surge of gratitude for this sensible, kind woman. I knew I'd been right about her. I felt like I could tell her anything. 'Well, I love wine, but at that time I was reaching for the spirits too and that really scared me. I needed something to do. My sister could see it, I was just a bit slow off the mark.'

Martha nodded.

'Anita told me how she'd read about me in the paper. Honestly, Martha, I hate seeing pity in people's faces when they look at me.'

Martha gave me an empathetic smile. 'People often don't know what to say to a grieving person. Death makes them awkward.'

That had certainly been my experience. 'Either they cross the road when they see you coming or they go all dewy-eyed and look at you like you're a child who's fallen over,' I said. 'Anita was one of those dewy-eyed ones, and I'll be honest, Martha, that made me squirm. She asked if I minded talking about it. There was no point lying, so I just told her yes. Anita looked genuinely sad and apologised.' I gave Martha a wry look. 'Naturally, I felt bad, especially because of how much she'd suffered, so I told her I would be okay, that I was getting used to it.'

Martha put her hand on mine. It felt warm and comforting. 'It was such early days for you,' she murmured.

'That's what Anita said. I was terrified I might tear up in front of her, so I couldn't get much out.'

'Anita wouldn't have minded,' said Martha. 'If there's one thing she's used to, it's people's tears.'

She removed her hand and I had an urge to reach for it but managed to restrain myself. I cleared my throat. 'Well, I'd have felt really stupid if I let my feelings show. Anita berated me for that. She reminded me she knew what it was like to lose someone.' I shook my head. 'A bit of a blunder on my part, but I was able to apologise and remind her that I was an accountant, not a talker.'

Martha smiled. 'Isn't it possible to be both?'

'Definitely not!' I insisted and we both laughed. 'Anyway, Anita told me she wasn't happy with the big corporate accountant the foundation was using at the time. She told me Lady Charmiane Cuthbert had recommended me. She's a charming old lady, as you well know, and I'd looked after her accounts for over twenty years.'

'Did you want to do the foundation's accounts or be on the board?' Martha asked.

I shook my head. 'I tried to wriggle out of it by telling Anita I was trying to wind down a bit. She assured me there wouldn't be that much to do. Board meetings were monthly, and in her words, "Martha does most of the work."'

Martha laughed, finished her glass and waved to the waiter for a refill. I declined.

'Anita persisted,' I told Martha. 'She reminded me I'd lost my wife and granddaughter because of the carelessness of a drunken driver. Full of fire and brimstone, she was, especially as the bloke only got a community order, but I told her I'd heard this so many times. I'm not into retribution. It doesn't help. But as you know, Anita is quite serious about it.'

I played with my glass and caught Martha's attentive gaze. 'I apologised to Anita, thinking at the time I'd refuse her offer. I told her I didn't know much about anything other than keeping books in order. I won't lie, I agreed with some of what she was saying, and I liked the foundation, but I just didn't think I'd be much use to her.'

'I can imagine how that went down,' said Martha. She gave me a warm smile.

I couldn't help but smile back at her. 'I told her I'd think about it, but Anita was persistent—in a nice way. The next day I got a call from Lady Charmiane inviting me to her retreat at Mt Martha.'

Martha looked impressed. 'I've heard it's a beautiful place.'

It wasn't my first visit, as I'd been her accountant for a long time, and I described the fantastic views of the bay for Martha's sake, and how over tea and cake I agreed to join the foundation. 'She wore me down. You know how persuasive Lady C can be.'

'I'm so glad you did join,' said Martha. 'You always have the books in brilliant order. You've taken a great load off my shoulders and I really appreciate it.'

I smiled at her, but it faded as I brought up something that had been on my mind for a while. It was, in fact, my true motive for taking Martha to lunch.

'There was something else I wanted to talk to you about today. Lady Charmiane's deeply concerned about the government's pursuit of charities, and I am too. Charities are starting to be tied in knots by regulation that's stifling their ability to do their work. It's discouraging benevolence.'

Martha nodded. 'Yes, I've heard her speak often on that subject. She says if charities express a point of view on social issues, like Anita does with victims' rights, they could be regarded as political activists.'

I nodded. 'And if that happens, they'll be caught by the strict regulations that apply to donations to political parties, and foundations could get caught up in that.'

'You don't think this will happen to us, do you?' asked Martha.

'I'll tell you the same thing I told Lady Charmiane,' I said. 'The Lost Lovelies Foundation doesn't have to be registered as a charity. It can be argued it's an advocacy organisation rather than a charity, thereby avoiding the scrutiny of the Charities Ombudsman, but as she pointed out, the foundation has to be a charity because of the tax breaks. She's right of course, most donors only cough up because they can claim tax relief. At some point the foundation may find itself under the scrutiny of the Ombudsman because Anita is so vocal about the Bill.'

Martha's brow creased. I think she understood where I was taking this. 'Gerard, is everything okay with the foundation?'

'The books are all in order,' I assured her.

She was so loyal to Anita that I couldn't bring myself to tell her my gut feeling that Anita was going to invite disaster on the foundation with her lavish spending. I wanted her to see beyond Anita's crusade. I wanted to her to see the fool sitting across the table from her. I wanted her to see that life could offer her more than just Anita's benevolence.

Martha was frowning, her glass paused in mid-air. 'There are a lot of charities out there. Every few months or so one of them crashes, and the media are full of stories of mismanagement and inappropriate spending.'

I nodded, thinking perhaps she was edging towards my own point of view.

'Anita is different. She has a vision that extends beyond self-aggrandisement,' Martha said firmly.

I didn't contest this. Martha abruptly called time. 'I have to get back to the office.' She gave me a warm smile. 'Thank you for sharing so much with me today.'

I returned the compliment. 'You're easy to talk to, Martha.'

Martha was kind and reliable as well as being good at her work. It was she who kept things going while Anita smiled and waved for the cameras. She wasn't the glamorous type like Anita but she was someone you could trust.

I grabbed for the bill, but Martha beat me to it. 'No, I've got a foundation credit card. This is a genuine working lunch.'

I asked if we could do it again. 'How about tomorrow?'

Martha laughed. 'I think I should actually do a bit of work tomorrow.'

'Sorry. I meant after work. Perhaps we could have a quick meal at the pub?' I was embarrassed by my little faux pas, but Martha just smiled.

'That sounds nice. I'll give you a call as soon as I know what time I'm finishing up.'

I watched her leave, unable to stop smiling. I whistled all the way to my car, feeling a spark of something I thought had long been extinguished.

10

Martha

I loved our office, located on the ground floor of Yarra River Hospital. Counsellor, telephone responder, donations officer and general dog's body, Leanne Lewis, worked here with our team of volunteers. Leanne was a good soul. We had done our nurse training together, and we were both on shift the day Heath Hammond-Jones was born and lost.

Our friendship was rocked by those events. The nurses' union lawyers advised us not to discuss what had happened until after the Coroner had made her findings. It was awkward for both of us to be working together yet having to avoid any conversation about Anita, Michael or Heath, who were always on my mind. I desperately wanted to apologise for any implication that she was somehow involved. In fact, I tried once to explain, but Leanne stopped me.

'Sorry, but you know the union has advised against any conversation between us on that subject. Please respect that and only communicate with me about our current work.'

I don't think I'll ever forget the look on her face as she said that. I feared I'd lost a friend and confidante, especially because the Coroner was expected to take two years to complete her investigations.

While I was wallowing in my guilt, Anita asked me to join her at the foundation. I didn't think that would be possible, what with the impending coronial inquest, but the union lawyers seemed to think it was a good idea. I left to help Anita with the foundation while Leanne stayed on at the birthing centre. I enjoyed the career change, but I really missed Leanne and my other friends in nursing, not to mention all the expectant mums and babies. They had been my life for so many years.

Leanne, however, was soon to be in the wars. Three years after Heath died, her daughter and two-year-old grandson were carjacked. A young thug jumped into the back seat of Heather's car, put a gun to the side of Liam's head and ordered Heather to drive fast. She did. The car went over an embankment and crashed into a creek. All three of them drowned.

The night before the funeral, I went to Leanne's house. There wasn't much conversation between us, but as I was leaving she allowed me to hold her tight and we cried together. The years apart meant nothing in that moment.

The funeral was a dismal affair. I recognised nurses I hadn't seen for years, many of them from our training days. It was good to see them all, despite the horrible circumstances. So much of what I had lost was restored that day, and once again I had friends. I was tempted to return to nursing at that time, especially as I'd been cleared by the Coroner, but what happened to Leanne only served to convince me why Anita's work was so important. I saw it as a chance to redeem myself in her eyes, those of the community and hopefully my own.

Eventually, I did start nursing again. It took a few years, and I had to fight through the stain on my reputation. There were some hospitals who wouldn't look twice at me, so I took the agency route instead. A day here, a week there … the upshot was I still got to nurse.

After the funeral, Leanne and I kept in touch. While I found my way back to nursing, she had left in the wake of everything that happened. She completed a counselling course and volunteered at a telephone help service once a week. When I told Anita this, she suggested we offer her a job. I thought it was a brilliant idea, so long as it wasn't going to be too much of a daily reminder of her own loss. Anita didn't see it that way at all and insisted I make the job offer.

Leanne worked long hours and never complained. She was calm, soothing and a bloody good listener—perfect for our callers. She and the volunteers kept the Listen Line rolling, but despite their herculean efforts they needed more help. We had no idea how many callers got tired of waiting to be heard and just hung up, disillusioned with us as an organisation. And the calls themselves weren't easy. On many occasions Leanne had to call the police and the crisis assessment teams, the hard-working folk who attend mental health emergencies.

Leanne also kept an account of the calls, including a log of adverse callers who, since Anita had started championing the Victims' Voices Bill, accused us of everything from disrespecting human rights to being akin to a hit squad. Still, it was the grieving ones who took the most out of her, she said, as we chatted one day.

'As nurses, Martha, you and I were trained to do blood, vomit, piss and shit, but not tears and grief. They rip my heart apart, but if I stayed at home I would never stop crying.'

Leanne transformed the Lost Lovelies office. She turned the hub of our activities into what I'd always thought they should be—a place where comfort and support were at the centre of what we did. Leanne located a small firm called Greenery Lives through the Down Syndrome Alliance. We all loved Jimmy and Bree. They were a lot of fun and we enjoyed their weekly visits. The plants gave the place a fresh and healthy atmosphere and Jimmy and Bree kept us well supplied with fresh red gerberas. They also handmade the red silk gerbera corsages we sold as our fundraising emblems.

The hospital got ten per cent of our annual donations so setting up shop there was an arrangement that suited them and us. It gave the foundation access to information about babies and children who died, because even though deaths caused by criminal acts were our primary focus, parents or relatives of any child who died, for whatever reason, were likely to be generous.

On Monday morning, I decided to walk to Yarra River Hospital because the spring sunshine was so inviting. At the kiosk I grabbed coffees for Leanne and myself and took them to our offices. Leanne was on the phones and gave me a grateful smile when I put the latte down beside her. We were to spend the morning recruiting for a new Listen Line worker. We had the space but not the funding, so we had to opt for a part-timer.

When Leanne was finally off the phone, we set ourselves up in the boardroom to work on the selection process. We went through twenty-five applications, whittled back from over one hundred. By lunchtime we had a short list of three terrific candidates to interview. We were both impressed with the CV of a young Indigenous man who ticked a lot of boxes. He was well qualified and the additional cred the foundation would get from having an Aboriginal man as an employee didn't escape either of us. Also, we needed a man for the phones because some of the male callers didn't find it easy to express their grief to women. But before any final decision was made, the successful candidate would have to be vetted by Anita.

I started to pack up, my mind already on the stack of filing waiting in my out tray. When I looked up, I saw that Leanne was giving me a cheeky smile.

'Was that Gerard I saw you with at the beer garden yesterday afternoon?'

I was nonchalant. 'Yes. He'd been in to do the books and suggested I should take a break. He's a lovely guy.'

Leanne continued to pack up the papers. 'Hmm.'

I put my hands on my hips. 'What's wrong with me talking to Gerard?' I demanded playfully.

'Oh, nothing, nothing. He's a lovely guy.'

I was about to snap back a witty rejoinder, but a flustered volunteer interrupted our banter.

'Leanne, I've got a complex call I need to escalate to you. It's urgent.'

Capable Leanne blew me a kiss and was back at her desk in a flash, ready to take over from the volunteer.

I'd been at my desk for barely a moment when my phone rang. My calls weren't nearly as dramatic as Leanne's; they were mostly business related and usually screened by one of the volunteers. However, the odd curly one occasionally snuck through.

'Is this Martha Mayne?'

'Speaking.'

'Do you understand the Bill you're supporting is full of human rights violations?'

I was momentarily stunned. 'I beg your pardon?'

'You support a woman who is so demented by her own grief that she's created a Revenge Bill. There's no justice in what she wants.'

'Who is this?' I demanded.

'Who are you?' the caller snapped. 'Are you a woman who was negligent on the job? Did you let a baby get kidnapped on purpose?'

I suddenly couldn't breathe. The man's voice was full of contempt.

'How messed up are you? How can you work for that woman after what you did? It's guilt, right? You feel so guilty you've become her slave in some twisted act of redemption.'

'I was cleared,' I whispered. 'I did nothing wrong.'

'Then how can you possibly agree that indefinitely detaining people is the right thing to do? They're not all vicious paedophiles. Nothing is ever that black and white. That girl who took your boss's kid was messed up. You were at the trial, weren't you? She was repeatedly sexually abused as a kid. Hell, she was only seventeen when her own baby died. She was a victim of rape and God only knows what else.'

I regained my wits. 'I don't have anything to say on the subject. I'll thank you not to call back.'

'If this Bill passes, she'll kill herself.'

I froze.

'This Bill kills hope, Martha Mayne. If it passes and she dies, it will be your fault. So will every other death because of this ridiculous law.'

The caller hung up and with trembling hands I put the phone down.

11

Martha

I tried to put the nasty phone troll out of my mind, but his tone was so vicious it haunted me all night. I barely slept. The following morning, I discussed it with my walking group and some of their feedback was also troubling. Sue had immediately agreed with the troll, which took me by surprise, and was hurtful to boot. I wasn't upset when she pushed ahead of us to walk with Judy.

However, Abigail stayed by my side. I particularly respected Abigail's opinion. As well as being a trained nurse, she worked in justice health policy. 'Those callers are often isolated and bitter with not much else to do. They get a kick out of putting the wind up people, especially those in public life. I bet he didn't identify himself.'

'No, he didn't. But he seemed to know a disturbing amount about me,' I said.

Abigail glanced at me as we powered along the path. 'Well, that's typical too. There's so much on the internet and that makes it easier for these pests to dig up dirt on people. Are you concerned he'll call again?'

I nodded. 'Yes, I am.'

'Let him know that if he persists, you will report him to the police,' she advised.

I thought about that as I puffed along, also thinking that I really must make the effort to walk more often. 'I can't stop him ringing a phone line that we set up to be accessible to the public.'

Abigail shrugged. 'Perhaps not, but you have every right to set some boundaries. It's an offence to use carriage services to harass people.'

Judy dropped back to stride beside us. 'What was his issue?'

'He accused me of trying to drive a patient to suicide because of my support for Anita and the Victims' Voices Bill,' I explained.

'Whew! That's pretty heavy,' Judy said. She gave me a sideways look. 'Martha, I've also got some serious doubts about this Bill.'

'Me too,' Abigail added.

'I'm not saying it's okay for him to make those kinds of pest calls, but if someone is facing the prospect of being locked up indefinitely they'd hardly be hopeful about their future,' said Judy hurriedly, when she saw the look on my face. 'Abigail, you surely have some concerns about the Bill.'

'Quite a few,' Abigail said. 'I've mentioned some of those to Martha before. I believe in judicial discretion, so it's a big issue for me.'

'And as a social worker,' Judy added, 'I know how important rehabilitation and good old-fashioned forgiveness is.'

I felt the bottom fall out of my stomach. They were defending him! At that point we arrived at the end of the walking track and I quickly waved goodbye to everyone without another word. I hurried off to get ready for work. It was better than dwelling on their opinions.

After sorting the invoices and expenses for the gala dinner, I grabbed everything that required a signature and knocked on Anita's door. I waited until she called, 'Come.'

It was a struggle to open the door without dropping any correspondence and I wobbled into Anita's office and stared at the desk, wondering where to put everything.

'Just shove those shoes and gifts out of the way. Grab a chair and we'll get started,' she said.

I dumped the papers on the chair and placed the three boxes of Italian shoes recently donated to Anita on top of a stack of other shoeboxes and came back to the desk and sat down.

'How much did we promise the musicians?' asked Anita.

'Twenty thousand,' I noted, checking my invoicing. 'That's not bad for a night's work.' I turned my attention to the paperwork, directing Anita's attention to the cheques she needed to sign. I also explained where Leanne and I were at with the candidates for the new Listen Line position. 'We've got three strong candidates short-listed. Two are social workers and the third is a guy called Daniel McIntyre who's a psychologist with telephone counselling experience and just happens to be Aboriginal.'

She listened with interest. I could tell she liked the idea of his presence in the office and she described Daniel as 'good value'. She glanced at his application.

'He is well-qualified, has plenty of work experience and would add diversity,' she said.

I agreed. 'Your dad called again, by the way. He seems to think I'm not giving you his messages.'

Anita grimaced. 'I should call him. It's just that his bloody dog is dying and he goes on and on about it. It's such a smelly old thing.' She pursed her lips and sighed. 'Yes, I should call him.'

'Well, you always say, "don't leave the difficult calls for last, do them straight away and they'll be done with",' I said. 'Why don't you call him now? I could get you a drink while you do it.'

Anita gave in. 'You're right, Martha, as always. What would I do without you? Will it disturb you too much if I put the phone on speaker? I'm sure they'd love to speak to you too. You were always such a favourite of theirs.'

'That would be lovely,' I replied. I did adore Stan and Margaret.

I took myself, the papers and the cheques over to the filing cabinet, filled a glass with gin and tonic for Anita who was already dialing. I handed her the glass and she flashed me a smile as she took it and switched on the speaker.

'Hello, Dad.'

I could tell from the excitement in his voice he was glad to hear from her. They were lovely country people, what my mum would have referred to as 'salt of the earth'.

'Anita? I thought you'd forgotten about us!'

I turned around and saw she was examining herself in the mirror. 'Oh Dad, you know I never forget you, or Mum. I'm just in so much demand at the moment. How's Jessie?'

There was a pause.

'She's gone,' said Stan.

A quizzical expression crossed Anita's face. 'Gone? Like lost?'

'No, she went to the big kennel in the sky.'

'Oh, Daddy. I'm so sorry, what happened?' Anita sounded genuinely shocked.

Her father sounded so sad. 'Well, she was getting older and more frail as you know.'

Anita added, 'And smellier.'

'She couldn't help that,' said Stan. 'Her kidneys went and she lost a lot of weight and your mum said it was time, so we had her put down. It was an act of mercy.'

'Oh, Dad! Why didn't you let me know?'

Stan explained it as though it had been his fault. 'I tried, but you weren't available. Anyway, she just went to sleep quietly, straight away. It was easy and peaceful. Your mum and I thought it was a pity you won't be able to do that for us when the time comes. You know, don't you, Anita, we don't want to be left lingering on?'

Anita turned to me and raised her eyebrows, held out her empty glass and faked a yawn. I got her another drink. She turned back to the phone, fresh glass in hand. 'Yes, I know, Dad.'

'Oh, hang on, here's your mother.'

I heard a shuffling of hands and feet and static, and Anita's mother come to the phone.

'Anita? You've been a bit of a stranger lately.'

'I'm sorry, Mum. The foundation keeps me so busy.'

'Yes, well, Dad would have liked to talk to you when we were losing Jessie.'

Although she didn't look it, Anita nonetheless said, 'Sorry.'

I wondered if she realised how lucky she was to have such lovely parents. Parents who probably wouldn't have any grandchildren. No wonder they were so fond of the dog.

'Anyway, love, it's good to hear from you. I'm off to bowls, so here's Dad back. We love you, and don't be a stranger. We don't want to only see you on the telly.'

I smiled at that. Margaret was a down-to-earth woman, all scones and homemade jams. She was someone who'd always put themselves out for others.

Anita put her glass on the desk and rested her chin on her manicured hand. 'Bye, Mum. Hello, Dad.'

'Me again, love. Anyway, you know how we'd like to take the same route as Jessie when it's time …'

Anita rolled her eyes in an expression of exaggerated tolerance because her parents were passionate advocates for euthanasia, which didn't really suit the world view Anita wanted to project. She pretended to sound compassionate.

'Yes, Dad, I have the power of attorney and I'm your executor. That side of things is all looked after thanks to dear Martha. But look I've got to run now. Martha's waving furiously at me. I love you both.'

My eyes bugged at the fib. I wasn't waving to her at all!

Stan ignored her. 'Oh, is Martha there? Say hello to her and tell her she's welcome to visit anytime. Anyway, Jessie's now at peace, and—'

Anita sighed. 'Bye, Dad.'

'Love you dear. Don't leave it so long next time—'

She cut him off. 'Bye, Dad! I love you.'

It was hard not to feel uneasy about Anita's flippant dismissal of her father. He wasn't just another fan nor was he some task to be crossed off her list. Margaret and Stan had been so kind and supportive after Heath was taken, not just to Anita and Michael, but to me too. They came to accept me as a family friend. They were nice people and I wondered if Anita was getting too wrapped up in her own world at their expense.

I checked my watch. 'We've got an hour before the Young Philanthropists meeting.'

'Okay,' she said, pulling out her compact and examining herself in the mirror before applying new lipstick.

I liked the Young Philanthropists. They were so eager and full of life. When I was their age it had never occurred to me that I could prepare myself for a life of generosity to others.

I got Anita to the meeting on time. She was in full flight that night, and as she spoke about going from surviving to thriving, her young audience was captivated. Although, I did notice she seemed a bit too high in her energy. I don't know why, she'd only had two drinks before we left.

My thoughts drifted back to Abigail and Judy, as they had for most of the day. That dratted call still played on my mind, and Gerard seemed to be trying to tell me something too. Was I being naïve? As I watched Anita open up the room to questions and start a dialogue with these young leaders, I put my doubts aside. She was inspirational and because of her these young people were going to do great things.

Leanne's dedication to the foundation and her support for the callers would have been an inspiring topic for the Young Philanthropists too. That's where the real action was and where the mission of the foundation was so apparent. I wished Anita spoke more about that side of the foundation.

When the event was over, Anita barely even bothered to say goodnight. She called Marcel and jumped in a taxi, leaving me standing on the kerb. It wasn't the first time she'd ditched me for Marcel this week; there'd been extra gym sessions and he'd picked her up from work last night too.

I was disappointed she was getting closer to that man. There was something off about him, and he was distracting her from the work of the foundation.

'That's a tomorrow problem,' I told myself.

I hailed a taxi and took my worries home with me.

12

Martha

The monthly board meetings were a big event for the foundation. Our board members were chosen carefully by Anita because of their philanthropy or 'personal interest' stories. I had no idea what she meant by this when I first started. She told me most of them had experienced personal suffering that made them sympathetic to our cause, so they were dedicated and attended all the meetings. Our board members were diligent. None of them were paid for the work they put in.

'That would be against the grain,' Anita had told me proudly. 'These people do what they do because they believe we are right. In return we give them a family of like-minded souls and some nice booze and food at the meetings.'

She had been right. We probably had the most stable board of any charity, with very few member changes.

That was about to change, with Anita having invited two potential nominees to the next meeting. It was a situation that made me uneasy. I got two fat files from the cabinet and placed them on Anita's desk.

'You need to have a look at the papers for the board meeting.'

'Oh, yes,' said Anita, looking blankly at the folders.

'Would you like me to guide you through them?' I suggested, following a pattern that had been ongoing for years.

Anita's face brightened. 'Yes please, dear Martha.'

'Right, first we have the apologies. Joan's not coming, she's got a medical procedure, otherwise everyone else will be there, including the new couple, Lilly and Mark Hartford. I've put their CVs here to remind you about them. I don't think it's a good idea to have a married couple on the board, but—'

'Why not?' Anita interrupted.

'They vote as a block.'

Anita disagreed. 'We rarely have votes on our board. In fact, I can't remember a time when anything went to a vote. We all get on so well, we just agree.'

Anita was right. In the time I'd been working for the foundation, all decisions were unanimous. This had always concerned me because I thought a well-functioning board was supposed have robust discussions and not just be a rubber stamp for the CEO. Still, the board always had the best interests of the families who needed us and the foundation in mind. So long as we kept putting the families first, Anita would probably go on being right.

Anita became reflective, cutting me off as I was about to launch into the agenda. 'Do you remember when Lilly came up to me after the speech I gave at The Hilton?'

'Yes, she told us it was the most inspirational speech she had ever heard in her whole life,' I said, remembering the almost zealous look on the woman's face. 'She and her husband had been crippled with grief ever since their little girl was murdered by a paedophile.'

Anita shook her head sadly. 'Terrible crime.'

'Isn't she a primary school teacher?' I pondered out loud.

'Not anymore. Her school principal complained the publicity around the murder was distressing the other kids. Lilly resigned and she and Mark started a business importing computer parts or guitars or something like that from China,' said Anita.

I was aghast. I didn't know about the school situation. 'That principal was a cruel, heartless bastard!'

'Yes, well, along with a sizeable donation, the Hartfords have agreed to say a few words at the board meeting about their loss before they're invited to formally join.' Anita must have seen doubt on my face. 'They want to get involved with philanthropic work, Martha, so I think they will be a good fit. That Mark Hartford is a good-looking man with sad eyes. He'll look good in our annual reports.'

I thought Anita was being too hasty. This was not good for the foundation but I kept quiet. In truth, I didn't know what else I could say that she would even listen to.

Anita waved a hand. 'They're grateful and excited and actually, I had only meant for him to be on the board, not her, but what could I do? Especially as she was the one who discovered me.'

This time I didn't bother to hide my concern. Anita tried to reassure me. 'Martha, they really are a good fit for us. I think it'll be okay.'

I pushed away my negativity and handed over the financial papers, which Anita brushed aside. 'I'm sure they're fine. Have you got anything more interesting for me to look at?'

I put aside the meeting paperwork and showed her the official photographs taken at the anniversary fundraiser and Anita's face lit up.

'Oh, these are fabulous. Look, there's me with the governor, and me with the board members, and me with the mothers. Andre is such a fabulous photographer; he always captures the essence of the event. How much did we pay him?'

'He donated his time,' I reminded Anita. 'In that sexy Canadian accent of his he told me that we couldn't afford him and it was a favour for you.'

'Oh, he is divine,' said Anita with a sigh, and then she looked at the clock. 'Speaking of divine, I'm meeting up with Marcel tonight.'

I suppressed a frown. Again? I had hoped the usual turn of events would happen where the relationship would be an enthusiastic rush that burned out quickly. How many men had there been since Michael? I'd lost count. Marcel was just another in a long line, but I did not like the way her eyes lit up when she spoke of him.

I decided to bring the conversation back to a more comfortable zone. 'How do you think the election's going? Should we be thinking about who we need to target for some last-minute lobbying?'

That certainly got her attention. If there was one thing that interested Anita more than men, it was the cause. She snapped to attention. 'Right, the next parliamentary sitting is not far away. We've been successful in getting the Bill onto the agenda, now we have to make sure it gets passed. I'm pretty sure the Premier is onside, but the Attorney-General is a bit of a leftie who likes to think of herself as an independent thinker. You can't tell what she'll do.' Anita tapped her manicured nails on the desk. 'See if you can get me an appointment to see her.'

'I'll get right onto it,' I told her, making a diary note. 'The polls are close. Do you think we should be visiting the opposition as well?'

Anita pursed her lips. 'It's likely the government's going to lose this election. That's why it is so important to get the Bill passed sooner rather than later. If it's passed into law and the opposition becomes the government, they won't dare campaign to overturn it—they'd be too afraid of losing the law and order vote.'

'So, should we concentrate on the government members only?' I asked.

Anita shook her head. 'We concentrate on all of them, but primarily the Attorney-General. The media will be paramount in this.' Anita jumped up and grabbed her vintage Leo dePons purse. 'Now, Martha dear, I must run. I have to get ready for my rendezvous with Marcel. Ooh la la.' She blew me a kiss and was gone.

I watched her go with a smile at her *joie de vivre*, but as I returned to my desk I was concerned by something Gerard had said about the consequences of foundations getting too involved in political lobbying. I made a mental note to talk to him more about that. I then made the appointment with Janet Johnson-Smythe's office, the hard-as-nails Attorney-General, and called it a night. I definitely needed a long, vigorous walk.

On the day of the board meeting I rang Anita first thing, well, 10.30-ish, to rouse her for the day. She was struggling to wake up, so I said I'd call back.

'Thank you, darling.' She muttered something about a late night.

When I called Anita again, she was still waking up. This time I had to press her more urgently to get her to understand she had to get up. 'Fifteen minutes to brighten up and be beautiful.'

I needed her in the office. Aside from the board meeting, we had our annual oration looming and I was getting stressed because we still didn't have an orator. It was particularly important this year with the Bill pending. We needed someone influential to show why the Bill was necessary, but Anita was going on about having some celebrity speak. I thought substance was more important than glamour for this event; I mean, what kind of celebrity would understand the intricacies within the law and present them in such a way that carries gravitas? I tried everything to convince her it was for the best. She was still thinking about it.

It was a shame that Peter Dickson, the soon-to-be retired copper on our board, wasn't better known. He would have been a great speaker. I was looking forward to hearing him talk about the Bill at the board meeting. He was going to share his thoughts on the possibilities that lay ahead for the Bill, including what would happen if it wasn't passed in time and the opposition won the election.

If this Bill passes, she'll kill herself.

I shuddered. That call was still playing on my mind, as was the opposition of my walking group. What would the Bill mean for people like Jennifer Harris and Helene Morton? I'd done a placement at Billabong when I was training and I knew how bleak the facilities were. Now that the Bill had a distinct possibility of becoming an Act, I couldn't help wondering how Helene would manage all those patients who'd done the wrong thing but had served their time. And the Billabong was crowded. It was back then and undoubtedly still was. Add to that the general understaffing that seemed to plague all areas of mental health services, and it sounded like a disaster waiting to happen.

I was shaken out of my reverie by the arrival of the caterers, nice and early, bringing us their magic. We'd used Tony and Toni many, many times. Tony kissed me on each cheek, European style, and I told him we'd be having a bottle of champagne or two to celebrate the success of the fundraiser luncheon.

Toni showed me the menu. To begin, the canapés were lobster with ginger and coriander. She lifted the corner of the cling wrap and invited me to test one and it was oh so exquisite! Then there was a single chilled anchovy on a flaky wafer sprinkled with Yarra Valley salmon roe, a squirt of lime and strawberry coulis. Toni gave me another sneak preview and oh yes, so good! Next came mini blinis served with duck, crispy kale and a drip of apple glaze. I scoffed one of those and once my taste buds had calmed down, I was able to groan in gastronomic delight. 'Tony and Toni, you have excelled yourselves!'

Tony bustled over. 'We can have the champagne prior to the meeting.

During the meeting we will be serving Marlborough District Sauvignon Blanc, Noble Heart 2012, or Mornington Peninsula Cabernet Malbec for the red drinkers. For the non-drinkers, there will be water with lime, cranberry juice with mint, coffee and tea, and Japanese quince tea for Lady Charmiane. Dinner is an antipasto platter, mini creamy rabbit and almond pies, and a single prawn served with Japanese noodles.'

I giggled, assailed by a sudden memory. 'Toni, do you remember the last time we had rabbit? We had palm fronds for the floral arrangement.'

'I prefer not to remember that,' said Toni with a miffed sniff, but she was smiling.

During one memorable meeting the palm fronds we had as a floral arrangement had suddenly decided to shoot out their seeds, blasting the whole boardroom with literally thousands of tiny seeds. They went off in sequence like a bloody marching band armed with machine guns instead of trumpets.

Ratta tatta tatta tatta.

There had been shrieks of surprise from the board members. Anita had saved the situation by bursting into laughter. She's got such a fabulously infectious laugh that soon everyone was joining in. Gerard grabbed a camera and took some great shots that we used in the annual report. It worked well, because as Gerard said, 'Our mission necessitates seriousness, but it's good to show the punters we also have a sense of humour and a positive outlook on our work.'

A polite knock on the boardroom door indicated Gerard had arrived. He was looking handsome in his suit and I was happy to see him. We chatted and for a while I forgot about time. He wanted to know about my walking group; I wanted to know about his penchant for old cars.

I checked my watch. 'Gosh, look at the time. I'll need to wait at the lift for the others. Can you go and get Anita from her office?'

'Certainly, ma'am.' Gerard gave me a small salute, and then said quietly, 'You look wonderful tonight.'

Once I got over the initial shock of being complimented, I was surprised at how good his words made me feel. I wasn't used to being praised about my physical appearance, especially when Anita was around. But there was something about Gerard's attention that pleased me. I hastily thanked him and hurried out to the foyer where I waited at the lift to greet the board members.

The Hartfords arrived first. I welcomed them and Lilly looked past me as though I didn't exist. 'Where's Anita?'

What a snob, I thought.

I plastered a smile on my face and guided them to the boardroom where I delivered them to Anita, who greeted them with a beautiful smile, clearly happy to see them. Lilly returned the smile and Mark shook Anita's hand and was introduced to Gerard.

I returned to the foyer. Lady Charmiane arrived in her wheelchair with her chauffeur and carer Donald, who glided her into the boardroom, helped her to her seat, flashed a friendly smile and took his leave with the wheelchair. I had offered to set a room aside for him, but he said he wanted to wait in the limo so he could listen to the footy. Lady Charmaine, ever the elegant lady, was wearing pearls, an embroidered white silk blouse, and a navy suit.

She took my hand in hers and gave me a warm smile. 'It's always lovely to see you, Martha. You're looking well.'

Anita introduced Lady Charmiane to the Hartfords just as Peter Dickson arrived. Peter was a proto-typical copper. His square head had corners shaped like it was designed to hold a police hat. His posture was upright, he had a steady gaze, and was quietly handsome in a rugged, working copper sort of way. He gave me a brief squeeze on the shoulder. 'How are you, sweetie?'

Bianca Mazzouri bustled in past us before I could answer. 'My dear lovely, Martha, I'm not late, am I? The traffic was awful. Took my taxi an hour to get over the bridge.'

I reassured her she was on time, saw that she got a glass of champagne and she was soon absorbed into the hive where Anita presided.

'Who are we missing, Martha dear?' Anita called out from the scrum.

I looked at my list. 'Just Wai Leung—' A movement out of the corner of my eye caught my attention and I saw our wayward final member. 'No, here he is. Right on time, as always.'

Wai bowed to me and held out his arms to Anita, who leaned in for air kisses. Her welcoming smile put everyone at ease, and soon they were all conversing cheerfully. I gave them a few more minutes and then invited everyone to take their seats.

The official business part of the meeting was brief, then the Hartfords were introduced formally to the board. However, they seemed cool towards Peter Dickson. Anita explained to Mark and Lilly that Peter had been a rock during the investigation into Heath's disappearance and had been a dear friend ever since. Lilly gave Peter a frosty look, which I noted with interest. Peter returned the look and I wondered if he knew them from their daughter's case.

Anita didn't seem to notice the tension. 'Lilly and Mark Hartford have shown a keen interest in our work and have asked how they can support us. I wanted you to meet them and consider them as prospective board members. They've lost a child through a vile criminal act. You will all be aware of their dreadful loss because of media coverage of the search for Anthea, and later for her body. I don't intend to impose on them to tell their story at their first meeting—'

'We would like to talk about Anthea,' interrupted Lilly.

'You have the floor,' Anita said graciously.

Lilly gripped her husband's hand and gave Anita a little smile. 'On that fateful day, four years ago, Anthea asked me to drive her to school. I had a doctor's appointment, so I suggested she walk around to her friend Tammy's place. It was just two streets away. I thought the two girls could walk to school together, or perhaps her mum could drive them. That was the last time we ever saw Anthea.' Lilly paused and I wondered if this was to compose herself or if it was for effect. It certainly rivalled one of Anita's pauses.

'I've had plenty of people have a go at me as a mother,' Lilly continued. 'Why did I put my own needs above those of my daughter? She was only ten. Should she have been on her own? You are all familiar with the myriad of opinions around that, from those who say we mollycoddle our kids too much to others who argue we live in an awful world and we need to better protect our kids. I have had a bad time with the media for the most part. I haven't been as skilled as Anita in dealing with them and I am hoping she will agree to assist me in that regard.'

Anita gave her a warm smile. 'Of course I will.

Lilly straightened up. 'Anthea was abducted that morning on her way to her friend's place. In all that has followed since, there is one thing I am steadfast about, and again, Anita has been a beacon in this. I know in my soul what happened that day was not my fault, not Mark's fault, not Anthea's fault. No, the blame has to be sheeted home to where it truly belongs. It must be pinned to the heart of Brendon Melton, the callous beast who raped my little girl and stole her precious life; a brute who arrogantly put himself in God's shoes and took what only God should take. He is in prison, where he deserves to be, and l will work until the end of my life to make sure he never returns to the community, never receives parole and never has the opportunity to hurt another innocent child!' Lilly's voice had become strident, and I think she realised it. She quietly cleared her throat. 'Thank you for listening, and I hope you will give consideration to including us on the board of your wonderful foundation. Thank you, Anita, for the invitation to attend today.'

Mark also addressed the meeting. He talked of the search for Anthea. 'I've never experienced anything like the terror and anxiety we felt while waiting for news. The days dragged on and the nights were even worse. Finally, two officers came to tell us they'd found Anthea. I had to identify her.'

Mark paused here and Lilly took his hand. 'This may sound a little callous, but in some ways the pressure eased once we knew what had happened to our little girl. The tension of hoping against hope every day, and of losing that hope, was unbearable. I don't know what it must be like for those poor souls whose loved ones' bodies are never found.'

Listening to Mark Hartford, I got the feeling he might have been able to live a more or less normal life if allowed to do so, but no, I didn't think anything would be normal for him again, not so long as he remained with his wife. I could see that Lilly had made the death of her child her life's mission and anyone or anything that got in her way would run into an immovable force. She had some of Anita's resolve in that regard, but little of her charm.

And worse, whereas Anita had let Michael go, Lilly was dragging her husband along with her.

The board thanked them for sharing their story, with Anita leading the way. I had some serious misgivings about how she and Lilly would function on a board together. I sensed strengths in Lilly Hartford that were similar to Anita's. She was certainly a competent speaker and her assertiveness was notable. Her husband seemed cowed by it. Not many men would take the back seat, not when they had lost a child. These two were also intriguing in the way they seemed to have worked out who played which role. Lilly, the martyred mother and vengeful guardian, and Mark, more practical and supportive, not as driven as his wife.

The rest of the meeting didn't progress as expected because instead of leaving as they were supposed to do, Lilly and Mark stayed on uninvited. I looked to Anita for guidance, but she just shrugged her shoulders and the meeting continued. Lady Charmiane had a glass of champagne and fell asleep. I woke her with a cup of tea when it was time to talk about donations. She surprised us all by announcing she would be contributing enough funding to ensure the Listen Line could continue for at least another three years and with an extra full-time staff member! There was an enthusiastic round of applause for our gracious and generous benefactor. Finally, Leanne would get the full-time help she deserved.

Peter Dickson's report on the Bill before the House was also well received. He explained the first reading of the Bill would happen at the beginning of next week and was really just a formality, with the most important stage being the second reading in the last week of the spring session of parliament. If it was passed it would be a dead set certainty to get through the Upper House. It looked as though it would get bipartisan support because, as Peter pointed out, 'What party is going to oppose keeping child killers in jail just before a cliffhanger election?'

Anita looked thrilled, but when she spoke it was with an air of caution. 'The opposition leader is a somewhat reluctant convert, but I believe she will support the Bill. I am more concerned about Janet Johnson-Smythe, who has been less forthcoming. Martha has arranged an appointment with her and I'll get back to you with an update about that.'

Peter turned to me. 'Are you still getting threats on the Listen Line about this?'

I looked to Anita, as I'm not a board member and have no real right to speak or contribute to board conversations. She nodded for me to answer.

'Yes, we have received some abusive calls and emails from the general public and people purporting to be human rights advocates,' I told him, thinking back to my call from the other day. 'It's hard to tell what organisation those callers represent as most of them are careful not to divulge their identities. I guess they don't want to risk being charged for using a carriage service to menace or harass, but the common theme is that we are nutcases who want to lock people up and throw away the key. There are also some callers accusing us of not going far enough, saying we should be calling for the death penalty.'

Anita intervened. 'I've been trolled on social media for being a control freak, a manipulative bitch, and the like, but I'll never let that kind of harassment deter me. Even if I was all those things, I don't care because if we save only one other family from having to suffer what we had to endure they can call me what they like.'

'You don't respond to them, do you?' asked Bianca. A frown furrowed her brow. 'You have to be careful with what you say on those platforms.'

Anita snorted. 'I tell them that as far as I'm concerned, the idea of not allowing a convicted killer to be free until those closest to the victims agree is first class law reform that strikes exactly the correct balance between civil liberties and the right of society to protect its most vulnerable, and I will continue to support it no matter what.'

Bianca still looked concerned. 'You know how social media can come back to bite. I've been through three PR teams at my other foundation.'

Now seemed like a good time to intervene, so I handed Anita a note to remind her we needed to make a decision about the Hartfords. Anita read it and announced to the room at large, 'Martha has just reminded me we now have to temporarily farewell Lilly and Mark.' She gave the Hartfords a warm smile. 'If you'd be kind enough to wait in the foyer, we'll get you back in to join us for dessert.'

As they took their leave, Lilly beamed at everyone, with the exception of me, who she ignored.

I knew it, I thought. I only hoped there'd be others who sensed the woman's two-faced nature.

Anita asked if anyone had any objections to the Hartfords joining the Board. Peter Dickson said he knew them in a professional capacity and wasn't impressed with them, but then he conceded that didn't matter too much to him because he was leaving at the end of the year anyway. He added, 'In general, I don't think it's a good idea to have married couples on a board because they always back each other up.'

'Does anyone else want to make a comment?' asked Anita, as I noted Peter's objection.

This was met with a shaking of heads, so she merrily declared Mark and Lilly accepted as board members. 'That ends the formal part of the meeting. Martha, please bring Lilly and Mark back so we can congratulate them.'

Dessert was served, and I talked with Lady Charmiane after the meeting. She entertained me with cheeky stories that had me in stitches until eventually Donald came to claim her.

'Oh dear, Donald has come to pour the old dear back into the limo and get her safely home.'

The other board members came over to say goodnight to Lady C and she called out to them cheerfully, 'Goodbye, I hope I'll still be around for the next meeting.'

Later, I accompanied Mark and Lilly to the lifts, where Lilly said she wanted an appointment to see Anita, on her own. I suggested 4.00 pm on Wednesday, but that didn't suit Lilly, so we settled on 10.30 am the same day. I suggested 45 minutes, she wanted an hour and so it was. Anita asked me later why it was one hour when we invariably make the meetings 45 minutes to allow her time to prepare for the subsequent meeting.

'Lilly was most insistent.'

Lilly had made herself clear to me during the meeting. I like to think that years of nursing had made me quite good at sussing people out and I trusted my instincts. I found her to be manipulative, and I thought she'd probably always been like that but her daughter's death, terrible as it was, seemed to have provided her with an opportunity to push people around even more. Anita shrugged it off, but I wondered if I should try harder to warn her. Yet my few attempts so far had been ignored. After all, people like Lilly Hartford are usually sweet as honey to those at the top, but really rude to those they consider below them.

The next day, as instructed by Anita, I drafted the documents and sent the Hartfords the relevant forms and information brochures on the duties and responsibilities of board members.

I had a gut feeling this would lead to trouble. I also made yet another mental note to get onto Anita about the choice of this year's orator because time was running out.

13

Jamie

Parents of missing and murdered children all react differently. Some are weepy, some are numb, but then you have those who get angry. Anita was one of the latter. Facing the mob, and in response to the inevitable 'how do you feel?' question, Anita had almost snarled, her eyes blazing. 'How do I feel? How would you feel? We lost our baby. He was robbed of his life and the chance to be loved.' She was firing on all cylinders. 'And the monster who did this? What did she lose? Five years because she's had trauma in her life. Oh, she didn't get enough love so that entitles her to rob us of our chance to love and nurture our child?'

Zoe Walters called out, 'Jennifer Harris got eight years.'

'Eight years with a minimum of five, and knowing our justice system, she'll be lucky to serve even that,' Anita shot back at her. 'But the fight isn't over yet. The Victims' Voices Bill is the key to that!'

I decided to step in at this point. 'And how were you treated by our legal system, Anita?'

Anita snapped around to face me. 'We were treated like we had no rights at all. We were told we were just "witnesses". We weren't even entitled to legal representation.'

Zoe persisted with her direct line of questioning. 'But you had the right to submit victim impact statements?'

Anita swung around to face her. 'Yes, we spent hours, painful hours, writing those. We don't know if the court even took any notice of them.'

'Did you request the right to read out your witness statement?' Zoe asked.

I watched on with interest.

'Yes. We requested the right to read our statements to the jury and our request was refused.'

'Why? On what grounds?' I asked.

Anita's pretty face curled into a sneer. 'The judge said if the court allowed the mother to read her statement that might unduly influence the jury and prejudice the rights of the defendant. The rights of the defendant? Nothing was said about my rights, only hers. It's wrong.'

There was babble of questions and Anita chose to recognise me over the mob. 'Do you intend to do anything about this?'

Anita spoke slowly and steadily. 'Oh yes, Jamie O'Dhea. You just watch this space.'

On the way back to the office I was surprised at how pleased I'd been when she remembered my name. It was like when she said my name everyone else vanished.

'Oh yes, Jamie O'Dhea.'

And I couldn't wait to watch this space. I rang her again. As I listened to the phone ringing, I also heard Jack's voice telling me to keep it in my pants, reminding me she's a story, not a friend. No answer. I left her another message, but this time she called me back. We arranged to meet at a bar in Little Lonsdale Street. She looked lovely and we talked for about an hour. I told her I'd love to see her again, off the record, as friends, and she said, 'How about we book into The Mansion Hotel this Saturday afternoon? We can talk there in private and see what happens.' She flashed that incredible smile and I was hooked.

We were an on again off again kind of affair that always kept me on the hook. Sometimes there'd be months with no Anita, in one case it was over a year. There was nothing regular about what we had. I'd run into Anita at functions where I was covering her for *The Watcher*. If I was lucky, she'd agree to meet up with me after the event and we'd go to a motel. I enjoyed the hit and miss nature of the whole thing. It had its disappointments when she was too busy for me or just got sidetracked. And I had my life and my family to work around too. That certainly had its moments, especially if Daisy was in one of her periodic investigative moods.

Still, Anita could reel me in whenever she wanted, and she knew it. But lately? I saw her leave a big event with some French dickhead called Bouverie. I called her a few days after and left a message.

She still hasn't answered that message.

I don't know if it's the distance opening up between us, but when I saw that Bouverie, the urge to do a little research came to me. I enlisted Jack and decided if she wanted to keep me at bay, I'd find some way to reel her back in. That guy she was seeing was a deadset fraud. Had to be. I can smell them a mile off. If I could get rid of him, she'd be back.

It seemed like if she was supposed to be just a story to me, I was just a reporter to her.

I didn't like that.

14

Michael

The kids were in bed and Naomi and I were doing the dishes. Because I was deep in thought, Naomi stopped and watched me, her free hand on her left hip, dishwashing mop in her right hand. It seems I was putting the dried dishes back on the side of the sink where the dirty ones were. She waved the dish mop at me.

'How long have you been doing that for?' she demanded. 'No wonder the dishes are taking so long to do! You've got me re-washing the ones I've just done.'

'I'm sorry,' I said sheepishly. 'I was thinking about Anita.'

Naomi paused, looking concerned. 'Why? What's wrong? Do you want to share?'

I sighed. 'The Lost Lovelies was on the news and that damn Bill is close to passing. Everyone was talking about it in the staffroom.'

'Yes, I saw it too. How did it make you feel?'

'Oh, mixed feelings,' I said, absently drying a dish. 'You know. After all, this has come about because our son died.'

Naomi stared at me for a moment and flicked on the kettle. 'Want a cup of tea?'

She always knew what to say. She took the tea towel off me and we sat down together at the kitchen table.

I knew how lucky I was, as my beautiful wife poured me a tea. We sat silently for a few moments, just savouring our time together. I smiled at her. 'You and the kids are everything to me. The past is always there in the background, but because of you I've been able to move on and concentrate on the things that matter.'

Naomi smiled. 'I love you, Michael. You know that, right?'

I took her hand and kissed it.

'I have an early morning,' she said, tossing back what was left of her tea.

'Don't stay up too long. Oh, and Margaret rang to wish Little Michael a happy birthday.'

I smiled. 'Did he get to talk to her?'

Naomi laughed. 'Yes, and as usual they talked for ages. Ben got jealous because he wanted to talk to her as well. Margaret and Stan have invited us to stay in the cabin on their farm during the school holidays.'

'Do you want to go?'

Naomi snorted. 'Are you kidding? I don't get any say. The boys have already decided, but I said I'd discuss it with you.'

'Well, we can't disappoint the boys. I'll call Margaret tomorrow and make arrangements,' I said with a smile.

Naomi paused for a moment, her expression uneasy. 'Does Anita know?'

I shrugged. 'I've got no idea. Anita's too busy to bother with her old friends and family. Last I heard, she hasn't been back home for years.'

Naomi shook her head sadly, kissed me again and went off to bed.

It was a warm night, so I left the kitchen and sat outside in the garden, enjoying the light of the moon on the plants and the scent of jasmine. Our spoodle, Snow, bounced through her doggie door and followed me out. Dear little Snow. That dog could read your thoughts and knew just when to cuddle up beside you. I couldn't have a dog when I was with Anita. For reasons I never understood she didn't like dogs.

The news reports came back into my thoughts. As I watched Anita's media presence growing over the years, I had become increasingly uneasy.

And now?

This was an Anita who was a stranger to me.

I was her professor when we first got together, so it was all a bit awkward. At the time I was living with Marcia and although we had been very much in love, things were going a bit stale. When I met Anita, I was swept off my feet. She was tremendously good-looking. We started an affair and although we thought we were being discrete, I soon got a tap on the shoulder from a colleague who warned me I could lose my job if the university authorities got wind of my relationship with my student. So, I told Anita it wasn't ethical for me to be involved with her and we would have to stop seeing each other. She cried and cried.

The next day she begged me to come to her flat. I said I couldn't, it was too risky. My job, my reputation, everything important was at stake. Anita decided to drop out of university so we could go on seeing each other. I told her that wasn't fair to her. But Anita had made up her mind, and nothing could ever stop her when her mind was made up about something.

'Michael, the only thing I care about is us.'

And that was that. So, Marcia left and Anita moved in.

We were happy, and soon we were pregnant. We bought a house by the river and renovated it together. Everything was perfect, especially the nursery.

I can't even bear to think about what that room looks like now. Probably filled with promotional materials.

Sometimes I loathe my memories.

The week before Heath's funeral two formidable people visited us. Margaret and Stan were staying with us at that time. One of our visitors was Lana Palmer, the founder and CEO of Survivors of Crime, and the other, Sean Brookes, held the same position at Parents' Rights. Margaret made tea and cupcakes while Palmer and Brookes argued about what colour envelopes would be distributed at Heath's funeral. Palmer insisted Anita and I were primarily survivors of crime and her charity should cover the costs of the funeral and therefore get the right to have their pale blue collection and information envelopes handed out at the church. Brookes insisted this was an instance of denial of parental rights and he would be paying for the funeral from his foundation and handing out bright purple envelopes. I politely asked them both to leave.

That evening when I turned on the news, to my horror there they were, Palmer and Brookes, arguing publicly on the television about which of them had the right to support us. Anita was still sedated at this time, so I couldn't speak to her about it. Luckily, we had Margaret and Stan.

Margaret was furious. 'Let them both bugger off. Stan and I will be paying for our grandson's funeral and we won't be handing out any begging letters.'

The next day, Margaret phoned Palmer and Brookes to tell them to get out of our lives. Palmer tried to argue with her, but Margaret said, 'If you don't leave us alone you'll be seeing a grieving grandmother on national television telling the world how the CEO of Survivors of Crime has made our suffering so much worse.' She told Brookes something similar and that was the last we heard from either of them.

Now, ten years later, Anita's championing a Bill that can stop a perpetrator of child crime from ever being released. I wonder if she realises how like Palmer and Brookes she's become.

Naomi and I had spoken a lot about the proposed legislation. This was not the way I wanted Heath to be remembered because it seemed to do nothing but perpetuate misery. I don't believe in retribution. I believe in rehabilitation and there's no room for that in Anita's scheme.

No amount of punishment is ever going to bring back Heath.

The night had lost its warmth, so I patted Snow, whose warm little body wasn't enough to keep out the cold. We went quietly back inside, Snow back onto Little Michael's bed and me to slide in next to my warm wife.

15

Martha

Wednesday started out as a gorgeous spring morning. I had a bracing walk with the ladies of my walking group at the crack of dawn, where the Bill was thankfully not a topic of discussion. I then showered and dressed with care because Anita and I were going to the races. It was perfect Melbourne racing weather; a clear blue sky with an expected high of 26 degrees and a slight breeze.

I took the tram to Yarra River Hospital and on the way, I picked up *The Watcher*. There was a story about the Bill that I read nervously. I needn't have been concerned because the interview, conducted by Jamie O'Dhea, was with Jessica Wilkinson, the leader of the opposition. It was a positive piece. She didn't exactly say she was supporting the Bill, but she was seeking legal advice from her shadow Attorney-General. She obviously considered the matter important, and, of course, Jamie had spun it favourably towards us. Anita would be pleased.

Anita arrived looking gorgeous but grumbling about the early meeting. She was wearing a dress with a full white skirt embroidered with crimson, yellow, orange and pink gerberas. It had been specially made for her by an admirer and it was a stunner. Apart from the exquisite embroidery, it was just like what my grandmother used to wear, but I didn't say so. Anyway, Anita's dress varied from Nan's as it had a plunging neckline.

'You look wonderful,' I told her.

She did a cute little twirl, looking positively girlish. God, she made me laugh sometimes.

Lilly arrived at 9.55 am for their meeting. She had also chosen a plunging neckline. I had to concede she looked good in her pale mauve spring suit, and she carried herself well.

Hmm. Cleavages at high noon, I thought, as I escorted her into Anita's office. I went to get the tea and when I returned the two of them were getting along like a pair of besties. Anita asked me to join them.

Lilly was telling Anita, 'I was a great admirer of your work and your passion even before we lost Anthea. Back then, of course, I never dreamed Mark and I would one day join the ranks of those who grieve for a lost child.'

Anita was looking pleased, but I doubted Lilly's sincerity. Despite her great loss, I felt like she was just trying to flatter Anita.

'I've crossed that line now,' Lilly said sadly. 'And, do you know, Anita, even before the terrible truth was known to me, I had this feeling you would be there to help me across this dreadful hurdle. I used to wonder how on earth you managed to cope and achieve so much?'

Anita rested her elbow on the table, her chin on her manicured hand. 'At first I was just numb. I couldn't feel anything. It was like being in a foggy bubble. You knew there was life outside, but you couldn't join it.'

I left them to it and went back to my desk. I was surprised at how much Anita was opening up to Lilly. These were sensitive issues and while she was willing enough to talk publicly through the media, she rarely spoke about them on a one-to-one basis. Anita wasn't a big fan of that. Although, she let me see more of her life than others.

I was about to start work on the accounts when I did a pivot and decided to do an internet search on Lilly Hartford instead. Call it a gut feeling. If I was going to convince Anita that she couldn't be trusted, then I needed proof. There were lots of entries concerning the disappearance of, and search for, Anthea and the subsequent trial. The horrible paedophile got life but the judge didn't exactly endear herself to the baying masses with her sentencing comments. 'The prisons,' she remarked, 'are packed, but the legislature keeps passing more and more mandatory sentencing laws without addressing the issues of where these prisoners are held and how they are supposed to be managed.'

There were plenty of interviews with Lilly, and while she presented well enough, there was footage of her at one event where she was caught in the background of the shot, rudely snatching a glass from a waiter and glaring at the poor man.

I shook my head. I knew it. The woman was horrible to those she thought beneath her, or who couldn't help her to get her way. Where did Anita fit into Lilly's grand view?

Gerard walked into the office, bringing me back to the moment. He greeted me with a warm smile and a compliment. 'I've come to do some work on the books. You look nice today, by the way. Going somewhere special?'

Anita and I are off to Flemington for the races.' I checked my watch. 'Oh blimey, I was supposed to rescue Anita from Lilly fifteen minutes ago!'

Anita didn't seem to be at all annoyed that I'd let the meeting go overtime. She was still listening patiently to Lilly's reminiscences about Anthea. I coughed and indicated the time and Lilly rose from her seat and picked up her bag.

'Thank you so much for your time, Anita. It's been a delight talking with you and I know I'm going to adore being on the Lost Lovelies board.'

Anita beamed and the two of them kissed cheeks—without touching of course, mustn't mess up the make-up—and I walked Lilly to the lift and tried to make polite conversation that she predictably ignored. It was a relief to see the doors close on her.

A limo was waiting for us when we got downstairs. The driver was dressed in a smart uniform and whisked us off to Flemington in style.

16

Martha

I'd never been to the races before and I admit to being thrilled. We'd been invited by the United Bookmaker's Association, or UBA, who were major donors to the foundation. A couple of the board members had initially been concerned it might not be a good look for the foundation to be accepting money from gambling, but, as Anita pointed out, bookmakers are parents too. She told the board, 'If we start discriminating against donors because of our own principles, we risk alienating people who may one day need our services. Besides, how would we determine who is allowed to give and who isn't?' The board had agreed and now Anita and I were guests of the UBA at Melbourne's most fabulous racetrack.

The crowd was fantastic, full of people from all walks of life. The fashion was wonderfully crazy. The girls were wearing short frocks, pastels and prints of every colour and style, and totally mad shoes.

Anita, who loved shoes, was spellbound by a pair of dagger pumps. 'How do they walk in such high heels?'

'A podiatrist's nightmare,' I agreed. 'There'll be some sore feet by this afternoon.'

We passed three girls who were struggling with a large esky, wearing ridiculously short dresses and jabbering into mobile phones, silly with excitement, one speaking so loudly into her phone that other racegoers stared and laughed out loud.

A man dressed like a lord with a top hat, striped pants and what was, I guessed, a dress coat came into sight. He was escorting three elegantly dressed women who walked behind him. He had a cane with a silver top and was tapping it loudly on the ground to warn off the hoi polloi. He copped some mocking. A guy dressed in tails and a tutu had the crowd roaring with laughter as he followed behind the lord, imitating him. Each time the lord stopped to look behind him, the mimic stopped too. When the lord resumed his tapping so did the mimic. What a hoot! The lord looked most indignant as he escorted his charges towards the gate.

Bruce, the CEO of the UBA, met us outside and escorted us efficiently—too efficiently; I wanted to linger and enjoy the crowd—to the members' lounge, where Bruce introduced Anita to other celebrities and their partners, and described me as 'Anita's loyal assistant'. I wanted to tell him that I had a name, but he had already moved on.

At our table were Barry Bradshaw and his wife, Charlotte. She was in a lilac linen suit, fake tan and her blonde hair brushed high, topped off with a spotted fascinator. She was wearing the same shade of lilac as Lilly had and I thought it must be the latest thing. Charlotte's lips looked all puffed up and there was something strangely stretched about her eyes. I tried not to stare. Anita and I knew Barry already because he had a prime drive home show and had given Anita heaps of publicity over the years, backing her campaign for victims' rights with great enthusiasm. He threw his arms out when he saw Anita, air kissed her, and said, 'You look gorgeous, my dear.'

His hands were a bit octopussy I thought, but Anita wasn't objecting and his wife didn't seem to notice, or perhaps she'd just got used to him over the years.

Next to the Bradshaws was retired jockey Steve Malone and his American wife Georgia, also gorgeous in a yellow frock with a floral garland encircling her dark wavy hair. The ex-CEO of the Flemington Football Club, Edward Jennings, and his wife Mary-Lou were next to them. He was resplendent in a fine Italian suit and Mary-Lou took his hand with a giggle. 'Oh, this champagne goes straight to my head.'

Georgia Malone was full of complaints. 'Steve was thrown from his mount two years ago and he hasn't been able to ride since because of severe back pain.'

'How dreadful!' Anita declared. 'Were you adequately compensated?'

'Hell no, he got a pittance, just the same amount as a bricklayer or a plumber would've gotten,' replied Georgia. 'And of course, we don't have any access to the black money now, so it's hit us really hard.'

I thought they didn't particularly look hard up. Her outfit was worth at least five of my mortgage payments.

Bruce encouraged Anita and I to have a flutter on the first race. She chose Sailor Boy and I picked Storm Cloud. Mine was a hundred to one, and the others laughed at me.

'Not a hope in hell, Martha,' declared Bruce, who had wagered $100 on the favourite. I felt a bit miffed—after all, I'd only bet $5 each way. Besides, I liked the name. It was certainly starting to match my mood.

It was exciting watching the horses being led up to the gates. The jockeys looked so swish in their colourful silk costumes and the horses were beautifully groomed with trimmed manes and tails shining in the sunlight. One horse refused to go into the gates and the attendants were pulling and pushing at it. I was reminded of a documentary I once saw of a queen bee being dragged back into a hive by worker bees. It was clear she didn't want to go and neither did this poor horse. Eventually she gave up and was locked in.

I felt vindicated when my horse won by a nose. I was jumping up and down with excitement until Bruce pointed out that my horse only won because two others bumped into each other.

Anita laughed. 'It doesn't matter, Bruce. A winner's a winner no matter how it got to the line. Martha's the one who'll be collecting the money.' She raised her glass. 'To Martha!'

Everyone at our table toasted and congratulated me. Bruce took it all in good style and estimated I had won over $500. Not bad for a five-dollar bet!

Jamie O'Dhea came over to our table, a suave smile on his good-looking face. I looked over at Anita, who seemed unconcerned. I wondered where they stood now that Marcel was on the scene.

Jamie gave her a particularly significant look, which Anita seemed to ignore, but Jamie handled it well enough. He was known to others at the table and spoke to several of them before saying farewell to Anita and me and joining an older man who was wearing a trench coat. I wondered why he had the coat on when it was so warm. We saw them again later when we went to place our bets, and I recognised him as Jack Ruler, another journo from *The Watcher*.

Overall, we had a good day. Bruce won hundreds of dollars and he gave all the cash to Anita for the foundation. I wanted to call it a day—my feet were killing me and I was ready to leave—but Anita wanted to stop by the betting ring in the public area.

I was surprised when she used some of Bruce's donation to place more bets, backing a horse called Redemptive Justice.

'Anita, what are you doing?' I asked her. 'Can you imagine the headlines if someone gets a snap of you doing that?'

Anita waved me off. 'We'll make it all back when the horse wins, Martha, and then Bruce's donation will have doubled in value.'

I kept my mouth shut.

The horse came dead last.

I was about to remark that she'd be best to cover the loss herself, when she immediately went and put a hundred dollars each way on Heavenly Angel, even though it was a rank outsider. I was fuming by this stage. It was no way to spend a donor's money, even if it was just a few hundred dollars. Luckily, she was assisted by the favourite being blocked by other horses and the jockey on her horse taking advantage of the situation by weaving around them, grabbing the lead and romping it in. Anita collected stacks of notes from the bookie. I couldn't see exactly how much because she spirited it away into her handbag, which she then clutched to her chest. 'Let's get out of here before I get mugged,' she hissed to me.

At the gates of the racecourse there were two young backpackers collecting for charity. Anita pushed past them. 'Piss off! I can't stand being mugged by charities.'

I stopped when I noticed they were collecting for The Lost Lovelies Foundation. I asked one of them how much they were being paid, as Anita stalked off.

The girl said, '$2.50 an hour.'

I put some gold coins into their collection cans and hurried after Anita. I had every intention of letting her know just who it was she had insulted, but when I caught up with her, she grabbed my hand with a delighted laugh.

'Oh, Martha. What a beautiful day. You're always such good company.'
The driver opened the doors of the limo and we sailed away.

17

Helene

Conrad and I arrived together at the activities room at six. Conrad's grant writing had proved successful. It convinced Della Chen, the director of the Diamond Foundation, to provide a small grant to support the clients as they created their musical. Della and two of her peer-support workers came out to Billabong to work with the seven participants who agreed to be in the musical. The workshop was to be led by a wonderful musician called Carmen. I introduced everyone and noticed that Conrad and Carmen immediately hit it off, bonding over guitars.

Jennifer was actively engaged. She was a bit tense around the strangers at first, but she started showing some enthusiasm when Conrad invited her over to look at the instruments. I was hoping this would take her mind off the Victims' Voices Bill. Anita Hammond-Jones was in the news a lot lately, so I hoped the preparations for the performance would be a distraction.

I got the attention of our small little group and invited Della to explain the role of the Diamond Foundation.

Della rose and was immediately warm and friendly. 'Hello, everyone. The Diamond Foundation works with clients of various facilities in our state. We don't go into places and force you to watch us perform, we work with you to develop an honest, authentic, and above all, entertaining show from your perspective. We've been doing this for many years now, and it is our honour to help you create a Christmas musical. I look forward to working with you all. In the meantime, allow me to introduce Sally.'

Sally moved to the front and gave the clients a friendly wave. 'Hi, everyone. I'm twenty-three years old and a solicitor. My father had schizophrenia and he heard voices. When my sister and I were kids, we'd lie in bed at night and hear him shouting at them. I didn't know there were other kids who had parents living with mental illness; I'd only ever experienced it as our family's personal shame. After our father died, I came to a Diamond Foundation workshop and

I found other scared and lonely kids just like me. I've stayed with Diamond ever since and now I help the newbies who come to our programs. I'm thrilled to be able to perform with you.'

I could see the clients take an interest in Sally. They'd all experienced shame—and shaming—in the way mental illness affected their own lives. I loved bringing in people like Sally. They were able to show the clients that it was possible to remain optimistic.

Carmen then took over and suggested we do some warm-up exercises to get things loosened up a bit. She had us rolling our shoulders, stretching, swinging our arms from side to side. We had to poke our tongues out as far as we could and say our names and dates of birth. It was so funny and led to many giggles, a welcome sound at Billabong. Carmen then asked us for ideas about what we wanted to do for the musical.

It was enlightening and challenging for me to hear the ideas that came from our clients.

Jason had a suggestion. 'Let's write a musical that tells the truth about being jailed on the pretence that therapeutic services are being provided by the state.'

I was secretly horrified, though it wasn't the first time I'd heard such talk. Conrad looked alarmed, but quickly hid his feelings. He knew how hard we worked for the clients.

Maddie gave a keen nod. 'Yeah, that's cool. It might be pretty fun to have some of the staff included in the cast telling the audience how much they love and care for us. We could give a counterpoint about what we really think of therapy in a setting like this. Jennifer's written a song that would be cool as in a show like that!'

Carmen asked Jennifer if she would sing it for us. Jennifer said she didn't feel up to it.

Conrad encouraged her. 'I'd love to hear your song, Jennifer.' He was such a lovely young man. She eventually agreed and sat down at the piano.
Her song had us all spellbound. The ending was chilling.

When
You've cried all the tears you can cry,
And
The last of your tears is dry,
Even
God can't bring you back.
So,
Why should he even try?

When Jennifer finished singing and the last overtone faded there was absolute silence in the room. The hairs on the back of my neck were standing up.

Eventually, Jennifer, her eyes downcast, asked, 'Didn't you like my song?'

We burst into applause and told her it was brilliant.

Carmen's face was full of admiration. 'Jennifer, you are wonderful.'

Jennifer didn't look up.

Conrad sat beside her. 'It's true. Don't let anyone ever tell you otherwise.'

Carmen led us through several of her songs and Conrad sang two original songs of his own that went down really well. I marvelled at him—I had no idea he was so talented.

The presence of Della and Carmen was like a shot in the arm. By the end of the session, the room was full of enthusiasm. We managed to talk the clients around to writing songs that were a bit more hopeful, but still honest. It looked like we were on track for the Christmas show. It was deeply moving to see the group so excited, so positive. Even Jennifer had lost her dark attitude. There was hope in the room on that night and I'll never forget it.

However, the Bill hovered at the back of my mind, like a dangerous disease-carrying mosquito. After the Diamond girls left, I invited Conrad into my office to talk about the Bill further. I'd asked him to keep track of its progress as part of his work experience.

He pulled out his phone and started scrolling through what I assumed were his notes. 'The Bill's already been tabled and had its first reading today,' he said. 'It goes to the second reading soon, and that's where the real debate happens.'

I felt a stab of fear and looked at my computer screen. I'd sent more than a dozen emails and letters to Anita and none had been answered. It was time to take stronger action. 'I'm worried there won't be much real debate on this one. I'm praying some of the politicians will oppose it, but I'm not confident they will.'

'Why not?'

'There's an election coming up,' I said. 'There are no votes to be won trying to protect the human rights of people who've been convicted of hurting children.'

Conrad was silent for a while. 'But when children who've been hurt themselves become, for want of a better word, perpetrators, because of the trauma they've been through, shouldn't that be, like, an important consideration too?'

I stood up and stretched my aching back. I smiled weakly at this bright young man. 'Yes, mate, spot on. But nothing's going to change until there are more people like you in parliament or on the judiciary.'

'You have a lot of insight into people, Dr Helene.' Conrad grinned at me.

I smiled back at him and sat down. 'Have you been thinking about which area of psychiatry you want to specialise in?'

'I had wanted to go into private practice for a while, but I'm finding forensic work really interesting. It's frustrating though because of the lack of resources. Maybe later I should follow in my father's footsteps, he was in politics,' said Conrad, with a shrug. 'Time will tell on that. In the meantime, I'll keep watching the Bill.'

'You do that.' I squared my shoulders. 'In my experience hope begets hope, but hopelessness only breeds despair.'

18

Peter

Look what the dog dragged in! Lilly and Mark Hartford. I'd been hoping I'd never bump into those two again, then bugger me dead they pop up at The Lost Lovelies Foundation. They haven't changed. After the board meeting, I stewed over what to do about them. At first, I thought I'd have a quiet chat with Anita, but it was clear they'd seduced her already. I figured it would be a better idea to keep a watch on things for a while and maybe talk to the accountant fella, Gerard. Next thing I knew I got a call from Lilly asking me to meet with her.

When I asked why, she said, 'I'm meeting individually with all the board members.'

'Oh yeah? Why's that?'

'I believe it's important that all the board members get to know each other so we can work better together.'

'Don't you think that should be a matter for the president and/or Anita?' I asked her.

'No, I don't. Good relations between board members will enhance good governance. So, when are you free?'

'Oh, not for ages,' I replied. 'I've got a big workload in the lead up to my retirement.'

Lilly was annoyed. This woman liked getting her own way, so I told her, 'Look this is a terrible line. I'm gonna have to hang up.'

And I did.

Next day she called me back again with the same story. This time I told her I was working on a top secret case and had to give it my priority. She seemed to swallow that, but said she'd get back to me. I decided it was time to ask Gerard the accountant to have a beer with me over lunch. After all, when breaking ranks, it's best to have an ally.

We met at The Dog and Shark, my favourite haunt for steaks and parmies. I got us a couple schooners and ordered our meals.

'What are your plans for the near future?' Gerard asked.

Now this was a topic of conversation I liked. 'Retirement. I'm looking forward to going fishing and spending time with the missus and grandkids. My youngest daughter has just presented us with a new little tyke. She and her partner named him after me!'

'Oh, that's lovely,' said Gerard with a warm smile. 'They must think a lot of you. Retirement is nice when you have grandchildren.'

'Yeah, I suspect I won't miss the job much.'

'How long have you been in the police force?'

'All my working life. I served nearly fifty years all told.'

'Martha told me you've been given three bravery awards,' said Gerard.

I took a swig of beer, couldn't quite suppress a burp. 'Being a copper's been my life. I've loved it, which is just as well because I know bugger all about anything else.'

A loud voice announced our numbers, so we went up to get our meals and helped ourselves to the smorgasbord of salads and vegetables. This old fella was hungry.

Back at our table I hacked off a chunk of steak cooked just the way I like it—charred. It was chewy but nice, full of flavor and I devoured it with a satisfied groan. 'Oh yeah, that's the stuff.' I watched Gerard as he delicately sliced into his chicken and sniffed. 'These days there's no time for real policing. I can't wait to de-camp.'

He looked up from his grub. 'How long have you been in homicide for?'

'Twenty-three years. I had plenty of hard cases to deal with, and you never get used to the horrors human beings can inflict on each other. The Heath Hammond-Jones case kicked me right in the guts. The total innocence of the parents and the baby, the vulnerability of the offender—it was a shocker.'

Gerard listened quietly. I like a good listener, that's how you learn things. I learned a long time ago if you want people to listen to you, you've gotta listen to them.

I took another swig of beer. 'At first it was dealt with by Missing Persons, but they quickly handballed it to us, not because they thought it was a homicide, but because they knew we had better resources and that'd speed things up.'

Gerard gave me an odd look. 'Funny thing that—we pay more money to find dead people than we do live ones.'

I agreed. 'Yeah, mate, well you're the money man. In the end it didn't matter how hard and fast we worked, we failed. Records got information on Jennifer Harris real quick because she was a ward of the state. When we couldn't find them on that first day, I thought we were in trouble. We got a break when Sergeant Jane Baker noticed that on several occasions when Jennifer had gone missing she was found at building sites. The sarge identified all construction sites within proximity of the birthing centre and we had teams searching them all.'

Gerard picked at his salad.

'Sarge Jane and I went to check out a site near the Botanical Gardens. It was an apartment tower where work had been stopped because of legal action, some rubbish about the building blocking sunlight to the gardens.'

Gerard smiled. 'I remember that.'

I took another drink, a big gulp, pausing to dampen the pain I always feel when I remember that day. 'It wasn't long before Jane called out to me. I went over to her and at the back of an almost completed room I saw what looked like a girl with a doll. As we got closer, I heard her singing softly and rocking it, and I swear the girl looked like a broken little fairy. She didn't resist. She just handed the baby over to Jane and we got her out of there.'

Gerard just nodded. His eyes, though, were full of sorrow. We both had a drink as I told him the rest of the miserable story. 'Me and Jane took Jennifer Harris to headquarters. She answered all our questions as well as she was able, after that we arrested her and she was taken to the police cells. The next day she appeared before the magistrate. There was no bail application and she was taken to the women's prison.'

'I suppose the next stop after the arrest was to see Anita?' Gerard asked somberly.

I nodded. 'Sarge Jane and I went to see her. Anita was heavily sedated, sitting between her parents looking like one of them classical paintings. The husband was pale. We told them what we had to say and left them in tears.'

Gerard nodded sympathetically as I wound up. 'We got back to the office and the normal procedure was to get in a few drinks to celebrate case solved. Instead, the sarge and I just sat in silence. Eventually, she got up and asked if I wanted a drink, but it was one of the few times in my career when I said, "No thanks." I just wanted to go home.'

We didn't speak for a while, just ate.

Gerard broke the silence. 'Thanks for sharing that, Peter.'

'No worries.'

Gerard looked like he wanted to say more so I waited patiently. Eventually he spat it out. 'Why did you ask me here? Is there something else on your mind? Is it the Bill?'

'It's one of the reasons, sure.' I was glad he'd asked. I had reservations about the Bill that I didn't get a chance to air at the board meeting, so the opportunity to run them past him was good. 'On the one hand,' I told him, 'I like that victims are being given more of a say. As a copper you work so bloody hard to catch the villains and all too often they get pissy little sentences and are out on parole in a few years and—bang, bang—someone else's dead.'

Gerard nodded. 'Yes, I remember that horrible rape and murder of the young woman who was grabbed by a man just as she left her grandmother's nursing home. He had a shocking criminal record.'

I remembered that case only too well. Nasty business. 'Yeah, let's hope he never sees the light of day. He was always going to re-offend. But you can't put Jennifer Harris in the same basket as him, and that's where I have issues with the Bill. She's no serial killer, she was a troubled kid who'd been through the wars.'

Gerard looked concerned. 'That's true.'

'In policing there are many shades of grey, mate.'

'So, if the Bill is passed do you think some bereaved parents will keep people like Jennifer Harris behind bars just because they can? Out of anger?' asked Gerard.

That was a fair enough interpretation. I sighed. 'Yeah. And this is the other hand. Maybe it is important for judges to have discretion in sentencing. I just wish the buggers would use it more wisely. We coppers work our guts out catching the bad guys and the judges go, "Oh poor fellow, he didn't really mean to hurt anyone." Frankly, Gerard, when it comes to most child killers, I'd put them away forever. Most of them aren't rehab material.'

'Perhaps that's so,' said Gerard. 'I think I read in the paper there's no money for more prisons. What do you think would happen if our justice system was properly funded for a change?'

I nearly choked on my beer. 'That'd be the bloody day! If I had my way, I'd start by paying coppers a fair wage right now. Next, I'd build more prisons. We could do with at least two extras.'

Gerard nodded, and eyed me critically. 'So, what's your real conclusion about the Bill then? Because I suspect we got the sanitised version at the board meeting.'

'That's worth another drink in itself.' I grinned.

He quickly offered to get me another schooner, but I declined regretfully.

'I won't. I'm driving.' I really did want to say more at the meeting, but Anita wouldn't have liked it. I looked into Gerard's calm eyes. 'Look, governments won't cough up enough to support the criminal justice system and when the shit hits the fan they're the first to start blaming poor sods like the parole officers. Mate, I get fed up with judges sitting halfway up the wall pontificating in phony English accents—even though they were born in Bacchus Marsh— about whatever horrible offence has been committed, but then they give a sentence that wouldn't deter a 14-year-old shoplifter. But I reckon the Bill goes too far. In my experience, if you go in too hard there'll be a rebound. Law enforcement has to be able to make some compromises to allow for the fact that everyone's circumstances are different.'

Gerard pushed away his empty plate. 'That's what I think too.'

It was time to change the subject. 'Anyway, I think that's enough of me carrying on. I had another reason for asking you to meet with me today, mate, and it's the Hartfords.'

Gerard looked surprised. 'Oh, you know them?'

'Know them, know them? Yes, I do and I wish I didn't.' I probably jumped in a bit strong there because Gerard was looking alarmed. I moderated my tone. 'I was on the team that investigated the disappearance and death of their daughter.'

Gerard's mouth fell open. 'Oh, I see.'

'The homicide squad's always been small and we're a tight knit team,' I told him. 'I've worked on nearly every big murder on this side of town.'

'Well, what was it about the Hartfords that bothered you?' he asked.

I scratched my head. 'Where do I start? Look, mate, when a child goes missing the police need every bit of help we can get from the families, school, friends, members of the public, and the media. It's really important that everyone works together, but frankly you can't work with Lilly Hartford. That woman's a manipulative bitch.'

Gerard looked troubled. 'To tell you the truth, she makes me feel uneasy and Martha is uncharacteristically down on her.'

'I know people are erratic and difficult when they're distressed, but this one was a piece of work,' I said, enlightening Gerard to that snake's true nature. 'She pretended to take our advice on things like dealing with the media but then ignored us. She called her own press conference and grizzled to the media, saying we'd hardly bothered to speak to her and her husband, but that was straight after the bloody chief commissioner and I visited the Hartfords at their home. We were there for three hours! And that was just the start. She's one of those people who come on all dependent and grateful and then stabs you in the back. Passive aggressive through and through.'

Gerard shook his head. He looked concerned. 'Looks like the foundation has a problem.'

'Too bloody right, mate,' I confirmed.

Gerard looked thoughtful. 'Do you mind if I share this with Martha?'

'No worries, mate. That's fine with me.'

'Martha's smart and Anita listens to her. Maybe it isn't too late.'

I wasn't too sure about that. Gerard and I shook hands, vowing to keep in touch. I headed home to grab my fishing tackle, hoping to have time to drop a line before the threatening black sky opened up.

19

Martha

Every year Anita and I scrutinised the grant applications. It was one of my favourite times of the year. The foundation had a dedicated fund established with a generous one-off donation in the will of Delia Morrison, a squillionairess whose daughter had been killed on her way to the library. The donor specified that the interest raised from her beneficence could only be used to support evidence-based research into understanding crimes against children. Unfortunately, this restricted us from using any of the Delia Morrison Fund money for staffing, but I loved that we had a hand in ensuring evidence-based academic research. It gave us legitimacy, and some of the papers of past years were fantastic.

I got the applications sorted into those I thought should be shortlisted. Anita usually agreed with whatever I ended up choosing, but the applications this year were particularly interesting. I took them into the boardroom so we could have lots of space to spread out the documents.

My top pick was an interesting application from a law student who wanted a grant to complete research for her Masters. Her topic was: *The impact of advocacy and legislation on sentencing.*

'Sounds interesting, who's the applicant?' asked Anita.

I read out loud. 'This application is made on behalf of Elissa Mustaffa who is a Masters student in criminology at The Bluestone University, supervised by Professor Louisa Moore. They were at the fundraiser, remember?'

Anita sniffed. 'Professor Moore's a bit of a sceptic concerning victims' rights.'

'She's signed the declaration that she'll be providing impartial support for her student, and they aren't asking us for too much, just $10,000 to do a literature search, and to identify and conduct interviews with families whose children have been harmed by released prisoners. It is part of a larger project in which she's interviewing and scrutinising decisions of judges and magistrates,'

102

I told her, skimming through the synopsis.

Anita looked thoughtful. 'This could be a great way to prove to Louisa Moore we're right! Elissa's research findings could erode her misgivings about victims' rights.'

I nodded but tried to caution her. 'What if her findings don't agree with our cause?'

Anita turned to peer at me, eyebrows raised in mock horror. 'Why, Martha dear, if the research is evidence-based it must agree with my lived experience of criminal acts against children.'

I suppressed a wince. That opinion sounded rose-tinted to me, but nevertheless, I made a diary note and turned to the second application, which was from an advocacy group supporting victims of crime. They were old favourites of ours called Hands Up. Anita was happy to support them whenever they applied, so long as they included a research component in their application to meet the terms of the fund. Their president was a young law graduate who had lost her brother to a violent assault when he was just eight years old and she was ten. She was now in her early twenties, as bright as a button, and a tireless activist for the Victims' Voices Bill. I read through the application and my eyes nearly fell out of my head. This quarter they wanted $100,000 to employ a full-time research assistant.

'Isn't that outside the terms of the grant?' Anita asked. 'It's not supposed to be used for staff.'

'It's not meant for staff,' I agreed. 'But it is a research assistant, so they must be doing research.'

Anita shook her head. 'No, they want too much. Get Melita in for a meeting and we'll look for a compromise. I'll also fire her up for the Bill.'

I grumbled to Anita, 'What a pity we can't use any of this fund to provide more help for Leanne.'

'Leanne's fine,' said Anita casually. 'She loves the work, and anyway we've got Lady C's donation to get someone full-time. How's that process going? Has the Aboriginal man accepted the position?'

I couldn't hide the wince this time. 'His name is Daniel McIntyre, and not yet. I rang him yesterday, but I haven't heard back yet.'

'Make it a point to follow up then,' said Anita, perusing another grant application. I put this on my to-do list.

At least today Anita was focussed, involved and making the kind of decisions that had given the foundation such a good reputation. I wished there were more days like this one, but with Marcel in the picture they were becoming a rarity. She'd come in hungover, again, and while I felt tired because I'd picked up a graveyard shift at Mount Minai Hospital, she had no such excuse. I was also annoyed because Anita hadn't brought back any of the money from the races. Initially, I thought she'd deposited it directly into the foundation bank account, but I saw no record of it on our statements. I suspected Marcel had fleeced her of the cash.

When we were finished with the grant applications, I took the papers away and called Daniel again. He answered straight away and he gave me the good news.

'I'm in,' he said. 'I'll have to give a month's notice, but that won't be a problem because I kept them advised about my application with you.'

'When could you start?' I asked.

Daniel paused. 'One month's notice takes us close to the end of the year and I promised my mother I'd go to see her in the Top End. Would it be okay if I started at the end of January?'

I would have preferred he started earlier, but I agreed because wanting to see his mum was fair enough. I just hoped we'd have enough volunteers who could cover the holiday period.

Daniel said he'd pop into our offices to fill out the paperwork. Things were working out well and I skipped across to Leanne to relay the good news. She was taking a difficult call, so I stood behind her, massaged her shoulders and listened.

'I'm so sorry to hear that,' she said softly. 'I understand how you feel … no, the Victims' Voices Bill hasn't been passed yet. If it had you would have been consulted about whether he should have been released … well, we're always here for you if you want to chat again. Yes, I'm here nearly every day, but we have some great people on the Listen Line. Yes. I understand. You're welcome.'

Leanne said goodbye to her caller, and I spun her seat around and gave her the news about Daniel, which pleased her greatly.

'The downside is he can't start until the end of January.'

Her face fell, her tired eyes shutting in a show of exhaustion. I spun her back around and gave her another gentle shoulder massage. 'How are you holding up?' I could feel her muscles start to relax.

She touched my hand gratefully. 'It's been busy. We've got callers from all sides wanting to express an opinion about the Bill.'

I sat down beside her. 'What are they saying?'

'Some love it, some hate it,' she said with a shrug. 'I had one caller today whose son got done for manslaughter for breaking up a fight. She's pretty sure the other family will never approve parole, despite him doing every possible rehab program and his intentions being pure. She needed to vent and chose us.'

I sighed. 'This bothers me. It's not Anita's fault that this young man got into trouble.'

Leanne rubbed her tired eyes. 'Yeah, well the woman might have a point. She's knows her son better than we do.'

The phone began to ring and Leanne turned away to take the call, leaving me to wander back to my desk. Leanne wasn't wrong. The call that I'd taken came back to me.

If this Bill passes, she'll kill herself.

I thrust the words away. Was the Bill perfect? No, but the lawmakers would sort that out, that was their job. We'd done ours and got it on the agenda. We found support for it and supported those families who desperately wanted it. I was still mulling over this when Gerard came in to look at the books. He had a copy of *The Watcher* in his hand and pointed out a couple of articles.

The first was by Jamie O'Dhea, and the second was by Jack Ruler. Jamie's story was, as usual, favourable towards us. It gave a brief history of the Bill and included a recap about Heath's kidnapping and death. As always, my stomach churned when I read about those events. The article included a brief history of how Anita had established the foundation and praised the work we did.

Jamie didn't seem to be at all concerned about impartiality; he described the Bill as 'inclusive' and 'an example of restorative justice in action'. He praised Anita's work and encouraged readers to support the Bill.

'Hmph. Sounds like he's trying to win Anita back,' I muttered.

Gerard threw up his hands. 'I can't keep up with Anita's paramours. When did he come on the scene?'

'Years ago. Best not to try to keep up,' I counselled. 'Mind you, I'd rather have Jamie hanging around than that Marcel. He creeps me out.'

Gerard agreed with me. 'He was on *Today, Tonight and Tomorrow* last night carrying on about being a spiritual healer and a shaman. I thought he was a personal trainer? He sounded like a total sham.'

I mimicked Marcel's accent. *'Je suis le Rasputin de France.'*

'How far from France do you think Collingwood is?' Gerard rolled his eyes.

I laughed and went back to the paper. Jack's piece was more probing. It questioned the wisdom of restricting a judge's discretion at sentencing and claimed the Bill was totally biased towards victims' rights. He'd also done a second piece that mentioned Marcel and criticised his alternative therapies, going so far as to call them snake oil and mumbo jumbo. I couldn't stop the laughter that burbled up from within.

Gerard nodded. 'I thought you'd enjoy that. Well, he's nailed the charlatan. Let's hope Anita reads it,' he remarked and wandered off to check his beloved books.

I was pleased Jack Ruler had got stuck into Marcel, but his article did not reflect well on Anita. It made her look shallow and easily led. I promised myself to have a conversation with her about their relationship. It was starting to impact the foundation, and that was a problem for all of us.

As it turned out, events took over and I never really got the chance.

20

Martha

As I put my jacket on to call it a day, I felt something in the pocket. I pulled out an envelope, wondering what it was, and quickly realised it was the letter Dr Helene Morton had sent to Anita. I'd been so busy I'd forgotten all about it. I put off leaving and made myself a cup of tea.

> *Not a day goes by that she doesn't express her deep remorse at what happened. An important part of any offender's rehabilitation is facing up to the pain they have caused to victims. If Jennifer had the opportunity to meet with Anita, she could learn about how much pain her actions have caused.*
>
> *I would be eternally grateful if you could contact me about this matter.*
> *Yours respectfully,*
> *Dr Helene Morton*

Just as I was finishing the letter, Leanne popped into my office with her own cuppa.

'Have you turned the Listen Line off for the day?' I asked.

She nodded and I handed her the letter. When she finished reading, she looked up at me, her eyes wide and her mouth open. She stabbed her finger at the page in her hand. 'I think this is a good idea.'

I shook my head. 'Anita won't like it.'

'No, but you could talk to her about it.'

I was doubtful. 'She saw the letter and read a line or two before going into a rage. I was supposed to destroy the damn thing, but I forgot.'

'She's called, you know,' said Leanne. 'Dr Morton.'

'When? What did she want?'

Leanne's tone was conciliatory. 'She's rung several times. I always took messages because Anita's never here anymore, but she called again this afternoon. That's what I came to tell you. I felt inclined to listen to her this time. She was really nice. She wants a chance to meet with you.'

I froze. 'Me? Surely, she meant Anita?'

Leanne shook her head. 'It was you she wanted to talk to.'

My cup was suspended in mid-air. 'Why would she want to speak to me?'

'Likely because Anita won't meet with her,' Leanne suggested.

I agreed. 'Then neither should I. Anita would be furious.'

'It doesn't have to be like that. It might be worthwhile just finding out where she's coming from,' said Leanne thoughtfully. 'If there's one thing I've learned it's that you can't understand people unless you listen to them.'

'The Bill's before the house. There's nothing I can do stop that, not even Anita could do that.'

Leanne shrugged. 'If you talk to her, she might stop trying to contact us.'

'Well, there's that.'

We finished our tea and Leanne went to pack up for the day.

I had enormous respect for Leanne, and I'd worked with Dr Helene Morton briefly, early in my career when I did my psych placement. I liked her back then. I thought she was one of those martyr-types who does the job no one else wants to do because it's too hard and always under-resourced.

I was washing my cup when Leanne called out, 'Dr Morton on the phone for you.'

I poked my head around the door. 'Shit! I thought you'd turned the Listen Line off?'

Leanne shrugged. 'I did, she's come through on the office phone.'

I didn't want to talk to her, but Leanne was right. If I just had a conversation with her, we probably wouldn't hear from her again.

I wandered back to Leanne. 'Will you tell Anita?'

Leanne gave me a pained look. 'Of course not. I look at it from this perspective. You're both medical professionals, and discussions between medical professionals are in confidence.'

I paused for a moment, grateful that she'd think of it in such a fashion. In some ways, I still felt that Anita was my patient, so I was okay with stretching the justification. 'Okay, I'll take the call.'

I stared at the phone for a moment, waiting for the transfer, before picking it up on the fourth ring. 'Good afternoon, Lost Lovelies Foundation, Martha speaking.'

'It's Dr Helene Morton from the Billabong Centre. Thank you, Martha, for taking my call. This is most kind of you.'

She sounded relieved to be talking to me, but I was still guarded. 'Dr Morton, Anita will not approve of you calling the foundation. She was most displeased with your letter.'

'I don't want to put you in an awkward position, Martha, but my client is in a desperate situation. I'm deeply concerned for her.'

I paused. 'I'm sorry, but I can't take sides in this.'

'Oh, and I would never ask you to. It's just that you have some influence with Ms Hammond-Jones, and I—'

Did she want me to intervene with Anita? I cut her off. 'She's my friend, my benefactor and my boss. I support her organisation and its mission.'

'But you are still a registered nurse, Martha. Please, all I'm asking is a chance to discuss Jennifer Harris's situation with you so you have the full picture.'

'This is a betrayal of Anita's trust, Dr Morton. And I can't help you with the Bill, it's gone beyond our influence now.'

'She doesn't need to know. Besides, this isn't just about stopping the Bill, I know it's too late for that. I'm asking you, as a nurse, to meet with me, a doctor, on a confidential basis, to discuss the wellbeing and possible life-threatening situation of my patient, and what you might be able to do to help her.'

If this Bill passes, she'll kill herself.

I pushed the voice away.

I hesitated. 'I understand you're concerned about your patient's wellbeing, but I don't see how I can assist.'

'You can still help,' insisted Dr Morton. 'Will you please give me a chance to talk to you about the clinical issues relevant to Jennifer's situation?'

I thought Helene sounded tired, and I sympathised, but I needed to be strong. 'I work for The Lost Lovelies Foundation. I'm not working with Jennifer. She's not my patient. I'm an administrator, and happy to be so.'

'And you are a midwife and a nurse. You have been trained in medical ethics, you understand how important it is to listen.'

I sighed. 'Listening is a two-way street, Helene.'

'I agree. Will you give me a chance to talk to you? Please, Martha. This is so important.'

'You can't come here,' I told her eventually.

'No, of course not. We could meet on neutral ground.'

'Where?'

'I can book the appointment room at the Jamieson Centre?' she suggested.

I stifled a sigh. 'That doesn't sound like neutral ground to me.'

'Please, Martha,' Helene said, her voice full of resolve. 'I am imploring you to give me the opportunity to make sure you are fully briefed. I have a free hour tomorrow at three and can book the room right now. Will you be there?'

I was silent for moment, debating with myself about the best course of action.

If this Bill passes, she'll kill herself.

'I'll be there,' I said.

'Thank you, Martha. I appreciate this more than I can say.'

I hung up the phone, not really sure what I'd agreed to. Anita would think I was meeting the anti-Christ.

I'd never gone behind Anita's back like this before. The feeling was an unsettling one, but there was a part of me that was adamant I was actually protecting her in doing this. It would get Helene off our backs.

Leanne popped into my office to say goodnight. 'I've got to run, got my support group meeting tonight.' Her smile fell away. She could see I was troubled. She gave me a thoughtful look. 'When I have a difficult issue to deal with or a conflict of interest, I find a friend to have a drink and a good talk with.'

She waved goodnight. I stared at the phone for a moment, then I called Gerard.

21

Martha

Gerard suggested dinner at the pub. I told him I needed to talk about sensitive issues privately, so he asked if he could come to my place instead.

I was hesitant. 'I won't have time to cook anything nice.'

'That's what delivery services are about. I'm an expert on those.'

'Oh Gerard, my place is in a mess. I've been so busy with the foundation and my nursing shifts.'

'That's not important, Martha. I'd be there to listen, not judge your housekeeping. I'm not a great talker, but I am a good listener.'

I agreed and raced home. I had just enough time to do some quick tidying up of the living area, and myself, before Gerard arrived. He brought with him an excellent bottle of pinot gris and opened it just as the butter chicken, saffron rice, raita and roti arrived. I had no idea there was even an Indian restaurant near my house, let alone such a good one. Goodness knows how he found it.

I got straight to the point. I told Gerard about Dr Morton's call and how conflicted I felt in agreeing to see her.

Gerard seemed surprisingly sanguine about the whole affair. 'Why not forget the assistant role you undertake for a moment? You and I are both professionals, Martha. If another nurse wanted to talk to you about a patient on the ward, would you listen?'

'Of course, but this is different. I think Dr Morton wants me to try to influence Anita, and I don't want to do that.'

'I understand. All you've agreed to do is to listen to what Dr Morton's got to say. There's nothing wrong with that. You can make up your own mind about what to do with that information.'

He made a lot of sense. 'Thank you, Gerard. You're right, of course.' I stared at my plate. 'You know, I always liked Helene Morton. If it wasn't for Anita, I'd likely never have refused to listen to her.'

Gerard lifted the bottle of wine and I nodded for him to refill my glass.

'It's good to have someone to talk to,' I noted. 'At times like this I miss Alex.'

'How long has he been gone?' asked Gerard gently.

'Oh, years now,' I said, seeing my husband's cheeky face staring back at me from a frame across the room. 'He was gone long before I met Anita, so over twenty years.'

Gerard winced. 'He was young. What happened to him? If you don't mind me asking?'

I didn't mind, and that was an interesting feeling in itself. I'd only been on a few dates after Alex passed and they'd been disasters. None of them made me feel the ease I experienced around Gerard. For the first time in a long time, I wondered if lightning would strike twice.

I gave him a little smile. 'I don't talk about Alex much because his death was such a shock. We had a great marriage. We fell in love when we were teens and never got the chance to fall out of love. Life was simple for us: I loved nursing and he loved being a mechanic. We weren't in a hurry to have our own kids, possibly because it never entered our heads we would ever be apart. And, well, there was an accident.'

Gerard topped up my glass. 'A car accident?'

I shook my head. 'No, nothing like that. Alex was interested in microlights. You know, the light planes? We were down at Hideaway Bay, which is where my family is originally from, and he went over the edge of a cliff. He died on the rocks below.'

I could still see it. I didn't really want to go with them that day, but an impulse urged me to go and take the first aid kid with me—just in case. Alex and his brother carried the plane to the cliff site, and the dog was doing doggy things and sniffing out rabbits. I'd been so nervous. The wind wasn't too bad, but I had severe misgivings about either of them plunging off the steep cliff over the sea. I remember asking them if they were sure about a dozen times.

I wish I'd asked a dozen more.

Alex had started the plane, a look of absolute joy on his face. He jumped on board, the engine sputtered, and the plane inched towards the cliff edge, only to plunge straight down and smash to pieces on the rocks below. Sean and I raced down the track, but there wasn't much left, certainly nothing that my skills could bring back to life.

Strangely, the most vivid memory I have is of the dog howling.

'Martha?' Gerard gave me a little nudge. 'Those must be painful memories for you.'

'Yes, sorry,' I said with an apologetic smile, jolting myself back to the present.

He placed a warm hand over mine. 'You have nothing to apologise for.'

'After Alex died, I went back to what I knew, which was nursing. And that's how I ended up delivering other people's babies and never my own. I didn't remarry. It was always work for me, and then the foundation. I've made other people's family's my life.'

He smiled. 'You're very good at it. I can see when you choose a cause, you apply yourself to it entirely.'

We sat in companionable silence for a while, then I got up and cleared the table.

'You're a good listener, Gerard. Thank you.'

He rose, pushing in his chair. 'My pleasure. Perhaps we can have a coffee before you leave for the Billabong Centre tomorrow?'

I smiled. 'That sounds wonderful. Any more advice for me on the Dr Morton situation?'

He shrugged. 'Perhaps all you need to do when you meet Dr Morton is just listen. I know you're worried about Anita and you feel bad about going behind her back, but I think you're doing the right thing.'

I bit my lip. I really didn't know why I felt so uneasy about this meeting. There was nothing so extraordinary about Helene's request. I suppose it was just the tension in my own heart and mind at having to listen to her point of view, rather than just Anita's.

I guided Gerard to the front door, and when we were on the threshold, he took my hand. He was looking at me curiously, and a strange thrill ran through me. I thought about removing my hand from his, but I didn't because it was nice and I felt safe.

'See you tomorrow,' he said quietly. He gave me a gentle kiss on the cheek and then disappeared into the night.

22

Jamie

While some people might think journos just get handed stories by their sources or editors, a lot of planning has often been done in the months previous. I was always trying to crystal ball the future to ensure there would be stories to tell. For instance, despite a strong law and order policy, the government was looking shaky. Cabinet ministers were beginning to jump ship which is always a good predictor of election results. I really wanted to get an interview with Janet Johnson-Smythe, the state's conservative Attorney-General, but my calls to her advisers weren't being answered. I needed to build up a relationship with her to get an interview about the Victims' Voices Bill, then, if the government lost the election, I'd get the opportunity to re-visit her for a follow up story on life after government.

A smart lawyer with a criminal law background, she'd campaigned on a law and order platform knowing there were plenty of votes in her white collar electorate to be had by cracking down on criminals. We were running a concerted campaign in *The Watcher* on home invasions by feral youth gangs and voters were taking notice. However, as soon as she got her shapely bum onto the Attorney-General's chair she softened her position and was listening to advice from the progressives in her office. Her head of department was known to be keen on restorative justice where offenders got to meet their victims. The offenders were given a chance to understand the harm they did to the victims and apologise. I wanted to get the inside story on why she'd gone soft.

It also seemed to me she wasn't keen to go along with Anita's agenda, and this made for great copy too. Anita rubbed Janet up the wrong way and their public meetings had been less than cordial. This was particularly so after Anita accused Johnson-Smythe of being a backslider on breakfast radio.

The host, Willy Walker, had asked Anita if she was pleased a woman had been appointed Attorney-General. Anita had replied, 'She has to do more

114

than just be a woman to prove herself. She must demonstrate she is able to take advice from victims and act on their experiences and in their interests. We need stronger laws to protect innocent children and to make sure child killers are given appropriate sentences. Appointments to the parole board have to be people who have the courage to do their job and protect the community. She's got to ensure victims are given the opportunity to participate fully in decision-making when consideration is being given to releasing child killers on parole. Most importantly she has to stop putting the perpetrators' interests above those of the victims.'

Anita really impressed me with that interview.

Janet Johnson-Smythe wasn't so impressed.

She'd spoken to me off the record about the soundbite and her derisiveness has stuck with me to this day. 'What a laugh, Anita Hammond-Jones posing as a feminist! She wouldn't know a feminist from a misogynist. She's totally self-interested and is incapable of understanding the need for balance in anything, let alone government policies.'

Juxtaposing the views of each of the two women would make good copy and get me another headliner.

Trouble was, Anita wasn't answering my calls either. I missed her. And her copy. Jack had been warning me about getting too close to her and I knew he was right, but Anita wasn't easy to shake. But at least we'd started to shake the tree on Bouverie. That conman pissed me off, and having Jack take the torch to him was immensely satisfying.

And then there was Jack. Even though he'd got out a few good stories, his drinking was worse than ever. He'd made a right mess of himself at the races recently, and I'd found him unconscious at Aunty Thelma's twice since then.

On Thursday I met Jack at the Journo's Club. I got there as early as I could so he wouldn't be too wrecked. He was into his third schooner but was coherent. He asked me about the Victims' Voices Bill, as if he hadn't just written about it last week.

'The lobbying on the part of the victims' groups is really revving up,' I told him.

'Especially by that foundation woman friend of yours,' Jack growled.

I let that go over my head. 'Jack. Mate. You're not looking after yourself.'

'Oh, good hand pass, mate,' Jack sneered, emptying his glass and looking beseechingly at me for more.

I shook my head. 'I'll do a deal with you. One more today and I'm taking you home.'

'Home to what?' Jack growled. 'Home to top myself up with whisky? Be safer to stay here and have a few more beers with you, mate.'

My old mentor looked rundown and right on the edge. It wasn't the first time I'd dragged him from the fire and I knew what to do. 'Hey, listen to this, mate. The Lost Lovelies Foundation and their Bill is a big story, whether the Bill goes through or not. I'm gonna need a hand to tie it all up.'

'Yeah?' Jack looked interested.

'Yeah. We know that things at the foundation aren't going well. Anita Hammond-Jones is still showing up places with that French bloke. We need to out him for the charlatan he is with another article or two. I've found two women who made complaints about him to the police, but the coppers don't seem interested in doing anything. I've also got a source within the foundation who volunteers on the phones. She tells me Anita's been skipping work, but the snappers in Gossip told me that her and the fraud have been to every event on the social calendar, whether it relates to her foundation or not.'

'Hmm.'

I knew he was listening intently. I went in for the kill. 'Look, I spoke to my cop source about Bouverie. They seem to think these women are adults and if they got conned by a good-looking man, well, that was just tough luck. I'm going to interview the women, but I need to you call up your sources to see if we can dig up any more dirt on Bouverie. This story's gonna blow sky high. A conman, a foundation, tragic women, the cops who did nothing, and so on. You and I could share the by-line on this one.'

'Why? What's the quid pro quo? What do you want from me?' Jack narrowed his eyes. His journalist's instinct was intact, even if his brain was saturated with grog.

'Aside that it's too big for me alone? The quid pro quo, mate, is that you agree to go into rehab for a spell.' I paused for a moment to give it a chance to sink in. 'You don't need to give me an answer right now.'

Jack was silent for a moment, but I could see his mouth tighten and his eyes go flinty.

'And if I say no? Tell you to get fucked and mind your own business?'

'I'll have no choice but to share the story with Stella.'

Well, that put the wind right up Jack. It was my ace in the hole. Stella Steele had only been with *The Watcher* for a few months, but she'd come from the UK where she'd won a big name prize for exposing sexual harassment of female journos by their bosses. It had caused a sensation at the time and led to the closure of a major newspaper. Jack hated her guts.

He banged his glass on the table. 'That fuckin' amateur cunt! She wouldn't know a good story from her own arse'ole.'

Jack's reaction was predictable, but his language awarded him a look of icy disapproval from Aunty Thelma. She shifted her gaze to me, so I gave Jack a nudge.

'C'mon, mate. Let's get you outta here. The moment you're in rehab, the story's yours.'

He mumbled some inaudible reply but managed to shuffle to his feet.

I was pleased. This was going to be a breakthrough. It could save Jack's life and produce a series of great stories. If I could steer Jack more towards the foundation stories, Daisy would be less suspicious. She'd been giving me a few unsubtle hints about my absences and how much interest I seemed to have in Anita Hammond-Jones. I was far from being the world's best husband, but I loved Daisy and the kids and I didn't know how I'd cope if I lost them. My protestations that Anita was just a story didn't seem to convince her. I needed a smoke screen. Jack could do the sensationalist side of the story and I could counterbalance that with an analysis of the Bill and take over the Bouverie part.

Anita would come around when that French shit was exposed for the fraud he was.

A win-win for me in every way.

23

Gerard

I drove to the offices at Yarra River Hospital for coffee with Martha who suggested we go across the road to the café that wasn't so noisy. I happily agreed. I noticed she looked really nice. She was wearing a tailored suit in a slightly brighter colour than she usually favoured. I got our coffees while she found us a table.

'I didn't get a chance to tell you, but I had a chat with Peter Dickson,' I said, handing her a coffee.

She looked up at me as I sat down. 'Oh? What about?'

'Lilly Hartford. Peter is not a fan. He described her as passive aggressive. Said she continually got in the way of the police investigation into her daughter. He called her "a piece of work".'

Martha sniffed. 'I didn't like her from the start. There was something about her that set off warning bells for me. I tried to warn Anita, but she wouldn't listen.'

'At least you tried,' I said. 'What was off about her?'

She swirled her spoon in her drink. 'I think it was the way she ingratiated herself with Anita. She is also impatient. She's demanded meetings and wanted everything on her own terms. It's not right.'

'She's on the board now,' I said. 'Perhaps it's not such a bad thing.'

Martha's brow shot up. 'Why?'

'We can keep an eye on what she's up to.'

Martha scowled. 'You can't mean that! She'll destroy the foundation if we let her!'

I held my hands up in a soothing fashion and diverted her to a topic that interested me far more, especially after our dinner last night. 'You have been very loyal to Anita for a long time now. Do you ever think about what life might be like for you if there was no Lost Lovelies Foundation?'

Martha frowned at me. 'What do you mean?'

I was feeling a bit like a skater on thin ice at this stage, but I stumbled on. 'Anita is totally absorbed by her own loss. She feels so wronged that nothing else matters.'

Martha frowned. 'Of course she does. Are you saying she's wrong to feel that way? I thought you were onboard with her mission, Gerard.'

Oh dear, in for a penny in for a pound, here I go …

'All I'm trying to say, in my usual clumsy way, is, and of course I understand the enormity of Anita's loss, it's just that she is so absolutely sure she's one hundred per cent right. She doesn't recognise any other point of view.'

Martha was staring at me. 'But you understand why?'

Feeling more than a bit flustered I answered, 'Yes, of course I do, but Martha, no one person can be absolutely right. They may think they are, but there's always another perspective on things and if we have a closed mind we can't see the bigger picture.'

Martha nodded slowly, then looked at her watch. 'We should get going. I have some more work to do before going out to Billabong.'

I took her hand to stop her from rising. 'Have you ever thought about what you would do if the foundation folded?'

She looked astonished, first at finding my hand on hers and then at the question. 'Why on earth would it fold?' I took my hand away from hers.

'Well, the day might come when all the work's done, or you might want to move onto new things,' I said, feeling foolish.

Martha laughed. 'I love working with the families. Besides, I don't think Anita would ever accept that the work is over.'

I didn't quibble because she was right. 'Yes, Anita's got her own strongly held views and wouldn't change them easily, and I know you love the work. However, I'm interested in what your life might look like without the foundation. Not Anita's.'

Martha stared at me incredulously, but then her expression calmed to something thoughtful. 'I've never really thought about it. I've never even imagined a world without the foundation—or her.' She looked tired for a moment and gave me a gentle grimace. 'I suppose I should be thinking about my own future. After all, none of us is getting any younger. My friends in my walking group have been at me about retirement.'

'Dare to dream, Martha,' I said, giving her an encouraging smile.

She shook her head and laughed. 'If I truly dared to dream, it would be of buying a house on the dunes overlooking Hideaway Bay. The kind of house the filthy rich have as their country getaways.'

'And what would you do there?'

Martha's eyes sparkled so beautifully at that moment and I knew this old fool was lost. 'I'd grow old watching the sea, the birds. I'd breathe in fresh, salty air and shiver at the chilly wind blowing in from the Antarctic every day. I'd go for long rambling walks, find fresh mushrooms and berries, and I'd grow my own veggies.'

'Do you think you would ever get lonely?' I asked, my heart in my throat.

She didn't seem to notice, if her shrug was anything to go by. 'Well, I might, so I'd get a couple of rescue dogs to accompany me.'

'How many?'

'Oh, probably two.'

'Could you imagine that being three?' I placed my hand over hers and looked into her lovely eyes.

Martha smiled at me, and this time there was no mistaking her. 'Yes, I could dare to dream of two dogs and a friend. But, dear Gerard, it's just a dream. Anita and her foundation are going nowhere, and neither am I.'

24

Martha

The Jamieson Centre still looked gloomy and foreboding, just as it had when I was a young, green nurse. The administration building was red brick, tuck-pointed, and although old and damp, the nicest part of the whole facility. I felt a chill in my bones as I stared at the building. Typical bureaucrats taking the best for themselves and leaving the grey concrete and barbed wire for the patients. I presented myself at reception at the Billabong Centre and was directed to the waiting area. It wasn't long before Dr Morton came to get me.

Her hair, which was once a warm brown, was now flecked with grey. She had a natural look, no make-up, clear skin and bright green eyes. They hadn't lost their glow. Her brow had more crease lines than I remembered, but they lifted as she smiled at me and indicated that I follow her to a room.

'Martha, this is so very kind and professional of you. I know how difficult it must be and I wouldn't have begged you to come and talk to me if it wasn't so important,' she said.

'What's the urgency, Dr Morton?' I asked, not wanting to draw the interview out. 'You said it was life-threatening.'

She directed me to a seat. 'Please, call me Helene.'

I relaxed a bit as I sat down. 'Sure, Helene.'

'Thanks, Martha.' She still had an alluring smile and a peaceful way about her. I could see how her patients would respect her.

I pressed the point. 'What did you want to talk to me about?'

The smile quickly vanished from Helene's face. A serious expression darkened her features. 'I've cared for most of the state's forensic patients, everyone from child killers through to mass murderers. Some of them have no regrets about what they did. Some have their own justifications and rationalisations. Most probably wouldn't offend again if released, but a few have a high probability of doing so and I would never recommend their release.'

I nodded. 'Understandable.'

Helene sighed. 'But Jennifer Harris is different. I've conducted many examinations on her and I've had the most respected forensic psychiatrists in the country examine her too. They all share my opinion. Jennifer Harris has no sign of mental illness and she is utterly contrite about what she did.'

'Anita would say she should never be released because of the gravity of the crime she committed,' I said. 'My understanding is she is being appropriately held under the law.'

Helene looked sad. 'I can understand why she feels that way, but Jennifer has told me she never had any intention of taking Baby Heath.'

I shook my head. 'I'm sorry to hear about her troubles, Helene, but she did take him. She kidnapped him and he died.'

'You're aware of her medical and mental state on the day,' said Helene. 'You know what she went through. Jennifer says she was groggy and distressed from her own failed birthing and she just wanted to get out of the hospital as fast as she could. Against medical advice she discharged herself. As she was leaving, she saw Anita's door was open and she was unsupervised—'

I suddenly felt like she had jabbed me with a sharp knife. My deeply held guilt flew to the surface and I burned with an unexpected resentment. I spoke before I could stop myself. 'Are you saying it was my fault? That if I'd stayed on duty and not left my patient, Jennifer wouldn't have done what she did?'

Helene looked genuinely surprised. 'No. No, that's not what I intended at all, Martha. All I meant to point out was that Jennifer acted spontaneously; it wasn't planned in any way. In no way was I trying to criticise you or your actions that day.'

My body seemed to make a decision for me. I stood up and grabbed my bag. 'The Coroner cleared me.'

'Oh, Martha, please don't misunderstand me,' said Helene hurriedly, as she jumped up and followed me as my legs took me to the door. 'I have read the Coroner's excellent report and I agree with her. It was a resources issue. How were you supposed to take care of all those patients with so little back up? I was just trying to advocate for my patient because I truly fear that if all doors are closed to her, she might open that final one herself.'

I heard the implication of those words, but I pushed it away. This was all too much. 'I've got to be getting back now.'

Helene tried pleading with me one last time. 'Martha, will you please just think about what I've said? Will you consider the implications of the Bill's passing? When all hope is gone, some patients will take matters into their own hands. This doesn't end with Jennifer Harris.'

If this Bill passes, she'll kill herself.

That pulled me up short. I glared at her, begging my heart to stop racing. I just wanted to go and get away from everything. 'Anita is a strong-willed woman and has a mind of her own. She's also not alone in her views on this matter.'

Helene walked me to the front door. 'Yes, I realise that, but she depends so much on you, Martha, and I know what she believes, but I'd like to know what you really think. That's why I asked you here.'

I spun around to look directly at her, realising that some of what I felt was fury at being manipulated. 'No, I think you asked me here to use my influence with Anita to get her to recommend Jennifer's release when it's next considered by the tribunal. Well, I believe in the work of The Lost Lovelies Foundation, Helene. I believe the community has a right to protect children from those who want to harm them. What guarantee can you give that another disappointment to your patient, if she was released, won't send her spiralling into the same state that was behind her actions ten years ago? You talked about your patient. Well, I have a patient to support too. Anita's still suffering under the weight of her grief, and she's not the only one. We have a whole foundation of people who are suffering, and more join us every day when those convicted of a violent crime are released and reoffend.'

Helene nodded, her expression sad. 'We all want to protect children. I'm only asking you to think about what happens to the patients in this facility when all hope is gone. The numbers at Billabong won't decrease with the passing of this Bill. They'll increase exponentially.'

I gave her a terse nod and left, cursing myself for agreeing to meet with her in the first place. I stormed down the path back to the car park.

A surge of guilt swamped me as the adrenaline started to wear off. Some of Helene's words were sinking in, and the implications weren't good. The Bill likely could lead to patients going from shorter terms in prison to a lifetime sentence in an institution. I shuddered, remembering what the Billabong Centre was like in winter, let alone summer or any other season. It was a depressing place and being incarcerated in its damp, concrete embrace for a lifetime would be ghastly. Might that lead patients to doing the unthinkable? Was Helene right?

Helene's insinuation that I shouldn't have left my patient engulfed me in memories I'd done my best to suppress. I decided not to go back to the office, and instead went home, where I spent the evening with a bottle of red and looking at old photos of Mum and Gran, wondering what really did come after the foundation.

25

Martha

I slept poorly after I met with Helene. In the cold light of day, I started to see I'd let my emotions run away with me. I dressed for my morning walk with a heavy heart, disappointed with myself. Abigail was the only other member of the walking group willing to brave the light morning drizzle, so I confessed my worries to her.

'You're too hard on yourself, Martha,' she told me, as we powered around the park. 'You were willing to listen, and isn't that what she asked of you?'

I agreed, but I couldn't shake the heaviness in my heart. 'I'm annoyed that she wants to use me to get to Anita, but I think the real problem is I know that some of what she says is true.'

'And that stings because it goes against the aim of the Bill,' concluded Abigail intuitively. 'It's distressing you more than you're willing to say because it goes against what you stand for as a person and a nurse, and it is not in line with what your foundation is advocating.'

'Anita, not the foundation,' I said quickly. 'The foundation is supposed to be there to support families.'

'What she stands for is what the foundation stands for,' said Abigail through her puffing.

I almost tripped over. 'Come again?'

Abigail stopped me, a serious look in her dark eyes. 'You know what I mean. Look, you know I don't agree with the Bill, we've had conversations about this before. You've always been neutral on the whole thing, encouraging everyone to have an opinion, but Martha, I know you well enough to know that you can't love this Bill.'

'The lawmakers will sort out what doesn't wor—'

Abigail sighed and pushed through the tired excuses I always gave. She put her hand on my shoulder and gave me a sympathetic smile. 'What happened to Heath was not your fault. You don't need to champion Anita's every move, and it's okay to admit that you don't always agree with her. You have no debt to pay.'

I looked away, the acceptance on her face too much. 'The families are worth the effort,' I whispered.

'And so they are,' she said. 'Just don't forget that you're allowed an opinion too.'

We finished the track in silence and parted friends. I thanked her and rushed off to get ready for work. I dropped off a latte to Leanne and sat at my own desk looking at my to-do list, which involved finding a way to distance the Hartfords. Lilly Hartford was keen to be involved with the Foundation.

Too keen.

In fact, I'd barely sat down when she called. She was always wanting more information about the foundation and even had the cheek to request the financial records for the last five years. She also wanted to spend a day in the office. I told her we didn't expect board members to come to the office, but she wouldn't back off.

'I'll need to run this past Anita,' I told her.

'There's no need for that because Anita has already told me she wants me to be involved with the running of the foundation,' she said in that haughty tone of hers.

I queried 'running of' in the privacy of my mind. 'It would be most unusual for a board member to do that, and if you check the information booklet I sent you, you'll see that the running of the office is not a board function.'

Lilly didn't like that.

Anita was surprised when I told her about Lilly's request. 'Why does she want to spend time in the office?'

'Who knows? I don't think it's appropriate. The running of the office is your role and you delegate that to me,' I told her. 'It's not what board members should be doing.'

Anita agreed. She looked sheepish. 'I think I may have misled her by saying we'd welcome her involvement in the foundation. She seems to have read much more into that than I intended.'

Lilly called back later that morning and seemed to have forgotten all about the office. This time she wanted Joan Murphy's phone number.

I felt my skin prickle. 'I'll have to get Joan's permission first.'

'Oh really!' Lilly snapped. 'All board members should have each other's contact details without having to get permission.'

'Our privacy laws prohibit the sharing of personal information without consent of the person whose details are being requested,' I patiently explained, even though I was getting more frustrated by the second.

'If that's the case I don't see how board members can do their job effectively,' Lilly snapped and abruptly hung up.

I relayed this back to Anita, suggesting we should put the issue of sharing personal details on the agenda for the next meeting. Anita looked alarmed. 'Let's not. I'd rather board members met with each other at the meetings or at our events rather than privately.'

I thought I'd been discrete, but my antipathy for Lilly must have been showing because Anita was staring at me speculatively.

'Don't you like Lilly?'

'It's not that I don't like her, I just think it's important we stick to what's set out in the information booklet,' I said, then I admitted, 'I don't trust her, Anita. She seems overly interested in the foundation's finances.'

'In what way?' Anita asked. She finally looked concerned.

'Well, she's been demanding to see the books—'

Anita's eyes widened. 'What! Well, that's not on. We'll have to keep a close eye on her, Martha. Good on you for standing up to her.'

During my lunch break, I read *The Watcher*. There was an article by Jamie O'Dhea about the Bill, where he complained that Janet Johnson-Smythe was refusing to be interviewed about whether or not she supported the Bill. He also wrote, 'The Premier, on the other hand, has expressed the view that she is sympathetic to all parents who have lost a child through crime and they deserve the government's full support.'

I rushed back to the office when I saw what else she'd said and dashed over to Anita's desk. 'Anita! There's an article in *The Watcher* on the Bill.'

She looked up from her computer. 'Who by?'

'Jamie O'Dhea.'

'And what does the foundation's best friend have to say?'

I put the paper down on her desk. 'He asked the Premier what she thought about the Bill. Jamie wrote that the government's economic record was—'

'Yes, yes,' Anita interrupted. 'But what did the Premier say about the Bill?'

I smiled. 'She hinted that their good financial management would mean there was funding for additional projects including a new prison because, in her words, "We'll be needing it".'

Anita looked delighted and pushed back from her desk. 'This calls for a celebratory drink! Please do the honours.'

As always I went to oblige, but I stopped when the phone rang. I saw Anita's eyes light up as she answered.

'Marcel, darling, yes of course. Where? Great! I'll be there in fifteen minutes. Of course I'll cover the costs, darling. See you soon.'

'Raincheck, Martha dear.' Anita stood up and checked her lipstick in the mirror, then she looked over at me. 'Do you mind finishing up the letter I was drafting for the unsuccessful grant applicants? Oh, and I haven't done my column yet for our newsletter, and I need some ideas for a few articles. I've been asked to write for *Mama Loves You*, you know, that big news and parenting site? They want four short articles, one a week. Oh, and if Gerard calls, just tell him I'm out. He's been at me all week.'

'What does he want?' I asked her.

She shrugged, slipping on her coat. 'Something about expenses.' She grabbed her bag, blew me a kiss and rushed out the door.

I put the bottle back in the fridge and went to the kitchen for a cup of tea. I sincerely doubted I'd see Anita again for the rest of the day. And now I had her work to complete as well as my own.

My conversation with Abigail came back to me as I returned to my desk. As ever, she saw things clearly. My guilt was clouding my vision.

I would always be loyal to Anita. She was my friend and I cared about her, and I would support her until the end. But not everything was black and white.

I was mired in conflicting shades of grey.

Helene's concerns and Anita's were poles apart, and if I knew Anita, they would never fall into alignment. So where did that leave me?

I needed time to think.

26

Conrad

We had our second music workshop with the Diamond group in mid-November. The creativity was totally buzzing and Jennifer had an awesome new song for us all to learn, so Carmen helped us with the harmonies.

Just as we were packing up, one of the clients turned on the television and the Premier came on. She was making an announcement about the introduction into parliament of the Victims' Voices Bill. The Attorney-General was standing beside the leader of the opposition. Both wore red gerberas.

I had a really bad feeling. It was realised when she opened her mouth.

> 'I am pleased to announce I have come to an agreement with the leader of the opposition on a most important initiative. I can only imagine what it must feel like to be a parent who has lost a child because of a crime. I am a mother myself. Our children are the heart and soul of our nation. They are the centre of the universe for all parents.'

I turned to see the colour draining from Dr Helene's face. She looked really upset, so I moved beside her as we watched the Premier continue with the spin.

> 'This is why both the government and the opposition have agreed to put our full support behind the Victims' Voices Bill. The initiative will mean no-one who has committed an offence leading to the death of a child will ever be released from custody without the express consent of those closest to the child, the parents or carers.'

Dr Helene and I looked at each other in horror. Dr Helene put her hand over her eyes and heaved a sigh, as if she just couldn't bear to watch.

'In the past, our laws have not been fair to victims. It is only in recent times that they've been represented in trials and respected as parties, rather than just witnesses. Previously, judges did not hear directly from them. The voices of grieving parents are powerful and should never be excluded. These days, the voices of victims are heard in trials and in sentencing, however they remain excluded from decision making by parole boards and other decision makers. The Victims' Voices Bill has the potential to change this by ensuring parents of slain children get the final say before any such offenders are released. It will act as a deterrent to future offenders and help to keep our beloved children safe. I thank the leader of the opposition for her support.'

As our two elected representatives embraced, I looked desperately around for Jennifer and saw her walking out the door. I ran after her, but she was out of sight. There was nothing I could do but go back to help the others pack up.

I knew what this announcement was going to mean for the Billabong Centre, and especially to Jennifer. I never felt so useless in all my life.

I promised myself a long session at the gym to work off some of the frustration.

It was starting to get dark as I walked to the car park with Dr Helene. The rest of the day had been, like, muted, and she seemed sad.

'Can I help with anything?' I asked her.

She gave me a weak smile. 'Thank you, Conrad. You are a blessing. We'll need to have a crisis meeting tomorrow morning first thing to discuss the implications of this. We have to put some plans in place to provide additional support to the patients.'

'Especially Jennifer?' I asked.

'Especially Jennifer.'

Dr Helene fumbled about in her handbag for her keys. I helped her put her stuff away, wishing I could do more to support her. I felt so inadequate. We stood around for a moment, while I tried to find the right words to say.

She didn't bother to mince hers. 'This Bill stinks to high heaven.'

'Won't someone at the top put a pin in it?'

She eased herself into the front seat of her car, winding down the window. 'I doubt it, Conrad. This is an election year.'

'But it's such a bad law, surely there will be politicians who will vote with their conscience despite the election.' I knew I sounded naïve as soon as I said it, but Dr Helene was always generous to me.

She smiled. 'If only there were people like you in parliament, Conrad.' She started her car. 'Get plenty of rest. The remainder of your placement is likely to be much harder than it has been.'

I watched her drive away. The magpies were caroling up in the trees, but they were soon drowned out by the cawing of huge crows.

27

Michael

I was in the staffroom having lunch when the television news came on. I saw the Premier standing alongside the opposition leader, both of them wearing red gerberas. My heart sank as they announced their united support for the Victims' Voices Bill.

I wasn't the only one watching the news, nor was I the only one disappointed. I was sitting in a corner, so I don't think two of my colleagues even realised I was there. One was Bob Brent, the Dean of Law, and the other was Louisa Moore, the noted criminologist.

'What a bloody disaster!' Bob groaned, shaking his head in disbelief.

Louisa shook her head. 'This government must be really desperate to hang onto power if they're backing something as ridiculous as this bloody Bill.'

'The opposition's just as bad. They're a bunch of useless turncoats!' Bob snorted derisively.

'They're supposed to be the party that supports civil rights,' Louisa added.

'Civil rights? Precious little of them around when there's a tight election to fight,' Bob grumbled.

They left without noticing me, thank goodness, still debating with each other as they walked away. I was relieved to avoid what would have been an awkward moment for them and I didn't want any pity.

I somehow got through the rest of my day but the news hovered over everything I did. It was everywhere. My phone sent a news alert, it was on television screens as I walked through campus, and my students were talking about it in class. Most of them were too young to realise just whose son and ex-wife they were speculating about. To them I was just Professor Jones.

As I walked home, I realised I couldn't just hope it would all go away. I'd probably be forced to make a statement at some point. Some reporter would likely jump out at me and ask for a comment. It was best to be prepared, so I started to compose one in my head.

I'm glad that Anita has been such an influential advocate for change. She—

No, that's not right, I thought.

'How about "let my son rest in peace you vultures",' I muttered out loud.

It was a thought unlike me, and when I examined it, I saw the ugly emotions underneath it.

Guilt. Anger. Defeat.

I felt complicit in this unfortunate fruition of Anita's ambitions. I knew it wasn't my fault, but I wished I'd done more to try to talk some sense into her at the time. I could have, I knew it. She was still responsive to me then; we hadn't yet been torn apart by the pain of losing Heath.

I sighed. Pushing the memories away wasn't helping, so I let them flood me. It was all such a haze of pain and bureaucracy. There were police interviews, witness statements, court appearances, dozens of official documents to read and sign. Anita, in many ways, seemed to cope better than me. Her wrath at Jennifer Harris was tangible. I think it gave her strength. For me, I felt no vindication at seeing the pale young woman being led from the court in handcuffs. I just felt sick.

Then there was that awful Coroner's hearing. That mess dragged on for two long years, and every time we had to tell our story to someone new, the pain resurfaced. The police and lawyers all said they were sorry, but they had no idea how to help someone come out of the pain that reliving horror inevitably causes. Every time I had to tell the story, it felt like I was having stitches ripped out of a wound. I know Anita felt the same pain, but for her it seemed like with every stitch they removed they added another one, leaving the wound to fester.

I sighed again, turning down my street.

I was so proud of Anita at first. She emerged from her grief with a growing vision of how the world should be and of herself as a leader. I loved that she had put herself back together again and wanted to make a difference.

The problem was I couldn't show her how proud I was. The pain and loss of Heath made me hunker down inside myself. I smiled, we had sex, but nothing was the same. I honestly don't think Anita noticed how I was feeling, not when she was so wrapped up in her own emotions.

She started drinking again, and after going to some seminar she began talking about establishing a foundation dedicated to Heath, as if this would be a magic elixir to eradicate our pain.

At the time, I didn't realise how important it was for Anita to have an outside interest. I was too busy nursing my own wounds and as soon as I was able, I threw myself back into work. If her dreams of a foundation were Anita's redemption, mine was in the laboratory and the classroom.

I checked my mailbox, noting with relief that my house seemed to be media-free. Although the street was empty, my mailbox was not Anita-free. I hastily scrunched up a political flyer that advocated for the Victims' Voices Bill.

It certainly hadn't taken long for Anita to become popular with the media. I would often come home to find the living area set up like a studio. Cameras and microphones would fill the house, and Anita was forever talking about clever tricks with lighting to make her look better. She seemed to love sitting in the middle of the mass of equipment, the star of the show. It all felt really strange to me.

I was there for the birth of that lousy Bill, even though I didn't really understand what was happening at the time. I was trying to get to the fridge as quietly as possible during one of those interminable media interviews, when the genesis occurred.

'Anita, you say victims are not given the prominence they deserve in legal proceedings. What changes are you calling for?'

She had replied in a clear and confident voice, 'I want to see a law that prevents any person who has offended against a child being released from prison, unless the parents of that child give their express permission.'

As I stood there holding the carton of milk, staring at nothing, the only thing I was sure of was that I didn't want a draconian law to be our son's legacy. I also knew right then and there that my marriage to Anita was done.

I tossed the flyer and other junk mail into the bin and decided I needed to write out my reaction to the Bill in a media statement. It was time I stood up for what I believed in and I knew Naomi would support me.

Grief can affect our ability to think clearly, and, in the end, to forgive. You can't heal if you can't forgive, and if you can't heal then life means nothing.

As I opened the door to my home, Little Michael came running at me for a hug and Naomi met me with a glass of white and a kiss on the cheek.

'Tough day?'

'Not now I'm with you,' I told her, gathering her to my chest and holding her tight.

Snow bounded up to us for a pat, and Naomi said, 'No telly tonight. Let's have a barbeque and enjoy this great weather.'

28

Martha

I got a call from a hazy-sounding Anita on Thursday morning.

'Martha, darling, I can't get out of bed. I think I've got the flu.'

This was not good news.

'Anita, you're speaking at the Green Valley Town Hall tonight,' I reminded her.

She groaned. 'I can't do it, Martha. I'm sick.'

I thought I could hear Marcel snoring in the background. I tried to dampen my frustration. She was clearly hungover. 'There are a hundred people coming to hear you! We can't cancel.'

This was a disaster. It was the third event she'd cancelled in recent weeks. Anita had been booked a full year in advance for this one. She'd been reluctant to accept the gig, but I'd persuaded her we shouldn't just be city-based and we needed to support rural people who'd lost a child to crime too. As it had the potential to expand our influence she'd finally agreed. With the assistance of local clubs and associations, I'd managed to get an audience of a hundred people, which was a big effort for a regional centre. I didn't want to disappoint everyone I'd enlisted to help organise this event.

'Do you want to wait until this afternoon to see how you feel?' I suggested hopefully.

'No, no,' she groaned. 'I'm too sick, Martha. You'll have to do something.'

Reluctantly, I told her I'd think of a solution and that she should rest and get better, otherwise she'd be unfit for other upcoming functions.

She thanked me and hung up before I could even respond, leaving me staring at the phone in irritation.

I wandered over to Leanne and told her what had happened.

She rolled her eyes and shook her head. 'Oh, Martha! You'll have to cancel. Those people will be so disappointed.'

With a heavy heart I called the Green Valley mayor's assistant and told her because of illness we had no choice but to cancel. She sounded disappointed, but less so than I'd anticipated.

'When something like this happens, we hold the meeting anyway and the mayor can describe the role of the foundation and the Victims' Voices Bill. We'll then debate it among ourselves.'

'There's quite a lot of information on our website,' I told her lamely. Internally, I was boiling. This was sheer neglect on Anita's behalf, and it did not look good for the foundation.

After I'd hung up, I got another call, this time on my mobile.

'Martha! It's Sophie from the nursing agency. I've got a few night shifts for you at the Melbourne Private Maternity Centre, if you want them.'

I smiled and accepted with pleasure, even though I knew I'd be tired. 'I do want them, thanks, Sophie. You always come through.'

She disagreed with me cheerfully. 'No, you always come through, Martha. You've never once refused a shift, even though you slave away in an office all day. You know, I have better contracts, ones that will get you on day shift where you're needed, rather than stuck in some office.'

I laughed. 'There are plenty of people here who need me too. But I'm grateful, nonetheless.'

'Yeah, well, all you have to do is ask.'

I put her suggestion aside as I returned to work. I had a whole heap of credit card statements to reconcile, and while Gerard usually took care of the nuts and bolts, I would often put things in a semblance of order for him. I frowned as I looked at Anita's foundation credit card.

'Jesus,' I muttered. She'd really been running up the wining and dining. There were massive bills for restaurants and hotels around Melbourne. I frowned when I realised she'd spent multiple nights at the Grande Hotel. She had no foundation reason to be staying there.

I gasped when I saw cash transfers on the card.

'Anita, what are you doing?' I murmured, getting out my highlighter. I circled at least seven occasions where hundreds of dollars had been sent to an unknown account. I looked for corresponding invoices in the pile of paperwork sitting next to me but saw nothing.

A sense of foreboding filled me. 'Marcel.'

No, don't think like that, Martha, I told myself. Don't jump to conclusions. I decided the best course of action was to make a copy of everything and email it all to Gerard. I knew he'd written off sundry expenses before, but I had no idea what he'd make of these latest charges.

I hurriedly wrote a couple of articles for Anita, and when I left at the end of my shift I was perversely relieved she was out of the way for a day or two because, frankly, I was getting a lot more done with fewer interruptions.

Sophie had sent me through the details for my shift at the maternity centre. I was helped by the handover nurse who reminded me where documentation and equipment were kept.

We had just the one birthing mother on the ward, a lovely young woman called Marika who was having her second baby.

Marika was amazing. She was admitted at 6.30 pm and by 10.00 pm was sitting up in bed with a tiny little girl in her arms.

'We are going to call her Rosalee, after my mother,' she said, her doting husband hovering with his phone, taking a million and one pictures.

It was such a magical experience. I never left her side until the handover nurse took over at the end of my shift.

As I left the hospital, I felt tired but also happy. I was doing what I was trained for and it was work I really loved.

I was suddenly struck by my sense of relief when I'd escaped the foundation's office earlier that day, compared to now, full of satisfaction and contentment. I always got that feeling after a nursing shift, but I realised with some dismay it had been some time since I left the foundation feeling that good. Even more so since I'd been to see Helene.

Of course, the joy emanating from Marika and her husband could have something to do with my good mood now. Her future was full of hope, whereas the future of Jennifer Harris was all but hopeless.

I vowed to have a serious talk with Anita. Judgement day was coming for Jennifer Harris and as I pulled up in my driveway, I suddenly realised why I was feeling so tense and anxious. Abigail had suggested it was guilt, but it was more than that.

Complicity.

I was complicit in Jennifer's plight. I shuddered and leaned over my steering wheel, taking deep breaths.

But if I was complicit, what did that make Anita? She might have been at every glamorous event in town, but she was in the office less and less, and was now skipping important grassroots events. It was time to face a few truths and confront Anita about her neglect of the foundation and her total self-indulgence.

29

Martha

Anita gave me little opportunity to talk to her over the next few days, and my resolve lessened as I was just too busy. We had events coming up and we needed to get the foundation back in the public's eye. If there was one thing Anita was really good at, it was getting publicity. She had a knack of making friends with journalists and never refused an opportunity to give interviews. One of those friends was Amelia Hooke, a journalist who worked for a glossy weekend magazine. She wanted Anita to find a victim for a lead article on the Bill and the foundation.

Anita, looking bleary-eyed and tired after yet another late night, sounded out Leanne and me on her chosen candidate. 'Matty Morris would be brilliant, but I'm worried he might not want to do it.'

Leanne looked at me, her head to one side. 'Who?'

'He's the one who lost twin babies four years ago. His wife suffocated them while they were sleeping,' I told her. I could never forget that awful business.

Leanne shuddered. 'I remember that one now. Messages from God, right? Babies being abused by paedophiles or something? Had to kill the poor babies to protect them?'

I nodded, my lips twisting. I still remembered the dazed look on his wife's face as they led her to the divvy van in cuffs. 'Indefinite sentence, I think.'

Anita nodded. 'Yes, and she's in a psychiatric institution where she belongs.'

'The last time I spoke to him he said things were looking up,' I said, not liking the look in her eyes. 'He's remarried and his wife has just had a baby, Anita. He specifically mentioned he wasn't interested in doing any more media.'

'It'll be fine,' said Anita with a wave of her hand.

'I think we should leave them alone,' I told her. 'He's been through intensive psychiatric counselling and is only just now back on his feet.'

Anita ignored me. 'Amelia's particularly interested in featuring a male because most of our victims are women. I'm going to call him.'

I exchanged a look with Leanne, who only shrugged.

Anita picked up the phone and dialed, looking much more awake now. 'Hello, Matty darling, how are you? How is your dear little girl and Sarah too, of course?'

Leanne and I exchanged a glance. We couldn't hear his responses, for which I was glad.

Anita pressed on amiably. 'Matty, we've been working hard to get real law reform for victims. We are so close to getting the Victims' Voices Bill over the line. It would be of tremendous help if you would do this one story for us with the *Weekend Colour* magazine.'

There was a long silence at the other end of the phone while Anita held up her hand to show me her crossed fingers.

Anita's voice oozed with sympathy. 'Matty, darling, I understand how you feel, but I beg you to consider the bigger issues. If we're ever going to stop violence to families we need radical law reform. We can only get that through stories like yours to shake the politicians out of their lethargy. We need you, Matty.'

Anita could be most persuasive when she wanted and it seemed as though she'd got what she wanted. A big smile crossed her face.

'Oh, that's fantastic, thank you. I'll be there, of course, to offer you anything you need and to support you. It'll be fabulous. Yes. Of course. Next Friday. Okay. Of course. Yes, see you then.'

Anita hung up the phone and sat back with a satisfied sigh. 'Wonderful. It's all coming together, ladies.' She got up and grabbed her bag. 'I have a lunch, so I'm out for a while. Martha, dear, could you please run your eye over those articles you wrote for me and then get them off? Also, find me something on the rack for the Women in Business luncheon tomorrow. I promised Korin I'd wear that new dress of his, but I can't match it with any of those bloody shoes and I don't want to go and buy a pair. There's got to be something in the pile of freebies that goes with chartreuse.'

She shouted a dozen more instructions over her shoulder and then disappeared, likely for the rest of the day. My shoulders slumped and I shook my head. She hadn't spent a full day in the office for ages.

As soon as Anita left, Leanne sighed. She looked as tired as I felt.

'Matty told me it never ends with the one interview,' I said. 'As soon as a story about him is published he gets dozens of follow up calls from radio shows and other media urging him to talk to them.'

Leanne shared my concerns. 'I wish Anita would just leave him alone to recover.'

'I agree,' I said. 'He's got a right to live his own life without being hounded.'

Despite my misgivings, I drove Anita to Matty's place in Aspendale the following Friday. We pulled up outside a rendered brick house that had hollyhocks and banksia shrubs in the front garden. I felt embarrassed to be disturbing this peaceful suburban scene, but Anita marched up the driveway and rang the bell.

Sarah met us at the door and gave Anita an icy glare. 'Matty's in the lounge room.' She was holding her car keys and pushed past us with the baby's bassinet. Anita cooed at the baby as Sarah stormed past.

I went after her to see if she needed me to hold the bassinet while she opened the car door, but she ignored me. In any event, Anita was calling for me.

'What's eating her?' She looked bewildered.

I turned back and watched Sarah take off at speed. 'Perhaps she's angry about the interview.'

Anita rang the doorbell again. 'Why would she be angry? It's just one interview.'

I didn't get a chance to respond as Matty called out for us to come in.

Anita let us in and hugged Matty. 'Darling, you don't know how incredibly grateful I am to you for doing this.'

Matty stepped back, putting her at arm's length. 'I want to make it crystal clear to you, Anita, this is the last time.'

The doorbell chimed and Matty let in the reporter and her photographer. With lights and shades, the living area was quickly transformed into a studio. Matty was placed on his own couch like a ventriloquist's doll, Anita next to him, holding his hand while he answered the interview questions. Amelia didn't hold back. She took him right back to the night the kids were killed.

I was squirming in my seat. It was all just so uncomfortable to watch. He clearly didn't want to be talking about the loss of his kids, and Amelia was a hard-headed reporter who left nothing to the imagination. She wanted it all from Matty: his feelings, his anger, and every little detail of the discovery of the bodies. She even wanted to know the words he spoke to his wife when he caught her. She asked if Matty ever visited her, which he didn't, and she wanted to know why not.

I almost gasped out loud at the audacity of that question. It wasn't anyone else's business.

Amelia delved into his decision to divorce his former wife, and his involvement with Anita and the foundation. Brett was clicking away with his camera the whole time. As Matty's distress increased, so did the number of shots Brett took. He was especially busy when Matty started to cry.

I was hating all of this.

Anita, on the other hand, seemed to be lapping it up. To me, it felt like dragging a battered boxer back into the ring when all he wanted was to be left alone.

After what seemed like hours, Amelia finally closed her notebook, turned off her recorder, and beamed at Matty, thanking him profusely and apologising hypocritically for his distress. Amelia and Brett beat a hasty retreat and we weren't too far behind them.

As we were leaving, Matty had hissed at me with a fury I'd never before felt coming from another person. 'I don't ever want to see you or Anita again. Fuck off and leave me and my family alone.'

I mumbled an apology as he slammed the door in my face.

Anita didn't seem to notice. In fact, she was ecstatic the whole way back to the office. 'Fabulous!' she declared. 'This is going to make such a difference.

It will get us heaps of coverage and will force that bitch of an Attorney-General to sit up and take notice.'

I couldn't even bring myself to comment. We were supposed to be supporting families, not inflicting more pain on them. How long would it take for Matty to recover from this? I fervently hoped we hadn't damaged his relationship with Sarah. It must have been so hard for him to find a woman he could trust after what he'd endured.

I stewed all the way back to the office.

30

Martha

Usually, I loved organising events such as the Oration, but I was under pressure because of the Bill and I still had my usual workload. Worse still, we hadn't settled on who was going to be the speaker for this year's event.

It didn't help that Anita was spending a lot of time with Marcel. Even worse, she had planned to bring him to the Oration. Whenever I called Anita, he would answer the phone with a 'Martha, cherie!' before finding Anita, who in turn was doing less and less work at the office.

I had to press her to go to lunch with the Hartfords to celebrate their ascension to the board. Lilly said they needed a dog friendly restaurant for their poodle Pom Pom, so I arranged for them to have an outside table at Ripples.

Apparently, it was not the most enjoyable lunch.

'I told them I wasn't a dog person,' Anita told me later, when she was back in the office. 'They didn't seem to mind that I sat as far away from it as I could, but I could smell the little thing. I hate doggy smells. Also, Lilly bugged me about the finances again, oh, and they think they can find a speaker for the Oration.'

'Oh? Who was their suggestion?' I asked, as I sat in the chair opposite her.

'She and Mark have a personal friendship with Judge Clifford Jamieson, who was the prosecutor in the trial of Anthea's killer. She offered to ask him, but I wasn't sure. Mainly because I don't know if he's one hundred per cent on side with the Bill. Lilly seems to think he is.'

'Well, I think you were right to be cautious, Anita,' I said. 'The wrong speaker could sink us.'

Anita nodded. 'That's true, but getting a Supreme Court judge to speak would be an absolute coup. But because I don't know him personally, I told the Hartfords I'd have a think and get back to them.'

'A judge would be good,' I agreed reluctantly.

She sighed. 'A celebrity would get bums on seats.'

I nodded. 'True, but we could save the foundation some money here. The judge would be free because, as a judicial officer, he's not allowed to charge us anything, and if he was once a prosecutor then he should be on our side. Why don't we call Peter Dickson to check him out? As an ex-copper Peter will know what this guy's like.'

'Martha, that's a great idea.' Anita was beaming. 'Can you get him on the phone?'

I rose from where I was seated, went to Anita's desk where she sat within reach of the phone, dialed and handed the phone to Anita when it was ringing. After a quick conversation confirming the judge's suitability, Anita then got me to give Lilly the go-ahead and call the judge.

Anita was so excited and hopeful that I was caught up in her enthusiasm. It reminded me of the early days when we had to fight and scrap for every little chance. Going with her everywhere. Booking her events. Standing back while she shone. Admiring her hard work and praising her after the shows. She'd worked so hard for the foundation.

Even now, she seemed focussed and was pouring over details. 'Okay, we can't seat Edwin Singh with Leila Mastiani, they're political rivals and may cause a scene. We don't want that, so put Leila with Malik Omar and Ken Mason.'

I nodded and started making notes, hiding a sudden surge of guilt. I'd thought the worst of her lately, but when she was present, really present, she was everything we all still hoped she would be. I'd been wondering about life after the foundation and my growing attachment to Gerard. The Bill was nearly passed and Anita was probably wondering what came next too.

I put my worries away and happily got on with work.

Bloody Lilly had pulled it off! The judge agreed to do the Oration.

The next few weeks were frantic with final preparations for the Oration going at full speed. Leanne and the volunteers were on overdrive writing out name cards, designing the brochures, and filling show bags with gifts and a red gerbera.

Anita never got to meet with Justice Jamieson prior to the dinner. I tried my best to arrange it, but his associate kept saying he was in court or he was interstate or he was busy writing up a judgment.

I met Gerard at the local pub that was becoming our regular catch up outside the office for a meal or a drink.

'Lilly is driving me nuts,' I told him, after sharing a few of Lilly's actions in recent weeks. 'Sorry to be unloading this on you.'

He just smiled. 'Unload as much as you like.'

'She wants to stick her nose into everything from policies to finances.' I gulped a mouthful of white wine. 'Anyway, let's not let her spoil this lovely evening.'

'Yes, let's drop her. I haven't seen much of you lately, Martha. I miss you.'

Gerard's frankness made my heart reach out for him. 'I'm sorry. There's been the Oration, and I've been doing extra shifts at the maternity centre.'

'How's that going?' Gerard asked.

'I love it,' I said without hesitation. 'It's where I feel at home.'

'No doubt. Are you seeing much of Anita these days?' Gerard's question was unsettling. He didn't miss much. I didn't need to answer as he could read me exceptionally well.

'When she deigns to bless the office with her presence, yes. Did you see the email I sent you about the credit card statements and the recent uptick in sundry expenses?'

Gerard gave me a terse nod. 'I did. And I agree with your suspicions. I think the so-called Frenchman is behind it. I mean, she's always been a lavish spender, but this is the first time she's started to make cash transfers.'

I nodded. 'Did I tell you that Anita's coming to the Oration with Marcel?'

He shrugged. 'Don't worry, we'll figure it out. I'll see you after the event?'

'Absolutely,' I agreed.

There were no pre-event drinks at the Oration, and the venue was set up theatre style, with seats facing the front. Anita and Marcel arrived on time, as did Lilly, who was all over the judge when he arrived. When all the guests were seated, Anita went to the lectern and acknowledged the traditional owners and then introduced the distinguished guests. She introduced the judge and beamed as he was enthusiastically applauded.

His Honour, Clifford Jamieson, walked to the lectern. I'd seen pictures of him in the papers, but I'd never seen him in person before. He was in his fifties, tall, had salt and pepper short cropped hair, and was wearing an immaculate Italian suit and the shiniest shoes I have ever seen. He cleared his throat and adjusted the microphone.

'Good evening, everyone. I would also like to acknowledge the traditional owners of the land we are meeting on and pay my respects to their elders past, present and emerging. My topic this evening is common law, sentencing and the role of legislation.'

'Yes!' Anita whispered in my ear. Her eyes were shining with pride and anticipation and I shared her excitement.

The judge began by outlining the principles behind common law sentencing. 'This is a system that has evolved to meet the needs of society in a fair and equitable manner; a system that strives to be just as well as comprehensible, a sensible system allowing judges and prosecutors the flexibility required to make the punishment fit the crime.'

Bloody hell, what is he saying? I could feel my nerves start to hum with foreboding. I glanced nervously at Anita whose smile had begun to fade. Lilly's mouth had fallen open and Mark was frowning, looking puzzled.

The judge paused to survey his audience. 'Common law is not perfect but an elegant feature of it is its ability to adapt and change over time. We have seen this happen in response to advocacy for victims' rights. Victim impact statements have now become standard practice and are of great assistance to our judges and juries.

'Voices critical of existing legal structures matter and must be heeded. However, their claims, like any others, must be tested and they must be well informed and balanced. Fixed and narrow perspectives focusing solely on retribution miss the opportunity for reasoned and helpful debate. We must have some forgiveness built into our legal processes. If there is no forgiveness, there is no incentive for rehabilitation.'

Yikes. I started to run through contingency strategies in my head. If Anita didn't blow up with this, then the media would. The judge didn't seem to care about the restless murmur growing around him, he just kept on speaking.

'It is regularly asserted that the sentences given to convicted felons are grossly inadequate. A check of the Sentencing Institute's annual reports over the last ten years reveals that, in fact, common law sentencing has resulted in increased sentences to allow them to reflect the expectations of the community at large. The increases have not been huge, they have been almost imperceptible, and this is why it is so important to check, to test the evidence and not to carelessly broadcast inaccuracies.'

If Anita was boiling with rage she hid it well. She was sitting bolt upright and the expression on her face was unreadable. I took my cues from her and tried to look as implacable as she did. I couldn't see Lilly's expression as she had her head in her hands. I saw Mark put his arm around her shoulder. The media table was busy as tablets and notebooks were hastily scribbled in and I noticed that Louisa Moore's student, Elissa, was also taking notes. Other audience members were becoming restive, probably wondering what was going on and if someone was going to stop the judge.

The judge ignored the undercurrent of unease and continued. 'Recent changes to sentencing laws are an example of imbalance in legal reforms. Mandating baseline sentences restricts judges from applying appropriate sentences that are cognisant of all relevant factors. Taking account only of retribution, while ignoring other important sentencing principles, will lead to injustices.'

I looked around the now silent room and then back at the judge.

'Yes, retribution has validity, but not exclusivity,' he continued. 'Yes, victims matter, but we cannot have our sentencing jurisprudence determined solely by their experience because to do so will throw everything else out of balance.'

This made me gasp out loud. Anita stopped trying to look impartial at this stage. She raised her eyebrows, shrugged her shoulders, and looked over to the media contingent, sighing loudly. Lilly looked like she had been struck.

Judge Jamieson took a sip of water, replaced the glass with a steady hand and went on. 'We should never underestimate the genius of the rule of precedence—the wellspring of our criminal and civil justice systems. Precedence gives us continuity and enables some degree of predictability in sentencing decision making.

'Some of us have been unfortunate enough to be victims of crime while others are the parents, families, carers, and lovers of the accused. Sometimes, the people who come before our courts are victims as well as perpetrators. Complex human interactions are rarely black and white.'

Anita shook her head in disbelief and coughed loudly.

Judge Jamieson ignored her. 'I conclude by reminding you that judges and prosecutors must have flexibility in sentencing and be allowed to exercise the extraordinary skills their years of study and experience have imparted to them. Sentencing is a balancing act. To achieve balance, we must take account of the total spectrum of beliefs, ideas, expertise and experience. I reiterate, common law is based on common sense and the common good. Parliamentary intervention through legislation is an important part of law reform, however we are also witness to emotive lobbying, particularly close to an election where the desire for retribution can overshadow other important sentencing principles such as proportionality, the offending history of the accused, deterrence to others and rehabilitation. Thank you.'

I heard chairs legs scraping, creaking and a collective drawing in of breath. The judge wiped his brow with a cleanly pressed handkerchief to polite, restrained applause.

There was an uncomfortable silence before he asked for questions. This annoyed me as he had expressly requested of us that there be no questions.

There was silence and then Anita got to her feet.

'Have you ever lost a child?' she demanded in a shrill voice.

She didn't bother waiting for an answer. She turned on her beautiful heels and left the room to the flashing of cameras. This meant there was no one to thank the judge, so he simply left the lectern and he was joined by Professor Louisa Moore.

Lilly looked as though she was weeping, with Mark hovering over her. As I wandered past, I could just hear her words. 'How could he? I thought he was our friend.'

Jamie O'Dhea was nearby and had seemingly overheard her comment. 'You can never be friends with a judge,' he said.

Gerard appeared like magic next to me. I gave him a grateful smile.

'I think a strategic retreat could be in order,' he whispered.

I nodded. 'I'll find Anita and meet you in the west car park.'

'Roger, that.'

Gerard took off and I turned to take stock of the room. Board members were chatting in low voices, and I saw Elissa Mustaffa in intense conversation with Louisa Moore, who'd returned and was conferring quietly with her student. Most of the media contingent had disappeared, so I figured if I found them, I'd find Anita. I walked quickly outside to the gardens where I spotted her. She was framed by the pillars of the law school and the magnolia trees that just happened to be in bloom. She was facing a barrage of questions from the media.

As I watched from the sidelines, Marcel came and stood close to me in an overly familiar way. I wanted to tell him to piss off but restrained myself because of the media.

'Did you expect the judge to take the position he did?' asked Zoe Waters, thrusting her microphone at Anita.

Anita shook her head angrily. 'No, I did not expect the judge to attack us. I wanted to meet with him prior to inviting him to address this meeting, but he was unavailable. He gave no indication he was hostile to victims of crime.'

Zoe nodded. 'Do you regret inviting him now?'

'No,' said Anita. She was more composed now. 'While I obviously disagree with him, it is important for all views to be taken into account. We need to have an intelligent, progressive debate on these difficult issues. I would say, however, the newly appointed judge has years of experience as a prosecutor.

It is interesting how quickly his views have changed since he was appointed to the Bench.'

Rufus Fitzgerald, an experienced senior journalist for the Australian Public Broadcaster, asked, 'What do you think of the judge's remarks about important legal traditions such as the law of precedence?'

'The law of precedence is flawed,' Anita responded confidently. 'Just because someone did something a certain way once, why does that make it right forever? Why should judges be forced to wear straitjackets buttoned up by ghosts of the past? Where are the opportunities for reform, change, and progress? Following precedence confines our judges to repeating the mistakes of the past.'

'Is that why legislation is so important to you?' asked Rufus.

'Absolutely,' declared Anita. 'Legislation has the ability to put the brakes on a judicial game of Three Blind Mice. We don't need judges who are blindfolded. We need judges who can see the future with courage and relevance. Legislation is the parliament expressing the voice of the people.'

Another question came from the pack of the press. 'Why do you think those voices are more important than the experience and expertise of judges?'

Anita smiled patiently. 'Those things are important, but if we allow only the voices of the judiciary to prevail, we risk sentences determined by a privileged, unelected elite.'

More questions were thrown at her, but Anita ignored them and riled up the bystanders who had gathered with the media throng. 'Listen to the victims!'

The cry was taken up enthusiastically and this allowed her to escape from the media mob.

I ditched Marcel and slipping through the crowd, I grabbed Anita's arm and led her through the university buildings where Gerard was waiting with the car.

We jumped in and the second the doors were shut, Gerard took off.

'Get me out of here, Gerard. I need a drink,' said Anita. 'Where's Marcel?'

'No idea,' I told her. I felt bad for a moment, but it was technically true. Who knew where he was now?

'Let's go to Rocky's, no one will find us there,' said Anita. She was fuming. 'That rotten judge!'

We headed towards the coast. 'You were brilliant,' I said. 'The public won't be swayed by him. He came off as just another arrogant and out of touch official.'

'He talked about bloody elegance even though he used to be a prosecutor,' she complained. 'There wasn't much elegance in the horrible crimes committed by the cruel bastards he got convicted.'

I agreed with her. 'How can someone change his views so quickly?'

Anita gave me a droll smile. 'He became a judge, that's what did it. He probably thinks he's sounding oh so judicial. And I suppose he wants to be accepted by the other judges. And did you hear that fucking little bitch Zoe Waters? I thought she was on our side too. I felt like saying, "Listen, bitch, my baby wasn't murdered just so you could get a good story".'

I winced. This brought Matty Morris to my mind and I wondered if there was one set of rules for her and another for other parents who'd suffered.

On our arrival at Rocky's, we were guided to a window table with a full view of the sea. It was beautiful, many shades of turquoise, with rippling patches of liquid gold as the sun set on Melbourne for another day. Anita ordered champagne and Rocky himself brought it to us with his engaging smile.

He kissed Anita. 'Darling, we were watching you on the news! We thought you'd be far too busy to grace us with your gorgeous presence.'

Anita put on her martyr's face. 'Rocky, darling, we have come to your haven to escape from the throng and unwind. Do you have lobster tonight?'

Jamie walked into the restaurant just as we finished our superb meal. Anita looked pleased to see him, so Gerard and I said goodnight and left them to each other.

31

Jamie

I'd stayed at the venue after Anita walked out. I knew the rest of the media would run after her and it'd be a waste of my time to try to compete with them. Jack had gone after the judge for a comment, which meant I had a whole lot of rich donors, sponsors and Lost Lovelies board members at my mercy. There was audible shock in the room with everyone talking at once.

I tried to speak to the board members, but they were all tight mouthed and said Anita was the spokesperson for the foundation. That was disappointing, but the parents of a child who had been kidnapped last year—and thankfully survived—did talk to me and I got some great quotes from them. The wife, Voula, was natural talent.

'We can't speak about what happened to us because the matter is still before the criminal courts, but we can say we were appalled by the judge's accusations, his bias and his appalling manners in being so very rude to his hostess. He should immediately resign and apologise to Anita for increasing her grief.'

It was gold. The husband wasn't so good, but he had useful things to say about the foundation. 'We were so lucky our baby was saved, but the outcome could have been horribly different. That is why we support The Lost Lovelies Foundation and Anita, who is our absolute heroine.'

I noticed Mark Hartford had gone to the toilet and his wife was sitting alone with her head in her hands. The people who'd been consoling her had left, so I saw my chance to move in. She wasn't willing to speak on the record, but I did get her card. There was something about that one … I put her in the back of my mind. Right now, I had more important things to do.

I took off and quickly filed my copy, then decided to drive out to Rocky's for a drink and time to think. To my delight Anita was there, as were Martha and one of the foundation's board members.

Anita looked happy enough to see me, and when I joined them the other two took off.

'You haven't been answering my calls,' I said.

Anita, as usual, didn't shy away. 'I've been busy, darling.'

'Well, I've had news to pass on. The Attorney-General appears to be changing her views about the Bill,' I said. 'And it also sounds like she's going to be changing her job.'

'How do you know that?' Anita demanded.

'Now, darling, come on, you know I can't reveal my sources.'

Anita gave me a saucy look and we clinked glasses.

'So, is she jumping ship?' Anita asked.

I sipped the excellent champagne. 'I believe so, according to a little bird, but before she does she'll be championing the Victims' Voices Bill.'

Anita was thrilled. 'Oh, Jamie, we're so close. The Bill's bound to get up!'

'I also wrote about a possible new prison facility,' I said.

'That would be a good sign. And it could undermine our opponents who keep saying we can't keep offenders in jail because there's not enough space for them.'

She let me take her hand and I slipped my other hand across her thighs and rested it on her knee.

Anita ignored my explorations and expressed her contempt for the judge, but she brightened up when my hand slipped higher. She always did. 'Let's forget about all that for a moment and concentrate on us.'

I wondered for a moment where the French fellow had gone, but it didn't matter. We smiled at each other and the sky blazed as the sea gobbled up the sinking sun.

32

Louisa

I arrived at my office early to check out the media coverage of the judge's speech. Unsurprisingly, the Oration was the lead story with O'Dhea in *The Watcher* describing the judge's words as 'anti-victims rights'. The story was totally biased towards the victims' point of view and quoted supporters of Anita who were demanding Cliff's resignation. It didn't present any analysis of the issues raised by him and there were no checks of the data. I thought it was lazy, sensational journalism. In a perverse way this was useful because it would be an excellent teaching tool for my students.

O'Dhea's piece was flanked by a short analysis written by Jack Ruler. This was a good piece of work. Ruler had done his research and had checked the sentencing statistics and compared them with what Cliff had said. He published the facts and left the rant to Jamie. Very clever, and opportunistic, of the editors to print puff and quality side by side.

By contrast, the reporting and analysis by Rufus Fitzgerald in the public broadcaster's news reports and podcasts dealt with the underlying issues in much more depth. He had checked the judge's statistics and identified changes in legislation that would have influenced sentencing, and carefully contrasted and compared the judge's remarks about common law versus legislated law and concluded that both had merit. He expressed disappointment that the judge's speech had set common law and parliamentary law up against each other as adversaries.

Yes, this would be an excellent teaching tool, not only for Elissa but for the whole of my student cohort.

Elissa, as always, arrived on time looking smart, though her hair was wet. She unnecessarily apologised, explaining she had come from the pool.

I asked Elissa what she thought about the judge's oration.

'It was a surprise to me; however, his words about common law make a lot of sense,' she said.

'What did you think about his views on victim advocates?'

'Not very well disguised, were they?' she remarked. 'I think it was impolite to accept an invitation and end up seeming to attack the hostess.'

'Oh? Do you not think it's necessary for the judiciary to explain their processes to the public?'

Elissa conceded the point. 'I still think he would have been wiser to have refused.'

I didn't disagree with that. In fact, when I caught up with Cliff later he did wonder if he'd done the right thing. Oh well. What's done is done. I smiled at Elissa. 'Have you thought about your thesis?'

Elissa sighed, looking lost. 'I think about little else. I have spent hours and hours reading relevant High Court cases.'

I took a sip of my tea. 'And what conclusions have you come to?'

'Please excuse me, Professor, but I concluded that Australia's judges engage in much verbal gymnastics. This is probably because English is not my first language.'

I smiled and indicated that she should start to eat her food, as I loaded up my own fork. 'Your English is not the problem, Elissa. Why do you think the High Court judges' decisions are so long?'

Elissa ate with youthful enthusiasm. I liked the way she was beginning to relax.

'Well, I suppose there are many competing views. And there are highly paid barristers—the best in the land—who get to argue their cases at the highest court in the land. So, they have to be thorough. But thoroughness can sometimes include a lot of nonsense.'

This made me smile. Having had to trawl through hundreds of pages of judicial verbal gymnastics myself over many years I understood all too well what she meant.

Elissa finished her salad and put her bowl aside. 'I suppose the judges have to respond to and carefully analyse the nonsense before they can rebut it, but at 2.30 am in the morning when I am becoming tired, I wonder if the judges aren't getting seduced into the nonsense when they could have said a whole lot earlier something like, "spare me the bullshit".'

I had a slight coughing fit at that. 'As I mentioned before, Elissa, there is nothing wrong with your English, and there is absolutely nothing wrong with your reasoning. Have you been thinking about a hypothesis for your thesis?'

She nodded. 'I was thinking I might be able to test to what extent the pattern of judges' sentencing is altered over time by legislation. I would like to compare sentences for similar offences pre and post the introduction of victim impact statements and mandatory sentences. Hopefully, I can compare cases in states where there has been no legislative intervention with those where there has; I would also like to interview some judges and ask them what they think about this.'

'Brilliant, Elissa!' I said, drawing a smile from her. 'This week our real work begins. We will design a methodology to test your hypothesis.'

'This makes me happy.' Elissa smiled with enthusiasm.

I reminded her of something she'd said to me at a previous meeting. 'Do you remember how you talked about people who know they are right?'

She nodded. 'Yes, Professor Louisa. I believe Anita could fit into that category.'

'Well, I'd like you to think about how that mindset could be influencing the way people can take a position and refuse to budge, even when they are presented with evidence that rebuts their beliefs,' I said. 'Judge Jamieson made some pertinent points about that in his oration.'

Elissa agreed. 'Policy makers also can ignore evidence because they have their own beliefs.'

'Yes. And if the Victims' Voices Bill is passed it would seriously limit the ability of judges to use their discretion in sentencing.'

Elissa nodded. 'I think that would be most unfortunate. It also would mean no freedom ever for some people. I don't think this is good justice.'

I picked at my plate. 'Why?'

Elissa's face hardened. 'Because a system that allows only for retribution, and ignores rehabilitation, will not work. Also, a system without any forgiveness cannot be a good system for society as a whole.'

We clinked teacups and agreed to meet again in a few days.

33

Martha

Anita had an appointment with Janet Johnson-Smythe on Monday morning, the day before the Victims' Voices Bill was to be debated in parliament.

My own doubts and worries had been growing. The media had kept up a steady stream of coverage since the Oration, most of it unflattering to the foundation, despite the judge's inflammatory remarks. Even so, Anita had been taking advantage of the coverage to be seen at every event. She did what she could to spruik the Bill, but she was barely in the office at all. The Listen Line was blowing up, with Leanne's stress levels through the roof. I regretted allowing Daniel to take the time he needed to go home. We desperately needed him in the office.

I wasn't sleeping well either. It didn't help that I was taking on extra shifts at the maternity centre and I was missing my walking group, but I knew that wasn't the heart of my problems.

If this Bill passes, she'll kill herself.

I still heard that man's voice and it haunted me. I had tried, many times, to rationalise him as a nutty troll with nothing better to do with his time, but his words had a ring of truth about them. And just like I'd done, many times, I pushed away my fears about the consequences of the Bill because the families who relied on the foundation needed us. I had to serve them as best I could.

It probably wasn't necessary for us to visit Janet Johnson-Smythe. She'd already publicly declared her support for the Bill, but that didn't necessarily mean she'd vote it through. Besides, Anita wanted to be seen to be at the heart of the action.

'It's probably not going to change things this late in the piece,' Anita told me. 'But don't cancel the appointment because it'll be a good look to be seen at the Attorney-General's office so close to the vote.'

After being cleared through security we took the lift to the thirtieth floor of the justice building where we were kept waiting for about 45 minutes.

161

Eventually, a young man in a designer suit came up to us.

'Good morning. She can see you now.'

No apology or explanation for the wait was forthcoming. We were offered coffee. Anita refused so I did too.

Janet Johnson-Smythe was seated at her large desk in a roomy office. She was wearing a smart black designer pants suit with a white silk blouse. There were framed photos of children on the desk. She nodded to us to be seated.

Anita came straight to the point. 'Attorney-General. We are both busy women, so I won't beat about the bush. My supporters and I would like to be reassured about what your position is on the Victims' Voices Bill.'

Janet Johnson-Smythe tapped her nails on the desk. Her body language said it all really. The Attorney-General was clearly not a fan. 'I haven't fully made up my mind yet. I am waiting to see the lay of the land when the House sits tomorrow.'

I knew Anita well enough to know that she was holding her temper at such a response.

'I'll be at Parliament House for the debate with some of our supporters,' she said civilly.

I scanned the Attorney-General's made-up face, trying to gauge her reaction to this, but she only raised her arched eyebrows and looked slightly bored. 'My final position will be revealed on the day the votes are cast. We still haven't seen the final draft of the Bill that is with parliamentary counsel. There may also be some amendments proposed by the opposition.'

'Those things sound like minor details to me.' Anita sounded terse. 'I represent people whose children have been harmed by criminals. They need to know if their Attorney-General proposes to support them.'

'Of course, I am fully aware of their distress, but there are shades of grey.' Janet Johnson-Smythe looked at her watch.

I winced.

Anita coloured up. 'If I can't reassure my supporters that you'll commit to allowing them to have a say before perpetrators are released, they will ask me to make that clear to the media.'

The only reply she got to that was, 'I don't react to threats.'

Anita snatched up her bag. 'Come, Martha,' she snapped. 'We need to get to the Channel 909 studio to do a live interview on the *Julia Jones Show*.'

She glared at the Attorney-General and in a voice laced with sarcasm, she said, 'Goodbye, Ms Johnson-Smythe. All the best for the election.'

We didn't actually have to go to the studio. When we hit the street, she wondered out loud whether Jamie's O'Dhea's latest bit of information was accurate. 'He told me the Attorney-General was one hundred per cent on side,' she complained. 'She stood beside the Premier for their press conference.'

'Perhaps she hasn't made up her mind yet,' I said, trying to be reasonable.

Anita was fuming. 'Or the bitch just hates me and is enjoying making me crawl to her. I'll see you tomorrow, Martha. I'm going to the gym and I'll dine with Marcel this evening.'

I tried not to look resentful. 'It's going to be a big day tomorrow.'

'You betcha it is,' she replied, more cheerful now. 'Bring it on!'

I didn't want her turning up bleary-eyed, so I hinted at my own plan for a sedate evening. 'I plan to have a red wine, a steak and an early night.'

Anita waved me off, completely ignoring my muted warnings. 'See you tomorrow, Martha. Keep your fingers crossed.'

'Will do,' I promised.

I'd never been to Parliament House for a live debate and I was excited by the prospect of true politics in action. We'd worked so hard for this day and it had been a rollercoaster of a ride, especially because of the fiasco at the Oration. I was swinging between pessimism that all our efforts would be to no avail and optimism that Anita's vision would finally be fulfilled.

Things were even more confused by my emerging doubts about the Bill. I thought about the judge's speech. One of the things he said, just a simple line, had stuck with me. 'We must have some forgiveness built into our legal processes. If there is no forgiveness, there is no incentive for rehabilitation.'

In a way, it added weight to what Helene was trying to get across to me. At first, I'd thought giving parents a say at hearings was sufficient. Parents could decide it was okay for an offender who had served their time to be released.

But I knew in my heart of hearts that Anita didn't fit that mould. It was clear if she had the final say there was no hope for Jennifer Harris.

I spent yet another restless night grappling with my thoughts. I was looking forward to the morning where I'd be with Anita and some of the board members who were able to attend the debate. I needed their reassurance to quell my nagging doubts, their strength and belief to show me that my own reasoning was flawed.

The next morning Anita and me, Lady Charmiane and Donald, Gerard, Lilly and Mark Hartford, and Bianca Mazzouri met at the café across the road from Parliament House. It was a lovely spring morning so we sat outside with our drinks.

Gerard ran us through what to expect. 'The introduction of a Bill is always a formality. Today is the big day because the Second Reading is when the real issues are debated.'

'How long do you think it will take?' asked Bianca. 'I have a dental appointment this afternoon.'

'Hard to tell,' Gerard said. 'It depends on whether the opposition decides to oppose all or any of the sections. They could also use the delaying tactic of putting up their own amendments.'

'And if the Bill is passed today?' asked Mark.

'It will still need to go to the Upper House, but given the government has the numbers that's pretty well a forgone conclusion,' said Gerard. 'If the Bill passes the Lower House, we can relax knowing it will sail through the Upper.'

Anita urged us to behave impeccably. 'When we're inside let the human rights activists yell and make a fuss. We sit together in quiet dignity.'

Lilly, who had been uncharacteristically quiet since the Oration—I'd not had any phone calls from her at all—squared her shoulders. 'We're all with you one hundred per cent, Anita,' she declared.

I thought she had a cheek purporting to speak on everyone's behalf, but I held my tongue as Anita gave her a quick hug.

The others climbed the steps to parliament while I went with Donald to take Lady Charmiane to the lifts. When we had all arrived in Queen's Hall, I saw that Gerard was looking indignant because security had made him put his harmonica in a locker.

'Did they think I was going to throw it at somebody?' he muttered.

Anita said, 'No, Gerard, they thought you might play it!'

We all laughed and Gerard grinned sheepishly at me.

Inside the House we were a bit like a bridal party. Those who supported the Bill sat on the wooden polished benches on the right and those against it on the left. Just as Donald got Lady Charmiane seated, a young activist rose up out of his seat and shouted, 'This Bill is evil. Everyone will suffer if it is passed. Liberty before retribution!'

The House Speaker leapt to his feet. 'Where the blazes is security?' he shouted. I made a mental note to check if those words would be included in the official parliamentary record, the Hansard. I later found out they weren't.

The external noise soon abated and I was left with my own thoughts for company, as Anita was talking quietly with Lilly on one side, and Gerard was explaining something about passing legislation to Bianca on the other.

My first experience of a parliamentary debate!

The drama of the whole thing was thrilling. Seated above the main arena we could see the politicians circling around below us like restless gladiators, eyeing each other off across the dividing bench. Several came over and reached up to shake Anita's and Lady Charmiane's hands. It seemed like they were anxious to be associated with the people who were the originators of the Bill. History was either going to be made this day or the Victims' Voices Bill would just fizzle out.

The debate was initiated by the Premier rather than the Attorney-General.

Gerard noted this in a subtle whisper. 'You'd expect the chief law officer would have had the lead running with this Bill, given its subject matter.'

There was a golden moment as the shadow Attorney-General got up from her seat, walked past us, gave Anita a little wave and strode across to the government benches to shake the Premier's hand, indicating her support for the Bill. The Attorney-General, seeing this, looked up to Anita and smiled and nodded. That's when we started feeling really confident. I felt Gerard take my hand and give it a quick squeeze. I exchanged a quick glance with Anita—she beamed at me.

The Speaker called for order. 'I invite the Premier to speak.'

A hush fell across the chamber as the Premier rose, paused for dramatic impact, shuffled her papers, and began. 'I have particular pleasure in introducing the Second Reading of the Victims' Voices Bill. This Bill has the potential to finally allow victims of the worst crimes—those committed against their children—to have the final say over the fates of the offenders who commit atrocities too unbearable for most of us to contemplate.'

The Premier spoke at length, including a complimentary word on Anita. I saw Anita's face glowing with pride as she received the accolades of the Premier. I also saw the look on Lilly's face. She was smiling and full of congratulations, but there was ambivalence there too. Could it be jealousy?

The Premier resumed speaking. 'The Victims' Voices Bill will complete the inclusion of victims in proceedings of justice by allowing them the final say over whether offenders are detained or released. I commend this path-breaking legislation to the House.'

There were some 'hear hears' and the Speaker called on the Attorney-General to speak to the detail of the Bill. She did so, accurately and concisely, but stopped short of actually saying that she personally supported it and she had nothing to say concerning Anita's role or that of the foundation.

The shadow Attorney-General tried for some minor amendments and one serious one. She wanted to add a right of appeal to a higher court in circumstances where the views of a parent or carer of a child victim could be challenged on the grounds they were not reasonable. Anita looked furious at this, especially when Jessica Wilkinson rose to support it. The Speaker asked if anyone else wanted to speak on the proposed amendment and there was silence. He then called for a vote on it. We held our breath as the numbers were tallied, but we needn't have worried. The amendment was defeated: 35 votes were in favour and 40 against with three abstentions.

The time came for the final vote on the Bill. The chamber was silent and tense as two members, one from each side of the House, used their index fingers to count the vote. They compared notes and took the result to the Speaker.

The Speaker stood tall as he announced the results. Anita reached out and grabbed for my hand and held it tightly. I was holding my breath when the tally was announced.

'In the affirmative 68, and the negative 20. The ayes have it and the Bill will now proceed to the Upper House.'

It was only when I heard everyone around me bursting into applause that I realised we had won. I exhaled.

Anita's eyes were shining as bright as headlights. 'Yes, this is for Heath!'

As we filed into Queens Hall, the board members and other supporters came up to congratulate a jubilant Anita.

Gerard and I stood to one side of the crowd. My thoughts were racing. 'What happens now?'

'Do you mean what happens to Jennifer Harris?' asked Gerard.

I nodded. 'Yes, but I was also wondering what difference it will make to The Lost Lovelies Foundation once the Bill is a real Act and operational.'

Gerard regarded me curiously. 'Well, it certainly took a lot of time and effort to get it through, so hopefully you'll be able to slow down a bit now.'

I grinned. 'And have more time for you?'

'Yes.' Gerard laughed. 'More time for us.'

'Let's talk about that tonight?' I suggested. 'But I wonder what this means for Anita, because you're right. The Bill was all consuming.'

Gerard had a serious look on his face now. 'Perhaps the work of the foundation is completed?' he suggested.

I mulled this over in my hyper-stimulated mind as he went to security to redeem his beloved harmonica. For me the work of the foundation was more than the passing of the Bill. It was about the families we supported, the Listen Line and the work of our volunteers. No, that work wasn't finished, probably never would be.

We joined the crowd of people leaving parliament and spilling down the steps where Anita, overjoyed, spoke from the midst of a media scrum and ignored the protests from a group of people she later described as 'bleeding heart human rights activists'.

'This is the moment we have been working towards for years,' she told the media. 'Ever since I lost by beloved baby to a criminal, I've been committed to the rights of victims and now we have the tools we need to ensure parents are empowered.'

Zoe Waters thrust her microphone forward. 'But how will this help to reduce crimes against children?'

Anita looked at her like this was a complete no-brainer. 'Potential child killers now know their behaviour will not be tolerated. If they harm a child, they'll be held to account by the people they have hurt. The message is crystal clear. Don't commit a crime against a child in this state because if you do no parent will ever let you out.'

Anita had a busy media day, giving interview after interview to radio shows and television in Australia, and also overseas to the United Kingdom, the United States and Canada. She also invited the board members and donors back to the Lost Lovelies boardroom for what she described as a 'spontaneous celebration'.

I muttered to Gerard, 'Her "spontaneous" means it's my job to organise it!'

Gerard looked sympathetic.

'I don't really mind,' I said quickly. 'Just having a bit of a grumble. We'd better get back so I can get some nibblies in. There's plenty of booze so we don't need to worry about that.'

Word had spread quickly and many people turned up at our offices. There were volunteers and donors, victim support groups, and other people who wanted to show their support or just get a free drink.

Anita stayed for an hour and then left because Marcel was taking her out for their own private celebration.

Lilly had gently castigated her. 'Oh, Anita, shouldn't you be celebrating with us?'

'I have celebrated with you, Lilly dear, and now I need some me time.'

Anita was so happy that Lilly's words just bounced off her.

After Anita left, the celebration fizzled out and everyone, except Gerard and me, left. We chatted about our big day, and far from feeling any kind of exhilaration, all I felt was tired and numb. I had a feeling we hadn't seen the worst of it yet.

34

Martha

As I lay in bed doing my stretching exercises, I thought about the day ahead. Gerard was coming into the office to check the books in preparation for the financial reports. That was nice. As I wondered what to wear, I thought about the last few hectic weeks. Anita had done it. The Victims' Voices Bill was now, finally, the Victims' Voices Act, having been rubber stamped by the Upper House.

The passing of the Bill affected the work of the foundation. Promoting and fighting for the Victims' Voices Act had been so central to our mission that its passing had left something of a vacuum for me in terms of event planning and management. This meant I had time to help Leanne on the phones, which I knew she appreciated, as the calls about the Act had not died down. Leanne was still logging dozens of abusive calls on a daily basis.

It was going to be a lovely, warm day, so I put on a light dress with a crocheted cardigan. Coffee in hand, I went out the front to get the papers and cursed at the unnecessary tight plastic that was a bugger to unwrap.

Over muesli I scanned the coverage of the Victims' Voices Act. It was no longer front page material, but there was still some analysis and two opinion pieces, one by Helene and the other by an independent candidate in the upcoming election, Felicity Palmer.

Helene's piece wasn't that much different from the conversation we'd had at Billabong. I felt a pang of guilt as I read her words. She painted her patients as child abuse or neglect victims who had caused great harm but hadn't intended to. She wrote about individual liberties and the futility of trying to provide treatment and rehabilitation to people who had little hope of ever being free. She also raised the issue of people being able to move on with their lives and that forgiveness is a powerful force for recovery of victims, writing, 'hard hearts cannot heal'.

Anita's face crossed my mind. She hadn't forgiven Jennifer, and probably never would, but she'd achieved so much for other parents who'd suffered so terribly. But since the Act had passed, she'd been gadding about with Marcel in ways that were, frankly, embarrassing for the foundation. As I flicked to the social pages, sure enough, there they were, champagne flutes in hand, at a frivolous, petty function that had nothing to do with our work. They were an ugly parody of themselves and a crass contrast to the seriousness of the opinion pieces gracing the main pages. I was angry now as I turned back to Felicity Palmer's article.

Felicity slammed the Act. She described it as vindictive, draconian and counter-productive, and questioned the limits of the state's power to punish. She decried the use of long sentences, saying the state should not be able to punish a person to the stage where they are left with nothing except hopelessness. 'A state without mercy is a threat to all its citizens,' she wrote. She promised, if elected, to repeal the Act and provide much more funding for the victims' compensation fund, the forensic mental health services, and the courts.

Well, no one who knew anything about the state of our forensic mental health services could argue with the suggestion for better funding. I wondered, while clearing my breakfast table, if the Act was going to make this even more urgent.

When I arrived at work, Leanne accepted the coffee I bought for her with a grateful smile. I sat down in her chair and took the next call, as she closed her eyes and took a sip of her coffee.

The caller wanted to know if we could recommend a counsellor for her. She'd been left in a state of shock after witnessing the hit and run of a child. I listened to her tell what was a horrible story and thanked her for sharing her experience. I gave her the name of three counsellors known to us and wound up. I turned to Leanne. She looked so tired.

'Things will improve when Daniel joins us,' I told her, not for the first time.

'Thank heavens for that!' Leanne exclaimed. She rubbed her eyes and looked at me with an approving nod. 'You look nice today. Got something special on?'

'Nothing special, it's a lovely day and I just felt like a bit of colour,' I said. I tried to turn the conversation back to her. 'I love your top. Did you—'

'Gerard's coming in today, isn't he?' Leanne asked with a cheeky smile.

I pretended to be surprised 'Oh yes, I forgot about that. I'd better get the books ready.'

Leanne shook her head. I was relieved when the Listen Line rang and Leanne responded. She gave me a knowing look and returned to her work.

I didn't have many preparations to make, but I had been keeping an eye on Anita's foundation credit card and noticed a few more mystery transactions. Gerard would know what to do with them, so I put them out of my mind.

He arrived on time, as always, and we went through the books and then to the café for lunch where we talked about the new legislation and the media coverage. I asked Gerard if he had seen the opinion pieces. He had read them.

He paused, sipped his coffee and sighed. 'They both raised some really important issues. Dr Morton makes an excellent point when she suggests that relentlessly reaching for retribution can actually punish the seeker of that retribution as much as it does the perpetrator.'

I raised a brow but said nothing.

Gerard shrugged. 'I tried to tell Anita at our first meeting that I don't believe retribution helps. She claimed her focus was not so much on victims as individuals, but rather on the broader societal status of all victims. I suppose at that time I was really only capable of thinking about my own situation.'

I wanted to hug him at that moment. I settled for putting my hand on his, which he immediately clasped.

'I do believe in the work of the foundation and I'm not sorry I've supported it, but I was disappointed when I watched Matty's interview. I felt that Anita's agenda was more important to her than Matty's wellbeing. She's lost the ability to listen to others.' He gave me an apologetic look. 'I'm sorry, Martha, if that sounds harsh.'

'I hated her pushing Matty into doing that interview too,' I admitted. 'I thought it was a terrible thing to do to him and his family. It wasn't what the foundation was set up for. We're supposed to help people who've lost kids, not use them.'

Gerard, looking sad, nodded. 'She exploited him.'

'Yes.' It was hard to accept, but I agreed with him. Anita was wrong on that occasion. 'It wasn't Anita's best moment.'

I stood up and straightened my skirt. 'I need to get back to the office. There's a lot to do.'

'There always is,' he agreed, and stood up. 'But surely things can slow down now that the Act has passed.'

I picked up my bag and put the strap over my shoulder. I couldn't quite look him in the eye. 'We have the Mental Offenders Review Tribunal next week. Jennifer Harris has what may be her last hearing. Anita wants me to do some preparation.'

'Really?' Gerard looked surprised. 'I would have thought Anita knows exactly what she's going to say.'

I nodded. 'That's so, but I still have to be on top of the finalised Act. I've got to read every section to make sure Anita is fully briefed.'

Gerard was solemn as we walked back to the hospital. 'Have you ever met Jennifer Harris?' he asked.

I shrugged. 'I've seen her a few times, but I've never spoken to her. She was the patient of another nurse at the hospital at the time of her stay, not mine. I also saw her at the trial, though her guilty plea had meant a short trial.'

'I see.' He looked troubled.

I put a hand on his arm. 'Gerard, what's wrong?'

I thought he wanted to say something, but instead, he shook his head.

'Nothing. You know that I worry about you, right?'

I flushed. 'I'm fine, everything's going great.'

'Are you sure? You just seem troubled by the morality of Anita's Act more than usual,' he noted.

I hastened to reassure him. 'No, it's fine. Healthy discussion is necessary for honest conversations.'

He studied me for a moment, and then leaned in and kissed me gently on the cheek. 'Then I'll see you again soon.'

I smiled and touched my cheek where Gerard's soft kiss had landed. I watched him walk away. His tread was firm and steady. He wasn't a spring chicken, but neither was I.

I smiled and went back to the office, telling myself to stop being dozy and to get back to work. My good mood dissipated when my thoughts drifted back to Helene and her patient. I had promised myself I would try to talk to Anita, but I'd used being busy as an excuse to avoid facing up to it. I knew Helene wanted me to persuade Anita to give Jennifer some hope for the future by softening her stance, despite her denials.

God, how that meeting challenged me. And after my shift at the maternity centre later on when I'd realised what that awful feeling within me was; that feeling of complicity.

It hadn't left me.

Well, I was running out of time if I wanted to change anything. It challenged me, forcing me towards a confrontation with Anita, but I had to do something. I had to try.

If I didn't, I'd have to live with the words of the troll on my mind for a very long time.

35

Helene

I was pleased Conrad was coming with me to the Directors of Psychiatry meeting. His youthful presence would ease some of the stuffiness in the room, and it was an excellent learning opportunity for him. It was much less of a burden having Conrad for company than coping with the usual clash of egos on my own.

The meeting was held at The Royal College of Psych Services. There were the usual formalities peppered with squabbles over who got the most funding and who was refusing to take on the most difficult patients. It wasn't until we got through all that nonsense that I was able to raise the subject of the Victims' Voices Act.

The President, Professor Roger Brandt, pontificated with his usual pomposity. 'Oh, Helene. I saw you wrote an article for the popular press.'

A few of his sycophants sniggered.

'Are your referring to my opinion piece?' I asked. 'Because if you are, I would like to express my extreme disappointment that the College has had so little to say on this topic.'

'This is a respected and learned institution! It is not a seeker of popular opinion!' Brandt barked.

I sighed. 'This College has a justifiable reputation for promoting research and practice excellence. However, I fear its focus is inward, rather than patient-centred. The new Victims' Voices Act has the potential to take away all hope from many of my patients and when hopelessness replaces optimism, as you gentlemen should all be well aware of, we end up with despair, serious mental illness and suicides. I believe these are issues this College should concern itself with.'

Brandt snorted. 'Patient-centred? That's what we do all the time. We always place our patients at the centre of what we do.'

Dr Aimapt Dennhu interjected. 'Dr Morton, I am wondering if you have a different definition of patient-centred care from Professor Brandt?'

'Yes, thank you, Dr Dennhu,' I said. 'I am not for a moment suggesting that any of you don't care about your patients. I am referring to patient-centred care that puts patients' needs first and involves them in decision-making about their care.'

Dr Dennhu nodded. 'I see. Yes, this is an important concept for us to be aware of. May I say, Dr Morton, that I am incredibly impressed with your work at Billabong. I would also like to thank you for the invitation to your Christmas concert which my wife, my daughters and I are looking forward to attending.'

I groaned. 'That may have to be put on hold now that the Victims' Voices Act has been passed. There's been a big drop in morale.'

'That is a shame,' Dr Dennhu said. 'What action do you want from this meeting?'

I saw my chance. 'A letter to the papers supporting my opinion piece would be a good start. We need wider community support if we ever hope to repeal the Act, which is what I think we should all be behind. We didn't do enough to stop the Bill and now we're stuck with the consequences.'

'I agree,' said Dr Dennhu.

I watched as Brandt's face turned the colour of rhubarb. It looked quite amusing under his white hair.

'We can't write a letter of support. Not everyone shares your views, Helene,' Roger snarled at me.

Dr Dennhu beamed. 'Why don't we put Australian democracy to work and take a vote!'

'Yes, why don't we?' I agreed, with a significant glance at the president.

Brandt's voice was calm but icy. 'This group was established to encourage support for psychiatry and to learn from each other—'

Dr Dennhu slapped the table, causing teacups to bounce. 'Precisely!' Dr Dennhu roared. 'And this is such a good opportunity to do just that. Who is for supporting Dr Morton by writing a collective letter of support that I will be more than happy to draft, and then get your comments on, for approval?'

Slowly, most of the members in the room raised their hands. The president, seeing the numbers, had no choice but to join them, and then everyone else raised theirs.

I could have kissed Dr Dennhu.

Conrad and I grinned at each other as we practically skipped to the car park after the meeting. 'That's the best meeting we've ever had.'

'The president is a total dictator,' noted Conrad.

This made me smile. 'Yes, well observed, Conrad.'

'And Dr Dennhu, he was, like, awesome, no?'

Conrad's lovely blue eyes were sparkling. He was so young and loved learning, it really was a joy to have him around.

'Yes, Conrad, awesome indeed.' I hadn't felt this good in months. 'This could be a real turning point. I'm always regarded as the one who gives Roger a hard time. I know some of the others agree with me, but they're too obsequious to say so. We just might be seeing the old guard challenged at last, and not just by me.'

But my mood deflated as I unlocked the car and we got in. 'Jennifer. The tribunal hearing is coming up. I really hoped we could finally get her released, but now that bloody Act has been passed I'm feeling pessimistic.'

'You've prepared her as well as possible. She knows what to expect from the hearing, she has all the paperwork, and we've got families lined up who will support her in the community,' Conrad said, ticking off the points on his fingers.

I started the car. 'I'm sure the tribunal will see everything clearly, but you and I both know where the real danger lies.'

He sighed. 'Anita Hammond-Jones.'

36

Bianca

When I was CEO of The Young People's Foundation, I was so busy I hardly had any time to think about myself. I loved my work caring for children, but my own kids complained that their children hardly ever got to see their grandmother. This stung. It was brought home to me vividly when young Willow and I were reading about an aircraft accident.

'What if Mummy and Daddy's plane crashed? Who'd look after me?'

She was only six years old.

I tried to reassure her as best I could. 'Planes very rarely crash.'

She looked up at me with her brown eyes sparkling and clear, a frown creasing her little brow. 'But they do sometimes, so who'd look after me?'

'Well, there's me and Grandpa.'

She looked at me incredulously in that honest and pragmatic way kids have. 'You? You couldn't look after me!'

I was taken aback. 'Why not?'

'You're too busy.'

Well, that did it. I resigned as CEO of The Young People's Foundation. I debated whether or not to dump the rest of my positions too, such as my role on the board of The Lost Lovelies Foundation.

I wasn't called on for much at the foundation; just to attend the monthly meetings and take an occasional call from Anita, Martha, and sometimes Leanne, if she needed an appropriate referral for a Listen Line caller.

So, it was a surprise to get a call from Lilly Hartford asking to meet with me in person. Apparently, she'd been trying to chase me down for some time, but I had been busy. And I was annoyed because when I finally got a free couple of hours to spend with the grandkids, Lilly snatched them from me.

I'd asked if there was any particular reason for the meeting and Lilly said she planned to meet with all the board members individually to get to know them. This sounded a little strange to me, something a CEO rather than a board member might do. In the end she was so persistent that I gave in.

We met for afternoon tea at the Hilton. Lilly congratulated me on my work at The Young People's Foundation. 'I've long been an admirer of yours. I like the way you stand up for kids regardless of competing interests.'

I was puzzled. 'Competing interests?'

Lilly was reading the menu. 'Yes, like the criticisms made of the residential care sector by the Children's Ombudsman.'

I shrugged. 'Oh, that! Well it's alright for him to put the boot into resi-care, but where else are these kids supposed to go?'

Lilly waved impatiently for the waiter. 'Foster care, he says.'

I sighed and waited while she demanded a full list of the types of coffee available from the waiter. She settled on a soy latte and asked for a description of the cakes. I waited patiently and ordered a long black.

'Lilly, do you know how hard it is to get foster parents for most of these kids?'

She smiled in a patronising way that I found irritating. It was like she was being deliberately annoying. 'I heard there were waiting lists.'

'The waiting lists have blown out,' I told her, despising her ignorant, overly confident assumptions. 'The kids who miss out are the ones with the most difficult behavioural issues. Many have had horrible experiences, such as their parents using meth or other substances, and worse. Most have suffered through inconsistent parenting, so the kids are always on high alert.'

'How tragic,' she said unconvincingly, while she stirred her coffee.

I was just about ready to leave. She was so wrapped up in herself she didn't see what was going on around her. 'Yes, it is tragic actually. We provide residential care for kids who don't have anywhere else to go except the streets and the Ombudsman gets stuck into us, instead of sheeting the blame home to the government for not coming up with better funding to attract foster parents—' I stopped dead, noticing Lilly had suddenly gone terribly pale.

'Lilly, are you okay?'

The woman looked like she'd seen a ghost. 'Sorry, I just had a bit of a flashback. I think I need to leave.'

'Oh, I'm so sorry. Let me help you out. Do you need me to call someone for you?'

She shook her head and seemed to be recovering. 'No, a taxi will be fine.'

I took Lilly outside and flagged down a taxi. Realising I'd left my phone inside, I hurried back to get it. Luckily, it was still sitting safely on the table. I put it in my bag and went to pay the bill. That's when I noticed Anita sitting at a table near the window. She was with a man—Mark Hartford.

I decided to get out of there fast. I really didn't want to know what was going on, and I didn't need the drama. What I did know was there would likely be trouble ahead at the foundation, and it would be far from lovely.

It was time for me to retire from the board.

37

Martha

I woke up feeling nervous after yet another night of broken sleep.

Jennifer Harris was listed to appear before the Mental Offenders Review Tribunal, or the MORT, as it was commonly referred to, and I was going along to support Anita. The Victims' Voices Act was now in force and Anita was to be the first parent to address the tribunal under the new law.

I took a taxi to her place. I'd been feeling rotten lately because of everything going on, but today I was positively jumpy because I had decided I would try to raise the issue of Jennifer with her. It was my last chance.

I got her loaded into the taxi and we took off for the tribunal. As we rounded the river, I decided to work up to the topic of Jennifer. 'We've been getting some really nasty calls on the Listen Line.'

'Oh? What are they saying?' she asked casually.

I felt a surge of anger. If she was in the office a bit more, she'd know. I forced myself to calm down.

'There's a few trolls, but one persistent one who says we're going to force Jennifer into suicide.' My stomach tightened, waiting for the response, and when it came it wasn't at all what I'd hoped for.

Anita sneered. 'Sounds like a good idea to me.'

'Anita,' I ventured carefully, 'if that happened it would be a terrible look for the foundation. It would sully our reputation and spoil everything you've worked so hard for.'

She snapped her head around to look at me. 'What are you suggesting, Martha?'

My hands were clammy. 'Well, it might make you look much more noble if you backed off a little.'

'Backed off? How?' she demanded.

I rushed my explanation. 'Just by leaving the door open a bit, like saying you couldn't bear for her to be released just yet, but that you might feel differently in a year.'

'But I wouldn't. I wouldn't feel better in a year's time.' She glared at me and there was something in her gaze I didn't recognise. It was too shiny, too bright, and I wondered which one of us was going off the rails. What had she and Marcel had been up to? Was he giving her some weird snake oils?

I decided to drop the subject for the moment, hoping the seeds I'd tried to plant might quickly take root and grow.

When we arrived, camera crews were already lurking like scavenging birds. I counted ten journalists, including Jamie O'Dhea and Jack Ruler. Zoe Waters and Rufus Fitzgerald were also there.

We didn't linger for long. I noticed Jennifer Harris enter the building, flanked by Helene and a young man, but I didn't really get a chance to study her in the chaos. She was a thin, short and rather awkward looking young woman, not that much different from when I'd last seen her at court.

We went inside to wait and I saw Jennifer again outside the hearing room, biting her fingernails. She had done her best to dress well, but I guess the Billabong had a limited supply of clothes. She was wearing a pleated tartan skirt, a white blouse with a man's black vest, and black tights with a pair of lace up brown shoes. As she waited, she seemed to be going over what she should tell the tribunal, with Helene and the young man listening. Occasionally, she would turn her big eyes to one of them, and they'd give her a reassuring smile.

Guilt filled me at the sight of her; even more so when Anita turned her bright eyes towards Jennifer. To me, Jennifer looked so small and vulnerable, but all Anita could see was a monster. It wasn't the first time Anita had seen Jennifer in person; however, on this occasion she gave her a devastating stare full of hatred. I don't think Jennifer noticed but Helene did.

Anita seemed unusually elevated, even though this was the hearing she had always wanted. I'd heard Jennifer being demonised so many times and I'd once even blamed her for causing my troubles with the Nurses' Board, but here before me was an elfin-like woman with luminous eyes. Helene was caring for Jennifer as best she could, just as a good doctor, or nurse, was trained to do.

I was suddenly ashamed of my behaviour at our meeting. I had acted poorly and from a place of emotion when all Helene wanted was the best for her patient. I hoped to catch Helene's eye so I could perhaps repair things a bit, but she was too busy with her patient. She didn't notice me.

Truth is, I felt sorry for Jennifer.

It was clear to me now that somehow, during all that time I'd been supporting Anita, I'd managed to compartmentalise Jennifer in my mind. I was so concerned with my own problems that she became a convenient scapegoat. She just hadn't seemed like a real person, so it was daunting to see her in the flesh looking so vulnerable. She was so thin and pale. I looked over at Anita, who was still glaring at Jennifer.

I felt my stomach tighten into a knot.

This tribunal hearing was a farce. Jennifer Harris didn't stand a chance.

The door suddenly opened and the clerk called, 'Jennifer Harris!'

I saw her take a deep breath before she entered the hearing room. We all followed. There was a beautiful wooden bench, probably mahogany, shaped a bit like a coffin, about a metre higher than all the other furniture. The room filled up quickly, and a loud banging of the gavel announced the entry of the three tribunal members who marched in line, took their places behind the bench and bowed. We all returned the bows, waited for them to sit and then took our seats, but Jennifer was asked to remain standing while the legal member introduced herself and the other members.

The lawyer was Professor Bettina Williams, Professor of Law at Eastern University, specialising in international commercial law. She looked over at Jennifer and gave her a cordial nod.

'Good morning, Jennifer. My name is Professor Bettina Williams and I am the presiding legal member of the Mental Offenders Review Tribunal today. Assisting me are Dr Joseph Speck, the psychiatrist member, and Jade Smith, the social and welfare member representing the community.'

The two other members smiled and greeted her. She nodded to acknowledge them.

'I'll just explain the role of the tribunal. Jennifer, as you are aware this tribunal is independent,' explained Bettina. 'We are appointed by the Governor-in-Council and our role is to determine whether or not you should be released into the community and, if so, under what terms. We must therefore determine if you appear to have a mental illness or if you constitute a danger to anyone in the community. To decide these issues, we will be asking you a number of questions based on the psychiatric report supplied to us by your treating psychiatrist, Dr Helene Morton. Have you been given a copy of Dr Morton's report, and, if so, have you read and understood it?'

Jennifer confirmed she had received, read and understood the report.

Bettina nodded briskly. 'Dr Morton is satisfied you no longer have symptoms of a mental illness and you do not constitute a danger to any member of the public. Do you want to say anything about the psychiatric evidence?'

'No, Professor, just that I'm grateful to Dr Morton and I believe her report is entirely accurate,' she said in a quiet voice.

'Thank you, Jennifer. Our community member will now ask you some questions designed to allow us to get to know you better.'

Jade smiled down on Jennifer from her position on the raised dais. 'Hello, Jennifer. As you know, I'm Jade, and my role is to make sure community opinion is represented rather than just that of lawyers and medical people. How are you feeling today?'

'Okay,' replied Jennifer in that same soft voice.

'It must be intimidating with all these people asking you questions?'

'No.'

'So, just relax, no one is trying to trick you, we all want what is best for you.' Jade smiled. 'If you were to be released from the forensic centre, what would you do?'

I didn't like this. I felt anger surge through me, especially when Anita snorted from where she sat next to me. Jennifer wasn't going to be released. This whole hearing was a cruel set up.

Jennifer looked puzzled. 'Do?'

'Yes. Where would you live? What would you do with yourself?' asked Jade.

'Dr Morton addresses that in her report,' Jennifer said, trying to reply respectfully.

Personally, I thought Jennifer was trying not to appear defiant.

Jade nodded. 'Yes, but I'd like you to tell us.'

Jennifer shivered as though she was cold, even though it was a warm day. Perhaps she knew what was coming too. She soldiered on. 'I'd like to get my own place. There are several people willing to help me get on my feet and have offered housing. I hope to find work in the law. I'm sure if I get a bit of help, I'll do well.'

Her response was excellent and I saw only too well what Helene saw. This young woman was no longer mentally ill, if she ever had been.

Jade waved her off. 'Oh, well, I'm sure you can talk to the social workers about that if the time comes. I'll just hand you back to Professor Williams.'

I was startled. Was that it?

The Professor looked glum. 'Now, Jennifer, here comes the difficult part for you. Under changes to the mental health legislation in this state, the tribunal is bound to give weight to any views expressed by your victims, in this case, Anita Hammond-Jones. I shall read here from the Victims' Voices Act:

> "If a court or tribunal is satisfied any victim of the detained offender would, on reasonable grounds, be convinced that the release of the offender would constitute a real or perceived danger to any member of the public then their release with or without parole must not be granted.'"

Anita was called to the stand to take the affirmation and face the questions. She quickly squeezed my hand as she rose and gracefully moved to the front. Unsurprisingly, she was brilliant, but it was a hard brilliance, more like a flint stone than a diamond. She remained calm and spoke steadily, telling the tribunal members she still cried every day for her baby and had nightmares about Jennifer coming to hurt him.

I looked at Jennifer to see how she was taking this, and she appeared even paler than before. She turned to Helene with an 'I told you so' look on her face.

Anita went on. 'To release someone who has behaved so heinously in the past would, in my opinion, be devastating. I don't believe I would ever be able to sleep peacefully again.'

The tribunal called a break for lunch after her turn at the stand and I went to find the toilets.

It had been a long morning and I felt sick to my stomach. Much to my discomfort there was a long queue, so I went around the corridor and found a more private bathroom marked Members Only. It was unlocked, so I let myself in and leaned on the wash basin, trying to still the waves of nausea.

I raised my eyes to stare at my image. My vision was suddenly blurred and my face looked anguished, with tears sliding down my face like paint running down a canvas. I filled my hands with water and splashed my face.

I stared back at my dripping reflection. 'What have I done?'

On my way out, I passed the room where the tribunal members were gathered. I heard Joseph Speck talking to his colleagues.

I froze. I knew I shouldn't have been listening, but there was no-one watching.

'God, they might as well hire a hitman to kill Anita because that's the only way Jennifer's ever going to get out under this legislation.'

Professor Williams sounded horrified. 'Dr Speck, as chair of this tribunal I must remind you that kind of talk is inappropriate for a member. You realise, under the Judiciary Behaviours Act, I have no option but to report you to the Judicial Conduct Board.'

'Oh, for heaven's sake, Bettina, it was just a joke,' he protested.

'It nonetheless breaches the law and I have no choice.'

I heard his savage retort. 'You know something, Bettina? You can stick this tribunal up your bum. As soon as this hearing is over, I resign.'

I slipped away and went back to my seat beside Anita. I told her what I'd overheard and she laughed out loud, causing a few journalists to stare at her.

I stared ahead of me as if nothing untoward had happened.

38

Martha

Unsurprisingly, the tribunal refused to release Jennifer. How could they have decided otherwise? The Victims' Voices Act was clear and Anita had won. Jennifer showed no reaction when Professor Williams advised her of the tribunal's decision.

'Following careful consideration of all the evidence before us today, and I thank Dr Helene Morton for her detailed and compassionate report, the tribunal is bound by the Victims' Voices Act. It is clear that Anita Hammond-Jones has established that she is a "victim of the detained offender" and as she is convinced your release would constitute a danger, we are unable to release you.'

The members stood. We bowed, they bowed, and Jennifer was whisked away by two security officials.

Anita grabbed my hands, her eyes blazing with triumph. 'Yes, yes, yes! Now she'll never get out!'

Again, I was alarmed by the brightness of her gaze. She looked almost manic. She floated away and I felt flat, unable to feel the same triumph.

We left the hearing room and Anita skipped up to the media scrum. Usually I loved watching her perform for the cameras, but not this time. All I saw was her swollen self-satisfaction.

In response to the inevitable 'how do you feel' question, she said, 'I feel vindicated. I feel we saw true justice in action today.'

I disagreed.

Zoe Waters called out to Anita. 'Is it justice to keep a young woman, who has also suffered a great deal of distress, locked up forever?'

Anita drew in a long breath, as though she was a mother about to talk to a recalcitrant child. 'Today we have seen, for the first time, a tribunal being obliged to listen to the victim's perspective. This is an exciting development in the victims' rights movement, and I want to say thank you to everyone who has supported this long and difficult battle.'

'But Anita, you aren't answering the question,' Zoe persisted, rising above the throng of voices. 'Is indefinite detention of a young woman who has served her time fair?'

Anita glared at Zoe and snapped, 'Of course it's fair. The offender knew what she was doing. The consequences of her selfish actions have been devastating. My baby had no chance, no choice and ultimately no life. Is that fair?'

The surge of guilt that rocked me was painful this time. The baby, Anita, Jennifer … it was too much. There was no good answer to any of it.

Zoe backed off as Jamie O'Dhea pushed past her. 'The Victims' Voices Act has been tested today and proved effective. What plans do you have for The Lost Lovelies Foundation now?'

Anita beamed at him. 'The Lost Lovelies Foundation still has much work to do. We will continue to assist victims in need whenever a child has been harmed by a criminal act. We urge anyone in such a situation to call our Listen Line to speak to our skilled counsellors, or you can email or write to us if you prefer. The Lost Lovelies Foundation is there for you and we will never let you down. Thank you, ladies and gentlemen, for your support.'

Poor Leanne, I thought. It wasn't like she didn't have enough to do. I had to talk to Anita to get her to recognise other people's needs not just her own.

Anita stepped away from the cameras.

'Are you coming back into the office?' I asked, as the media contingent disappeared. 'We haven't seen you much this week and we have a lot of work to catch up on.'

A taxi pulled up beside us and she smiled at me and slid into the back seat. 'I've got a bit of headache, Martha darling. I need some time out at home. I'll call you, and you just take care of things for now.'

The taxi pulled away from the kerb, leaving me standing there alone. I stared after her for a long time. Whoever that person was, she wasn't the Anita I agreed to help all those years ago. Her heart had hardened and was merciless.

Scrambling in my bag, I found a couple of aspirin and threw them down with a swig from my bottle of water. My nausea had eased, but my head felt squeezed.

Get it together, Martha, I thought to myself. I knew it was time to stop asking, 'What have I done?' and instead address the bigger question, which was 'What do I do now?'

I decided to take a tram back to Yarra River Hospital. As we rattled down Collins Street, I overheard a conversation between two young women. It seemed they had been at the tribunal hearing too.

The dark haired one said, 'I really don't know what to think about this. It feels all wrong to me.'

'What do you mean?' asked her friend.

'Jennifer Harris is about the same age as us. I feel sorry for her.'

'Do you feel sorry for the mother who lost her baby?'

'Surely it's possible to acknowledge the mother's grief and also allow there to be some forgiveness in the legal system? Can you imagine how it would feel to be told you are never going to go free? You might as well top yourself.'

I was startled by the response and pressed the bell to get off. I didn't want to hear the rest of the conversation.

Staring at her screen, her friend added, 'Well, she could go free if Anita Hammond-Jones decided she'd been punished enough.'

'Yeah, right!' said the other one. 'We both saw her give her evidence. She's creepy. She doesn't want to ever let go.'

'What, she, like, gets her power from her victimhood, or something?'

'Definitely.'

Her friend laughed. 'I told you to stick to legal studies. This psychology stuff is really changing you.'

The tram jolted to a stop and I got off in a daze. There was nothing I could do for Jennifer Harris now. Anita was walking down a path I couldn't follow, and wallowing in my guilt would get me nowhere. There were still bereaved families to support.

I went back to work.

39

Martha

When I got back to the office, Leanne immediately hustled me to one side. She was alone, the volunteers had finished for the day.

'What happened? Where's Anita?'

God, I was tired. 'Come to the café with me and I'll tell you everything.'

Leanne was reluctant to be away from the phones, but she needed a full briefing to answer the queries that would inevitably come from the public as a result of the media coverage.

Leanne shook her head. 'Too late. The calls have already started. The shock jocks are having a field day.'

'What's their angle?' I asked.

Leanne grabbed her bag. 'Some are really happy with the outcome, others are cautious, and quite a lot are horrified. They reckon the whole thing has become a witch hunt against Jennifer Harris and it's time Anita learned to forgive and forget.'

I thought of her blazing eyes and grunted. 'Well, that's not going to happen in a hurry.'

I told her about the hearing as we walked to the café. I dumped my bag at the first table I saw and got out my purse, indicating for Leanne to sit down while I got our coffees.

'Can I have a blueberry muffin as well?' she asked. 'I missed lunch today.'

I left to order and when I returned to the table, Leanne was watching Anita on the muted café television. I resolutely ignored the screen.

'Anita looks unusually elevated,' Leanne observed.

I nodded. 'She was strange today. Her mood was off.'

Leanne picked at her muffin. 'Well, I suppose it's a big day for her.'

'It was more than that, she was really off. Elevated, like you said. I thought she might actually be manic,' I said.

Leanne looked alarmed. 'Did you say anything to her about that?'

'I didn't dare, she wasn't in much of a mood for listening today. On the way there I tried to suggest she back off on Jennifer Harris.'

Leanne winced. 'How'd she react to that?'

'Predictably,' I said. I heaved a sigh. 'Why do I feel so flat?' I asked her, as I stirred my coffee. 'Watching Jennifer today was gruelling. Did we really want to lock her up for the rest of her life?'

'That's precisely what Anita's always wanted,' Leanne said without any hesitation. 'You know that.'

She said it without rancour or blame, but her words still stung. Even worse—she was right.

I did know. I always knew.

I suddenly wished I'd gone home. I just wanted to shut the curtains and curl up in bed.

'Hey, cheer up,' said Leanne. She reached across the table and took my hand. 'I can see where your mind is going. You can't go back into that whole guilt thing again, Martha. We need you more than ever.'

I brushed a hand across my face and busied myself with my coffee. 'Not sure about that,' I said in a trembling voice. 'What good am I now?'

'Don't talk like that. You're the one who has kept the foundation going all these years.' It was Leanne's time to complain. 'Where is Anita? Frolicking with her toy boy. She hardly turns up anymore. She's got no idea what's going on at the office. If it weren't for you the place would be in shambles.'

I had no answer to that.

'She doesn't have any idea how every time she opens her mouth to the media our workload increases. I'm run off my feet and the volunteers feel unsupported,' said Leanne.

I frowned. 'Unsupported? I always acknowledge them.'

Leanne put her hand across the table and squeezed mine. 'I know you do, Martha. That's not what I meant. They joined the foundation for lots of reasons, but Anita was the main one. Now they think she's deserted them and there's no leadership anymore.'

'You think we're lacking leadership too,' I noted quietly.

She nodded. 'Anita's not supporting us. The phones are running hot and I'm just about burned out.'

This alarmed me. Leanne held up the most important part of the organisation. Without her, the whole counselling service would collapse.

'She's off at events with that weirdo Marcel, and the callers are commenting on it,' she added. 'And when she does come into the office she looks tired and hungover.'

And possibly something else, I thought to myself, thinking of her shiny eyes.

'It's time she came down to earth,' Leanne said with determination. 'Can you call her and make it clear she has to be here tomorrow? We've got the monthly support meeting for the volunteers. She's missed the last three.'

'I'll read her the riot act and tomorrow I'll set up the room for you and get some catering in,' I promised.

Leanne smiled. 'There's no need for catering. Everyone's bringing a plate, so it should be really nice. Ranjana's bringing in *kalakand*.'

'What's that?' I asked.

Leanne shrugged. 'No idea, but I was assured I'd love it.'

I smiled and shook my head. No doubt she would—Leanne had always been a foodie. My smile faded away and I sighed.

Leanne raised a brow. 'Out with it, Martha, what else is bugging you?'

I fiddled with my napkin. 'Do you ever feel like chucking it all in?'

She stared at me. She shoved a bit of muffin into her mouth and took a gulp of coffee. 'Yes, I do,' she said eventually. 'Many times a week and especially so lately.'

'Why do you stay?'

'The callers and volunteers.' She shrugged. 'I was a nurse and now I'm a counsellor. They're similar roles in many ways, and it's what I'm good at. They need me. The work we do is important. That's why I stay.'

I sighed. 'I've been thinking about leaving.'

She thumped her cup down on the table. 'Don't you bloody dare leave me! It's bad enough for me now. If you jump ship how am I supposed to survive?

I might love the work, but I can't do it if you go.'

I jumped in shock. 'Oh, Leanne.' I took her hand. 'I'm so sorry. Of course, I'll stay, but we need to think ahead.'

Leanne squeezed my hand and leaned back in her seat. She looked at me thoughtfully and shook her head. 'Anita really did a number on you today, didn't she?'

I frowned, and Leanne made a pacifying gesture.

'Look, we love her, we all do, but she took advantage of you, Martha. She used your better nature and blindsided you to the truth of things,' she said.

I didn't want to hear this. I closed my eyes, but when I opened them my old friend's face was sympathetic and kind.

'She has power over you because of your self-doubt and residual feelings of guilt over Heath.'

I blinked back tears. 'I should never have left that room,' I mumbled.

Leanne leaned across the table and took my hand. 'But you did, and you were exonerated by the Coroner for doing so. Perhaps it's time you forgave yourself?'

'Easier said than done,' I said.

We walked back to the office and Leanne returned to the phones while I called Anita. Her phone just went to the answering machine, so I left a message telling her it was imperative she attended the volunteers meeting. I was proud of myself for being so firm with her.

An hour later she texted me to say she was feeling exhausted and would be taking a couple of days off.

I nearly threw the phone at the wall.

I was so angry! It was like she hadn't taken any notice of my message. She was tired? What about us? What about the foundation? It sounded like she couldn't care less.

I stormed over to the phones to show Leanne, who was beyond disappointed, she was downright angry.

'It's time she got her priorities sorted,' she growled.

I rubbed my eyes with the back of my hands. 'Are there any priority actions waiting?'

Leanne nodded. 'There's a family who desperately need a cash hand out. They meet all of the approval requirements; we're just waiting for Anita's sign off.'

'How much do they need?'

Leanne consulted her notes. 'Their government support doesn't kick in for a few more days, so enough for a motel and basic supplies.'

I knew exactly what I needed to do.

'Did they leave their banking details?' I asked.

'Yes,' she said. She saw the look on my face. 'Please tell me we're going to do something about this.'

'We are. Gerard's coming in shortly. He's not only the money man, but a board member. He can sign off on it. Give me the paperwork and let the family know the money will be in their account before close of business today.'

'But Martha, how—'

'I'll get it fixed, you just take care of that family,' I told her firmly.

If Anita wasn't going to do her job, then I bloody well would. We promised to support families in need. I intended to keep that promise.

40

Lilly and Mark

I saw you at the Hilton with Anita Hamilton-Jones.

I didn't see you.

No, Mark, I know you didn't. You were too enticed by Anita.

I was no such thing!

Don't lie to me. I know you too well.

I don't think you do.

What do you mean?

Since our daughter died you hardly even notice me.

Is that why you've been seeing Anita?

I haven't been seeing Anita.

But I saw you together at the Hilton.

Lilly—

I was with Bianca Mazzouri. It was so embarrassing.

Lilly, we were just talking. There's nothing else.

How many times have you two been just talking?

Look, there were just two times. Once when I went to help Martha and Anita set up for a meeting—

No, you didn't.

Martha didn't turn up.

Martha is reliable. If she says she's going to show up, she does. Martha wasn't invited to your little meetings.

Please, Lilly, there was nothing in it.

Nothing?

I just needed a friendly ear. Someone to talk to.

And did Anita offer you more than her friendly ear?

Yes, she did. We were waiting for Marcel. She said he could help me.

Help you? How?

He was going to talk to me about his healing techniques. He's helped

Anita a lot, so she's helping him to build up his practice.

Why did you keep this a secret from me?

I didn't. I was always going to tell you.

And you just didn't get around to it?

How could I? You're always too busy to talk to me.

I don't deserve this.

You think I had sex with her, don't you?

I don't know what to think.

I didn't have sex with her. I never wanted to. I only want you. Do I have to die too, before you can move on? Sometimes you make me feel like I'm Brendon.

Brendon.

My daughter's killer.

Our daughter's killer, Mark. I have never heard you speak like this. Is this coming from her?

No.

Does she tell you, during your little chats, that I treat you badly?

No. We only met twice and Marcel was at the second meeting.

I'm beginning to understand why most marriages don't survive a trauma like ours.

Okay, Lilly. First, I love you. But there are some things I don't like about us.

What things?

I don't like the fact you can't move on and you won't let me move on either.

Why don't you move on? Go on! Move on, right out of here.

I'm not going to leave you.

Can't you see how this looks? You know what a shit childhood I had with my crazy mother.

Yes, I've heard you talk about her many times. Perhaps it's time we talked about your feelings, Lilly. I mean talk properly and not just in platitudes.

When we got married you promised you would always protect me.

I have and I always will.

So why have you betrayed me?

Lilly! I have not betrayed you.

Other people would have seen you with Anita.

So what if they did?

How do you think that makes me look?

Oh shit, I'm going to have a drink.

Me too.

Whiskey?

Yes.

You never drink whiskey.

I'll have one now.

We can't go on like this. Bundling up feelings.

We survive.

Yes, and that's about all we do. On the rare occasions you let me in it's like making love with half a person. You're not with me emotionally. You make love like you're doing it out of duty.

I don't dare risk getting pregnant again.

Well, perhaps it's time you did. Here, have another scotch.

You don't love me.

I do. I always will.

Will you be seeing her again?

Not without you.

You mean it?

I want only you. I want you in my arms and I want to feel your passion.

Like we used to?

Yes.

And only me?

Yes, only you and all of you.

41

Jamie

The write up on Jennifer Harris's indefinite incarceration was one of the most explosive pieces I've ever worked on.

The election was imminent and the polls weren't looking good for the government. Commentators were indicating that the Victims' Voices Act and the hard line on crime wasn't working in the government's favour. The polls showed them losing in a landslide to the opposition. Shock jocks were ranting about a lack of leadership and internal factional warfare. Perhaps sensing a defeat, Janet Johnson-Smythe was the first minister to jump ship.

The Premier tried to ameliorate the damage by appointing her as the inaugural Charities Ombudsman. Her role was to ensure charities distributed their funds in accordance with the Charities Control Act. That law was passed following several high profile charity scandals. I'd covered them all but The High Flyers Assistance Fund was a stand out.

A famous rock singer and his mate, a stunt pilot, established the High Flyers and raised millions of dollars to assist people injured as a result of high-risk public entertainment accidents. Two whistleblowers from within the foundation talked to me about drunken parties, sex with prostitutes, some of them very young, and failures in record keeping. I published an exclusive on page one of *The Watcher* and the government immediately ordered an inquiry.

The subsequent public hearings revealed the High Flyers had spent a disproportionate amount of its donations on administration, events, travel and plush offices. Precious little donated funds ever went to the intended injured parties. The results of the hearing were not pretty. There was a total lack of accountability, a culture of bullying and sexual harassment of staff, and downright theft. The founders were charged with criminal offences, found guilty and given suspended sentences, hefty fines and barred from ever running a charity again.

There was a public furore, of course, and the government decided the recovered funds would be invested and put towards the establishment of the Charities Ombudsman.

Later, the scope of the Charities Act was quietly extended to include foundations.

I wondered if Anita was aware of this.

I didn't think Anita was in the same category as the crooks who ran the High Flyers, but I was keeping a close eye on the negative public response to the passing of the Victims' Voices Act. The opinion pages were full of commentaries blasting her. Stella Steele had got in on the act, and a group of psychs, led by Roger Brandt, called out the recklessness of passing the Act without proper consultation.

I was forced to acknowledge that Jack had been right all along. He was immune to Anita's charm and better able to recognise something was rotten at The Lost Lovelies Foundation. He'd been good since coming out of rehab. His work was focussed and he'd been doggedly sticking with the substance stories, while I took the more commercial angles. It was an approach that was working well, and the editors were satisfied, which was all that mattered.

Kayla in Gossip had been keeping me in the loop on Anita's social life. I hadn't seen any new snaps since the Jennifer Harris hearing, but I'd seen dozens of other photos in the weeks prior of Anita with Bouverie at lots of events, most of them unrelated to the work of the foundation. She always had a drink in her hand, and worse, she didn't seem to realise that it wasn't a good look. She was losing some of her glamour. A story in *The Women's Magazine* had noted she'd been cancelling events on short notice with little reason given. Jack advised this was something we should keep an eye on.

'It's falling apart, lad,' he told me.

I tried to call Anita. I had to let her know that she was losing all the goodwill of the last decade, but again, I got her bloody voicemail.

'Anita, you have call me back. You're getting torn to shreds in the media and you don't seem to realise it. Call me.'

I was surprised at how pissed off I was. Could that odd emotion be jealousy? Surely not. I had no right to demand anything of Anita, certainly not fidelity, after all I was married, and we'd never been a couple. Our relationship was opportunistic. If the opportunity arose to be together and she was willing, it was a done deal. I was certainly up for it, but it had happened only once since the shaman had come on the scene.

I sighed. Jack had been right all along.

I called Daisy and said I'd be home early.

She sounded surprised. 'Is this a no news day? The kids will love that. Let's get fish and chips down at the jetty.'

The kids were at the gate waiting.

Fionn was grinning at me. 'Daddy, daddy! You're home early.'

I held out my arms and both he and Rosie were all over me. I laughed and hugged them tight.

'Alright, that's enough. Get your scooters, we're going to get fish and chips,' said Daisy.

They ran away, screaming in delight, and I dumped my briefcase inside. Daisy locked up and then we walked down to the jetty to get fish and chips.

We ate, sitting on the sea wall, fighting off the seagulls. As the kids played in the sand, Daisy and I talked.

'I'm sorry I've been an absent husband and father of late,' I said quietly.

Daisy nodded, but she wasn't looking at me. I followed her gaze and we watched a fisher reel in a reasonable sized snapper, its scales shining mauve and gold in the setting sun.

'I knew when I married a journalist that life was not going to be ordinary,' she said, and I thought I was off the hook.

'I've been on a big story. Big stories, I should say,' I corrected myself. 'There's been a lot going on.'

'You could share the workload with Jack,' she suggested. 'Perhaps even let him be the lead on the Lost Lovelies story?'

She knew more than I thought she did. 'I've already done that.'

I looked at her and she looked to the kids. 'Best get these kids home now.'

Later, over a glass of wine, we talked some more. Daisy reminded me of what was happening in her world. 'The kids we get at school now have such awful lives. Alcoholic parents, druggie parents, druggie alcoholic grandparents.'

'I'm never going to let our kids do drugs,' I said firmly.

Daisy looked mildly amused. 'How would you ever know if they did? You're never here.'

Well that certainly stung. 'I know I've been away a lot, but that's gonna change.'

'How is that gonna change?' she demanded.

'I've given up the stories that are taking too much time. I told you, Jack's got the whole Lost Lovelies mess.'

'That's a good start.' She drained her glass. 'Listen, Jamie, I'm doing it tough at the moment. I come home at night covered in scratches and bald spots from where the kids pull my hair. Despite that, I love the work I do. I want to keep doing it, but I need more commitment from you.'

A strong sense of shame flowed through me. 'I didn't realise it was so bad. Things will be different from now on, I promise you.'

'I'm going to bed,' said Daisy.

I went with her.

We lay side by side for a while and then I reached for her.

Daisy rolled over on her side, away from me, and said, 'I'm tired. We'll see how this story pans out.'

42

Martha

I'd had a good long cry the night of the tribunal hearing, and every night since. Gerard had wanted to come over, but I didn't want him to see me in such a mess. I knew he wouldn't judge me, but still.

When I took the time to examine how I was really feeling, the ever-present guilt was still there, but now there was also anger. At myself, at the system, at the Act, and at Anita.

Eventually, I picked myself back up again. I went out with the walking group, taking the time to actually enjoy the walk. I told them straight up that I didn't want to talk about the Act, and they respected that. Abigail gave me an empathetic smile that spoke volumes, but judging by the looks on the faces of Judy and Sue, they had no pity for me.

I couldn't blame them.

I later went into work and got busy. I prepared draft statements for the media on the efficacy of the Act for when Anita did return, and I approved the priority requests in her absence. There was no way I was going to let the foundation's most needy go without so she could romp with Marcel.

After a week off, Anita came back to work. She looked tired and untidy. She wasn't shabby or anything like that, but she seemed less interested in her appearance. I rose and followed Anita into her office. 'I've got a whole list of things to run through with you. We have several media outlets requesting statements. I've drafted some options; they're in your inbox. I also need you to sign off on a number of documents, and more besides. We've also got a board meeting next week.'

'Can this wait?'

'No. Leanne and the volunteers have also requested a meeting,' I told her. 'They're unhappy at the lack of support you're providing.'

'Yes, fine, whatever,' she said tiredly, sitting down at her desk, head in her hands.

'Oh, and you have Lilly Hartford arriving shortly for a meeting.'

I felt cruel dumping that on her, but it had been in her diary for the last few days. I'd been so frustrated by Anita's lack of communication, so I'd barely even fought Lilly as we haggled over the time.

'Martha, you know I hate morning meetings,' Anita mumbled.

I shrugged. 'Lilly wouldn't have it any other way.'

Lilly arrived soon after looking smart in a purple suit, the blasted poodle tucked under her arm. She ignored me and marched into Anita's office as though she owned the place. I hastily grabbed my notebook and followed her. Anita looked surprised at the unannounced entrance. She glared at the dog but invited Lilly to be seated.

'Can we close the door?' Lilly asked.

Anita raised a brow. 'Why? I never close the door. There's only Martha here and I don't have any secrets from her. Leanne is right down the end, so we won't be disturbing her.'

I hid a smirk. 'Do you need me to take not—'

'No, this is a private meeting,' interrupted Lilly.

Anita was annoyed. 'Excuse me, Lilly.' She gave me a hard smile. 'Please sit down, Martha. I would like you make a record of this meeting.'

I took my seat and pulled out my recorder.

'Have it your own way, Anita,' snapped Lilly. 'I was merely trying to save you embarrassment in front of your staff.' She moved the poodle to her lap. 'We have to talk about the anomalies in the foundation's finances.'

My jaw dropped.

Anita was aghast. 'What anomalies?'

'Well, there are some pretty big problems—'

'Lilly, what are you talking about?' Anita demanded. 'Everything is perfectly in order. Gerard has done regular audits.'

I was appalled at the cheek of Lilly Hartford. Who did she think she was?

Lilly was fondling the poodle's ears. 'Anita, there are big claims for personal services for you.'

My jaw fell open in shock. She knew about those mystery transactions.

Anita glared at her. 'What do you mean "personal services"?'

Lilly gave her an accommodating smile. 'I mean the hair styling, Italian and Spanish shoes, handbags, holiday accommodation for you and a journalist, alternative therapies from an unregistered provider—'

Anita's voice trembled with outrage. 'How dare you question me! I started The Lost Lovelies Foundation. I have worked my butt off for it. I've worked day and night, 24/7, for ten years. I've given 120 per cent. And why? To help other people who have suffered. People like you and Mark. I have made this foundation. I am this foundation. My work has been exemplary. I have been internationally acclaimed, I've been given medals and an honorary degree.'

A traitorous part of my mind didn't quite agree.

Lilly persisted. 'True, however, the expenses—'

Anita threw her arms up. 'For heaven's sake! I have to be on television and do heaps of public speaking. I've got to look the part.'

'Anita, as a board member of the foundation I am deeply concerned.'

Anita glared at her. 'All I do is for the victims of crimes against children. I don't know what game you're playing, Lilly, but The Lost Lovelies Foundation would be nothing without me. Now, please leave.'

I smiled. This was the old Anita, passionate, committed—a fighter.

'Anita, please listen to me. I am a director of this founda—'

'Yes, and I am its founder, its inspiration, its soul,' retorted Anita.

Lilly stared at her. 'As a director of the board, I have a duty to bring my concerns to your attention. After all, the directors would be personally liable if there were proceedings against the foundation.'

'Proceedings, what proceedings? What bloody proceedings, Lilly? What are you up to?' Anita demanded furiously.

'I have spoken to some of the other directors and we agree that under corporate governance principles we are bound to—'

Well that did it. Anita lost the plot. She rose up out of her seat and I heard her inhale vigorously. 'Corporate governance principles? What would you know about those? You're just a primary school teacher. A trumped-up nose-wiper.'

I sensed movement out of the corner of my eye and saw Leanne standing uncertainly in the doorway. The ruckus must have drawn her from her desk.

Lilly's voice hardened, the smile well and truly gone by now. 'I will not be spoken to in this way. We need to work as a team, Anita. You've become increasingly despotic, you refuse to discuss important issues with us, and you don't consult or advise the board on your actions.'

Anita had had enough. 'Bugger off, Lilly, and take your pissing poodle with you. It shouldn't be in a hospital. That's against the health regulations! Perhaps I should get Martha to call security?'

I blanched. This was getting out of control. I got up and moved to the office door.

Lilly stood up, smoothed down her skirt and picked up her dog and bag. 'Okay, we clearly aren't getting anywhere. This discussion has not concluded. I shall be raising these issues again at the board meeting next week. I tried to do the right thing and raise them privately with you. I wanted to do the decent thing to save you embarrassment. You've not allowed me to do that, therefore it will need to be considered at the meeting.'

'How dare you threaten me!' Anita hissed at her. 'The directors are loyal to me. You'll find yourself on your own with your treachery.'

Lilly didn't bother to respond to that. Leanne and I shifted just outside Anita's office, standing side by side, making space for Lilly to depart.

As Lilly stormed off, Anita followed her to the door of her office and called after her, 'The public, the donors and the media will never love you like they love me. Love will override corporate governance every time!'

Lilly didn't bother to look back.

Anita slammed the door.

After Lilly had gone, we heard Anita crying.

I didn't know if I should go to her or not. I certainly felt bad for her. Lilly had clearly gone behind her back, but a part of me wondered how much she'd brought on herself. Leanne whispered that we should give her time to collect herself, so we went back to work, both of us feeling unsettled. Eventually, Anita called me into her office.

I took a seat. I had no idea what she would do. I suppose that was a sign of how far apart we were growing.

She was looking into the mirror, tidying her hair and dabbing some powder on her face. 'Martha, can you get me a taxi?'

That really concerned me. Running away? That wasn't like her. I didn't want her going off on her own until I was sure she had pulled herself together. I was even more fearful of her going to Marcel while she was so vulnerable.

'Are you sure? Why don't we take a bit of time out and just talk?' I suggested. 'We could go for a walk along the river, get some fresh air.'

Anita smiled and came around to where I was seated. She touched me gently on the shoulder. 'I'll be fine, dear Martha. Just call a taxi.'

So, I did. I let her walk out of the door, her vulnerability radiating off her in waves.

I watched her go, not at all comfortable with the situation.

Leanne took off her headphones and came over to me. 'Are you okay?'

I pushed away my worries. I gave her what I hoped was a reassuring smile. 'That was a ding dong row, wasn't it?'

She ignored my feeble attempt to pretend nothing was wrong. 'What do you think is going to happen?' The furrow in Leanne's brow showed how concerned she was.

I just shook my head because I didn't know.

'Do you think Lilly will follow up on her threat to raise it at the next board meeting?'

I nodded. 'I think she will. She's nasty enough to do it.'

'And what will the board members do?' she asked anxiously.

I thought for a while and shook my head. 'Look, I'm sure everything will be fine. Gerard always has the books in order.'

'But Lilly's got a point about how much Anita spends.'

'I know. But Anita does have to look the part to promote the foundation.'

Leanne wasn't entirely convinced. And neither was I.

I put a reassuring hand on her shoulder. 'I'm sure the board members will support Anita. They've known her for much longer than they've known Lilly. At the very worst there might be some suggestions for restraint but nothing more. Let's just hang in there until after the meeting and we can reassess things then.'

Leanne nodded and went back to the phones.

Meanwhile, I blocked out some time to discuss with Gerard if there was any way of removing Lilly and Mark from the board before they could do any more damage.

43

Martha

There was a rather official looking letter in the morning's mail. I was horrified when I scanned the contents and realised it was from Janet Johnson-Smythe—she'd been appointed as the inaugural Charities Ombudsman.

The letter enclosed a brochure advising us of her role in receiving and investigating complaints about registered charities and foundations. My heart thudded anxiously when I read that the foundation had an obligation to make quarterly reports to the Ombudsman of its fundraising and expenditure and had failed to do so.

She was going to audit the foundation!

I frowned. Anita was not going to like this.

Naturally, Anita wasn't in yet, so I called Gerard to get his advice. He wasn't fazed.

'Don't worry, Martha. The Charities Ombudsman doesn't have jurisdiction over Lost Lovelies because it's a foundation, not a charity.'

'But her letter says she does have jurisdiction and she's sending her auditors to inspect us on Monday.'

Gerard sounded surprised. 'Does she say where her authority comes from?'

I read from the letter. 'Schedule 17 of the Charities Act extends the jurisdiction of the Charities Ombudsman to foundations and organisations supporting individuals affected by the Victims' Voices Act. This includes all charities and foundations.'

Gerard groaned. 'They've snuck it into a schedule without consultation. No wonder I didn't see it!'

I felt trapped. Anita and the foundation were going to need me more than ever, but was I even up for that? Anita had been sullen since the confrontation with Lilly, and the foundation was still getting pounded in the press.

Anita didn't end up coming to work that day—which made Leanne mad, as she missed seeing the volunteers again—so I had to corner her the following day.

I was dreading telling her about the letter, but she was smiling when saw me. Maybe it would be okay.

'Martha, dear, I suppose it's too early for a champagne? I'd love a mimosa.'

I didn't return the smile. 'I think it would be a good idea to wait because I have some news for you. '

She laughed at my serious tone. 'What is it?'

I handed her the letter. 'We're being audited by the Charities Ombudsman.'

She sat bolt upright and snatched the letter. 'I'll bet that treacherous bitch Lilly Hartford has dobbed us in out of spite. She hates me. She's so jealous. I think she wants to take over the foundation for herself.'

I frowned. 'Why would she hate you?'

Anita tried to be casual, but I could see a touch of guilt in her expression. 'Oh, I met with her husband a couple of times.'

I was startled. First Jamie, then Marcel and now bloody Mark Hartford. What a stupid choice. I tried not to show my irritation. 'Was Lilly there on those occasions?'

Anita sighed. 'No. He's a lonely man and he needed someone to talk to. Martha, why are you looking so serious? It was just to talk, that's all. I introduced him to Marcel who thinks he can help Mark.'

'That woman would never think it was just a talk.' I didn't try to hide the urgency in my voice. 'And Anita, it's *Janet Johnson-Smythe* auditing us. She was the one appointed Charities Ombudsman. She's sending her auditors here on Monday.'

At last I had her full attention. The colour drained from her powdered cheeks and she dropped the letter. 'Oh shit. What are we going to do?'

I hated seeing her so upset. And as always, I tried to think of ways to fix it. She might have made some poor decisions lately, but the foundation still mattered. 'I can work through the weekend to make sure everything is in good order. Gerard can help me.'

Anita looked incredulous. 'Of course everything's in order, isn't it? Why wouldn't it be?'

'The books are in order. Gerard makes sure of that,' I reassured her.

Anita raised her upturned hands in a question. 'So, what's the problem?'

I stared at her in disbelief. 'Anita, it's about your spending.' I tried to explain it to her, realising that she'd barely listened to Lilly Hartford's diatribe about personal expenditure. I also waved the letter with the explanation. 'Before she left office, the Attorney-General snuck in a schedule to the Charities Act, meaning we're now within her jurisdiction.'

'The cunning bitch!' Anita snapped. She pushed her chair back and stomped around her office. I watched as she muttered curses, but she still didn't seem to realise how serious this was for the foundation.

'Anita, do you see? We could have problems with some of the expenditure.'

'What expenditure are you talking about, Martha?' demanded Anita.

'Well, there's a lot of expenditure on things like clothes—'

And that's where I lost her. I didn't even get to whatever money she was spending on Marcel. She was already close to hysterical and now her arms windmilled in indignation.

'Christ! I have to look good in this job, otherwise how am I going to convince people to donate to us?' she shrieked.

I tried to placate her. 'I agree. I know you have to look the part, but perhaps we are vulnerable when it comes to trips and accommodation expenses, and support services.' I watched her face turn from bewildered into something darker.

Anita's self-denial was turning to hostility, her hands now on her hips, such as they were, and she glared at me. 'Oh, am I supposed to stay in shared accommodation or a fucking dormitory or something?'

I felt like I was sinking. 'Anita, I'm just telling you what might happen. I'm not making any judgments about it. They're also going to look at other things. Our catering expenses are high, especially for alcohol.'

She laughed, her mood instantly moving from hostile to convivial, which in itself was a big worry. I could still sense that undercurrent of hysteria under the smiles and bright eyes. 'Oh, fuck it, Martha dear. Let her come. Open a bottle of Möet and we can talk about how to get Lilly and Mark thrown off the board.'

As always, I did what I was told.

44

Conrad

I was so sorry our Christmas concert had to be cancelled. After the tribunal hearing Jennifer became withdrawn. She refused to come out of her room and wasn't eating or drinking. Dr Helene had to use all of her persuasive powers to even get her to drink water. On Friday afternoon, Dr Helene asked me to come with her to Jennifer's room to see if we could talk to her; I was nervous, but Dr Helene brushed off my worries.

Jennifer was sitting on her bed, staring into space. Dr Helene asked if she could sit on the bed and Jennifer nodded.

'I have to leave shortly, but I didn't want to go home without saying goodbye and checking if you're okay,' said Dr Helene gently.

Jennifer spoke bluntly. 'You can go home. I can't.'

'I'm sorry, Jennifer.' Dr Helene's voice was soft and kind. 'It's rotten what happened.'

Jennifer rolled her eyes. 'No wonder they call it the MORT. That's French for dead, isn't it?'

Dr Helene's brow creased. 'Jennifer, have you been thinking about self-harming?'

'No.' Jennifer drew her legs up to her chest, her thin arms around her knees clasped by long, entwined fingers.

Dr Helene was calm but concerned. 'Any thoughts of suicide?'

'What would it matter if I did?' Jennifer sighed. 'I shouldn't be here. I should be free.'

'I can get you some extra sessions with the psychologist,' Dr Helene suggested.

Jennifer sneered at her. 'Can't you understand? It's not me who's the problem! I don't need your behaviour therapy, or your talking therapy or your drug therapy, your shock therapy, your music therapy, or your fuckin' art therapy! What I need is to have been born at a different time, in a different world. After all these years, I should be forgiven. If you can't help me with that, you can't help me with anything.' She glared at us. 'Get out of my room.'

We did.

I didn't know what to say. I'd never seen her so cold, so dark.

Dr Helene arranged for Jennifer to be given thirty minute checks by the nurse on duty and seeing I was troubled, she suggested we have a coffee. The kiosk was almost empty.

'The usual Friday afternoon desertion,' Dr Helene remarked, as she called 'hello' over the counter to see if anyone was there.

A voice shouted back, 'We're closed.'

'Sorry, I was just after a couple of coffees,' said Dr Helene.

A jovial face appeared from behind the counter. 'Oh, it's the lovely Dr Helene. Sit down, sit down. I get you coffees and crostoli on the house.'

Dr Helene thanked him and we sat down. She explained why she was so concerned. 'I've tried to increase Jennifer's mood stabilsers, but I think she's been spitting them out. Her depression is spreading to the other residents.'

I agreed. 'It doesn't help that the Christmas concert was cancelled. They are losing interest in doing anything now.' I crossed and then uncrossed my arms as our coffee arrived. 'I don't understand how things got so bad.'

Dr Helene sighed. 'Yes, you do. You read the Victims' Voices Act. You know how unforgiving it is.'

I played with my cup. 'I'm starting to think I'm not cut out for psychiatry.'

Dr Helene shook her head. 'You're going to find that every specialty in medicine has its price, Conrad. All I can I do is point you to the information you need to make up your own mind.' She smiled at me sadly. 'Medicine is a part of the society we live in. You can't understand a field like psychiatry if you look at it in isolation. Social movements that focus on civil rights, human rights, consumer rights, women's rights, and the LGBTQI movement all change society and, along with that, the way we practice medicine. Their influences have taken us away from medical paternalism to a more open and shared decision-making model of practice. The law is an important part of that. Unfortunately, we now seem to be living in a time of retribution. Much of what I would see as gains have been co-opted in the search for vengeance.'

I felt totally sad. 'Jennifer did say that she was living at the wrong time.'

Dr Helene gave me a tired look. 'Jennifer may well be right. You head on home, Conrad. You're a first class student and it has been a great help having you around.'

I just couldn't get Jennifer out of my mind. 'Isn't there anything else we can do for her?'

Dr Helene gave me a bleak look. 'Pray the ice age that has settled on the cold heart of Anita Hammond-Jones melts, pray that someone has the guts to repeal the Victims' Voices Act, and we need to use the skills our training gave us to provide what little comfort we can.'

45

Louisa

Once Elissa had her methodology sorted, she went at it like a trooper. I'd expected it would have been hard to get any judges to talk to her, but armed with my letter of support and her own charm, she was soon able to interview six sitting judges, five sitting magistrates and ten retired judicial officers. She accessed sentencing data for a ten-year period before the passing of the Victims' Voices Act which would be really useful for future comparative research.

We speculated about this, and in light of what the judge interviews revealed, we had enough to suggest that juries were reluctant to convict in all but the most serious cases because they were so worried about constraints on judicial discretion and mandatory sentences. The judges were certainly down on the Victims' Voices Act. They considered it draconian.

This was such exciting research! It set a clear pathway for future inquiries into sentencing in these cases.

Anita Hammond-Jones was unlikely to approve of Elissa's findings, given her foundation had part-funded the research.

Too bad, I thought.

'We won't worry about the politics for the moment, you should just get on with your work,' I told Elissa, who had been concerned. 'If you maintain the rigour and excellence you've already demonstrated the research will speak for itself.'

The following Monday, I took Elissa out to the Billabong Centre. Helene Morton was an old friend and she was very interested in Elissa's work.

For her part, Elissa was apprehensive. 'I've never been to a residential forensic facility. This visit will give me some real life experience of the impact of the Victims' Voices Act.'

I reassured her. 'I'll be with you and Helene will show us around.'

On our way out there, Elissa told me about media reports she'd been analysing on sentencing.

'In 93 per cent of articles where the author claimed sentencing was too lenient, the sentence that was cited was the non-parole period, not the full sentence. And in 92 per cent of articles where the sentences were said to be too severe, the full sentence, not the non-parole period was cited,' she said. 'Do you not find this to be misleading and deceptive?'

I nodded. 'I most certainly do. Great detective work on your part.'

She looked troubled. 'I believe it is unjust.'

'Okay,' I mused. 'So, your thesis will show everyone why that is so?'

'No. I feel most strongly about this, but the main aim of the thesis is to establish that fettering the discretion of judges has a detrimental effect on sentencing.'

I nodded. I noticed that our stop had arrived, so we got off the train and walked the short trip to Billabong. It was a rainy day and we sheltered under my umbrella as we made our way to the reception area of the Jamieson Centre.

Helene had sent her work experience student Conrad to meet and guide us to Billabong. He arrived with an extra umbrella and apologised. 'It's right down the back I'm afraid.'

We were guided through the intensive security measures and deprived of our bags. Elissa gave me a beseeching look. She wouldn't be able to take notes. Once through security, Conrad showed us to Helene's office.

Helene met us at the door, a tired smile on her face. 'Hello, Lou. It's good to see you. And this must be Elissa, your wonder student?'

Elissa blushed as she shook Helene's outstretched hand.

'Indeed, she is,' I said proudly. I gazed at Helene. 'How are you going? I can imagine your disappointment when the Act passed.'

A fleeting storm cloud crossed her face. 'It's dreadful.' Helene turned to Elissa and handed her a notebook and pen. 'Ask any questions you like. I'll post your notes to you so you don't have to do any explaining to the security guards on your way out.'

'Oh, thank you,' said Elissa gratefully. She asked about the number of clients, the types of offences and the average length of stay. She was particularly interested in whether the Victims' Voices Act and its predecessors that introduced mandatory sentencing and indefinite sentences had any impact yet. I was curious too.

Helene looked troubled. 'We have one client, Jennifer Harris, who, after serving her jail time, came here five years ago. She didn't have a mental illness when she arrived and is only here because Anita Hammond-Jones argued vehemently for her confinement. Jennifer has been confined at Billabong, even though every psychiatric report recommended she should be released.'

That bloody woman, I thought to myself. Helene did not look at all happy. She tried to offer an encouraging smile.

'Perhaps you'd like a tour.'

Elissa gratefully accepted. The bleak facility was more like a stagnant swamp than a billabong. We stayed long enough for Elissa to complete her notes.

I took Helene's hand. 'Perhaps I can buy you a drink the next time you're out my way.'

'Thanks, Lou. I'd like that,' she said with a smile.

We went back to the station wiser but sadder. Elissa was very quiet.

'What's troubling you, Elissa?' I asked gently.

She sighed. 'I fear that Anita is on the wrong path and she doesn't know it. She won't like my work.'

'So long as your work is thorough and well-researched it doesn't matter what Anita thinks. That's why we do research—to test hypotheses and dispel myths.'

'Would any evidence ever persuade Anita to see that she is wrong?' Elissa asked.

I vehemently shook my head. 'No. Not her. She's the type who is so convinced she's right she'll never listen to others.'

46

Martha

I started work early on Saturday. The first thing I had to do was pack up all the expensive shoes and bags cluttering Anita's office, many of which she had only worn once, if at all. I hadn't realised how many there were until I got into the chore. I filled several large boxes, but I didn't know where to put the jolly things. In the end I called a storage firm and asked if they could send someone around to take the shoes, bags, paintings, the wardrobe of designer clothes in Anita's dressing room, and all the boxes of jewellery.

Gerard came into the office with a smile, and I called the café for coffees. He said the books were in good order, but the big problem was expenditure on personal items, the accommodation, trips and administration costs. 'Anita's been chalking up some big items. She's been calling a certain guru's costs "personal training and spiritual renewal". It's not too hard to guess who those funds are going to.'

I gave him an exasperated sigh. 'Every time I try to broach the subject of expenditure with her she gets really hostile.'

He looked around the office at Anita's myriad of possessions. 'Yes, it can be difficult to reason with her when it comes to personal gratification. Martha, I've been giving this a lot of thought. I don't think you should hide this stuff.'

I stopped what I was doing and looked at him. 'What?'

'If I don't tell the whole truth to the Ombudsman, I could be struck off the Register of Accountants. I'd be part of a cover up and held responsible as a board member,' Gerard said. 'You are in a similar situation. You're still registered as a nurse and midwife. You need to think carefully about this. I fear your loyalty to Anita might tempt you to try to soften your evidence.'

'But the books—'

'Tell the truth about Anita's spending.' He shrugged. 'Hiding stuff won't change that. And if it was Lilly who blew the whistle, both she and Mark can provide ample evidence of Anita's spending. If you testify otherwise, you could get in trouble.'

I had a sudden flashback to the Coroner's Court and felt my legs go wobbly, so much so that Gerard reached out his hand and steadied me.

'Easy.' He guided me to a seat. 'Are you okay?'

I sat down at Anita's desk and grabbed a tissue. 'Sorry. I just remembered what it was like being hauled before the courts after Heath went missing.' I shook my head. 'It's all gone wrong, Gerard. This foundation was perfect. Anita was the right leader for us, and what we've achieved has gone far beyond what I would have thought ten years ago. We're close, we're supposed to be friends, but I don't feel like I know her anymore. I see flashes of the old Anita, but … oh, I don't know.'

I felt that awful, clenching twist in my stomach, a feeling of panic. 'Oh what a mess. What am I going to do? Anita's my friend and I care about her; she's had her issues lately, but I don't want to hurt her.'

Gerard sat down opposite me.

'Martha, you are a truly good person and you've been a great friend to Anita, the board, the donors and the parents who have lost children.' He took my hand. 'For once, you need to think about yourself. You need to think about how this is going to look in the press and where you'll be positioned.' He looked around the room. 'I suggest you put back all those items you've packed. The Charities Ombudsman needs to see things as they are.'

I reluctantly nodded.

'It's an offence to conceal evidence, Martha,' he said softly. 'Perhaps I can come to dinner at your place tomorrow night and we can talk.'

I nodded my agreement to dinner and paused, torn between duty and fear. I didn't want to get in trouble, but I didn't want Anita harmed either. She may have made some questionable choices but she wasn't a criminal or anything like that.

I picked up the phone, cancelled the storage and unpacked the boxes I'd already sorted.

Was I throwing Anita to the wolves or was I protecting myself?

I wasn't sure.

How on earth did I let myself get dragged into this mess? What was I thinking?

Gerard was watching me. 'I think you know how much I care for you. I don't want anything bad to happen to you.'

I blushed and turned away to hide my face from him. Gerard gently placed his hand on my shoulder and turned me around to face him. I stared into his reassuring brown eyes.

'Promise me you'll think about yourself for once, please? And consider a different future, one I hope I'll be in when all this mess is over.'

I felt a calming wave of relief. I smiled. 'I promise.'

I did another enjoyable shift on Sunday at the maternity centre and raced home to get the food on for me and Gerard. I cooked two poussins. As I stuffed the little birds with rosemary leaves, a bay leaf and quartered limes, my thoughts circled back around to Anita, much as they had all weekend. Was I going to have to betray her? Or was Gerard right when he told me it wasn't my doing, that Anita had made her own decisions?

I shoved the poussins in the oven. Anita used to listen to my advice, but as her confidence grew she often did just the opposite. She stopped listening to Leanne too. Somehow everything had become increasingly all about her … or was that how it was right from the beginning and we'd been too enthralled by her to recognise it? And if Anita was going to put herself first, where did that leave the rest of us?

Thoughts of Gerard invaded my mind and brought a clarity and sense of peace that I hadn't felt for a long time. He made me feel so safe. I wanted to feel that way all the time. I didn't like how I felt at the foundation anymore, nor did I like the direction it was taking.

I froze, a brace of carrots in my hand.

I'm not happy.

I didn't even realise I had dropped the carrots.

I'm not happy at the foundation.

'I want to leave,' I said out loud.

A strange flurry of sensations flew through me. Relief, guilt, so many things. It was like a weight fell off my shoulders as I finally admitted the truth to myself. But then what came next?

A knock on my door revealed Gerard and he came bearing a bottle of white. When dinner was ready, we sat down to eat and discuss the future.

'What do you think will happen with this investigation?' I asked him.

He'd been about to put a forkful of creamy poussin into his mouth but stopped in mid-air. 'The books are in good order, but Anita's expenditure has been pretty over the top.'

I toyed with my meal. 'Is that a capital offence?'

He smiled. 'No, it's not a capital offence, but it is serious. Unfortunately, she's made it worse by giving Marcel so much money.'

My heart dropped. 'How much?'

'A lot.' Gerard chewed slowly on his poussin and raised his glass in approval. We clinked glasses and I finally tried the meat too. It was delicious.

Gerard took another bite, a look of pure delight on his face. 'Oh, Martha, you have excelled yourself. This is delicious.'

I was pleased. And for the rest of our meal, we forgot about the foundation. It was nice to talk about my maternity work, wineries we both liked, and other things that mattered to us. I told him about my beloved mother, he told me about his poor wife. We talked about our past pets and laughed over their silly antics.

Later, after we'd tidied up, we sat on the lounge close to each other. Gerard slipped his hand across my shoulders and I leaned against him.

'You know how you said you wanted me to think about a different future?'

I could feel him nodding, but he said nothing, so I looked up at him.

'Well, I've been doing that. I think I'm ready to leave the foundation.'

I could hardly believe what I was saying. Leaving the foundation would have been unthinkable a week or so ago. 'But I believe I owe it to Anita to see her through this difficult time that's coming up,' I added. 'I won't abandon her.'

He squeezed my shoulder. 'Fair enough. I think it would look bad if you and I both jumped ship at this stage.' Gerard softly stroked my arm. 'It would be a much better look if you stayed until the findings of the investigation are known. That way you'll still be the loyal Martha you've always been, even if the Charities Ombudsman does find Anita culpable and censures her.'

'Do you think that's all that will happen?'

'Yes, I do think that's going to be the outcome,' he admitted.

I sighed. Public censure would ruin Anita. What would happen to the foundation then? All the families?

'What are you thinking about?' asked Gerard.

I leaned in closer and breathed him in. I pushed away the foundation. There was something I had to know. 'Are you thinking about a different future too? One with me in it?'

Gerard paused, and for a moment I thought the worst. I stiffened and went to move, but he stopped me. 'You know I have. Right now, what I really have to decide is if I call a taxi or not,' he ventured, a hopeful note in his voice.

I blushed. 'Best not,' I said, and he kissed me.

Gerard stayed the night and we made gentle love. It had been a long time for me and I was pleased at how natural and easy it all happened. In that moment with Gerard I was able to let everything go, to be touched, and to touch and to love in return.

But while I could have floated in a lovely dreamland forever, I knew life had to go on and there were some rocky times coming up.

I hoped Gerard was right. While the public scrutiny would be demoralising and embarrassing, it was better than Anita facing criminal charges. Once it was all over I could help Anita find someone else to take my place and I'd be free to find my own place in the world, far from the city and with Gerard at my side.

Janet Johnson-Smythe arrived early on Monday. She had two men with her. One was an accounts auditor, the other a senior investigator. Anita arrived about half an hour later, dressed simply and without expensive embellishment. She looked lovely, and my hopes rose at seeing her mood more like her old self.

Anita looked around the office in dismay. 'Oh Martha, I thought you were going to clean up the office. I didn't want the Ombudsman to see it in such a mess.' She looked confused and even a little ashamed.

Although she smiled at me it was a rather grim smile and her eyes told a different story. And even though I knew where I stood, I still felt conflicted.

Janet Johnson-Smythe was having none of it. 'Ms Hammond-Jones, under the Charities Act I am empowered to investigate any complaints about charities and foundations. I have received complaints about The Lost Lovelies Foundation. It is my duty to carry out a complete audit of your donations and expenditure. I intend to make my enquiries retrospective to when the foundation was first established. My team require full access to your records. I estimate the process will be completed in about a fortnight.'

Anita still had a little defiance left. 'May I inquire about the source of the complaints?'

She smirked at her. 'I'm sorry, the whistleblowers have requested anonymity under The Whistleblowers Act.'

Anita stiffened. 'I see.'

It was clear that Janet Johnson-Smythe was pleased with Anita's discomfort. 'You may wish to consult your legal advisors.'

And so the investigation began.

47

Martha

Gerard and I were at my place listening to the radio when the Premier announced a public inquiry into The Lost Lovelies Foundation. I turned the radio up.

'The Ombudsman's preliminary investigations reveal disturbing allegations that must be openly and thoroughly investigated. People have donated their money and placed their trust in this organisation whose remit is to protect and nurture families who have suffered intense loss. We will not let them down.'

Gerard and I looked at each other; he took my shaky hand in his. 'It'll be okay, love.'

I flinched at the sound of Janet Johnson-Smythe's voice. 'My initial audit of the foundation's accounts reveal satisfactory record-keeping; however, there are a large number of expenditures that appear to be in breach of the Charities Act. As requested by the new Attorney-General, I shall be conducting a public inquiry. Anyone who wishes to participate is invited to make a written submission and/or to appear in person to give oral evidence under oath. It will be an independent and fair process designed to ensure transparency and determine if all donated funds were utilised in the way donors intended and were entitled to expect.'

I shook my head. 'You were right. It's an inquiry.'

I caught the tail end of Johnson-Smythe's announcement. 'Xavier Kelly QC will be counsel assisting the commission.'

Gerard looked concerned. 'Kelly has a formidable reputation. The media call him "The Revelator".'

I was startled. 'Why?'

'It's because of his style of questioning,' said Gerard. 'He looks really calm and quiet but his questions are persistent and insightful. Some say he is so seductive he can get witnesses to like him even while he's destroying their credibility.'

I turned off the radio. 'I'm so afraid for Anita,' I confessed. 'Do you think they'd allow her to be legally represented?'

Gerard also looked concerned. 'She can apply for her own legal representative, but there are pros and cons to that. It might stop her shooting off her mouth, but only if she decides to actually take advice and we both know she's not always good at that.'

'I wonder if having her own lawyer makes her look guilty right from the start,' I said, as I got up and made us gin and tonics.

He took his glass and agreed. 'There is that, and it would cost heaps.'

In the end we agreed it would give Anita more credibility if she appeared unrepresented.

'What's it been like in the office lately?' asked Gerard.

I threw up my hands in a gesture of resignation. 'We're all treading on eggshells. Anita's not herself. I mean, she could always be a bit snappy if she didn't get her own way, but this is different. She's trying to be diligent and involved and we've been seeing a bit more of her, but she's also vague and scatty and she contradicts herself.'

'Late nights with Marcel?' Gerard asked.

I shook my head. 'It's more than that. True, she looks tired, but she'll decide to do something and then doesn't finish it. Honestly, sometimes I don't know whether I'm Arthur or Martha around her.'

Gerard laughed. 'I can tell the difference.'

I had my own suspicions on Anita's state of mind, but it didn't do to speculate.

Gerard suddenly took my hand in his. 'I know this is terribly difficult for you, but it will be over before too long. It's important for us to keep in mind that we have our own future. Anita is an adult who is responsible for her own excesses.'

'That's true. I just hope that Janet bloody Johnson-Smythe won't be too brutal with us. After all she's got history with Anita,' I said.

'History. That's yesterday's news,' he said. 'How about you and I spend a bit of time together in the present and the future can look after itself?'

Dear Gerard. He was an easy man to love. He put down his glass and took my hand, smiling that lovely smile that made the crow's-feet around his eyes crinkle merrily. We kissed gently and then more passionately, and I led him into my bedroom.

Gerard took my clothes off, fumbling a bit with my bra, and then I helped him undress. We fell together and made love gently and slowly at first but with increasing passion and delight.

'Ohh,' he moaned, 'feels so good.'

Afterwards, we lay side by side and before too long Gerard drifted off to sleep. I stayed awake for a while savouring the moment, feeling supported and protected and loved.

I slept like a baby that night, not waking until well after dawn when Gerard brought me a steaming, aromatic cup of tea, kissed me goodbye and said he would see me later at the office.

I would have loved to just lay in bed and sip my tea, reliving the lovely night we'd had together, but as always there was a lot to do in the office.

Things were tense when I got in. Gerard had been coming in daily to help us prepare all the papers the Ombudsman wanted. Board members had to be contacted and advised about what was happening. Gerard had asked Anita if she thought we should call an extraordinary board meeting, but she shook her head. 'Not necessary. They'll already have read about it in the media, and besides, we have a meeting coming up soon.'

Gerard and I shot glances at each other. 'I think they would expect to be contacted personally. They're sure to have questions.'

Anita shrugged indifferently. 'Okay. Martha can just tell each one individually by phone.'

I froze, trying hard to suppress my anger.

Gerard indicated that I follow him out to the main office. I think he could see that I was miffed and needed to blow a fuse. I fumed as I paced the office.

'Good old Martha will look after it! She's got no idea how busy Leanne and I are with everything that's happening. The phones were busy enough before, but the investigation has got what's left of our donors feeling edgy. I can't even help Leanne because of all the extra work generated by the Ombudsman.'

'When's Daniel starting? I'm sure he'll be a help,' Gerard noted.

I grabbed some files to take to the photocopier. 'He's not back from his trip home yet. I hope all the bad publicity doesn't scare him off.'

Gerard took the papers off me. 'I'll do the copying. Do you want to start ringing the board members?'

I felt a surge of relief. He was fast becoming my rock. 'You're a star. I'll get onto that right away, and guess what?'

'What?' Gerard asked.

'I'm not going to call Lilly and Mark Hartford.'

Gerard smiled knowingly, and I returned to my desk and picked up the phone. Most of the board members were concerned but polite. Some of them even managed to surprise me with their response.

Bianca was the first person I rang. 'I've been thinking about resigning from the foundation, but it looks as if I've left my run too late. If I go now it'll just look bad for me and the foundation,' she said, and I realised that her approach wasn't too different from my own.

Lady C didn't sound surprised. 'Martha, dear, I've seen worse than this in my long life. Stay strong, we'll get through this.'

Peter Dickson was matter of fact as usual, and I felt justified when he said, 'I knew things were going off the rails when those Hartfords joined the board.'

The rest of the responses were all much the same, and it left me wondering why none of them had spoken up earlier.

The hearings were upon us before we could turn around.

On the first day of the hearing Anita greeted me warmly. It was almost like she'd forgotten every tense moment since Janet Johnson-Smythe's visit. She decided it would be a good look if she and I arrived at the hearings by tram rather than taxi. Ironically, the hearing was being held at the casino, as that was the only large venue available at such short notice. We took the Victoria Harbour tram down Bourke Street.

As the tram rattled to a stop at the corner of Queen and Bourke Streets, to our horror, we saw Lilly and Mark Hartford boarding. My blood pressure always rose when I saw Lilly and today was no exception. Fortunately, they didn't notice us. It was good. I was in no mood to play nice. I thought Anita might have a muttered comment about them, but she was unaccountably calm. I hardly knew what to make of it.

I felt sick when we arrived. There was media all over the place. I was relieved when Gerard came to greet us and tried to shield us from the media mob. Anita didn't seem to want any shielding. She beamed at the media as though this was some kind of promotion. Her inappropriate attitude made me even more nervous and I wondered if she had any idea how serious this was. For my part, I hadn't felt so bad since Heath was taken.

We were seated and the morning was taken up with legal argument, setting the agenda and other official matters. Xavier Kelly, The Revelator, was just as Gerard had said he was and more. He was probably in his early fifties, good-looking with a friendly smile, and creases around his eyes. I thought that perhaps Janet Johnson-Smythe was sweet on him, the way she followed him around with her eyes. And he did indeed have a seductive voice. I can only describe it as melodious with a touch of gravel. He sounded like Leonard Cohen.

In the afternoon, things livened up. The first witness to be called was Lilly Hartford. My blood pressure began to spike again. I shot a knowing glance at Gerard. 'I reckon this confirms she's the one who went to the Ombudsman,' I whispered.

Lilly took the oath and Kelly asked her to identify herself, to state the date she joined the board of The Lost Lovelies Foundation and her motivation for doing so. You could have heard a pin drop.

'I wanted to join the foundation because I really believed in what Anita Hammond-Jones was doing. To me, she was a saint. I admired the way she was able to establish the foundation after the devastating loss of her baby. Listening to her make a speech at a Lost Lovelies fundraiser last year was so moving. Her experience struck a chord with me and my husband Mark and we decided to see if we could make a contribution to the work of the foundation by donating a substantial sum of money to its work. I wanted to support others who'd lost a child as a result of a crime, and to be part of law reform around these dreadful atrocities.'

Kelly didn't ask Lilly many questions, he just let her talk with a brief prompting here and there.

'Were your expectations met?' he asked.

'At first, yes,' said Lilly. 'Anita was brilliant at public speaking and garnering support for the foundation. But I became concerned about the way she controlled the board. She ruled with an iron fist under a cloak of geniality. Questions about expenditure were evaded. Alcohol was always served at board meetings. I didn't think this was appropriate and I told Anita so. She just said the board members were not paid for the work they did so the least the foundation could do was to provide them with good quality wine and food.'

'Why were you concerned about the drinks?' asked Kelly.

'I didn't think board members would be as alert as they should be if they were drinking. The drinks were served by waiters and they would just fill people's glasses without asking. Some of the members were red in the face and a bit wobbly by the end of the meetings,' said Lilly.

Kelly paced in front of her. 'Did you have any concerns about the information board members received prior to the meetings?'

Lilly shook her head. 'Martha was always very good. She would get the papers to us at least a week prior to the meetings. They were professionally prepared and well ordered, but I didn't think they contained the kind of detail board members require to do their job.'

You patronising bitch, I thought, and reminded myself to take slow, deep breaths.

Kelly stopped and turned to his witness. 'What kind of information was missing?'

'The financial details were under broad headings like expenditure, but the kind of expenditure wasn't stipulated. There were lots of vague headings like sundries or general,' said Lilly.

'Did you query this?'

Lilly put on a poor little innocent me look. 'Yes, I mentioned it to Anita and I was not well received. I asked her if she was spending money on Marcel Bouverie and she just about pushed me out the door. I also raised it at a board meeting. I thought we should get more detailed financial reports. Anita said something like, "Well, Lilly, no-one's ever complained before and the board members are busy people."'

Kelly moved back to his table and shuffled some papers. 'Were you given any orientation when you first joined the board?'

'No, nothing like that. Mark and I had a meeting with Anita, we attended one board meeting as guests and we were appointed. There was no training, you just had to learn on the job,' said Lilly.

The lawyer was so impassive. I couldn't read him, and I was worried about facing him myself.

'Were you concerned about any personal expenses accrued by Ms Hammond-Jones?' he asked.

This seemed to please Lilly, who practically smirked. 'Yes. She always had expensive clothes, designer shoes and bags, and original paintings for the office. She got her hair and make-up done either as gifts from patrons or from foundation funds. She hired limousines to take her to functions and stayed at five-star accommodation paid for by the foundation. I asked about this and she got really angry, saying I didn't understand how hard she worked and she had to always look good to convince people to donate to the cause. When travelling, she said she needed somewhere nice to stay so she could get enough sleep to do her arduous work.'

I looked over at Anita, expecting to see her blow a fuse, but she was unaccountably calm.

After leaving time for that to sink in, Kelly resumed his rather annoying pacing. 'Did you discuss your concerns with any other board members?'

Lilly the Innocent looked pitiful. 'I tried to, but they were incredibly loyal to Anita. They wouldn't listen. I spoke first to Peter Dickson because I thought a retired police officer would understand the need for integrity.'

'What did Peter Dickson say?'

'He said he had known Anita ever since her son was kidnapped. He had worked on the investigation and was largely responsible for bringing the perpetrator, Jennifer Harris, to justice. He wouldn't hear a bad word about Anita. He talked about how distraught she was when Heath disappeared and how incredibly brave she was.'

Kelly took his glasses off. 'Did Mr Dickson say anything else?'

'Peter claimed Anita had done so much for other families who've lost children and is a major force for law reform,' said Lilly.

'Did you approach any other board members?'

Lilly was trying to look humble, but she didn't fool me.

'I tried to get an appointment to talk with Lady Charmiane Cuthbert, but she was always busy and I gave up in the end. Bianca Mazzouri, on the other hand, was a good listener and understood how foundations should be run because she was the CEO of The Young People's Foundation. I felt she shared my concerns, though I think she was a bit scared of upsetting Anita, so nothing changed.'

I was boiling as Lilly gave her evidence. She wasn't actually lying outright, but she was certainly exaggerating and trying to make herself look good at Anita's expense. I shot a glance at Anita, who didn't seem to notice what was going on. She seemed a bit spaced out and I grew alarmed. Didn't she realise that Lilly was sinking her?

Lilly blathered on. 'Wai Leung listened politely, thanked me but said goodbye, so I approached the Charities Ombudsman—'

At this stage Janet Johnson-Smythe hastily intervened, reminding Lilly that whistleblowers to her office were entitled to remain anonymous. There were a few chuckles from the audience that caused Johnson-Smythe to glare at them, but it was bleeding obvious that Lilly was the whistleblower and she didn't give a toss who knew it, so long as she was getting attention.

Gerard gave me a look that seemed to say, 'That settles that.'

Kelly said he had no further questions for Lilly. Mark Hartford was called to give his evidence. He didn't say anything that contradicted Lilly. Typical.

The Ombudsman called for an hour's break. I was relieved because Anita had almost been dozing off and that would not have looked good. I'd been giving her sideways glances, trying to work out if there was anything wrong with her.

Somehow, Gerard and I managed to get her past the media and went to a nearby coffee shop. Gerard ordered a tea for me, skinny latte for Anita and a long black for himself.

I expected Anita to be upset, but she was surprisingly upbeat and seemed much more awake now we were out of the casino. In fact, she was bright-eyed and rambling. 'I always knew Lilly Hartford was the one who undermined and betrayed me. She was jealous. She wanted to run the foundation herself. She's trying to make out I wasted donors' money. All I took was what I needed to do my job. You can't go around looking like a frump when you run a foundation and are trying to attract funding. You have to look successful to be successful.'

Gerard and I shot concerned glances at each other.

'Can you imagine me attending garden parties at Lady Charmiane's mansion not wearing designer clothes?'

I couldn't actually. It was hard to imagine Anita as anything other than designer.

'I've never taken a salary from the foundation, so it is only fair I use foundation funds to do my job,' she said. She didn't seem to see the concerned looks from those around her. 'You know that, Martha? I know you understand. Trusty, Martha. You always understood me.'

I looked away from her. It was so clear she hadn't a clue.

Gerard was called to give his evidence in the afternoon. He squeezed my hand before standing up and walking to the witness box.

Kelly asked question after question and Gerard answered them all with calm authority. He explained the processes he'd put in place to ensure accountability and how often he checked the books. He already knew the Ombudsman's preliminary inquiries had given his work the tick of approval. Even so, I admired the way he stuck to the point and wasn't distracted by any of the manouevering tactics from the Revelator.

There was only one other witness that day and that was one of our donors from the corporate sector. Frank Henry was in real estate and had been supporting us for years. I hadn't spoken to him for ages, and I guess he must have voluntarily contacted the Ombudsman to give evidence. His evidence was dry and focused on what kind of accountability donors were entitled to expect from foundations. He wasn't especially critical of us.

It was a long day, and while it might have been interesting from the outside looking in, I felt nothing but anxiety. Anita seemed dismissive of the whole affair and Xavier Kelly was expertly acquiring what he needed.

I knew I had no option but to be completely honest.

Tomorrow I was going to have to give my evidence. My stomach tightened with panic at the very thought.

48

Martha

I had a fitful, restless night. In one dream, I was clambering up a cliff that got higher and narrower as I climbed. Anita was smiling from somewhere higher up, urging me on, and Gerard was warning me to be careful from somewhere below. I woke up with a terrible start, balanced on the edge of a precipice, sweaty and trembling.

It was only 5.30 am, but I didn't want to go back to sleep.

I lay in bed thinking about what the day held in store for me. Ideas of how to save Anita kept popping into my head. We'd been friends for so long and I didn't want to let it all go to hell. Yet, if I supported her, I'd be making it look like the whole organisation had a bad culture. If I lied, that was perjury.

I didn't know how Anita was going to react today. Goodness knows, she was hurting herself enough by refusing to see how inappropriate her behaviour had been.

But what would happen if I gave away too much information? Would I lose her friendship? Would she sack me? What should I say about Marcel? Gerard had all but confirmed he'd been fleecing the foundation with his hefty bills for his phoney services.

I tried thinking of excuses. I could tell the Ombudsman that people kept giving presents to Anita. I could say it was me who booked all the expensive hotels when Anita would have been happy to stay in an ordinary motel. I could say that I was the one who urged her to use the foundation credit cards for every purchase.

Sick of going over the options, I dragged myself out of bed, had a shower and dressed.

Sitting at my kitchen table with a hot cup of tea, watching the steam curl in spirals, I knew what I had to do. Telling the whole truth was the only option.

I couldn't cover up Anita's behaviour. Anita was the problem.

She was her own worst enemy and I had to save myself.

My hands shook and I spilled the tea, burning my left hand. I got out the ointment on autopilot and smeared it across the burn before winding a bandage around it.

I decided it was best not to drive with my shaky nerves, so I booked a taxi and called Anita to let her know I was on my way to collect her. She told me not to worry as Marcel was going to drive her. I knew that was a bad idea, but I held my tongue.

You can't save her, I told myself.

It was the clearest thought I'd had in a long time.

I arrived at the casino early. There was a media pack waiting, but Gerard was there to shield me. I tried to hide my bandaged hand from the cameras.

'Where's Anita?' Gerard asked, pushing past Zoe Waters, who had a determined look in her eye, her microphone outstretched. Jamie O'Dhea was standing just behind her, and behind him was Jack Ruler. He stared at me with a speculative glint in his eye.

'Marcel's bringing her,' I hissed.

Our eyes locked. Gerard raised his eyebrows and shook his head. 'That's not a good idea.'

'That's what I told her, but she wouldn't listen.'

Gerard shepherded me past the last of the reporters and into the building. 'Well, it sounds like you did your best. If there's any fallout, it's on her head.'

I stopped Gerard and hesitated. 'I'm so bloody nervous!'

He took my unbandaged hand and looked into my eyes. 'I know you are, Martha, but I also know you can do this. Just be honest and true to yourself.'

I paused, looking over at the doorway where Anita waved at me. I looked back at Gerard. 'She's going to hate me.'

He ran a hand down my face. 'You tried to help her, Martha, and she's not doing anything to help herself. You did what you could. It's time for you to look after number one.' He kissed me on the forehead. 'Come on.'

I took a deep breath, pulled myself together and we went into the hearing room. We took our seats next to Anita, who beamed at us like she was at a party or something. Marcel was sitting beside her, holding her hand. He looked weird and just as spaced out as Anita did.

'Mademoiselle,' he drawled.

I turned away in disgust.

Eventually, after some complicated and boring legal submissions, my name was called. I made my way to the makeshift stand on trembling legs, hoping my hand wasn't shaking too much as I took the affirmation. The last time I'd had to do this was years ago at the Coroner's Court, and I could taste the same bitter bile that had racked me back then. I tried to remain calm, as Xavier Kelly QC, The Revelator, seemed to take an eternity shuffling his papers.

'It's Martha Mayne, right?' he eventually asked.

I tried not to fidget. 'Yes.'

'How long have you known Anita Hammond-Jones?'

'I've known her for eleven years. I was her midwife.'

'Could you explain what happened on the day her son disappeared?'

I hadn't expected this line of questioning. 'We were all so happy,' I babbled. 'It was an easy birth and then Michael, Anita's husband, went to get a coffee. Anita was sleeping. I got called by another patient, so I nipped in to see her just for a very short time. When I came back Heath wasn't there.'

I was shaking, so was my voice. Kelly moderated his tone. 'Take your time, Miss Mayne.'

I thanked him and tried to collect my wits. 'At first, I thought Michael must have taken the baby, but he came back empty-handed. It was a dreadful moment. It slowly dawned on me something untoward had happened. The police were called.'

He suddenly changed the line of questioning and it was then that I truly understood how he got the name The Revelator. 'How long have you worked with Anita Hammond-Jones at The Lost Lovelies Foundation?'

I frowned, thrown by the pivot. 'I worked with her from the beginning, ever since she established The Lost Lovelies Foundation and asked me to be her personal assistant. I didn't want to give up nursing, but I wasn't happy with the way the hospital had suspended me when the police investigation was happening. I was exonerated, of course, but it still rankled. Also, I had a deep admiration for Anita. She was beautiful, brave, charismatic and had a strong commitment to the cause of helping other parents who had lost children because of criminal behaviour. So, I gave up midwifery at that time and joined The Lost Lovelies Foundation.'

The Revelator was patient with my rambling, or at least he pretended to be. His next question was direct, even abrupt. 'Did you have a good relationship with Anita?'

'Yes, excellent. We were more friends than boss and employee,' I said. I felt like he was making even the most innocent of my answers sound suspicious.

'Did you ever feel bullied by Anita?'

I don't know why I hesitated before answering. 'No, never bullied. I worked hard and so did Anita.'

Anita beamed at me. She looked so proud and positive; unfortunately, she was still holding Marcel's hand.

'It was a successful and busy foundation and there was always heaps to do, what with running the Listen Line, organising fundraisers, dealing with the media, appealing to donors, looking after the board members, and more,' I added.

The Revelator checked his papers. 'You prepared all the board papers?'

My mouth felt dry, so I took a sip of water and nodded my agreement. 'Yes, and I always got them to the members in plenty of time so they could prepare for meetings.'

Suddenly, he looked stern. 'Did you decide what information the board members got?'

'No, that was Anita's role. She would tell me, and I prepared whatever papers she wanted.' That got me feeling a bit confused because it wasn't strictly true, and I worried I might have misled the investigation, so I stupidly added to my statement. 'Well, sometimes if Anita was too busy, I decided what papers should—'

He didn't appear to be interested in my explanation. 'Had you ever worked with a board of directors before?'

'No.'

The Revelator became thoughtful in his approach, displaying an almost genial curiosity. 'When the Charity Ombudsman's auditors visited the offices of The Lost Lovelies Foundation, they found dozens of pairs of designer shoes, handbags, expensive watches and jewellery. Why were they there?'

'Well, they all belong to Anita. She gets a lot of gifts,' I explained.

'Did she ever purchase any personal items using her foundation credit card?'

'Yes, all the time.'

'Were you worried?'

I didn't know what to say. I sought out Gerard's face and he looked calm and reassuring. Next to him Anita smiled broadly. I was in the grip of a fit of indecision, knowing the lawyer wasn't going to let me fudge this answer.

Further back in the crowd, I could see Jamie O'Dhea and Jack Ruler in among the large press contingent, taking notes, and I knew this was my moment of accountability.

The Revelator prompted me. 'Ms Mayne, please answer the question.'

My answer came blurting out. 'Yes. I tried to talk to Anita about it, but she wouldn't listen.'

'And why were you concerned, Ms Mayne?'

I fidgeted. 'I became worried when Marcel Bouverie came on the scene. She was enthralled by him. I didn't trust him.'

I didn't dare look at Anita, so I stared directly at the lawyer.

'Why was that, Ms Mayne?'

I answered unhappily. 'There were large amounts being debited to Anita's credit card and I wasn't sure what for.'

'But did you hazard any guesses, Ms Mayne?'

I took another sip of the water and then took a breath. 'I thought it was going to Marcel Bouverie. I thought he was fleecing her.'

'Thank you, Ms Mayne. There are no other questions at this stage.'

I was so relieved it was finished, but when I looked over to Anita … I can't describe the look she gave me. Actually, yes, I could.

Betrayed.

I put my head down and walked over to Gerard.

The day came to a close, and Marcel took Anita by the hand and led her out to the media contingent. Gerard and I followed at a distance.

Zoe Waters shot the first question at Anita. 'How much donor funding has gone to Marcel Bouverie?'

Anita responded calmly enough. 'Mr Bouverie is an extraordinarily gifted and talented healer. His services kept me going through difficult times.'

'Services? And what kind of services were those?' Zoe demanded.

Anita ignored the question, scanning the faces of the media for a more sympathetic questioner. She didn't find one, even though Jamie O'Dhea was in the pack. Eventually, Marcel took her hand and guided her through the throng.

Zoe called out to them both again. 'Marcel, what qualifications do you have?' This question hung in the air, unanswered. While the reporters followed Anita and Marcel, Gerard took me by the arm and led me in the opposite direction.

'Best we scarper before they turn on you,' he whispered.

This was advice I wasn't going to ignore, so we stole away.

49

Gerard

Martha paced around her living room. 'I had no choice,' she said.

'You did really well,' I said reassuringly. 'You didn't lie and you couldn't, not without risking being charged with perjury. Anita must understand that.'

She shook her head. 'I don't think she will. She's no fool, but she's led by her feelings and her own needs, and I'm sure, Gerard, I could swear she's on drugs.'

'Drugs?' I was horrified.

'I've suspected it for some time now.' Martha stopped pacing and frowned. 'She's all mixed up. She's always believed in her cause, and she never really sees anyone else's point of view but now she's not just inflexible, she's all over the place.'

I felt a surge of relief. I'd wondered if Martha would ever be able to see beyond Anita's shining persona to her real personality.

She gave me a helpless look. 'What do we do now?'

My heart went out to her. 'We wait until the Ombudsman delivers her decision.'

'And then what?'

I wasn't sure if I should reveal my own plans. I'd barely spoken to myself of this, let alone anyone else. 'I've taken certain … precautions … to make sure you and I will be alright.'

'What precautions?' she demanded.

I didn't want there to be any secrets between us, but Martha still had a lot to get through. I didn't think she realised just how uncomfortable the foundation's office was going to be in the coming week. I made a snap decision that it was best to not say too much until after the verdict was handed down. 'Best you don't know yet.'

I was treated to an angry glare.

'Gerard, don't treat me like an idiot.'

I threw up my hands in surrender. 'Believe me, I know you are no such thing. When I say it's best you don't know, I mean you might be called to give further evidence. You can't be obliged to give information you don't have.'

She backed off. 'Oh, I see.'

To change the subject, and because I was getting hungry, I suggested it was time for food. 'Do you want to pop down to the pub for a meal?'

She smiled but shook her head. 'I think it might be better if I just get something out of the freezer. There might be some roving reporter around.'

'Good thinking. What have you got?'

Martha went to the fridge. 'You remember we had those yummy flans left over from the last fundraiser? I've still got a few of them.'

I grinned. 'Sounds good. What flavours have we got?'

'How about West Australian marron?'

'Perfect.'

When we had finished preparing the meal we sat down to eat and to talk.

'Tell me again what might happen to Anita,' Martha said.

'The Ombudsman could find Anita has broken the law by accepting unlawful gifts and indulging in excessive personal expenditure,' I said, as she served me a slice of flan. 'Or, they might say she hasn't breached the letter of the law, but she behaved in ways inconsistent with the spirit of the law and not in accordance with the code of conduct. In other words, unethical rather than illegal.'

Martha helped herself to the salad and then handed it over to me. 'Where does that leave us?'

'The books are in order. We don't need to worry,' I said with a shrug. 'The board members may be criticised for not doing more, but it's highly unlikely there would be any formal finding against any of us. Ironically, the media attention has demonised Anita and taken attention away from the board.'

Martha was thoughtful, staring off into space as she ate. She shook her head. 'Poor Anita. What should we do?'

'Well, when this is all over, we should get married,' I said, calmly putting down my knife and fork.

Martha dropped her cutlery in shock, but a wide smile crossed her face. 'Is that supposed to be a proposal?'

She had a twinkle in her eyes, and I felt my confidence soar. 'Yes, my dear, that's precisely what it is.'

'So, why aren't you down on your knees?' Martha gave me a coquettish grin.

I put my hands up in defeat. 'Arthritis, Martha, rotten old Uncle Arthur Rightus.'

50

Jennifer

It doesn't matter what I do, how good I am, how useless. I'll never be free. They say what I did was unforgivable. The mother of the baby I took can never forgive me, so how can I forgive myself? Dr Helene says I'm a traumatised child, but that doesn't allow the baby's mother to ever forgive me. I am Jennifer, The Great Unforgivable.

I was five when dad lost his temper with the baby. She kept crying and crying and Mum was trying to shush her.

'Shut that kid up,' he yelled.

Mum took the baby into the bedroom. Dad jumped out of his chair and followed them. I heard Mum scream. I heard the baby cry out and a banging noise like someone thumping on a wall.

Someone knocked on our door. I opened it and the lady from across the hall was standing there. 'Is your Mummy alright?'

'I think Daddy hurt the baby,' I told her.

The woman held out her hand. 'Come with me, dear.'

We went to her house and she gave me colouring pencils and a book. I drew a baby girl with blood on her head. Then the police came and they took Mum and Dad away. The lady told the police I could stay with her that night. The police had a different plan.

'No, she has to come into care.' The police lady put me in the police car and we drove away into the night.

They put me into resi-care. There was a lot of scared kids there, but some real tough ones too. A bigger boy got into bed with me.

He hurt me.

I was six.

Then they gave me to foster parents. At first Mr and Mrs Harris were nice to me. Later, Mrs Harris said I stole money from the jar on the table.

'Paul, she has to be punished. That's your job, not mine. I do everything else around here.'

He took me to the shed and he hit me with a cricket bat.

I didn't cry.

I was seven.

A lady from the government came. Mrs Harris made her a cup of tea and gave her sweet biscuits. The lady smiled at me. 'Happy birthday, Jennifer. Are you happy?'

I said I was happy, but not when Mr Harris hit me.

She dunked her biscuit in her tea. It was a teddy bear biscuit and she was holding it by the ears. 'What did he hit you with, dear?'

'A cricket bat.'

'A cricket bat!' The lady gasped and the teddy bear broke and she was left holding its ears while rest of it floated in the tea.

Mrs Harris snorted. 'See, I told you that's what she says. She makes up silly stories.'

They laughed.

The government lady left.

I was eight.

Mr Harris said, 'I need to talk to you, Jennifer. Come out into the shed.'

I ran away, but the police found me hiding in a building site and they made me go back.

I told a teacher at school what happened. She didn't believe me. I told the other girls. No one believed me. I only told them about the beatings, not the other stuff. If they didn't believe me about the beatings, they wouldn't believe me if I told them what he did to me when he sneaked into my bed at night.

One day the government lady came with a letter. It was from my mother. It said she loved me, she was working in a factory trying hard to get enough money so we could be together. I never heard from her again.

I got pregnant when I was thirteen. The government lady took me to a doctor and she did something to me that made me cry out and then bleed. I got pregnant again when I was seventeen. This time I ran away and lived on the streets. There was a small group of girls who let me hang with them.

They were the only real friends I ever had. We used to go to Flinders Street Station where the food vans were. When my pregnancy got too obvious the government lady put me back in resi-care. It wasn't so bad, but I was shit scared of some of the other kids, especially the boys. I didn't cop it as much as some of the girls because I was so pregnant.

When I went into labour they took me to a birthing centre. I delivered a dead baby. The pain was so bad I thought I was dying.

I wish I had.

Later, I got up and dressed myself. On my way out I passed a room. There was a beautiful lady sleeping. There was a crib in the corner near her. I watched the beautiful sleeping lady and I wished I was her; I picked up the baby just to give it a cuddle. Someone was coming, so I bolted.

I still had the baby so I couldn't go back.

I went to a building site and I cuddled the baby and sang songs to it until the police came for me.

Now I am never going to get out.

I know I did wrong. I know I caused pain. I was punished.

She's locked me up forever.

Conrad's nice. He said I was wonderful. Told me to never think otherwise.

No, I can't think like that. The things other girls have aren't for me. Falling in love or getting married or having kids. I killed all those chances when I took the baby. My future died with him.

I'm scum. I don't deserve to live.

51

Martha

Leanne gave me a massive hug when I told her about Gerard's proposal.

'Oh, Martha! This is lovely news. I knew you two had become close, but I'd no idea you were this close!' She winked at me. 'Care to fill me in on the … you know?'

I blushed. 'I have to admit it was daunting going to bed with a man after all this time.'

'But it was okay?' Leanne, ever the nurse and counsellor, went to the heart of the matter.

I had to resist the urge to gush. 'It was more than okay. It was lovely.'

'We age, but our bodies don't forget.' She smiled her warm smile that I depended on so much. 'Skin on skin will do it every time. I hope you weren't wearing those daggy flannelette pajamas you used to like so much!'

Hell, I'd forgotten all about those old pajamas! 'Of course not!'

'Well, I'm glad you've got a good thing going with Gerard, because I think we both know it's going to get worse around here.' She held up *The Watcher*. 'Did you see this?'

There was a photograph of me walking away from the camera arm-in-arm with Gerard. I winced. It made us look like co-conspirators and I knew Anita wasn't going to like it.

'Damn,' I muttered. My good mood fluttered away.

The phones started ringing and Leanne was suddenly inundated. The publicity surrounding the hearings seemed to have prompted half of Victoria to call in with their stories. Many wanted to express their disappointment that Anita was being treated so badly. Others weren't so generous. Worse still, donations had dried up.

Leanne listened patiently as always, but it was getting chaotic. I could see she was under immense pressure, so I called four volunteers asking for support, two of them were happy to come in and help. The others made unconvincing excuses and I could tell their admiration for Anita was sorely bruised. I jumped on the phones myself until Julie and Ranjana arrived.

Anita turned up at eleven looking tired and not very well groomed. She went straight to her office and closed the door. She didn't look at any of us, nor say hello.

I admit that I breathed a sigh of relief. I'd readied myself for a confrontation, for a flurry of angry words. I supposed she was angry with me for my testimony, but she was giving me the silent treatment instead of a fight.

And suddenly, my relief turned to frustration. Yet again, she turned up when it suited her. She looked like she'd had a night on the tiles, and then she ignores the situation and barricades herself in her office. We needed an honest conversation, one where she could try to understand why people were so annoyed with her, not this avoidance tactic. She needed to sweet-talk our wayward donors and address our stakeholders.

I let it go for an hour, but there was a stack of paperwork that needed her signature and there was that board meeting to prepare for; with the whole investigation, this board meeting would likely be a hard one. I knocked on her door just after midday.

'Come!' she called.

I entered and decided immediately that Anita looked frosty. Well, she was just going to have to put it behind her.

'I got volunteers in to help Leanne; the phones were hot from the moment we opened,' I told her, as she glared at me silently. 'We also have to get things ready for the board meeting. I highly recommend we start preparing for every eventuality now. We both know Lilly is going to be a problem.'

I stared back her, willing her to be the Anita I knew—that bright, vibrant woman who could tackle anything and anyone. She looked away, bleary eyed, and then she put her head in her hands. I wasn't sure what was happening until she spoke.

'Martha, have we got any painkillers? I've got a bugger of a hangover.'

My irritation flared and then suddenly faded. I don't know what it was … acceptance? The nurse in me? The Anita I was looking for seemed to be gone.

It was like the Bill had been her spark and now the flame was dwindling. She'd pushed herself so hard, for so long, and for what? She'd had her vengeance on poor Jennifer Harris, but she didn't look any happier for it.

I sighed inwardly. 'Yes. Do you want a coffee?'

She nodded.

I quickly got her sorted out and asked if she wanted to go through the board papers. She shook her head and I could see that even that much movement seemed to cause her pain.

'Not right now, Martha. I feel shit, so I think I'll go and have a massage. If I feel better after that, I'll come back and we can take care of everything then.' She put on her big sunglasses, unsteadily picked up her bag and left. I didn't bother to stop her.

Leanne got off the phones and came to stand with me as we watched her leave.

'She's not coming back in today, is she?' asked Leanne.

I shook my head. 'I doubt it.'

Leanne gave me a sympathetic look. 'Was she angry?'

'Yes, but it was strange,' I said with a frown. 'She didn't have a go at me or really say anything. It was almost like she expected me to let her down. As though everyone else had, so why not me too?'

'Don't fall for that martyr act, Martha,' said Leanne firmly. 'She's in a situation of her own making. You just focus on keeping this office running.'

Unsurprisingly, Anita didn't come back to the office that day. I started to get through my workload, hoping there wouldn't be too many interruptions, but my wish was not granted. I got a call from Lilly Hartford.

'I'm deeply concerned with the way in which the foundation is being managed. I want an item on the agenda for the next board meeting,' she said.

I'd run out of patience with the woman. 'I'll need to discuss it with Anita first.'

Lilly sounded cross. 'Martha, I wish you would just do as you're told. You are an assistant, not a CEO.'

I bristled. 'Yes, I am Anita's executive assistant, not yours!'

'I have consulted my solicitor and there is a legal obligation under the Charities Act to include in the agenda items as requested by board members,' she snapped.

'I'm aware. The Act also states that two members have to be in favour of the request.'

'Yes,' agreed Madame Hartford. 'Mark and I. Put the item on the agenda, Martha.'

Another one of Anita's poor decisions coming back to haunt us, I thought. 'I will pay Anita the courtesy of being advised about this conversation. Now, I must get back to work,' I said, and hung up before she could speak again.

Leanne was busy on calls, so I rang Gerard to vent. I could almost see him shaking his head.

'She's right, Martha. Two board members are all that are needed for any issue on governance to be put on the agenda.'

I groaned. 'I know. That's why I tried to warn Anita about not having a married couple on the board. They vote as a block and Mark does whatever Lilly says.'

'Well, we're stuck with both of them for the moment. But enough about them. I was wondering if you might like to celebrate our engagement tonight and have a nice meal by the coast? We could talk about life after the foundation and where we'll live. Would you like that?' he ventured warmly.

I found myself smiling and tried to put the Hartfords completely out of mind. 'I would love that.'

He made me feel like a young thing again.

I fluttered about for the rest of the day, smiling at odd intervals and drifting off into daydreams. It was strange, especially as by the end of the day a dozen donors had dumped us. It was weird, the way worry and joy could co-exist in such a way.

Leanne came to say goodbye before she left for the night. She laughed at me. 'Martha, have you been on the happy pills?'

I gave her a quick hug. 'Yeah. Something like that.'

52

Martha

I wasn't looking forward to the board meeting. Anita was at work, but she was distant to everyone all week. She often came in looking as if she'd been drinking heavily the night before. On Wednesday morning I asked her if she wanted to go through the board papers for the meeting. She gave me a blunt, 'No.' I tried to persuade her to look at the agenda. I knew she was going to refuse me again, just as she'd been ignoring most of my memos that week, so I had to forcefully point out that Lilly Hartford had asked to be allowed to address the meeting on issues of corporate governance. That got her attention. She huffed out an irritated breath and tapped her fingers on her desk.

'I suppose we should cancel the usual catering and tone things down a bit. Can you call Tony and Toni?'

'I've already cancelled them,' I said. 'I figured it best we don't give Lilly any more ammunition.'

Anita shrugged. 'On top of things as usual,' she said, but her tone was bitter. 'I love the way you've always organised the meetings with such flair. But times are changing I suppose.' She looked around me surreptitiously. 'I think we're being watched, Martha. We have to be mindful of the lenses that are on us.'

'What?' I blurted out.

'Everyone's watching, all the time,' she said quietly. She stared at me and all I could do was nod. I did not like the look in her eyes.

I escaped to the quiet of my desk and took a deep breath. This was worse than not understanding the limits to personal expenditure, worse even than drug use. I just hoped she could keep herself in check until the meeting.

It would be an understatement to say the board meeting was tense.

Anita had managed to stay in the office for the whole day, but she didn't interact much. She signed everything I placed in front of her and was ready when it was time for the meeting to start. She welcomed the members without her usual flair, all of whom looked startled at her diminished state. Gerard wasn't the only one who shot me a look of concern. Joan and Bianca asked me if she was alright, and Lady C seemed to be eyeing her off too. Anita completed the formalities in a dull monotone and invited Lilly Hartford to speak.

Lilly thanked her with a false grace that played on my nerves. 'I am grateful to you for allowing me to speak. As you know, Mark and I have had some serious concerns about anomalies in spending. I have tried to discuss my concerns with Anita. I was not well received. Indeed, I was asked to leave in no uncertain terms. I felt bullied and alarmed.'

I had to suppress a disdainful sniff.

'My concerns involved large amounts of money spent on personal expenses and items by Anita, including massages and mindfulness therapy services provided by Marcel Bouverie. The foundation has now had to face the embarrassment of having its affairs examined at a public inquiry.' Lilly held up the papers that I had prepared earlier in the week. 'The financial papers Martha sent out before the meeting clearly indicate donations have dwindled away and our reputation is at serious risk. I am told the preliminary investigation has been completed and the Charities Ombudsman will be handing down her findings at the end of next week.'

Next week? I had no idea it was so soon. And how did Lilly know? Gerard looked at me with a raised brow.

'As directors, we are all at risk. Our legal obligations are extremely onerous and personal liability rules apply. Accordingly, we need to be able to show we are taking reasonable steps to mitigate any risks and get things into order as quickly as possible.' Lilly gave a heavy sigh, trying to look regretful. 'I propose that Anita stand aside as CEO until the findings from the inquiry are known. If Anita does not agree, we need to take a vote on the matter and ask for nominations for acting CEO.'

Anita finally came to life. She was livid. 'I will not be stepping aside. I am the founder and CEO of this foundation. There is no one else here who could possibly do what I do!'

Lilly ignored her and spoke to the board at large. 'Do you really want to see the media chipping away at the foundation, day after day, until Anita is thrown out of office publicly? Would it not be better for the foundation to solve this problem internally?'

Anita glared at her. 'Problem, Lilly? Am I the problem, or are you? We didn't have a problem until you joined us. Everything was fine. We were united in our cause.'

Bianca, ever the conciliator, spoke up in a grave voice. 'Anita is correct, but so is Lilly. We were too complacent, and things are done differently these days. We owe it to our donors to be squeaky clean. I propose we vote on whether Anita stands down temporarily and an acting CEO is elected. Does anyone want to accept this motion?'

Joan Murphy put down her knitting and raised her hand.

'Is there a seconder?'

Wai Leung, eyes downcast, raised his hand.

Oh no, I thought.

Lilly couldn't stop a smirk of satisfaction crossing her face. 'I forward the motion for a vote to remove Anita as CEO.'

I was horrified. This was deceptive! I rarely spoke at these meetings, but I couldn't stop myself. 'Sorry, but that's not what Bianca suggested. She suggested a vote be taken on whether Anita steps down temporarily.'

'That's correct, Martha,' Bianca said. She looked rather annoyed at seeing her words misrepresented.

Anita had turned pale under her make-up and feigned a cold indifference.

Lilly shrugged. 'Whatever!'

I glared at her. The woman was beyond disgusting.

Gerard raised his hand and then spoke in that measured voice of his. 'We need to be crystal clear exactly what it is we are voting for. Martha, could you please read out Bianca's precise words?'

I consulted my notes. 'Bianca said, "I propose the meeting votes on whether Anita stands down temporarily and an acting CEO is elected."'

No-one made any objection.

The room was silent for a moment as the vote was put to the room. All board members, but two, slowly put their hands up. Gerard and Peter abstained.

I tensed in frustration.

'Any nominations for acting CEO?' Lilly asked.

There was a long silence until Mark Hartford finally raised his hand. 'I nominate Lilly Hartford.'

Anita stormed out of the room.

I ran after her. She got into the elevator just before I reached her, and as the doors closed in my face I saw she was utterly enraged. I stared at the elevator doors for a moment and then turned around.

I returned to the meeting where Lilly had taken up the reigns. Smiling broadly, she hypocritically thanked the members for their confidence in her.

'I am going to close this meeting now. We can reconvene when the report from the inquiry is available and our lawyers have had the opportunity to appraise it. You'll be advised of the date of the next meeting when it is known. Thank you all very much.'

Aside from Gerard, I was left alone to clean up the mess.

53

Louisa

Elissa was amazing. I'd already seen an early draft of her thesis and had been impressed. She made me wonder how on earth it could have been that women had been held back for so long. She was an exemplar of how true the 'educate a girl and you educate a nation' movement was.

If she had one flaw it was that she was in too much of a hurry. Instead of our normal meeting, I decided we needed to have a long stroll along the river.

Elissa seemed doubtful when I invited her to meet me at the boatsheds. We wandered down to the river and the moment Elissa hit the path she took off. I stopped and waited for her to notice I wasn't keeping up with her. Eventually she looked back over her shoulder and smiled as she came back to me. 'Oh, I am too much in a hurry?'

'You tell me,' I said. I invited her to relax. 'Take a little time to just appreciate this beautiful city, the river and the freshness of the early morning, because sometimes slowing down helps us to think more clearly. Your work is amazing, but it's time to pause and think about where it's taking you.'

She sighed and took a deep breath. 'You are wise woman, Professor Louisa. I have been rushing like the river myself and not taken time for reflection.'

I suddenly spotted two ducks landing on the water. 'Oh look! Aren't those ducks gorgeous?'

Elissa looked startled but agreed.

We watched the ducks for a while then we resumed our strolling.

Elissa eventually opened up. 'I have been, as you know, a big admirer of Anita and her foundation.'

I acknowledged this was so. 'Are you having some doubts?'

She nodded. 'Many doubts, Professor. I have been reading about the investigation by the Charities Ombudsman. Things at the foundation don't seem good.'

That was true, I thought. They were being hammered in the press. 'Yes, they look rather bad actually. It's looking as if the foundation has let its donors and supporters down. And we're already seeing repercussions of the Act in action.'

Elissa shook her head 'My research is showing the sentences imposed since judges lost much of their discretion are unbalanced. They do not take into account the special circumstances that individual offenders are in. It's like one size is supposed to fit all.'

'And why do you think that's a problem?'

She shrugged. 'The law should be more flexible. Without judicial discretion it cannot be flexible, it is rigid, and, in any event, it has not achieved the objectives the victims' rights advocates wanted. Anita wants to reduce crimes against children, and she believes this can be done with the threat of tougher sentences and prolonged containment. This has not happened. There is no evidence to suggest crimes against children have reduced.'

I empathised with Elissa. She knew this research would be challenging, but I don't think she realised how much. She was an optimist, and Anita Hammond-Jones at her best was undoubtedly inspirational. It was such a shame she used her considerable powers so inappropriately. I turned to Elissa. 'So, despite your admiration for Anita, your research has filled you with doubt?'

She stopped walking. 'Yes, this is so. And I worry Anita will be angry with me.'

'Does that matter?' I asked her gently.

Elissa gave me a worried nod. 'She has been generous to me. I have had the grant from the foundation and they gave me access to people I could interview. Those people would not usually have been accessible to me.'

I invited Elissa to sit on a park bench and quizzed her about what this really meant. 'I'd like you to reflect on why we do research.'

'That's easy,' she replied. 'We use evidence rather than mere opinion. We test hypotheses. We try to get to the truth, the objective truth.'

'And have you any thoughts about whether objective truth is superior to, or different from, subjective truth?'

With her young brow deeply creased, Elissa took a moment to think. 'The law has evolved to take both into account,' she said slowly. 'It is different from science because it is able to take account of relevant subjective factors as well as using objective evidence based on research to do its best to adjudicate on human behaviour.'

I gave her an encouraging nod. 'And how has it done that do you think?'

Elissa didn't seem to have an answer for that. She held her head in her hands, her eyes wide. 'I have so much to learn!'

'And you are well and truly on your way to doing just that,' I assured her.

'Perhaps the law has evolved because it has allowed itself to learn and grow from precedence that is adjudicated by experts,' she said. 'I know that is simplistic—and the experts have their own prejudices—but if our judiciary is truly representative and fair, they need to be able to use their discretion to come up with the best decision-making they can.'

I smiled and pushed her thinking with an outrageous suggestion. 'Do you mean the judiciary need to be representative? Does that mean you support popular election of judges?'

She was horrified. 'No, definitely not! If judges were elected, they would have to take too much notice of lobbyists like Anita.' She paused. 'I know that is subjective, but my opinion has been informed by research.'

'Bravo.' I smiled at her and got to my feet. 'Shall we go back now? We can stop by the uni café for lunch, if you like.'

She gave me a warm smile. 'Thank you, and please don't think me ungrateful, but I would like to get back to my work now.'

'Why are you in such a hurry?' I asked her. I'd never had a student so focussed. 'You're months ahead of where you should be.'

This time her smile was sad. 'I miss my family. I want to get my work done and then go to Malaysia to see them. I am lonely.' She gave me a cheeky little grin. 'Now, is that subjective enough for you?'

I laughed and escorted her back to campus.

54

Helene

I was grateful to Conrad for accompanying me on an especially cold and dismal day to Jennifer's funeral. I gave him a sad smile. 'It's good to have your company. Your attendance swells the numbers in the congregation to nine, if you count the vicar.'

Conrad looked around. 'Who else is here?'

I peered at the other attendees. 'There's the funeral people, of course, two of our Billabong case workers, and those two women over by the coffin. The tall one in the suit is a barrister and the shorter one is the duty lawyer from legal aid. They helped Jennifer at her trial.'

Conrad pointed discreetly at a man off to the side. 'Who's the older guy in the trench coat?'

I was curious too. 'I don't know him.'

'He could be a journalist,' Conrad suggested.

I was startled. 'I hope not!'

Conrad turned to me. 'Why not?'

'Journalists don't usually publish details of suicides because of the risk of copycats,' I told him. 'If the other residents at Billabong read about this it would distress them even more, putting them all at risk.'

Conrad nodded somberly. 'Your job is hard enough.' He sighed and stared around despondently. 'Jennifer was wonderful. She was an awesome musician and her lyrics were strong. If things had been different, she could have made it as a singer/songwriter. What happens to her songs now?'

'They die with her,' I said.

'Why?'

'Patient confidentiality.'

'Oh.' He was silent for a moment. 'Why do you think she took her own life?'

I sighed, feeling gutted. 'She couldn't see any future for herself, so she gave up trying.'

'Could we have intervened more?' Conrad looked troubled.

I did what I could to console him, but the truth rarely brings comfort. 'We did what we could. We increased her medications and provided more counselling, but we couldn't give her what she needed most.'

'Freedom and forgiveness,' Conrad said.

'Precisely.'

'I heard Anita Hammond-Jones talking about that stupid Act in an interview,' said Conrad darkly. 'Said it was a great achievement.'

I grimaced. 'She thinks so.'

Conrad was still grumbling next to me. 'This feels so wrong. It's unfair.'

I stared at him for a long moment. 'Justice holds people to account for what they've done, vengeance never pardons them. I wrote letters, I wrote emails and I tried to call Anita. I begged her talk to me about Jennifer, but I never got a reply.'

'Do you think she got your letters?' Conrad asked.

I shrugged, 'I don't know. She might have read them, or she might have thrown them out. I'll never know. Come on, Conrad. Let's go in.'

He looked around, as we entered the cold and sparse chapel. 'Do we sign the visitor's book?'

There was no table, no memorial cards, nothing that showed a life had even been lived. I sighed, staring blankly ahead of me.

'There isn't one.'

55

Martha

After the last disastrous board meeting, I tried many times to contact Anita but was unsuccessful. On the first working day after the meeting, Lilly and Mark turned up in the office, like a two person tornado. Lilly demanded a guided tour, and, thankfully, Leanne joined us. I don't think I could have borne it alone.

Lilly looked around scornfully. 'How quaint,' she muttered to Mark. She noticed the plants and pointed at them disdainfully. 'Do those plants belong to the foundation?'

'No, they're leased. The company that supplies them refreshes them every month,' I explained. 'They employ people living with disability and we love them—'

'Get rid of them,' Lilly ordered.

'But, Lilly, we have such a good relationship—'

She cut me off. 'Is this where the Listen Line works from?'

'Yes,' I replied. 'It's only Leanne and whatever volunteers we can get on the day. However, things are really looking up as we have Daniel starting with us soon.'

'Daniel, who is Daniel?' she demanded.

'He is the new employee for the Listen Line,' Leanne explained.

'Funded by Lady Charmiane,' I added. 'Daniel's Indigenous and his appointment gives Lost Lovelies a fantastic opportunity—'

She cut me off again. 'He won't be needed.'

I was stunned, so was Leanne.

'Leanne's run off her feet,' I protested. 'She needs help. Lady Charmiane specifically made the donation to ensure that all our caller needs are met by qualified individuals.'

Lilly stared me down. 'He won't be needed. Mark will be helping out with the Listen Line.'

'Mark?' Leanne and I blurted out at the same time.

'Yes, Mark,' said Lilly. 'I want him to understand the work of the foundation so he can be my deputy.'

Leanne and I were speechless.

'Now, where is my office?' Lilly demanded.

I took Lilly to Anita's office with Mark tagging along.

Lilly gave him his marching orders. 'You stay with Leanne. She can show you the ropes.'

I gritted my teeth and whispered a suggestion to Leanne for a quick meeting at the pub after work. She nodded in mute resignation and took a quiet and awkward looking Mark Hartford over to the Listen Line. I couldn't even begin to imagine what a disaster that would be.

Things only got worse as the day dragged on. Lilly poked her nose into everything, demanding explanations about how we ran the place. She snorted at my answers and treated me like I was her maid. I got no useful work done all day. When she demanded I take shorthand, I nearly screamed. No one takes shorthand anymore! What planet was this woman coming from? I handed her the dictation machine.

'Anita always dictated letters if she was in a hurry. Otherwise she typed them herself and I'd check and tidy them up.'

Lilly glared at me. 'Anita's gone, Martha. I'm in charge.'

I struggled to hold my outrage in check. 'You are the acting CEO. Anita has temporarily stood down. It is your duty to hold things over until a final decision is made.'

We glared at each for a moment in a stalemate, but then luckily the phone on Anita's desk rang. Lilly stared at it as though she'd never seen a phone before. I sighed and answered it. It was a women's magazine wanting to interview Lilly. I knew that would distract her, at least for a while.

As I went back to my desk, preparing myself to make some difficult phone calls to those whose services were no longer required, I could hear her simpering away. 'Oh, yes. I'd love to. When?'

By the time she and Mark had left for the day, I was more than ready for a drink. At the pub, Leanne flopped into her seat, tired and cross. 'What a flipping bitch.'

'She certainly knows how to make her presence felt,' I agreed with more than a touch of irony.

We both threw back a decent swig of gin.

Leanne looked worried. 'Do you think Anita's going to come back?'

I could only shrug. 'I don't know. I'm hoping Anita will fight back. I keep trying to get her on the phone, but I only get the answering message.'

Leanne rolled her eyes. 'Not the one that includes Marcel, I hope?'

I nodded. 'The very one.'

'Do you think the Ombudsman will dump on her?' she asked.

I threw back my drink. 'She might. Or she might just admonish Anita without destroying her and the foundation. Janet Johnson-Smythe was a politician for a long time, but she never liked Anita. I'm just praying Anita will get the strength to reclaim what she fought so hard for; we can't have Lilly running the place.'

'We've got to do something to turn this around. How can we help do you think?' Leanne was looking at me in an imploring fashion, but I was at my wits end. We couldn't do anything about Lilly without Anita.

'What if we both go to see her, explain what's happening and tell her how much is at stake?' I mused. 'We have to join forces and bring Anita back to reality.'

Leanne leaned forward, both hands around her glass. 'Would Gerard be able to help?'

I nodded. 'I'm sure he will. I'll sound him out.'

'He could lobby the other board members,' Leanne suggested.

'Agreed.' I reached across the table and took one of Leanne's hands. 'He knows how tragic it would be if we lost you.' I was cheering up now.

Generous Leanne added, 'Or you.'

We clinked glasses. 'Here's to us.'

'Lucky I'm getting the bus home tonight.' Leanne giggled and drained her glass.

I called for another round. 'I can drop you off in a taxi.'

'Okay.' Leanne dreamily recalled the early days of the foundation. 'Do you remember how driven and enthusiastic Anita was at first?'

I smiled. 'I do. She was so passionate and loved what she was doing.'

Leanne nodded. 'Yeah. She swept us along with her. She'd suffered so much and yet she didn't let it get her down.'

I remembered those days so well. 'She was determined to make a difference and she did. She succeeded beyond all expectations, but it got out of hand. She lost when she stopped listening to other points of view.'

'True,' Leanne agreed unhappily. 'Although it's nice to see you recognising that fact. You and I both know it's the families who matter. She lost sight of that.'

I raised my glass. 'We have to get the foundation back on track for them.'

Leanne raised her fresh gin and tonic in salute. 'We do! We need the real Anita back. She'll be her old self and bring in the donors and we'll take care of the families.'

A vision of us at eighteen came to me. 'Do you remember that first body we had to dress?'

Leanne nearly choked. 'Oh cripes, yes! At Prince George's.'

'And we got the giggles!' I started to laugh at the memory.

She grinned. 'Even though it wasn't funny.'

'Not at all funny. We were absolutely hysterical!' I was laughing out loud now, and Leanne giggled.

'And we were so scared someone would walk by and see us laughing and think we were horrible,' I reminded her.

'And that made us laugh even more.' Leanne was wiping her eyes with the back of her hand. 'We were only laughing because we were so nervous.'

I gave her a reassuring smile. 'We'll get through this too, if we stick together.'

The rest of that week was a nightmare. The phones were ringing persistently, Lilly was rarely in the office, as much of a part-timer as Anita had become, and donations were way down. We were losing volunteers, and the media was relentless in trying to destroy the foundation with their coverage. Jamie O'Dhea and Jack Ruler featured the exodus of volunteers. Ruler interviewed one who was not complimentary about the foundation. Thankfully, she laid the blame at Lilly's feet, but she also indicated Anita hadn't exactly been reliable to work with either because she was hardly ever in the office.

I somehow got through the week. I even managed to get through a couple of shifts at the maternity centre, and on Saturday Gerard came around for dinner, greeting me at the door with a kiss, a bunch of carnations and a nice bottle of my favourite pinot noir. As he poured the wine, I poured out my concerns. In particular, the sacking of Jimmy and Bree and her dismissal of Daniel McIntyre. I also shared that she actually suggested paying Mark for being on the Listen Line.

'I wonder what Lady Charmiane would think about that?' Gerard mused. 'She didn't provide funding to pour it into the Hartford's bank account. I think I know what the Ombudsman would say given Mark is a board member.'

I shook my head. 'When I pointed that out Lilly backed off.'

'Good,' Gerard said.

'I felt so terrible when I called Daniel.'

'How did he react?'

'He sounded as if he wasn't really surprised. He actually tried to cheer me up by telling me he could easily get his old job back.'

'That's a relief.'

'Yeah, well, pity Leanne. She desperately needed his help and half the time Mark's not even on the phones,' I complained. 'Lilly is continually calling him away from the Listen Line to cater to whatever perceived need she's conjured up.' I refilled my glass. 'It's a mess. I'm having to help Leanne on the phones, which keeps me from my own work—work that's doubled by the way, because of Lilly's constant demands.' I hit my stride and my voice rose an octave. 'She's got no idea about managing people or running an office, let alone a foundation, but she's convinced she knows it all. You're expected to drop what you're doing and cater to her needs immediately. It's driving me nuts. Anita could be a bit scatty but at least she let me do my job. She trusted me and was sort of aware of what her own limitations were.'

I paused momentarily because that wasn't quite accurate, so I added, 'Well, actually, she got bored doing office work, but that was a lot easier to deal with than Lilly's incompetent interference. Donors are down, volunteers are dropping like flies … it's just no fun going into work anymore. Honestly, Gerard, I feel like walking away from the whole mess right now.'

I suddenly stopped rambling, as it occurred to me how bitter I sounded. I put an apologetic hand on Gerard's arm. 'I'm sorry. I didn't even realise how much I had bottled up. Thank you for being so patient and letting me get all that off my chest.'

Gerard smiled reassuringly, but he was concerned about Lilly going beyond her powers as well as her competencies. 'She was to be acting CEO only,' he reminded me. 'She was to keep things afloat until the Charities Ombudsman's findings are known. An acting CEO should not be implementing their own changes in this way.'

'Try telling her that,' I said. 'She's power hungry and incompetent and demanding. I have tried to slow her down, but it only makes her more determined.'

'A dangerous mix,' Gerard agreed. 'I think I'll have a quiet chat to Lady Charmiane.' He took my glass and then clasped my hands. He gazed at me with those serious brown eyes of his. 'Martha, I'm going to ask you to grin and bear it, just for a short while longer. I know you're feeling ready to move on, but I need to make sure everything is in order before you do. Without you the foundation will crumble and we can't have that.'

I squeezed his hands. 'Of course not. We can't leave the families unsupported.'

We moved to the couch where Gerard put his arm around my shoulders. I snuggled into him with a satisfied sigh.

'We also can't leave Leanne with such a terrible mess,' he added.

'She's the main reason I'm staying,' I reassured him. 'But how long do you think this is going to take?'

'Your guess is probably as good as mine,' he said. 'The findings are imminent. Janet Johnson-Smythe is a seasoned politician and she'll want to make capital out of this. She won't linger.'

'Will you talk to some of the board members? Tell them about Lilly and see what they can do to help?' I asked.

'Of course. Anything for you.'

I snuggled down into his embrace. I felt warm and relaxed, like something hard and cold inside me was melting away.

56

Martha

Leanne and I tried to keep things steady as we waited for the verdict. We were only able to tolerate Lilly and Mark because we had each other. Over a morning coffee Leanne told me she was deeply concerned about Mark's manner on the Listen Line. 'I heard him tell one caller that Jennifer Harris got what she deserved.'

I groaned and felt a pang of guilt. What with everything that was happening, I'd hardly given Jennifer a second thought, but her pale face and elfin eyes sometimes came to haunt me.

If this Bill passes, she'll kill herself.

I wondered how she was coping following the verdict. I wanted to tell Leanne how I felt about Jennifer, but she was so wound up about Mark Hartford that I couldn't get a word in.

'He keeps referring to his own situation and doesn't listen to what the callers are saying.' She groaned and ran her hands down her face. 'You don't do that!'

'Especially not to people who are traumatised,' I added.

'They need to be heard, they don't need his troubles heaped onto their own.' Leanne was worried. 'He and Lilly are so wrapped up in their own experience they just can't empathise with others. They can't see past what they perceive as their own entitlements.'

I agreed they were certainly self-entitled. 'This morning Lilly insisted I book a photographer so she could "have a photo shoot to update my profile".' I raised my fingers for air quotes.

'Isn't she just supposed to be holding the fort?' Leanne said.

'Exactly! But she seems to have a different definition of what that means than you or I do.'

Leanne snorted. 'Let's not forget Mark and his Listen Line antics.'

'What else has he done?' I asked.

'I heard him tell one caller, "Well at least you only had to wait for two days before you got an answer because Lilly and I—", then off he goes raving on about their experience and not paying heed to what the caller is saying.'

I was horrified. 'That is so unprofessional. Our callers don't need that!'

At that very moment Mark poked his head into the café and snapped at us. 'Lilly wants you back at the office immediately.'

I looked at my watch. We'd been at the café for 40 minutes! No wonder Lilly was looking for us.

I paid the bill and we rushed back to the phones.

Lilly was waiting by my desk with a smug reprimand. 'It was slack of you both, however I don't blame you entirely. Standards in this place have been dreadful thanks to Anita's poor management skills. I'll soon get that fixed. The mail is here and I need you to sort it.'

I glared at her.

'Shouldn't you be prioritising the mail that's already on your desk from two days ago? I've already sorted them for you and there are some urgent invoices that need paying.'

Lilly looked bored but agreed to do as I asked. However …

'I want to see today's mail first. There might be requests to do presentations or media. Those things are useful for attracting donors and winning new friends.'

I stayed mute. Thanks for the lesson in public relations, I thought. It wasn't as if I didn't know this.

I sorted the new mail and among the letters was a small package containing a Mior handbag.

'Oh, how lovely!' Lilly exclaimed, holding it up against her dress, admiring herself in the mirror. 'I'll be able to take this with me to my interview with *Women's Affairs* tomorrow.'

I looked at her with contempt.

Here we go again, I thought. I debated rebuking her, reminding her just how Anita fell into such a hole, but I shut my mouth and quietly left her office.

I caught Leanne just as she was hanging up after what seemed to have been a particularly difficult call. Her face was drawn and she looked tense.

'It was Sandra Jesson,' she said quietly.

She'd been a friend of the foundation for more than three years. Her young daughter went missing at a shopping centre but later showed up unharmed. As a result, Sandra had donated considerable time and effort to fundraising for the foundation. She was a good friend to the foundation.

'How is she?' I asked.

'She spoke to Mark yesterday,' she said quietly, not wanting the subject of our conversation to overhear us.

'Oh no. What did he say to her?' I dreaded the answer.

Leanne looked completely fed up. 'He said she didn't know how lucky she was because her daughter had only gone missing, unlike his daughter who was murdered.'

I put my arm around Leanne, who rested her head on my shoulder. 'I don't think I can put up with much more of this.'

57

Martha

I arrived at Yarra River Hospital early after an invigorating walk with my walking group. I'd been slacking off in recent weeks now that I had a wonderful bedwarmer in Gerard. The ladies were all chuffed when I shared the news of my engagement, none more so than Abigail, who noted that I looked happier than I had done in some time.

As I put my bag away and went to the kiosk to get a coffee, I saw Helene Morton.

I felt a pang of alarm and thought about avoiding her, but no, I knew better than that. I owed her an apology.

'Helene,' I called. She turned around, gave me a smile and a small wave. She came over to me without hesitation. That was encouraging.

'You wouldn't have ten minutes for a chat, would you?' I asked.

She looked at her watch. 'Of course. My Grand Round isn't until 9 am, so yes.'

I gestured out the window to the fine day outside. 'It's a mild morning. Should we grab a seat outside?'

Helene agreed and we made our way to the seats among the native shrubs. 'This is a lovely spot,' Helene remarked.

I agreed. 'It's always been a favourite of mine, especially when the shrubs are flowering and the honey-eaters and wrens are out in force.'

'The little birds. They're so precious,' Helene said, looking around with a smile.

I drew in a nervous breath. Best to get it over with. 'Helene, I wanted to apologise to you for my rudeness and stupidity on the last occasion we met.'

Helene immediately shook her head. 'Oh Martha, I've never known you to be stupid! Far from it. And there's certainly no need to apologise. I should have been more sensitive to your situation.'

'No, I totally over-reacted,' I admitted. 'I regret that. I can see you were just concerned for your patient.'

'Yes,' Helene looked sad. 'Poor Jennifer.'

'How is she?' I asked.

Helene was startled. 'Oh, Martha, you haven't heard?' She looked deeply concerned.

I knew immediately what she was going to tell me.

If this Bill passes, she'll kill herself.

'Jennifer died. The funeral was a couple of days ago.'

I fought to still the tears burning my eyes. I looked away to compose myself.

Helene took my hand in hers. 'Martha, dear Martha, please don't blame yourself. This is not your doing. There were so many factors at play.'

I couldn't look at her. 'I'm so sorry to hear that she's dead. And I'm sorry for the part the Act played in that.'

Helene nodded sadly. 'I'm afraid Anita just doesn't understand the system at all. She doesn't understand the value of psych services and how hard it is to support some clients.'

Guilt tore through me. 'But I did know and I should have known better. The Victims' Voices Act leaves people like Jennifer with no hope, just as you tried to warn me.'

Helene looked sad. 'The Act is bad, but Anita could still have left some hope for Jennifer.'

'I tried to talk to her about that,' I said weakly. 'I suggested she could tell the tribunal that by next year say she may feel less concerned about Jennifer.'

Helene gave me a taut smile. 'Thanks for trying, Martha.'

An announcement from the hospital's loudspeaker split the air. 'Dr Helene Morton, please report to reception.'

'Shit!' Helene said, looking at her watch. 'I'm sorry, Martha. I've got to run.' She gave me an empathetic look. 'I hate to leave you like this.'

I shook my head. 'No, please go. You have your meeting. A few moments alone will be good for me.'

'Will you promise to call me?' she pleaded.

I nodded. 'Yes, of course. Now you go, and all the best for the lecture.

What's it on?'

She either didn't have the time to tell me, or perhaps she didn't want to.

I sat alone, watching the little birds until a dark cloud swept across the sunshine and stole it away.

Anita got her vengeance all right. Jennifer Harris was dead, and I was the fool who didn't try hard enough to stop it.

But what could I do? Anita didn't want to hear any other point of view, she didn't want to know Jennifer's story, and while I understood Anita's reasons why—the girl had stolen her precious baby boy and he'd died as a consequence—it didn't mean that Jennifer Harris should have to die too.

How would Anita take the news? I shuddered. Imagine if the media got hold of this! Anita would be crucified.

I picked up my bag and made my way back to the office. I glanced at the hospital's events noticeboard and saw the Grand Round that Helene was presenting.

Managing a forensic psychiatric service in an unforgiving world.

58

Gerard

Martha wept in my arms. Poor thing. She was copping one thing after another these days.

'Helene tried so hard to advocate for her patient and all I did was wallow in my own guilt.'

My heart was breaking for her. 'I think you are being too hard on yourself, love,' I said. 'Suicide is so complicated. There is never just one reason and certainly there's never just one person who contributes.'

She took the tissues I offered and wiped her nose. 'I know you're right. I'm usually more resilient than this. I just … I don't know. This year has been so hard and so wonderful. It's been a real rollercoaster. Anita's changed, she's gone and put herself and the foundation in trouble, and Lilly is a nightmare. She's making life hell for me and Leanne …' She broke down sobbing again. 'Helene was just so polite about the whole thing!'

I pulled her in close and let her have a good cry. Sometimes, that's just the best way to push through pain. After a few minutes, she sat up and rubbed at her eyes, calmer and clearer in mind.

'I've got to get out of the foundation, Gerard. Or we have to find a way to get rid of Lilly. She's driving me nuts,' she said, grabbing another tissue.

I nodded. 'She's hard to take, that's for sure. A little bit goes a long, long way.'

'She actually gives me orders!' said Martha, throwing her arms up. '"Martha, I ordered you to get water for Pom Pom. When I order you to do something, I expect it to be done at once."' Martha's frustration was evident. 'I told her I wasn't accustomed to taking orders, and she said I'd better get used to it if I wanted to continue working for the foundation.'

This sheer audacity made me gasp. 'How dare she! She's only an acting CEO!'

Martha's eyes were flashing with resentment and pent up frustration. 'I lost it. I told her the foundation was built by Anita with a spirit of caring and cooperation, not orders and demands.'

'And what did she say?'

Martha raised her fingers for air quotes. '"What a mess the foundation is in as a result of that."'

I was taken aback. I knew Lilly was bad, but this was infuriating. Martha didn't deserve to be treated in such a demeaning way.

'I was so upset, Gerard,' Martha replied, wiping her eyes again. 'I know you told me to be patient, but I lost it. I told her she should start looking for someone else to be her handmaiden.'

I was proud of her, even though I wished she'd been able to hold her patience. My plans weren't quite ready yet. I buried my disappointment and gave her a reassuring smile. 'Good for you, Martha. That's the spirit! How did she react?'

Martha curled her lip. 'She backed off. Told me that change is always difficult, that she understood but my loyalty to Anita is misplaced.'

I sighed. I leaned across and squeezed Martha's hand. 'I'm really proud of you, love, but we need to soldier on until the report is available. I need you to hold on for just a little bit longer.'

Martha stared at me listlessly for a moment and then took a sip from her wine, well, it was more like a slug of her wine, really; understandable, given the circumstances.

'Why, Gerard? It's been too long already. Leanne's totally stressed, we're down to a small handful of volunteers and I've had enough.'

'I know it's just awful for you at the moment—'

'You don't know the half of it,' she said in a sulky tone.

I squeezed her hand. 'I promise you it will be soon. We just need to ride out whatever happens with the Ombudsman's report. I agree that working with Lilly and Mark isn't feasible, but if you can put up with them for just a bit longer, it will give me a chance to sort a few things out.'

'What things?' Martha demanded.

'Well, I still have to sound out the board members, get their take on the situation and see if they've got any ideas about how to get rid of Lilly and Mark,' I said, hoping to reassure her and allay further questions. 'I've already spoken to Joan Murphy. She'll stay on until the situation is resolved and then she's retiring.'

She stared at me, trying to perhaps figure out what I wasn't saying.

I ran my hand down her face. 'You know I love you, don't you?'

She immediately softened and nestled back into me. 'I do, and I know I love you. I can't believe how lucky I am.'

Dear Martha put her faith in me and I wasn't going to let her down. How wonderful it was to find out she loved me, as I did her. How surprising that it could happen twice to one simple old fool. This love was something I was determined not to lose.

I met with the remaining board members, as I promised Martha. All of them wanted to jump ship, but I managed to convince them to remain until the report came out.

As I walked back to the car after meeting with Wai Leung, I realised the bird had already flown. Lilly would get her way and take control of The Lost Lovelies Foundation. As I got in my car, an unexpected thought came into my head. Was that such a bad thing? Indeed, it might be good. Let Lilly have the foundation. I know Martha and Leanne worried about the clients, but anyone unhappy would find better support elsewhere. Martha would be free and I could take her away from all this madness.

It wouldn't be long. A few more transactions, and it would be done.

59

Jamie

Jack's story on The Lost Lovelies Foundation was on page one of *The Watcher*, gazumping the sinking of a refugee boat off Christmas Island.

It was a biggie, taking the cover and pages 4–5, and was written in anticipation of the Ombudsman's report. It was one of those primers for the reader. It started with the origins of the foundation, a timeline of events as the foundation grew to prominence, and a personal timeline showing the rise of Anita Hammond-Jones.

And the fall.

Jack tore into her questionable dating habits, with that Bouverie prick the star of the show. He also showed the readers the many times Anita had pushed her views on the then Bill with a vehemence that didn't allow for any other viewpoint to temper her opinion.

The kicker had been his piece on Jennifer Harris. That poor kid had gone and killed herself, and while we wouldn't normally print that kind of story, the editors decided it was such a vital part of the Lost Lovelies story that it had to be mentioned. Jack strongly hinted that Anita's inability to ever forgive Jennifer was a contributing factor in the girl's death. He detailed some of the abuses Jennifer had suffered as a foster and resi-child. Jack had even gone out to the funeral. I got the sense he was sorry for her. It was certainly a sympathetic story, although I wasn't sure if he was gaming the readers on that one. The sympathy generated for Jennifer Harris only played into Anita's downfall.

He speculated in the article, which was more of an opinion piece, that Anita's refusal to agree to Jennifer's release was directly responsible for Jennifer's suicide. It was a bold claim, but Jack didn't do half measures. He tried to get comments from Anita's parents, who told him to bugger off, as did Michael Jones, Anita's ex-husband. Dr Helene Morton, Jennifer's treating psych, was happy to go on the record with her response, and she called for the

Victims' Voices Act to be repealed immediately.

The Bouverie article was just as scathing. We'd researched that one together, and after going through a ton of records and buttering up a number of coppers, we learned that his real name was Allen Rogers. He was Collingwood born and raised and had never been to France. He'd been convicted of a string of fraud and deception charges. We found dozens of victim accounts, including one woman who had lost $100,000. Apparently, he'd convinced her to ditch traditional treatments for breast cancer and was using mindfulness, tantric techniques, and light therapy. I really hoped Anita hadn't given the fraud too much money.

At first, I ground my teeth at seeing Jack's name on what was essentially my story, but looking at how he'd framed the whole thing, I realised I couldn't have done what he did. He'd told the story alright, but I was seeing a full character assassination by a master. Jack did a ripper of a job.

As far as I was concerned, Bouverie was the real villain in this story. Anita was vulnerable so it was easy for him to take advantage of her. The fucking prick. And despite Jack's brilliant job, I was pissed at him for a while. He was too hard on Anita, but then that's probably proof I did the right thing in giving him the story. Anita was done.

But she wasn't done for me.

I wanted to see her one more time.

60

Martha

Lilly backed off after our little talk. She was still a first class bitch who I'd never like and certainly not trust. I told her I'd stay until we learned what the Charities Ombudsman's report came up with. She thanked me and I informed her, 'I'm not doing it for you. I'm doing it for the foundation and all the people who depend on it. Besides, if Anita is exonerated and comes back, I'll probably stay on.'

Lilly smiled at me. 'Or perhaps we'll get used to each other's ways?'

I didn't reply to that, but keeping Gerard's wishes in mind, I gave her a terse nod. Not bloody likely, was my thought.

She asked me to get Pom Pom's lead. She was going to meet her new publicist, wasting more of the foundation's funds promoting herself and trying to improve her image.

When Lilly and Mark left, I walked over to Leanne. She was on a call and I listened in.

'No, sir. Yes, I do understand, and while you can't believe everything you read in the papers—I know, it's difficult to see the foundation's name being dragged through the mud.' Leanne put her head in her hands. With a tremor in her voice she said, 'Well, we have to wait until the Charities Ombudsman hands down her findings and recommendations, but in the meantime I can assure you we're continuing to provide our full range of services and your generosity is being put to good use.' Leanne paused. 'Hello? Hello?'

Leanne sat back, a despondent look on her face.

'C'mon, you need a break.' I took the headphones off for her and she let me lead her out the door for a coffee. I told her what had happened with Lilly.

'I've got to hand it to you, Martha,' Leanne said with a smile. 'You're brave, standing up to her like that.'

I grinned. 'Hating her guts helps. I can say "Yes, Lilly, no, Lilly," while simultaneously thinking "go root your boot, Lilly!" How's Mark going on the phones now?'

Leanne shrugged. 'He's pretty hopeless, but in fairness to him, she keeps taking him off the phones to do her bidding, so he doesn't get much of an opportunity to learn.'

'But he wants to learn?'

'Yeah, he tries,' she said tiredly. 'He'll never be as good as that Daniel guy would have been, but if he doesn't know something he's not afraid to ask. I spoke to him about not using his own tragedy as a guilt trip and he seemed to listen.'

I sighed. 'That's something. Donations are way down, you know. I think everyone's just waiting for the verdict.'

'The donors are all so attached to Anita. They are never going to trust Lilly,' she said.

I clasped my coffee cup in both hands breathing in the comforting, pungent steam. 'Everything depends on the verdict. If the Ombudsman tears into Anita that will be the end of the Lost Lovelies as we know it.'

Leanne sighed. It was like she'd run out of energy.

'If Anita just gets a good rap over the knuckles, the board could ask her to come back.' I tried to sound hopeful while not feeling hopeful at all. 'There's been plenty of times where the leaders of foundations have been found to be tickling the till and they just tell the media how sorry they are and how everything's been fixed.'

'Sure, but times have changed, Martha. The rules are getting stricter. Will the board be willing to put up with her ways?'

'Not sure.'

'Come on,' Leanne said suddenly. 'Let's get back to what we both do well; me on the phones talking to the people and you running the place.'

I sighed. 'Well, there's precious little else we can do except keep the ship afloat and hope for the best.'

We finished our coffees and plodded back to the office. Would I still go if Anita returned?

If Anita returned.

That seemed less likely with every day. I still couldn't reach her and Jack Ruler, the bastard, had skewered her with his articles in *The Watcher*.

If this Bill passes, she'll kill herself.

The voice came upon me swift and unbidden and I pushed it away before I was swamped with guilt once more. It wouldn't do to burst into tears in the hospital foyer. Thankfully, I had a distraction.

As we approached the foyer, we came across a camera crew who were filming Lilly doing a walk-through. Well, several walk-throughs actually because she was so hopeless they had to get her to repeat it several times. Lilly was so absorbed in her own performance she didn't notice us as we paused to watch.

'She's got her bloody dog with her inside the hospital,' Leanne said, noticing Pom Pom nearby. 'And I thought we had to get special permission from the medical director and the privacy officer if we want to film inside the hospital?'

I sighed. 'Lilly makes up her own rules, you know that. I'll let security know in a minute and she can hoist herself on her own petard.'

'So long as she doesn't take everyone down with her,' Leanne added gloomily.

It was at that moment Pom Pom started sniffing the cameraman's shoes. To our horrified fascination he slowly lifted his leg and pissed on the cameraman's trousers. Leanne and I grabbed each other in glee, watching the wet stain spreading on the guy's trousers as he, oblivious, kept filming Lilly.

The cameraman suddenly pulled his head away from the camera and peered over his shoulder.

'Oh fuck!' he cried, as he saw what the dog was up to. He shook his trouser leg, disgust on his face, while Lilly looked mortified.

'Mark, take Pom Pom outside at once!'

Mark, who'd been lurking with the rest of the camera crew, dived into action. Leanne and I grabbed each other's hands, hopping from one foot to the other as we tried to suppress our laughter. A glare from Lilly sent us running.

Just before we entered the office, I saw the security guy striding towards the scene while Lilly was trying to pat the cameraman's wet pants with a tissue.

Once we were safely inside, Leanne and I erupted with laughter.

'She might be a pain the bum, but she's a freaking funny one,' Leanne said with tears streaming down her cheeks.

61

Martha

I'd just got off a shift at the maternity centre when I got a surprise call from Anita. I was so happy to hear from her. I'd been trying to reach her for ages, but she either hadn't wanted to talk or was ignoring me. Surprisingly, she didn't seem to be holding a grudge against me anymore. She asked how things were going in the office. What else could I say? 'Terrible.'

She suggested a catch up on the weekend and I happily agreed. It was good to hear from her, especially after having to put up with Lilly. I missed her in that sense. I also wanted to see if she was okay following the release of Jack Ruler's articles.

We met at the Riverside Café at eleven on Saturday morning. She was looking a bit tired, but I couldn't detect any dilation of her pupils or other signs of drug use. She was still beautiful, though she seemed to have toned things down a bit, looking slightly hippy. Mind you, it was upmarket hippy, rather than Beaconsfield Market cheese-cloth hippy.

Our conversation was hesitant at first. I inquired politely about her health and then Marcel. She eyed me curiously.

'You don't like him, do you, Martha?'

'No,' I told her simply. In days past, I might have hesitated, but I had no fear of telling the truth to anyone now. 'I worry about you.'

She smiled and sidestepped my concern. 'Dear Martha. You're always good to me. And so things in the office aren't good?'

'They're bloody awful!' I gave her a rundown of the drama. 'Lilly's behaving like a little tyrant. She's even put Mark on the Listen Line.'

Anita's mouth fell open in shock. She looked utterly horrified. 'Holy hell! Mark Hartford? On the Listen Line! I couldn't think of anyone worse. He doesn't even know how to help himself.'

When I told her how Lilly had been treating Leanne and me, Anita got really mad and said she was proud of me for standing up to her. She actually looked happy when I told her donations were down.

A triumphant smile spread across her face. 'They're still loyal to me, Martha. I told you they'd never love her like they love me!'

'She's hired a publicist to help improve her public image,' I said.

'Well, she needs to with that attitude of hers!' Anita retorted. 'I never needed one. I learned on the job. Do you remember that time when the elastic in my knickers broke just as I was walking to the lectern?'

I laughed. 'How could I forget? You weren't wearing any tights!'

'I had to do a kind of duck walk to get to the microphone before they fell off me.'

'And the audience thought you were just trying to entertain them and applauded.'

She shook her head. 'I don't know how I got through that speech!'

I grinned. 'You were brilliant. And after you finished, I scooped up the knickers and shoved them in my pocket.'

'And then I went back to the microphone and fessed up. I said, "Okay, we are now going to auction the knickers!"'

'I nearly died when you said that!'

'The punters loved it.' She frowned. 'Who won the auction? The Lord Mayor?'

I nodded. 'Yep, for five hundred dollars. And then you invited him up to the microphone to collect his prize—'

'That's right! I couldn't find the knickers. I thought could I still be wearing them, but I checked and they were gone.' She grinned. 'And that was when you—'

'I had to come up to the mike and whisper to you that I'd tried to hide them in my pocket!'

She laughed. 'And I told the audience "how's that for loyalty" and you got a huge cheer.'

I blushed just thinking about it. 'I was red as a beetroot, standing there, holding your knickers.'

We howled with laughter, causing several other customers to stare at us. We quickly calmed down. After all, it wasn't a good time to be frivolous in public.

I refilled her water glass. It was really good to be back in Anita's company. We'd been through so much together, and even though she'd lost her compass somewhere along the way, she was still my friend. We beamed at each other and a shadow left her face; that beautiful, bright, familiar smile of old suddenly broke through all of the awkward barriers.

'You're still booked for the gala dinner for the International Victims League,' I reminded her suddenly. 'Lilly told them she was going to do it, but they arced up. They said they had a contract and they'd be obliged to take legal action if you backed out.'

Anita wasn't happy. 'I don't know, Martha. I'm not looking forward to that while everything is in limbo.'

'Would it help if I came with you?' I asked.

She scoffed. 'What would Lilly Bitch think about that?'

'She'll be as jealous as a green goblin,' I predicted.

Anita laughed. She straightened up and smiled at me. 'I'm not finished yet, Martha dear. Far from it. The Charities Ombudsman likes to dress well too, and she doesn't skimp on spending money on herself. She'll understand that in a position like mine you have to look the part.'

I pushed away the sigh that threatened to rise from within. There was no repentance in that comment. I forced a smile onto my face. 'We should know what the Ombudsman's findings are well before the gala dinner.'

Anita took my hand. 'We will! And the rebuilding of The Lost Lovelies Foundation will start as soon as I'm back and Lilly's out on her arse.'

She was so full of hope that I didn't have the heart to ask her about Jack Ruler's articles. I wondered if she'd even seen them.

62

Helene

Conrad's placement at Billabong was coming to an end.

During his last week, the residents put on a farewell lunch for him. We had cakes and sandwiches that they'd made themselves.

'So, Conrad, have you come to a decision about your specialty?' I asked.

'I don't really know yet,' he said. 'I'm going to think about it over the summer. But I do know you've been awesome and taught me so much.'

'You've been an awesome student,' I said, and pulled out my ukulele.

Conrad grabbed his guitar and we had a singalong with the clients. One of the clients, Dylan, asked if he could say a few words.

We all cheered.

Dylan was nervous. 'I just, umm, wanna say, umm, like, yeah, a really big thanks to Con.'

More cheers followed.

He shuffled his feet. 'He's been good to 'ave around. He treats everyone real nice. He's a great musician, but he slows down to help others. We're all pretty wrecked because of Jennifer, and Con here, he helped us through that shit. Yeah, mate, so we, umm, just wanna say thanks.'

Conrad blushed and gave him a nod, but they weren't done yet.

'Speech, speech,' they all yelled.

Conrad looked surprised, but he gave it a shot. 'Wow, thanks, everyone. And thanks, Dylan, for those kind words. That's really cool, man. You guys have all been so awesome, even though things are tough for you. I'm, like, still sorting out what I want to do with my life. I'm just lucky to have so many choices and freedoms, but I promise you all, here and now, I'm going to learn how to put forward your cases so the system is fairer in the future.'

'Oh fuck!' Dylan interjected. 'Con's gonna be a bloody politician.'

There was a great roar of approving laughter.

My day wasn't quite over yet.

That afternoon I invited Conrad to meet the new resident who was moving into Jennifer's old room. I checked the file as we stood in the corridor outside. Akon was nineteen years old. She'd been charged with the serious assault of her brother and one of his mates. She claimed they raped her, but it was her word against theirs. Born in Africa, she'd witnessed the killing of her father by soldiers who raped her mother. After two years in a refugee camp they were finally accepted as refugees by Australia.

They moved into an uncle's house in Footscray. By that time, Akon was showing signs of a psychotic illness. She was observed responding to internal stimuli. A psychiatrist prescribed anti-psychotics and anti-depressants and she did well for a while. She got a job in a shop but was sacked; she said for refusing to give the boss oral sex; he said she was a thief.

I put the file down. I opened the door and we went to meet the real Akon.

63

Louisa

I try not to get too personally attached to students, but Elissa was different. She was alone in Australia and missing her family, but she was here to work and that's what she did.

Her research was thorough and revealing. The high distinction she gained for her thesis was well-earned and I encouraged her to publish an essay from it so she could reach a larger audience. Elissa was nervous about anything to do with the media, but she came up with a terrific piece of work that was accepted by *The Dialogue* online journal. It was picked up by the public broadcaster's *News Bulletin*, which led to requests for further interviews. She asked me if I could do them for her. I was happy to go with her to the studio and support her, but there was no way the producers of the shows would want to hear from me. They wanted her, the pretty, young academic gun who ticked diversity boxes. Especially the folk at *Today, Tonight and Tomorrow*.

I drove Elissa to the television studio. She was dressed in a neat dark jacket, white shirt, slacks and flat shoes. I asked her if she would like to borrow my glossy silk scarf to add a bit of colour, but she politely declined.

It felt strange walking into the fantasy land that was the studio. There were large glossy photographs of celebrities everywhere and everyone seemed to be in a big hurry. Wired up people rushed by talking to other wired up people. It was certainly different from the university. I watched from a monitor in an anteroom and nervously ate sweets from a bowl as Elissa was interviewed by Souzi Court.

'Elissa, thank you for appearing on *Today, Tonight and Tomorrow*.'
'Thank you for the opportunity,' Elissa replied softly.

I found myself urging her to speak up as Souzi continued.

'We have seen some dramatic events recently with revelations of financial irregularities at The Lost Lovelies Foundation. Do you have any comment on that?'

Elissa looked startled. 'No, I just want to discuss my research findings.'

'Your research was funded by The Lost Lovelies Foundation, wasn't it?' Souzi asked.

'Partly, I had a small grant from them,' Elissa conceded.

'Then why should we trust your findings?'

'My supervisor, Professor Louisa Moore, is very thorough. Her own research is internationally renowned. She taught me how to conduct ethical research and to stick to the evidence, even if the findings are unexpected,' said Elissa defensively.

'Or unpopular?' Souzi suggested.

'Yes, even if the findings are unpopular.'

Souzi seemed to be waiting for her to elaborate. She was left hanging, so she asked, 'And what did you find?'

'My research shows sentences have actually been reduced.'

Elissa was sticking to her guns and I let out a big sigh, not realising I'd been holding my breath.

'Because of public pressure?' Souzi demanded.

Elissa shook her head. 'The judges I interviewed insisted they were impartial and took no account of public pressure.'

Souzi dived in. 'Did you find that the Victims' Voices Act has influenced the decisions of sentencing judges?'

'It is too early to tell. However, the judges have expressed dismay at the Victims' Voices Act.'

'Why is that?'

'Before the Act came into force, judges knew offenders would be released when they had served their terms.'

'And after the Victims' Voices Act?'

'Now they can be held for as long as the victims' carers decide.'

Souzi frowned. 'And what does that mean?'

'Some offenders have received lighter sentences under the new Act because judges feared they would be held for longer than they deserve.'

Souzi glared at her. 'Do you see that as a problem?'

Elissa refused to be led. 'It is not what was intended, and not the way sentencing should be.'

'What do you think sentencing should be about?' Souzi asked.

'Sentences should be proportionate to the crime and consistent with those given to others convicted of similar offences. Punishment has to be fair and just and sufficient to deter further offending. They should allow for the rehabilitation of offenders and demonstrate the offending conduct is censured. Sentences must take account of the need to protect the community.'

'Did your research take account of the fact our jails are full and so are our mental health facilities?'

'I am mindful of that, yes,' Elissa replied, 'but that is a government responsibility. If they pass legislation, they have to ensure the resources are available to make it work because—.'

Souzi rudely cut her off. 'Thank you, Elissa, that's all we have time for.'

Elissa was quiet on the way back.

'You did well!' I assured her.

She shook her head. 'I answered as well as I could, but it was not enjoyable for me.'

I looked over at her, but she wasn't in the mood to say very much.

'You looked lovely, you know. And you spoke well. Souzi Court is known for trying to rattle people, so I think you should be proud of yourself. You presented yourself with integrity, and there will be a lot of people thinking about what you had to say.'

'You think so?' she ventured eventually.

'Of course!' I exclaimed. 'Don't confuse razzle dazzle media with good common sense. We need more people like you out there.' I patted her hand. 'Now, when you visit your family, I do hope you keep in mind that you have a future here if you want it. I know you could make a significant contribution to policy here in Australia.'

'If it's all the same to you, Professor Louisa, I might just actually enjoy my break,' she said with a wry smile.

I laughed. 'So, you're finally ready to just sit back and relax?'

She grinned at me.

'Good. Well, I don't think there'll be any more research funding coming our way from The Lost Lovelies Foundation!'

Elissa's lovely young face brightened. 'Ha! You are certainly right there. Today I will be sending a summary of the research findings and a link to my thesis to them. That ends my obligations to The Lost Lovelies Foundation.'

64

Martha

The days spent waiting for the Ombudsman's report went quickly. I'd been pushing myself harder and harder on my walks, at the foundation and the maternity centre. The future was uncertain and I was anxious to earn as much money as I could while I had the opportunity. Every spare second beyond that was given to Gerard.

Meanwhile, Lilly hired a communications officer. Colleen had worked for a private school, and that's where Lilly knew her from; Lilly had taught at that school.

I was furious. Colleen was being paid out of the foundation funds ostensibly to raise our profile but, really, to promote Lilly. They hired publicity people who invaded the office with their cameras and lights. Lilly was silly with excitement and invited me to watch. I snapped at her that I had too much real work to do, but she insisted I sit in because it would 'add to her performance' if she had Mark and me as an audience. I know Anita was vain, but Lilly was vain without having any substance. I could almost hear Anita's assessment: 'Talentless bitch!'

The film crew was charming; that's what they got paid for. I couldn't help noticing that the cameraman, Ned, was especially gorgeous. It was fascinating to watch what he did with the lighting. He turned our boardroom into a darkened set with the only light shining directly on Lilly's face.

All she had to say was, 'The Lost Lovelies Foundation exists to promote justice for children and their families, to keep them safe from criminals.'

That was all. It took more than fifteen minutes for her to get it right. Hopeless!

The crew were full of compliments as they packed up. 'Wonderful darling. You were fabulous.'

What balderdash! Lilly tried to not look too pleased with herself and failed. 'I think that went pretty well,' she gloated.

I wanted to vomit.

What's worse, her behaviour had finally pushed Leanne into taking sick leave. This was unprecedented for her and her doctor's sick leave certificates were written in general terms, so they didn't give much away. Leanne hadn't given any reasons to Lilly, but I knew the cause only too well. At first, she took a single day off, but the following week she'd taken another two.

I saw the signs and I worried for my friend.

65

Martha

A few days before the Ombudsman's report was due to be released, Leanne asked if we could go to the café. We took off, and looking across the table at her, I could see she was more tired and stressed than I'd noticed. I came to the sad realisation that this was it for her; she couldn't go on.

I waited for her to take a big sip of her coffee.

Her voice was wavering as she spoke. 'I'm used to distressed and angry callers, but the tenor of their complaints has changed. A lot of the callers are blaming the horrors they've experienced on us. They feel the perpetrators have failed them, the law has failed them, and now they've lost faith in us.'

I put my hand on hers.

Leanne started to cry. 'I'm not coping, Martha.'

My dear friend, ever generous to others, was breaking down before my very eyes. 'Leanne, love, what do you want to do?'

'I need out, Martha. I can't go on without risking a full-on breakdown.' Her hand was shaking as she picked up her coffee.

I sighed. 'I'm so sorry, love. Are you sleeping?'

'No'.

'Nightmares?'

'Yes.'

'Have you talked to your doctor?

She nodded. 'Yes. I've talked to a psychiatrist as well.'

That stunned me, but I managed to hide my shock. 'What did they say?'

'She said I'm suffering from stress. My blood pressure is way up and I have to find a way to deal with it before it gives me a heart attack.' Leanne took a deep breath and handed me a letter.

I opened it quickly and scanned the contents. It was a sick leave certificate from her doctor, and not one for just a few days. I looked up. 'Oh, love.'

She wouldn't look me in the eye. 'I'm taking my remaining sick leave and then I'm out. I'm finished with the foundation as of right now. Finished with Lilly and Mark.'

'But not with me?' I pleaded. 'Surely not.'

Leanne picked up her bag and smiled lamely at me. 'You and I go back a long way. Our friendship will endure.'

I stood up and hugged her.

'There's no reason to stay at work for the rest of the day. Let me walk you out to a taxi,' I said. I rifled in my own bag. 'Here, I've got a taxi voucher you can use. Is there anything you want me to get from the office?'

She shook her head and swiped tears off her face. 'No. Anything I've left there, stays there.'

We walked out through the foyer and into the bright sunshine.

Leanne took a deep breath, and when she looked at me, she already looked a little lighter in spirit. She gave me a weak smile as she looked out towards the street. 'Things will get better now that I'm free of The Lost Lovelies Foundation.'

I took her hand. 'You call me when you've had time to rest up.'

'Oh Martha,' she said with a sigh. 'I'll feel better when I know that you're free of this place too. Make sure you let me know when you're out.' She found the energy to waggle a finger in my face. 'I also wish to be the first advised if there's a wedding in your future!'

I smiled. 'First invitation is yours.'

She hugged me again. 'Take care,' she said quietly. 'And look after yourself.'

I nodded silently, battling to hold back tears. I watched her get into a taxi and leave the hospital grounds.

Last woman standing.

I walked back to the office alone and listened to Listen Line until it rang out, then I turned on the message machine.

A few minutes later Lilly and Mark arrived, and he switched the phone back on. He gave me a broad smile. 'I'm really getting the hang of this. I feel I've got great rapport with the callers.'

I couldn't even bring myself to answer him. I followed Lilly into her office and handed over Leanne's sick leave certificate. She read it and shrugged. 'I was thinking about replacing her anyway. She's out of touch with modern methods of managing a Listen Line. I'm going to introduce change management to this office.'

'Oh yes?' I didn't even try to hide my cynicism. 'And how are you planning to do that?'

'I'm contracting Charities for Change. They'll do a complete audit and check of our policies and procedures and make recommendations for improvement,' she said, ignoring my tone and placing the letter to one side.

'And charge the foundation a small fortune,' I observed.

'Every cent will be money well spent.'

Well, at least I had one ace up my sleeve. 'I have to remind you that if the contract is worth more than $10,000 it has to be approved by the board.'

She just smiled, looking at herself in the mirror, and agreed. 'Put it on the agenda for the next meeting.'

I walked back to my desk, but I was distracted when I noticed Mark gesticulating wildly at me. As I walked over to him, I heard him tell a caller, 'Okay, my supervisor is here now. She'll take over.'

I glared at him as he practically threw me the headphones. I took the call and let the caller vent her frustrations. I walked her through her anger and was as kind to her as I could be. If she was a marker of what Leanne had been dealing with day after day for months, then it was no bloody wonder she was so stressed. When the call ended, I put the Listen Line onto the answering machine.

Mark was mopping his brow and looking flustered, but he had the grace to thank me. 'Leanne is so good with these difficult ones.'

I agreed. 'She was, yes.'

Mark looked shocked. 'Was?'

'She's taken stress leave.'

'She can't! I need her help,' Mark said, his eyes wide. 'What are we going to do?'

'Why don't you ask Lilly?' I suggested acidly.

66

Martha

Lilly had been given a hand-delivered confidential draft of the Ombudsman's report to check and wouldn't let me see it. I pointed out that she wasn't really in a position to check it for accuracy herself because she hadn't been with the foundation for all of the period covered by the inquiry. 'Sorry, Martha,' she said smugly. 'Janet has given me a copy of the draft on a strictly confidential basis in the interests of natural justice. I must respect her confidence and show no-one else, not even Mark.'

I was boiling with rage. Oh, it's Janet now?

I left the office and called Gerard.

'If Lilly's been given a copy Anita will have one too.'

I immediately brightened up. 'Good thinking, Gerard!'

I tried to call Anita but got no answer. I was disappointed, as I'd been hoping she was climbing out of that dark hole she'd been in.

I'm not sure how I got through the day. I kept hoping Lilly would nip out and I could sneak a look at the draft, but she was too cunning for that. That only left me with one option.

After work I drove by Anita's place and saw that it was all closed up with the blinds drawn. The letter box was stuffed full, and among the mail there was a large envelope with a government crest on it. With a furtive glance around, I slipped it into my pocket and drove home where Gerard was waiting.

I waved the envelope at him. We went through the report and recommendations together and it was a bleak story. Anita was roundly criticised for blurring the lines between running the foundation as a charity, thereby gaining benefits including tax exemptions, and also as a political lobbying organisation. The Ombudsman found her to be 'unethical, unwise, ambitious and lacking in understanding concerning modern management methods'.

The report was a bomb. Anita's credibility was shot.

'She won't come back, will she?' I whispered.

Gerard shook his head.

Lilly would be staying and she would be unbearably triumphant. Gerard poured us a drink as I sat with my head in my hands, wondering what was to be done.

'We just go on as before, at least for the moment,' he said.

'How can we?' I demanded. 'With Leanne gone the office is intolerable for me, Gerard.'

'There was no criticism directed at you, me or the board,' he pointed out. 'We just have to weather the immediate future and then we get as far away from Lilly and her foundation as we can.'

'How long will that take?' I groaned. 'I'm supposed to be happy, celebrating our engagement, but this is like waiting for the results of a biopsy.'

Gerard pulled me up and held me by my hips, pulling me towards him. He kissed my forehead, my cheek, then my lips. 'It'll be no longer than two weeks, I promise.'

'Two weeks?' I murmured against his lips. 'You promise?'

'I promise.'

On my way to work the following day, I drove over to Anita's place. Gerard was on my mind, naturally. And while I loved and trusted him, I admit I had a few bitter thoughts. I didn't have any superannuation and my only assets were my mortgaged house and my pride. I'd worked hard all my life and I was ending up with bugger all. I'd put so much of myself into The Lost Lovelies Foundation and I'd be leaving with nothing. I hoped whatever he was working on was worth the effort.

I sighed. I was going to miss the foundation. But what had we even achieved after the fuss and bother, the lobbying and the publicity? Anita would be shamed and I'd leave with my tail between my legs. Is this what Jennifer Harris had died for?

When I got to Anita's place, I was about to put the re-sealed crested letter with the other mail when I was confronted by a microphone-wielding reporter with cameraman in tow. God knows where he came from.

'Are you a friend of Anita Hammond-Jones?' he demanded, shoving the microphone in my face.

'No, I'm just a neighbour helping with the mail while she's away,' I lied.

'Away?' he insisted. 'Where's she gone?'

'I don't know,' I answered, truthfully, as it happened.

'Can I see that letter?' The pushy bugger was grabbing at it. I pushed him away.

'No, you bloody well can't!' I exclaimed, shoving it in my bag. 'And please get that microphone out of my face or I'll pop one of your pimples!'

I made a dash for the car with them running after me. A quick wheel spin dumped mud on the reporter's suit and I took off.

The day had certainly got off to a shaky start. I pulled into a petrol station and filled up. Inside the shop I noticed bunches of carnations for sale. I chose a mixed bunch and breathed in their heady scent that reminded me so much of my mother. I decided I'd take the flowers around to Leanne's place, and even though this would make me late to work, I didn't care. Lilly could wait.

There was no response when I rang Leanne's buzzer, so I scribbled a note asking her to call me. The report was bad news for Anita.

67

Jamie

Jack and I went together to hear the official results from the Lost Lovelies inquiry. I didn't see anyone from the foundation there, but there was plenty of media interest; all the commercial television stations were represented as well as the public broadcaster. It was good to see some old journalist mates. Jack was a hero, welcomed by all. His coverage of the whole debacle had put him back on the map. He looked like he was enjoying himself as we helped ourselves to coffee and cakes.

The Ombudsman came in and sat down. She waited for quiet and when the noise died down, I flipped on my recorder.

'After receiving several complaints, I have conducted a comprehensive public inquiry into governance and behaviour at The Lost Lovelies Foundation. The foundation was established by Anita Hammond-Jones to raise funds and use them to support families who have lost a child as a result of a criminal act. She was a highly successful fundraiser attracting generous philanthropic donations and government funding. Ms Hammond-Jones has also been a vigorous campaigner for changes to relevant criminal legislation. It is these latter activities that bring The Lost Lovelies Foundation into the arena of political lobbyists and therefore under the scrutiny of legislation relevant to political donations.

'My final report is available in hard copy and online, so I'll just outline the major findings for you. In short, The Lost Lovelies Foundation has been well served by its board, and the accounts are in good order. There are, however, large amounts of personal expenditures by Anita Hammond-Jones. These include luxury accommodation, items of high-priced designer clothing, art works and personal services. The Lost Lovelies Foundation has spent large amounts of donor funds on alcohol. While some expenses have necessarily been incurred to assist with fundraising there have been disproportionate amounts spent on administration and personal expenses compared with other charities of a similar size.

'There were also large payments made to Marcel Bouverie, spiritual healer. His real name is Allen Rogers and he has numerous prior convictions for misleading and deceptive conduct.

'My recommendations include that the foundation needs to examine its culture and clarify its purpose and function. If the intention is for it to be a charity it must comply with the Charities Act. If it is also a political lobbying organisation, it must comply with the Political Donations and Expenditure Control Act.

'I recommend of the total donations received by the foundation, no more than 25 per cent should be spent on administration and fundraising with the remaining funds applied to the purposes for which the organisation was established: to assist the families of children who have lost their lives as a result of crime.

'I have not found any outright theft or fraud on the part of Anita Hammond-Jones, but I did find her behaviour to be unethical and self-serving. I recommend the foundation holds an extraordinary meeting by the end of the month and reports back to me on changes to remedy the situation. Are there any questions?'

I let out the breath I'd been holding. This justified everything that Jack had written and while he was beaming, I felt conflicted. I had a sudden flashback to the way Anita had handled that first media throng when her baby had gone missing, and her incredible courage. I'd watched her defiantly become a public figure, her growing confidence swaying the media to her cause. I remembered how good she felt in my arms, and now it had all gone to shit.

There were many questions, of course. Zoe Waters kicked off first, followed by the rest of the rabble.

'Why have you shown so much leniency towards Anita Hammond-Jones when she is clearly ripping off extremely vulnerable people?'

'What are your feelings towards Anita Hammond-Jones?'

'How does it feel destroying the reputation of a woman whose baby was kidnapped and killed?'

The Ombudsman became visibly angry at this last question and did a dummy spit.

'I have conducted this inquiry in accordance with the rules of natural justice and made my findings within the limitations imposed upon me by the Charities Act. I suggest you familiarise yourselves with the legislation and read the full report. Good afternoon ladies and gentlemen.' She gathered up her papers, rose, and turned her back on us.

There was an excited babble as journalists ran to file their copy.

Poor Anita. There was no finding of any offence against her, but she'd be rotten meat in the public relations department.

I needed to find her. I thought about asking Jack to track her down, but I wasn't in the mood to be torched by his cynicism.

Nope. I'd just have to do my own detective work on this one.

Michael

'Are you okay, love?'

I nodded, turning off the television. 'I might take Snow down to the park for a quick walk.'

Naomi kissed me on the cheek. 'Be back soon.'

While Snow was busy sniffing the tree trunks, I restlessly tried to push away dark thoughts. Anita didn't deserve the sensationalist rubbish they were bandying about on the news.

Naomi was so different to Anita. She had a difficult pregnancy. She was even hospitalised at one stage. Her condition improved after the first trimester and life got a bit easier. When Little Michael was born, I was overjoyed but consumed with terror that something would happen to him. I couldn't burden Naomi with my irrational fears, so I discussed it with my doctor who referred me to a psychologist.

The psychologist taught me some coping skills that helped a lot. He also recommended finding a reliable person to talk to. A mate who would listen and not judge, and who would understand the need for confidentiality. I realised at that time I didn't really have any friends. I think the enormity of the loss of Heath repelled a lot of people and made me more guarded.

In the end, the one person who I could really talk to was Anita's mother. Margaret came to visit us at the hospital the day after Little Michael was born, and I could see pure love in her kind face.

I was saddened by what was happening to Anita. She was determined and dynamic and so charismatic, but she never could see the other side of an argument. And now it was ruining her.

Naomi considered Anita's views on sentencing to be one-sided. She understood the pain inflicted on parents whose child had been harmed, but she also recognised from her own work—as a child protection officer—that the perpetrator is often a victim too.

She once said to me, 'Anita never got the chance to learn that as a parent, you come to accept that you're not the main game, your kids are, and they will never love you as much as you love them.'

I told her I thought that was sad and she had only shaken her head.

'No, the sadder truth is your kids will never love themselves as much as you love them.'

It was getting dark, so I put Snow back on his lead and headed home to my family.

I was a lucky man.

Martha

On the day the Charities Ombudsman delivered her findings, Lilly held what she described as, 'My first press conference!' She couldn't have been happier and was so excited. Five reporters turned up with their camera crew and it was very crowded in our boardroom. I was surprised and impressed with how they cooperated with each other, with one channel even agreeing to share their footage with one of their competitors. That cleared up a bit of space, which was just as well, because Lilly's head was so swollen it nearly filled the room on its own.

She swanned in like she was a bloody film star, shoving her stupid dog onto me, gushing, 'Halloo everyone.' They showed her where they wanted her to sit and then the questions began. They wanted to know what her opinion of the Charity Ombudsman's report was, and I felt like she was punching me in the belly as she praised the report and her own role in bringing it about. She took a cheap shot at Anita.

'Well, I believe the foundation had lost its way. Instead of putting all its energies and efforts into helping people, it tried to be a political lobbyist with its own agenda.'

At least Anita had a vision, I thought.

'The then director, Anita Hammond-Jones, became distracted and stopped listening to the people who matter most,' said Lilly.

This almost made me laugh out loud. Who had Lilly ever listened to? Her only guiding light was her own sense of self-importance.

When she started talking about the future and how she had already implemented what she described as 'significant changes' and how she and Mark were a brilliant team, I couldn't stand it any longer and walked out, the restless poodle still under my arm.

I stopped in my tracks when Lilly mentioned Anita. I turned around.

'Anita Hammond-Jones should be congratulated for establishing The Lost

Lovelies Foundation in the first place. The good work she did should never be forgotten. The passing of the Victims' Voices Act was a triumph and that was down to Anita Hammond-Jones.'

Magnanimous bitch, I thought.

'Will Anita be returning to the foundation?' asked a reporter.

Lilly shook her head. 'No, Anita advised me last night that she feels her work here is now complete and she is happy to hand over to me.'

I nearly dropped the bloody dog. I didn't know Lilly had talked to Anita. Neither of them ever mentioned that to me, not that I'd heard from Anita lately. She'd gone back into silent mode.

Anita would have seen the final report by now and the media coverage. She must have, to have made her decision. I wandered out to the main office area and held up Pom Pom in front of my face.

The dog stared back at me.

'Well, boy, she's made things very easy for me.'

I don't know if it was because he actually had someone paying attention to him, but Pom Pom licked my nose. I felt sorry for the little bugger, so I took him for a run in the open park area near the hospital where he did multiple pees and sniffed the bum of every other dog in the park.

Back in the office, I put Pom Pom into his crate where he curled up and immediately went to sleep with a gentle snore. I left a letter on Lilly's desk, giving notice of my resignation.

I packed up a case of my belongings, planning to come back for the rest later. Gerard was waiting for me in the car park.

'It's done?' he asked with a warm smile.

'It's done.'

70

Martha

On the day after Lilly's press conference, Anita was scheduled to appear at the International Victims' League gala dinner. I met her at the venue and was horrified when I saw the state she was in. She looked terrible. Her hands were shaking, so I quickly diverted her to the kitchens and loaded her up on coffee. I almost had to force her to the lectern, where her speech was short, subdued and uninspiring. Anita later startled me by saying the audience had looked to her like a room full of poisonous jellyfish whose stinging tentacles were reaching out to grab her, pull her down into the water and strangle her.

I was dismayed. I'd hoped there would be some fight left in her, but she seemed done. I tried to get a good look at her pupils, worrying about what she might be on, but she evaded me.

'Why don't you head on home? Consider taking some time off and visit your parents. I'm sure Stan and Margaret would love to see you,' I told her gently.

'I'll think about it, Martha,' she mumbled.

I tried to drive her home, but she refused. A taxi arrived with Marcel on board and whisked her away.

The following day I couldn't get a response on Anita's phone, so I drove to her house. I'd slept poorly, and while I was finished with the foundation, I was still a nurse and, in some ways, she was still my patient. She was also my friend and she needed my help.

When she didn't answer the front door, I went around the back and found her lying on the grass in a pool of vomit. There was blood on her beautiful skirt.

I dropped to my knees next to her, heart pounding, but her pulse was strong. She was okay, just very drunk or stoned, or both. I got her into the house, cleaned her up and put her to bed.

'Oh, Anita,' I said with a sigh, pushing her fair hair out of her eyes and then rolling her onto her side. She stirred fitfully and I let her sleep while I packed her bags.

How did it come to this? My beautiful Anita, everyone's darling; stinking, drugged and dirty. I wanted to blame everything on Marcel, but Anita was an adult. She had all too willingly got herself into this and she was the only one who could get herself out.

Step number one was getting rid of Marcel. Allen. Whatever his name was. He had to be around here somewhere.

I found him in Heath's nursery, passed out on floor amid drug paraphernalia and hugging that precious little teddy bear. I shook him and got enough of a response to know he was alive. Fumbling in my bag, I found my phone and called Gerard.

Gerard arrived within twenty minutes. He didn't muck around. He emptied a tray of ice cubes onto Marcel's head.

Marcel sat up with a start. 'What the fuckin' hell's going on?' he sputtered.

Gerard crossed his arms. 'That didn't sound very French, did it, Martha?'

I gave Marcel a cold look. 'No, Gerard, not at all. Sounded more like Collingwood to me.'

Gerard shook Marcel's shoulder roughly. 'Listen you phony, you're out of here in five minutes or I call the cops.'

Marcel stumbled around, getting his gear together. Gerard was only too happy to slam the door after him when he staggered out.

I called Anita's mother to tell her I was bringing her daughter home.

71

Louisa

'Lou! How are you?'

I grinned down the line. 'Cliff! I'm well. Enjoying the mess that is the Lost Lovelies?'

He snorted. 'What a drama that turned out to be. Anita Hammond-Jones is a piece of work. The media coverage has been interesting. The latest account in *The Watcher* was actually fairly accurate.'

Now that startled me. 'You mean Jack Ruler's reports?'

'No. Not at all. Jamie O'Dhea actually did a piece on Jennifer Harris and the Victims' Voices Act that I thought was a well-balanced article.'

I agreed with him. That was a good piece and, unlike O'Dhea's usual puff pieces. Who knew he could actually write? 'It looks like Anita Hammond-Jones' reign has come to an end.'

'Yes, but from what I've read so far it sounds like the new one is even worse, and we're still stuck with that wretched Act.' Cliff sounded grumpy and who could blame him? That Act made me grumpy too.

'Well, here's to sunsetting,' I said.

When I said goodbye to Cliff I checked my mail. There was a small parcel from Elissa sent from Kuala Lumpur. It contained a letter, a silk scarf and some photographs. I was thrilled and put the scarf on straight away, admiring its bright colours. I picked up the letter.

My dear teacher and guide Louisa,

If you look at the photographs you will see I am so very happy. My parents introduced me to a man who turned out to be wonderful. I resisted being pushed into meeting him; however, I succumbed to the persuasions of my sisters and agreed to having lunch with him. It was amazing. We talked

I smiled.

A wedding sounded fantastic. I could spend some time in Sri Lanka, after exploring Malaysia. I'd always wanted to visit the elephant orphanage and the tea plantations. I wanted to climb Sigyria before I got too old, and lie on a lounge by the sea at the lighthouse in Galle.

I swished the ends of my pretty new scarf over my shoulders. Yes, life shouldn't just be about work. It was time I had a holiday.

72

Jamie

Tracking Anita down was easier than I expected. Her mother liked to talk and after revealing she visited Anita every day, I was able to find her quite easily. She was hidden away at a rural facility not too far from the family farm. I told Daisy and the kids I was chasing a story in the country and would be staying overnight. It was all too easy.

I was shocked when I saw her. She looked so different from the radiant star I'd known. Although she was freshly showered and made up, she'd lost her glow. Her face was drawn, almost haggard. Still, she greeted me cheerily enough and offered her cheek for a kiss.

I watched her curiously as she wandered into the small kitchenette. 'How long are you staying here?' I asked.

'As long as it takes for you to get me out of here. It's like a bloody prison. I always knew you'd come to rescue me,' she said, flashing me a ghost of a smile. She pulled a vase from a cupboard, filled it with water and arranged the flowers. 'They say I had drug-induced psychosis.'

'What do you think?' I asked her gently, leading her to the table.

She shrugged. 'It was just the drugs. I'm fine. I needed a rest, that's all. I worked too hard and I trusted people. That was my problem,' she grumbled, staring at the table. 'I trusted Martha and she let me down in the end. She didn't defend me at the hearing. She pretended to, but she shafted me, no doubt about it. Right from the start, I was taken in by her.'

I was mortified. Martha Mayne had never been anything but loyal. I decided to keep my mouth shut. Whatever was going on in her head, well, I didn't think it would have been possible to interrupt. And I didn't think it was just the drugs.

'Martha even tried to make me mistrust my dear Marcel. She said she never liked him right from the start. Martha doesn't know how much Marcel means to me. The man is a saint. When I first met him, I thought I was on top of things. But Marcel showed me I hadn't even begun the journey to discovery.

'It is Lilly Hartford who is responsible for what happened to me. I saw her on television last night. She was boasting. All prim and proper looking, talking about how she was saving the foundation!'

I nodded sympathetically, but I couldn't tell if she even noticed.

'She was jealous. Sure, her husband liked me, and I liked him too. But that's all it was. He needed someone to talk to because his wife was so absorbed in herself. Lilly's a control freak. She had to be the one in charge. She wanted the foundation for herself right from the start. The people will never love her like they love me. I made a difference. People loved me, especially the parents of the lost lovelies. She went behind my back. Making up lies. Conspiring with the other board members. Even Lady Charmiane seemed to believe her.'

She became teary. 'No-one cares. People are so fickle. After all the incredible work I did for them. All I ever wanted was to make the world safer for children and to support their parents. We've got a crazy system where someone kills a child, they go to prison for a while, they study while they're in there and they come out with a law degree! How is that fair? Mothers who've lost their babies, they get a lifetime sentence. Yes, I enjoyed the limelight, but I had to because that's how I got my message across. They said I loved the sound of my own voice. Well, so did they, once, before Hartford came along. People are so easily conned, especially by good-looking women.' She stopped. 'Actually, I don't think she is good-looking at all. I think she's plain. Yes, ordinary, that's what Lilly Hartford is. She's getting noticed now, but it won't last. No, it'll all be over for her soon enough. She doesn't have any depth to her. Shallow and power hungry. She'll get what's coming to her. They'll drop her. The foundation's nothing without me.'

I was filled with a deep sadness as I listened to her talk. It was so much more than the drugs. I looked around for some kind of buzzer, as she stared steadfastly at the table.

'Did you see that student Elissa on the television saying, "My research reveals … my findings are …". Duh. How can her cold facts and figures ever be more valid than what a mother feels when her child has been killed? What a boring interview it was. She's totally without talent. You could just about hear the interviewer yawning.'

I finally located the buzzer and pressed it. Anita was crying.

'I was the victim and they scapegoated me! They needed someone to punish and that was me because I reminded them of how evil and greedy people are. They had to hurt me to get themselves off the hook. But Lilly Hartford's not off the hook. Not her. When I get out of here, I'm going to get my revenge on her. I'll start another foundation. It'll be called The Anita Hammond-Jones Foundation for Heaven's Angels. That will soon knock silly Lilly Hartford off her perch. Everyone knows me. The donors will desert her. They'll flock to me. Oh yes, the sweetest revenge of all.'

I pressed the buzzer again, wondering where the bloody nurse was.

'The Anita Hammond-Jones Foundation for Heaven's Angels will support parents and carers of anyone affected by any crime against children. Yes, the children won't have had to be killed, because ... actually, there aren't enough of those to sustain a big foundation. No, affected by a criminal act. Yes, I like that. It will set my foundation apart from the Lost Lovelies. Let Lilly have it. Everyone knows I was the one who started it and now I'm going on to bigger and better things.'

Finally, there was a knock on the door and I hastened to open it.

A kind looking nurse walked into the room and went to Anita. 'How about you have a little rest now?' she said.

I beat a hasty retreat, jumped into my car and out onto the highway. I couldn't wait to get home to my family.

73

Martha

When I went into my office to collect the rest of my belongings, Lilly told me she was changing the name of the foundation. 'It's going to be The Hartford Family Memorial Foundation because our good name will attract donors.'

Well, it held no importance for me. She watched me pack up my desk, looking almost confused, and asked me to stay, as though she'd only just realised I was leaving.

'No, it's time I started my own life,' I told her, not regretting my decision for a single second. Lilly wafted off back to her office, and when I looked over at Mark Hartford on the phones he waved his arms frantically, the universal signal for help.

I turned around and finished my packing.

Colleen, with her fancy communications qualifications, had been relegated to my old role. All she'd done lately was pick up after Lilly, and she seemed to be as annoyed as I'd been.

She told me at the last board meeting that Lilly asked all the board members to stay on. 'Peter Dickson had said he preferred going fishing with his grandkids. Wai Leung had to go to China because his father was sick, and Bianca was too busy with consultancy work to stay on.'

'What about Lady Charmiane?' I asked.

Colleen had laughed. 'She said she was hideously old and had better things to do with her time.'

As I tidied up the last of my odds and ends, I thought about how exciting the early days of the foundation had been. There were so many challenges; we had such a strong sense of purpose and our belief in the mission of this new organisation we were creating was absolute.

It was all so fresh back then. Anita and I worked together like old pals and, despite the seriousness of our work, we had a lot of fun. We got a real buzz from the media involvement, and Anita was always in demand. I watched her growing in confidence, becoming a real star.

For a while.

I sighed, as I packed away a photo of me, Anita and Leanne at some event or other.

What went so wrong?

The media turned out to be even more enthusiastic in their condemnation of Anita than they had been when they'd adored her. Her popularity quickly turned to notoriety, and the gutter press published some awful photographs of her, deliberately making her look deranged. The headlines went from praise to demonisation. 'Anita the Cheater', 'Charity Queen Dethroned', 'She Threw Out the Babies with the Bathwater', 'Shafted by a Charlatan Shaman'.

Anita knew how to attract people but she lacked the substance to deliver what she promised them. People who had already suffered enough were duped into donating their time, money and faith into Anita and the foundation. They were bound to be disappointed.

Worst of all was the damage done to Jennifer Harris. I sighed. The girl had caused real and devastating harm to Anita and Michael, but she was no dangerous criminal.

If this Bill passes, she'll kill herself.

I didn't run from the voice this time. Yes, I told it, you were right.

I would always have to deal with my complicity in what happened to Jennifer. I would always blame myself, like I did for Heath.

But that's what guilt is. Something you accept. In time, and if you're lucky, it becomes less jagged.

I put a couple of bottles of Bollinger into my bag and decided to take the little ruby and pearl letter opener. It was so pretty and I didn't want Lilly to have it.

I switched off the lights in my office and locked the door behind me.

My new life with my husband awaited me.

74

Gerard

Being grounded with a twisted ankle gives me time to think. I was so proud to be able to get this house for Martha and me. There are worse places to be an invalid than here. I take a deep breath. Martha picked some wild garlic this morning from out the front and has hung it from the rafters. Its pungent aroma wafts through the house.

I was pleased when I could finally spring my ultimate surprise on Martha. I'd brought her here to Hideaway Bay for a weekend getaway, then blew her mind over sunset with a simple question.

'Should we buy this house?'

'If only,' she had said with a sigh.

I couldn't stop the twinkle of triumph. She'd thrown a pillow at me.

'Gerard, stop dreaming. We couldn't afford it even if it was on the market.'

I grinned. 'Yes, we could and yes, it is. I checked. Oh, and I already brought it for us. Welcome home.'

She was overwhelmed.

We married not long after in in a quiet ceremony at the registry office in Melbourne. Ranie and Leanne were our witnesses. Afterwards, we had a quiet lunch at The Windsor. The following morning, we piled into our packed car with Martha's two new rescue dogs, Lost and Found, to take possession of our home.

I take a deep breath and smile. I didn't think life would ever improve after I lost Mary and the kids.

I was wrong.

Martha has me propped up with pillows in front of one of the large glass windows. There are three others in the main bedroom to the south and eight frame the living area. The house is built of solid bluestone painted white to soften the darkness of the rock. It stands high on a heath-covered cliff. There is no other house in sight. It's a place where you can think, let the past drift in and out like the waves, carrying the echoes and shadows of the lives we lived.

The book Martha left me with before her walk is about Joseph Stalin. It's a fascinating account of how a grey shadow of a man took over a whole empire and ruled with a dictator's might. Perhaps in a small way he reminds Martha of me. People think accountants are boring people. We look after the books and control the statistics.

Well, accountants can be creative too.

Yes, a bit of creative accounting, good bookkeeping and knowing who's who and what's where in an organisation places one in a powerful position. With the two of us becoming a team it was a win-win situation. It was convenient of the crooked guru Bouverie to do a runner after nearly destroying Anita. It was clear he had fleeced her and the foundation of a large amount of money, but they could never be sure of how much.

As I watch the sea rolling to the shore and back again, I hope Martha would be home soon.

75

Martha

At the kiosk I collect the papers from Bobby and Shirley. Doesn't matter if it's yesterday's news here. I follow the tide line when I return home. In the afternoon sunlight, the beach is a great arc of pearly-pink sand. I stop to watch a gannet soaring along the edge of the waves. Its long, slender wings are raised like those of a dancer. The dogs are tearing around the sand chasing each other.

The city and its concerns are so far away from here. I have no desire to return.

Occasionally, I see things in the paper that remind me of the heady days of the foundation, but as time passes those memories recede as surely as the waves do. I suppose I should go and visit Anita at her parents' farm, but I keep putting it off. And despite my idyllic retirement, I just can't help myself. I do a shift whenever they need me at the local hospital.

Anyway, I'm more content to just stay here, savouring my freedom, the wild weather, and the beauty of Hideaway Bay.

I return home and wheel my husband outside for some fresh air and to enjoy the sunset. Gerard and I call the hour before darkness the glory hour. When it isn't too cold or windy, we sit outside with our drinks and watch the waves smashing themselves onto the rocks on the flank of the headland. Sometimes we can hear the roar of the blowholes. We see the reflected glory of the setting sun lighting up the capes.

This evening is spectacular. As the sun goes down the bay glows. The sky, so exciting, with orange and yellow lights explodes into ecstatic crimson. The shrubs turn into serrated dragons and the capes are black serpents. Day falls, night rises.

Gerard calls the dogs and we go inside. We enjoy our evening meal and sit by the open fire sipping a lovely shiraz, dogs snoring, while Gerard plays his harmonica softly and I sing along. He drifts off to sleep and I sit mesmerised by the burning wood in our fireplace, my thoughts winding down twisted roads.

I should have done more, much more.

But sifting through the entrails isn't going to help. All I can do is try to work out what to do with the knowledge I now have.

The ocean is booming away outside the house. The wind is knocking on the windows, and I hear the lonely sound of a hooting owl.

I stare into the flames, waiting for the fire to burn down low. I can clean up the ashes in the morning.

Acknowledgments

A psychiatrist colleague asked me why I was writing a novel. I told him I wanted to test, at seventy years of age, how well my brain was functioning and if it was possible for me to complete a whole book from beginning to end. He chuckled and said, 'Other people would find easier ways to do that Beth.' I thank him for his insight and, yes, it was a lot more difficult than I had expected. This was not because of my age, it's just because writing a novel is hard work. Fortunately I was able to enlist some wonderful people to help me.

Thanks to Dave Mercer who discovered Regina Lane and Laneway Press. Thanks to Regina for finding Rebecca, who supported me in the writing process. Thanks to Liz Harrington, intern at Laneway Press whose keen and questioning young mind provided inspiration. Thank you to Mary Dalmau for proof reading. Special thanks to Dr Sally Cockburn, Sally Bouvier, Dr Penny Webster, Dr John Serry and Bob McGowan for critique and encouragement. Thanks to Ashley Dickinson for ideas regarding the character, Peter Dickson.

Thank you to everyone who has shown interest in this project and who, hopefully, will maintain that interest long enough to read the book.

I'm not grateful to a broken foot, arthritis and a haematoma, nor for COVID-19 for grounding me long enough to get this done. However, I suppose if I had to be grounded this was as good a time as any. Was it worth the effort? The reader will have to be the judge but I'm happy with the way my brain functioned.

Author's Note

The Lost Lovelies Foundation is a work of fiction. Any resemblance to actual events, organisations or persons, living or dead, is unintended.

This novel is a fictional exploration of what can happen if egos and personal ambition take priority over more benevolent agendas. The majority of charities and foundations play a vital role in supporting people who experience disadvantage. I am a proud participant in several of these.